VERSION

by

Craig Jenkins

First published in Great Britain in 2014
by LionheART Publishing House

Science Fiction, Fantasy, Futuristic, Sci Fi, Aliens, Thriller,
Mystery, Apocalyptic, Suspense

Cover Design by Gareth Hughes
Technical Editing by John Goodfellow
Edited and Prepared for Publication by
LionheART Publishing House

YEAR 2216

EASTERN SAHARA
MURTON DAM

Forests and acres of farmland stretched for thousands of square miles where barren desert land had once stood. A powerful armoured truck, silver in colour, sped through the heavy downpour as its quad-light system created strong beams to perforate the dark.

The road leading the way had thick irrigation pipes either side which could be mistaken for safety barriers. Regardless of climate change they continued to pump water down from the Mediterranean Sea, through distillation centres and into the Murton Dam complex.

A sudden fork in the road caused the truck to career to the right, sliding in deep pools of water as it went. It continued up its new path along an increasing gradient until the forest canopy either side receded where the enormous face of the dam wall came into view. The vehicle sped on.

Gavin gripped the steering controls and pushed harder as the storm gathered force. Fork lightning lit the sky as a gale picked up and thrashed the vehicle.

The truck slid around precariously as it tore along the narrow road spiralling around the circumference of the dam's outer wall. The passage was steep and awash with flowing water across its surface where branches and all manner of debris impeded the vehicle's progress. There was no time to slow for this. Reckless driving in such conditions increased the chance of sliding into the forest canopy below. *No mistakes.* The fear and tension built within him as he approached the top of the artificial channel that rose a thousand metres above the parklands below.

1

He peered through the continuous flow of water which obscured his vision as it flowed thickly down the windscreen. Wipers vacuuming away water struggled with the workload, making it hard for him to see the reservoir on the other side of security barriers as he approached the summit.

The vehicle entered the visitors' parking area and slid to a halt in a shallow layer of pooled water on the smooth concrete surface. It was fortunate that he knew the area well from his days in retirement wandering this marvel of engineering. He used to bring his only son, Ologun, on weekend fishing trips here; today he'd be faced with the boy's stupidity and penchant for misadventure.

The man checked his watch to confirm how long the journey had taken. Ologun's friend had called twenty minutes ago, and under normal circumstances and with any other person in such trouble it would be too late. All he needed to do was find his son, then let him do his thing. His main fear was that he wouldn't be able to find his body and there was no way he could risk calling for help.

He had just retired from his commission as Admiral from the Ishima Misceri Corporation and could still summon a fleet of aircraft from Cairo's IMC station outpost to scour the reservoir's deep waters; ready to carry out the rescue with total efficiency. *Can't get them involved!*

The comms box on the vehicle's dashboard blinked: 'Gavin, are you there? Mr Jowett, it's the Sahara Park Authorities. Come in, over.'

Gavin ignored the comms and reached into the back seat of his transport to grab a long cylindrical object. He removed its casing to reveal a telescope with thermal-imaging assisted motion detectors. Exiting the vehicle he fought the weather to peer through the scope and saw the digitally enhanced version of the reservoir. His vision was immediately drawn towards the flickering motion of large fish which lit up in a red-orange colour beneath the navy representation of the water. The digiscope displayed readings of all solid objects by measuring and identifying them. Driftwood, fish and large clumps of vegetation flashed up on the screen's recognition grid. *Shit!* He'd spotted three crocodiles swimming near the dam's anterior wall. He lowered the device for a moment in order to take a deep breath and surveyed the expanse of water presented before him. He felt his body slouch a little and became overwhelmed by the magnitude of the place. It had never occurred to him on previous visits that he would stand at this very same place and in such different circumstances which would seem utterly nightmarish and no longer a sight-seer's dream attraction.

He banished the moment and continued to scour the area. If Ologun had drowned, his body would have been caught by one of the outlet filter channels which acted as overflow conduits to the dam's external face. At least they would stop his journey, ending it before the thousand-foot drop to the main river below. He continued the search by following the dam wall the full length around and underneath the water's surface. His fingers quickly pressed the small selection of buttons on the digiscope, fluent in operating its components. Still nothing: most shapes revealed under the water remained that of plant life or the odd dead carcass of some poor animal swept here from the network of reservoirs located further north. The crocodiles had no doubt come here to hunt for the rotting flesh and would soon find Ologun.

Gavin's grip tightened on the scope as it centred on the shape of a human body. He activated a function on the apparatus which scanned for height and weight. *That's definitely him!* As feared, Ologun had become trapped in one of the dam's filter outlet portals twelve feet under the forceful torrent. Gavin rushed to the boot of his vehicle for a rope before he ran blindly through the rain across the circumference of the dam wall. The path across the top of the dam was flat and wide with partition walls for safety either side. A layer of water, ankle deep, covered the path and was unable to drain away properly in the tempest. He breathed heavily, gasping as this temporary stream slowed his efforts. He knew he was physically fit but this storm seemed focused and unusual.

Eight hundred yards later, Gavin finally reached the juncture where he'd seen Ologun. He fumbled with drenched fingers and tied the rope to a nearby safety railing and then to himself. He took many deep breaths before leaning backwards, believing this to be his last few moments in the world of the living. He had to retrieve his son's body at any cost; even his own life was a fair price to pay. *Just get on with it!*

The inside face of the dam was slippery underfoot as he made his descent down thick algae which hung in a furry formation all the way to the water's surface. The mist from moving water mixed with heavy rain left Gavin feeling smothered. His son lay directly below him deep under the dark water, stuck within a tremendous level of suction inside the filter tunnel.

He plunged down into the torrent, immediately feeling his body tiring. He wasn't sure he could withstand the reservoir's deadly might. *To hell with it!* Gavin took what he considered to be his last deep breath and vanished under the surface.

YEAR 2136

LAUNCH

The sun rose from behind Earth and across the desolate moon landscape, causing the digital glass to adjust within the safety parameters for human eyesight. Doctor Rajendra sat looking out of the small window at the front of her cabin and squinted.

She thought about the day ahead; the past twelve years; then her overall feelings as she headed for the finish line. She was, in essence, depressed. This surprised her as in the beginning there had been no doubts; or rather the doubts had been superseded by ambition, arrogance, even by the gamble of it all. Diane's mind had always been consumed and now it was at a pinnacle, trying to hold her conviction for another twenty four hours until the deeds were done.

Diane Rajendra had become, at least for this moment in history, one of seven geniuses guiding an army of scientists, engineers and many other skilled technicians to develop and launch the frontier project. Such a project could never be achieved via any nation on Earth as the politics, along with the economics, would forever stay precarious. All governments, it seemed, were destined to be limited in such a regard for eternity. In the end it had taken the politics of business from one of the most powerful firms in existence to conquer deep space exploration or, should it be said, to gather the essentials together in order to attempt it.

Diane looked at her unfamiliar aged face staring back at her from one of the mirrors in her cubicle. Twelve years had slipped away only to be left with the pride that humankind could advance forward once again to a truly momentous time. *Progression, not distraction.*

She sat back down on her bed, thinking of her father; of how he'd been swept along, almost press-ganged into this project, and how the company had changed to push such an insane idea to its full conclusion. It hadn't been so long ago that living in a moon base would have seemed improbable. The real change had come when Diane's father accepted a job at the company's aeronautical systems division to create space probes fast enough and with enough scope to find something worth further attention. That was the first time anyone, including any government from around the world, had taken a serious interest in space for over two hundred years. Astronomy, cosmology and the science hadn't died; the funding with which it had once survived, however, had been far from available. Eventually Diane's father, as forecast by the company, had succeeded in discovering a planet possibly compatible with Earth's own atmosphere. Fortune Symmetry's small aeronautical division was about to begin the quest that would change human history forever.

Diane now worked for the IMC, which was the outcome of a merger of Fortune Symmetry and another powerful corporation: Misceri Plyologics.

Misceri had become the second most influential company on Earth in a very short time by producing advanced armour technologies. The innovative shielding had been devised by developing pliable metal-weave fibre plating to be installed on military vehicles. The technology was significant as it made all combat vehicles lighter by reducing the thickness of armour required for protection, while remaining robust enough to replace retrospective casts of bodywork. The fibre sheets were so malleable that the terrestrial military crafts' computers could momentarily contract the toughened fibres when in combat to increase their deflective attributes.

The newly formed IMC was ambitious and impatient at times, and Diane felt things had gone too far. She remembered the simplicity of being a journey calculations' officer and how it had been complex but simple to work with the idea that Symmetry wanted to send a few ships carrying mechanical drones to record more data. That was the ethically sound part.

When Diane had been promoted to Chief Operations Officer, the things she'd learned had unsettled her. Since the company merger Diane had grown suspicious of certain ship design alterations and was stunned when she'd found that the new terms of exploration would include sending a human cargo. The directors at Fortune had revealed these intentions when they'd appointed a new team to specifically work on living biological stasis development. Naturally the directors hadn't informed her of what was to be placed in stasis, although she had a strong sense that the units wouldn't be carrying monkeys.

Diane eventually found a copy of the manifest for every one of the twelve crew members allocated to each vessel. One hundred and forty six people, both men and women, would be suspended for the thirty-five-year journey to the planet. As probabilities went she tried to reduce the risk for the sake of the equipment; yet to her, equipment was an acceptable loss. People were not. The company she worked for seemed to have the exact opposite set of values.

Diane pulled her thoughts together; it was now 8:00 a.m. set base time. She made the usual hundred-yard walk past the science post and to the main deck for launch preparations. Rick Bussey, the journey ships' development commander and head engineer for ships' construction, stood high up on a platform overlooking numerous monitor screens which had been erected along one of the control room's concrete walls. Rick was busy and, as usual, shouted into his headset at the construction crew floating around the ships two miles above in the vacuum as they frantically worked to make final adjustments for the launch in twelve hours. Diane noted Rick's ability to slip into a mode of stringing so many swear words together there were no orders or requests to be deciphered, only simple and continuous abuse at the people around him. *It's the pressure.*

Rick looked up at Diane and nodded with a grin; he loved his job. He resumed his work and shouted even more aggressively than before. Diane looked at the same monitor as Rick to see what the fuss was about. One of the construction workers was frantically moving towards a welding rod that, if Diane wasn't mistaken, was headed for an emergency fuel tank near ship three.

The crowd of thousands stood in the now urbanely decorated hanger which had initially been used to construct components seven and twelve of the ships' hulls. The ship development centre, Kilo, had now become a rally point for the world's ruling elite and anyone else who could afford the tickets to watch the launch spectacle. All seven hundred members of the project's crew were also invited as it had become evident they'd been working indefatigably for over a decade now. They were ready for a real party, and many were already being shepherded away from sight due to being 'intoxicated beyond company tolerance'.

The ship hanger was brimming with noise despite the hundred-foot-high ceiling and the sonic absorbent material installed along the hanger's interior. All thirty IMC company directors were present and talking to crew members and other science officers about the project, while remote camera units buzzed around for maximum coverage of the event. Diane hoped they wouldn't notice her as she was ushered to the VIP stand. She moved among the crowd looking to slip away when a sudden screech from the speakers mounted on the hanger walls curbed much of the noise in the room. Diane looked to a very tall digital lens at the front of the hanger as its blacked-out field exposed a grey landscape and a black horizon filled with stars. Further inspection of the view revealed twelve objects floating way above in the distance. *They're ready!*

Everyone gazed at the frontier ships. The specifications for these ships to think, move and defend themselves against possible debris when they travelled through solar systems required a great deal of processing equipment, which in turn required capacity. The journey ships were three thousand metres long, two thousand metres in width, and five hundred metres in height. They were enormous in comparison to other contemporary forms of spacecraft, and larger than any of the military aircraft carriers dominating Earth's oceans.

Diane thought about the passengers. They'd been given rooms to sleep in no larger than one of the nuclear weapon loading ports. This, however, wasn't the real issue, for some secrets along with many lies had been woven into this whole endeavour whereby only certain people, including herself, knew an incredible truth. This truth would change reality and at the very least put to rest all criticism of the project's shortcomings. Digital lenses, atomic reactors, enhanced ion engines, and solar winds would not be enough for these ships to go the distance. It seemed anyone involved in this industry could sense that something was up, or that if the journey were to be a success some form of sorcery had to be involved. Diane smirked at the thought of the magic the ships' engines were using. It was so radical and had so many implications for humanity it seemed criminal to keep it a secret.

Diane hadn't noticed the voice coming out of the speakers until her name was mentioned. Now she listened with relative interest as a full monologue regarding the ships' quest was orated, while overhead the ships' protection sails were peeled off. They looked like giant guitar picks, wide at the back and narrow at the front. Diane had seen these ships on paper, on digital mapping, even bit by bit in the construction hangers. She'd also seen them in the vacuum; half built, in pieces. *The finished fleet is something else,* she thought. No windows to look out of – or into – and almost black from the heat-resistant panelling covering the entirety of each ship; they'd become invisible to the human eye after a few hundred metres of drifting away towards their launch mark.

The ships gently glided from view towards a satellite which flashed brightly, hanging high above the grey desert of the lunar surface. A countdown from sixty seconds began and it seemed as though the whole crowd gathered in the hanger bay were petrified as they stared silently through the window. The ships were synchronised perfectly, and all hit the journey starting point simultaneously. As the timer finished, a huge flash erupted from the direction the spectators' attention was fixed upon. The large digital window did its best to block out the violent light, yet still everyone flinched as though the whole fleet of ships had exploded into a nuclear fireball.

Diane felt numb as she mingled with the important guests. The ships were now well underway and they'd have to wait longer for ship status reports the further away they travelled. In a decade they'd have a three-year wait for a message, despite instant-link data pins being dropped en route every month. By the time they reached their destination, Diane knew she may not even be around to see the results. She would never know whether to despair or rejoice for the poor souls sent in their transparent caskets and buried alive in metal.

She would grieve now and for a while, just in case.

YEAR 2256

SON OF BLAME

The Global Earth Alliance Courts of Military Justice were grey, metallic and far more draconian than any other place of trial. The accused were displayed at the centre of an enormous triangular room and questioned by a chosen group of eight GEA high-ranking officers. Taking turns, they fired questions while sat in an evenly spaced octagon surrounding the defendant. It was unusual for an IMC soldier to be here under such circumstances, especially under prosecution for murder.

This trial was mostly political posturing as the IMC had become an incredibly powerful authority, winning most contracts in the arms race against the GEA, and now had just as many security contracts to police Earth along with other off-world colonies.

If anything, the trial was about a lost moral code between two giant institutions which had the will and the means to go to war. The term 'war' was no longer metaphorical either, as companies in the new age had far more means to wage war than the countries they were subsidised to represent.

The man on trial knew this to be the case even before he'd killed twelve GEA soldiers. No mixing of contractors had always been the rule. Now it appeared he'd take the brunt of a political uproar over the terrible atrocities existing on the newest irrigation plains of North West Africa. He'd taken a stand and could now be executed for what he thought had been the right thing to do. He'd given up hope of escaping this situation and realised his employers at the IMC had signed his life over with little fuss.

He stood in the centre of the room under a blinding spotlight which obscured his interrogators from his sight. *GEA nuts,* he thought. The clichéd lighting system of intimidation provoked him to yawn as a way of showing some defiance. *Why can't they have wooden furniture in here like other courts?*

His mind drifted away, ignoring the fuss in the room, to enjoy a daydream. He liked the one where he stood on a floor made of – *what is it exactly? Glass, maybe?* The floor glowed a strange orange colour and stretched on for miles in every direction with no buildings or structures of any kind to break the horizon. There was also a craft which gave the impression of sentience as it hovered above him, always facing him everywhere it drifted. It was so strange he could hardly believe his imagination had created such a thing.

It floated elegantly in the air with a vast wingspan, its aesthetics reminding him of a shelled creature from the ocean crossed with a vicious bird of prey. In his dream he always stood beneath it, facing in one direction as it moved around. The creature had organs or maybe engines underneath its wings which spun and pulsated with shards of light escaping in all directions.

He thought about the dream's significance and why it had been on constant replay whenever he slept. The nature of the dream itself was potent, even relentless, and somehow like a memory or something beyond – it was so vivid and clear. He could see the heavy rain pouring on to the strange glass-like floor, on to himself, and on to the aircraft dutifully hovering around. The rain bounced violently off everything as the sky above gave off a turquoise glow through a thick unbroken blanket of cloud. There was never any sun, or any real hint at what the sky may look like above a land of endless glass which kept that consistent orange glow.

His thoughts were rudely interrupted by a large crash a few feet in front of him. The judge wanted his attention. He was angry and critical as he pointed his finger in disgust. 'You have been found guilty by this military court, sir. Are you listening? You have been sentenced to the deep-sea mining facility, level seven, to spend the rest of your days. Please acknowledge that you understand, Sergeant Ologun Jowett.'

Ologun stared indifferently at the fattened gorb of a judge wheezing as he tried to elicit a response. The poor man couldn't quite believe Ologun's attitude, making him turn a purple colour as he became more hysterical. 'Your actions were barbaric, evil and callous. Your attitude to the whole proceedings in court have been—' The judge sighed, lifted his hands to his shoulders, and shrugged them in disbelief; there were no words it seemed.

'I hope your time on Deceiver will help you reflect on your actions, Sergeant Jowett. That is all.'

The judge had remained calm throughout the so-called trial. He had muttered his comments in soft tones of empathy and, against his best efforts, had slowly lost all patience over the past few weeks. He pressed a button which made the sound of a block hammer hitting wood, and stared furiously at the prisoner, who was rapidly escorted out of the room.

The court guards led Ologun along a dark corridor and outside into blinding daylight, eventually revealing a large garden area with a concrete circle in its centre. This circle was a landing point for the shuttlecraft that would soon take him away from Earth for good.

Ologun still thought his actions justified, regardless of ending up on the wrong side of military law, yet something about it all eluded him – he felt as though the whole affair were unreal. He'd always been a contractor, a mercenary, rather than the proper thing. Security forces of this nature made more money and had a more varied lifestyle compared to the grunts who made it into the GEA's international peacekeeping brigade. He had spent twelve years on missions within the IMC forces, working against the constant barrage of city violence which had escalated over the past twenty years. This part of his career, however, was the highlight, and he quickly thought about other things before remembering what he had once nearly become.

Twelve years and a sudden loss of the IMC tender of the Moroccan ecology contract placed Ologun in an impossible position both morally and ethically. He had risen to the point of being in charge of thirty IMC marines until the GEA had returned to one of the Sahara's most western plantation outposts to resume command.

His moment to ponder the past was rudely interrupted by the butt of a rifle hitting him on the bridge of his nose. He was beginning to realise that since the incident he'd been distracted with his own thoughts too often. Another hard blow to the top of his skull connected at the same moment his nose exploded with blood. As he fell to his knees, a boot kicked him in his chest, then another struck his face. Over and over he was hit with fists, a rifle butt, and steel-toed boots until he was left to kneel with blood pouring from his face.

He was blinded and his face swollen, but he felt nothing: no fear, no physical or emotional pain at all. He wondered about the court guards and whether they'd put the odd boot in for fun. The reality was that the people who'd done this were upset about the incident, the whole reason they were kicking him off Earth and to the planet Deceiver: one of the greatest mysteries of all time it was said.

Ologun knelt for some time, disorientated with acutely blurred vision. Occasionally he swallowed blood which slid from the back of his nose and down his throat. The midday sun was hot and warmed his scalp through thick black hair; he could only see its brightness as a hazy orange glow through his eyelids. He listened to birds chirping above and to his left, while insects buzzed around close to his head. He then heard something louder: a more powerful mechanised sound of a hollow voice which moved overhead and towards him until it came to rest a few yards away on the concrete landing circle. Without fuss he was pulled to his feet, still blinded by the swelling of his face, and dragged by his escort towards the ship. He gasped, trying to catch his breath and somehow compose himself from the battered mess he'd become. The guards were rough and forceful, yanking his arms and legs around so that he was quickly seated and held in place on the large chair while they shackled him by wrist and ankle plates. One restraint was then wrapped tightly around his forehead and another around his neck, causing him to choke and struggle for breath.

They'll say it was an accident. He'd never heard of a long-distance flight where the passenger was leaking blood down their throat just before forced hibernation which would render him unconscious in his chair. He was convinced, with little distress, that he would drown on his own blood as soon as he went under.

Version

Ologun tried to relax, banishing these thoughts, and listened for other passengers. He slowly regained his sight and found himself to be sitting in a large rectangular cabin in one of sixteen chairs facing each other rather than the traditional system of pointing forwards towards the cockpit. He took one look at the other, already heavily sedated, passengers facing him in their full splendour of ugliness, and became agitated.

Movement caught his eye and he flinched as two robotic arms pulled his trousers down. One arm moved quickly underneath to remove the bottom of the chair and Ologun knew what was next. He flinched as another robot pushed a metal-ended hose into his anus, then put a large nappy with external waste bags into place. The level of excrement a person produced while in hibernation was minimal, yet no one wanted to arrive even slightly soiled. He was at least glad the other prisoners were, at this point, all dribbling in their comatose states and unable to see him. The noise from the shuttle's engines increased to a high-pitched scream as they prepared for lift off. He knew this meant that he too would soon be forced into slumber.

His entire body tensed as two long syringes from a robotic arm injected him on each side of his neck. *The pain's worse than a kick in the face.* He grinned at the thought. The pain subsided, to be replaced by a numbing sensation which eased the rest of his aches from the beating. He slipped into a strange state of intoxication from the cocktail of hibernation inducers and his eyes rolled upwards to the ceiling of the cabin. Directly above him a small round window revealed Earth as it drifted away to become a small speck amongst the stars. He kept watching until all he could see was blackness, which in turn fuelled his fall further away from reality and into his dream of the glass floor, the rain, and the strange hovering aircraft.

The shuttle headed to the outer reaches of Earth's solar system and beyond with a dramatic acceleration. It had once taken over thirty years to reach Deceiver. This shuttle would arrive there in just one.

The choking sensation from restraints returned to Ologun as he regained consciousness. His deep sleep had been disrupted by the sound of a loud siren accompanied by a hollow digital voice: 'WARNING. DECELERATION INTERUPUPTED. WARNING.'

He felt quite fresh and alert and tried to look around but was prevented by the restraints still in place around his head. His eyes swivelled from side to side watching the other passengers waking up, and realised they weren't able to concentrate in the chaos. They were more like zombies: dribbling, swaying and moaning incoherently. One passenger, a large white man with a ginger beard, began crying loudly while he salivated all over his shirt – and the smell!

Ologun turned his eyes away from the pathetic display around him in disgust and glanced upwards out of the small portal he remembered was above him. He strained his eyes through the window, seeing a flat object weakly reflecting sunlight. He couldn't gauge its size, yet became puzzled, associating the debris to a thin piece of slate which appeared to give no true indication of a natural surface. There were no defects, craters, crevices or any features to give it any texture he knew.

The object passed from view to be replaced by Deceiver, a brilliant blue planet with one vast ocean which coated the entire surface. Warnings from multiple speakers within the cabin fought for his attention with the joyful information that they only had three minutes to impact and the ship had lost all power. Ologun had lost all interest in the computers' whining. He sat back and was glad of the view as they entered the atmosphere, only for the ship to burn with fire as it rushed down to meet the ocean. He tried to ignore the other prisoners who were still panicking and screaming as they re-gained consciousness. *There's no need to wake up now!*

He stared in fascination as the dark-blue–light-blue divide of the ocean and sky spun ever closer while ignoring the cruel knotting of his innards. He wished the passengers would be quiet: *whining maggots*. The robotic arms were no better as they too gave off the impression they were panicking. One such device rushed past and slowed to look at him as though in search of an answer, its robotic eye swivelling erratically. Then, as though in reply, a deafening smash ripped through the air as the cabin exploded in all directions. Two of the chairs occupied by prisoners broke free from the floor, hurtling to the front. One of the shuttle's hibernation monitors flew forward to hit some of the other occupied chairs, and the chaos and noise triggered Ologun to finally flinch, closing his eyes until all went silent.

The impact had caused such damage that even the ship with its internal robotic arms no longer had anything to say, and Ologun felt peculiar: deaf and convinced he was already dead.

He opened his eyes and was very still with shock. The cabin rocked and creaked wickedly, inflicting a nauseous cadence where relief should have been.

His head had broken free of the restraints, allowing for a quick probe at the carnage where the full power of the surreal aftermath became instantly overwhelming.

He continued to stare, wide-eyed. The man immediately opposite had been decapitated. The jaw of another to the right had been ripped off and blood pumped down from the roof of his mouth all over the cabin floor. The man with the thick ginger beard had lost an eye, which was now hanging from one of the ship's broken robotic arms which flopped lifelessly across a dead passenger's lap.

Ologun shook his head in disbelief that he was still conscious and witnessing such a mess, then looked out of the portal again and into the deep sea for his final moments. He was even more astonished as he noticed his reflection in the window. It appeared that a robotic arm had pierced deep into his chest and was twitching as though trying to free itself. He peered beyond his reflection in denial and ignored the spray of water hitting his face. He also ignored the buckling sound of the cabin around him as the water pressure rapidly increased.

He felt cold – very cold – all of a sudden and realised, at last, that he was about to die.

The view across Deceiver's ocean was clear to the horizon in all directions. High above the dark-blue ocean and moving rapidly across the lighter shade of the firmament, a blazing object streaked. Captain Notifoss stood looking out over Deceiver from on board an ore-extraction rig. He saw the distant spark falling and ran to the top observation deck to look through his binoculars. He barked orders for the station's submersible launch to rescue the stricken space transport immediately.

'Bloody shuttle's going to sink like a concrete block, sir!' one rig worker shouted as he pulled on his gear before running the full length of the mesh platform towards the sub.

The captain checked his watch. There was only one transport scheduled to arrive. *It's the prisoners.* He knew the rate at which this type of shuttle would sink in a saltless ocean. If it were up to him he'd let it go; yet, to be fair, the pilots deserved a chance. Deceiver's ocean measured twelve miles deep in parts and the sub could only withstand being seven miles down before succumbing to the water's pressure. If the sub missed, the shuttle would be lost.

Notifoss watched with little optimism as the submersible dropped into the water below. By his further estimations he knew the prisoner vessel had already sunk a couple of miles and would already have been crushed, killing all on board. Still, regardless of its passengers' wellbeing the Global Space Alliance would want the wreckage to be retrieved in order to investigate the cause of the crash and would be unimpressed if a rescue attempt on the vessel had failed to be initiated.

As the submersible sunk out of view, Notifoss caught sight of a large sea mammal surface for air three hundred feet away from the rig. He'd taken to using sonar to measure some of these monstrous aliens and was amazed how the submersible with its generous size of sixty metres hadn't yet become prey.

Searching the vista again, Notifoss saw something beyond the point where the ship had fallen. Way in the distance a strange formation of brightly lit cloud headed in the station's direction. Notifoss looked more closely through his binoculars and became very concerned. He quickly activated an intercom link hanging on a sensor mast which patched him through to the trace deck.

'Have you seen this weather front heading our way, Jack, what the shit fire is it? Could be here any moment judging by the speed of it.'

Version

The frantic voice of the rig's chief science officer crackled and hissed from one of the weathered speakers mounted nearby. 'There's an anomalous mass out there, it's freezing everything instantly, sir. I don't know what it is!'

Captain Notifoss remained focused, through his binoculars, on the ocean as it rapidly turned to glass underneath the white gas moving across its surface. He thought he'd experienced every variety of weather Deceiver had to cast over these seas. This thing appeared to be more of an attack that would soon be upon them. There was nothing he could say to his crew and he also knew there was no point in running for cover. The cloud could only be comprehended as some creature sucking the ambient levels of energy out of the water as it passed.

Notifoss gripped his binoculars tightly as he felt the temperature change approach. *It's insane*, he thought, *there are no signs. Where's the wind that carries it?* He checked one of the sensor readings from a buoy which was much closer to the incoming front, now only a mile away. *Minus one hundred and thirty!* He lifted his binoculars for another look in disbelief as the water solidified and cast a white vapour from its surface as the front passed.

As though an invisible wave had painted the entire ocean white, the negative force did the same to the metal framework of the rig as it flashed across the observation deck. Notifoss gasped with no chance to exhale, and was set in ice instantaneously along with the entire crew of the mineral rig. No one had time to move or prepare for the supernatural drop in temperature which held everyone in their final moments. The air remained still and silent as the captain stood; very much a memorial statue looking out over the now frozen landscape of Deceiver.

1

2338

BLACK BALL

Digital dusk engulfed the outpost in a deep pink, an emulated light which shone over seventy thousand square miles of the basin's carefully developed wilderness; or at least it had begun its existence in such a way. Eighty two years of established forest and farmlands fed through automated systems had allowed certain locations in the outpost to grow wild and unkempt.

He felt empty at this time of year; the anniversary was in only six days and, as always, it was time for a rest; time to think. He listened as the dense marble wall, over a thousand metres in height, echoed the sounds of the outpost and translated them into haunting songs like that of a blue whale from the deep. His mood deepened. He drank whisky from a small glass and combed thin fingers through his thick silver hair. He checked a small clock hanging on a chain attached to his navy waistcoat, and leaned forward over the railing of his balcony.

It had been sixteen years since he'd left it all behind. He was a different man here at Black Ball, and yet with every harvest it all flooded back to him. The IMC had plucked him for this role when he'd thought he had nothing left to offer. Yet typically, the IMC had offered him an amazing opportunity, one that was impossible to refuse, which in itself instilled a level of scepticism and caution. He still hadn't found the catch.

Such an empty place these days, he thought. He looked over the old mining town below made up of tall plasma-concrete towers and flagstone pavements which stretched in both directions halfway across the circumference of the outpost's northern wall. It was clean and quaint in many respects, yet no one lived here any more. Hundreds of buildings had once been used as hotels, shops, bars and leisure complexes; a fully functioning city which remained an abandoned waste.

The digital star lens flickered and dimmed to deplete the land of its managed sunlight.

He stared through the darkness, eyes adjusting towards the lake over a hundred miles away at the centre of the outpost which still glimmered and flickered with light on its surface. He breathed in the perfumed air from the forests still in bloom, and drank some more. This place was his salvation in every respect and had given him peace, yet he remained troubled by it, even after fifteen years as its steward.

A metallic clunking noise drew his focus to the wall of scaffold his cabin was perched upon. Only he remained in this particular row of fibre-plate cabins and metal-mesh stairwells and walkways. He liked the solitude along the north wall of the outpost where he lived two hundred metres above the old city on a vast framework of cabins. He had shunned the chance to live near the centre of the basin in which the outpost had been created, and where the tourists stayed.

He had no problem with the few hundred tourists who holidayed in their luxury resorts which surrounded the lake. If the IMC allowed them to stay here for six months at a time then so be it. He could see the attraction of travelling seven light years from Earth to enjoy sixty thousands square miles of forest parklands along with two thousand square miles of Black Lake. The outpost was simply paradise.

There it is again, he thought, contemplating life and this place. The IMC had been so bold and continued to be extremely ambitious. All the excitement and wonder of this outpost for the company had long gone before he'd even been born. It had all begun with Deceiver, the lonely planet within this solar system. The IMC had sent probes and found it hidden, spinning a glorious blue in a static position ninety two million miles from the star that had given it life. Without probes the planet would have remained concealed and things would perhaps have been different. That was all history, over two hundred years ago, and had led to the definitive struggle to reach and colonise the planet. Such hope, expense and effort would have been in vain, for Deceiver was completely covered by a deep ocean that would have scuppered any chance for steady colonisation; except for one thing.

Inter-dimensional metal ore, klenethium and asaronite made the planet not just a scientific point of paramount interest, but had created a new industrial revolution which had helped space travel to become an ever more feasible way of life. They said that such a find confirmed a number of bewildering possibilities, but he wasn't a scientist and held no real value for what they had called the impossible: extra 'stable' elements on the periodic table. They still wanted to know where this planet had been and where it had acquired the super materials that shouldn't exist in this universe.

The IMC had made him captain: *Captain Frank Sharplin,* he thought with cynicism. He wasn't a real captain, just a caretaker; a task master of sorts. He'd never been in charge of a war craft or mining frigate, and had only accepted the position out of curiosity for this place. The basin in which the outpost had been built belonged to something far more remarkable than anything else in existence.

Eighty two years ago a catastrophe had halted all mining production on Deceiver when the planet froze almost instantaneously; killing over a hundred thousand people on a vast array of floating ore rigs. The incident had remained classified due to the appearance of 'God's Blade': a colossal fragment of unknown origin which had come to rest midway between Deceiver and its sun. Its name was derived from it being akin to a large flint blade; at least it looked that way from the correct angle and distance.

Frank remembered arriving at Black Ball for the first time. He remembered the incredible view of the shard from his shuttle craft and that it had changed his perception of existence in some way. The shard's dimensions had stuck with him and had mesmerised him into realising how insignificant humanity could seem. He thought about the sheer size of this thing with its rough proportions of fifteen thousand kilometres in length, eight thousand kilometres at its broadest plane, and three thousand kilometres in depth. Such figures were impressive to think about, but to see such magnitude had instilled a new fear and wonder of the universe in him. It wasn't a moon, a planet or an asteroid, and had managed to arrive unannounced, circumventing all human surveillance operating within the system. He thought about this aspect and shivered, as he always did.

Sharplin sat back deep into his chair and hooked his ankles up and over the balcony railing which divided him from the considerable drop on the other side. He felt tipsy and relaxed in the warm humid air. Large fans attached to the scaffold structure at intervals along the basin's wall pushed cool air over his skin. He felt better and began to doze until a sharp echo jolted him upright. He drank his whisky and poured some more.

Fifteen years of an easy life of fishing, hunting and golfing had never taken him far from the reality of this place, even if everyone else took it for granted. How easily people forgot the paranormal aspect of this elongated shard. Two massive planes of a flat surface smoother than marble and which met at sharp edges the full way around.

One of its flat planes continuously faced the sun and yet remained stubbornly cold, impervious to solar radiation. All of this, however, came second place in his mind to the shard's most unnerving aspect. The IMC had found a perfectly grooved pocket on the shard's planes. A thousand metres in depth, it boasted an inner area covering roughly seventy one thousand square miles: the basin.

The IMC had given him a classified document before he'd arrived, when he'd agreed to become caretaker to the outpost. He could recite in detail the incredible goings on and the level of engineering the IMC had undertaken to develop Black Ball. To him the whole thing was absurd.

The first experiment within the basin had begun by detonating atomic weapons with ever increasing kilo-ton yields until, inevitably, they amped the experiments up into the mega-ton variety. Such a barbaric endeavour had had no effect on the shard, which was then considered to be composed of an indestructible substance. One other marked point of the unexplained phenomenon was that all radioactive fallout from these detonations somehow dissipated; had perhaps even been absorbed into the basin's walls and floor.

Hordes of insects gathered around and landed on Sharplin's arms and face. He activated a small device on the table next to him to deter them from being drawn to the light in his cabin. The irritants quickly moved on and he again relaxed.

He always thought about the shard and the basin a lot at this time of year. He questioned his faith in everything on this anniversary. Where he saw the need for caution and respect for the unknown, the IMC had found opportunity and chosen disregard. Take Deceiver, for instance. The catastrophe of its freezing had destroyed the mining infrastructure in a single stroke. The IMC had advertised its distress, but in reality had found it a blessing for they could mine through ice far easier than traversing the planet's deep ocean, so that in turn, ore extraction had increased tenfold in the subsequent years.

They could have moved the shard and restored life to the planet, but instead had chosen to reap the benefits. Where some had seen alien and paranormal significance from the shard's appearance, the IMC had found an opportunity to create an outpost; the engineering challenge of a lifetime.

They were the company which had grown rainforests within some of Earth's most arid regions, thus helping replace and aid the ones which had been felled near to extinction. They had created fundamental technologies to finally push humankind into the space age and at phenomenal cost; any price would be paid.

The IMC were also wasteful in many of their achievements. Sharplin hadn't believed his eyes when he'd finally arrived at Black Ball. He'd spent a day in his new abode suffering from space lag until he'd walked on to his balcony for the first time. He'd expected it to be jam-packed with construction, an industrial city landscape of concrete and machinery; instead the IMC had made Eden. They'd levelled the basin floor with plasma concrete and created a circular dip of eighty metres with a fifty-mile diameter at its centre. They'd filled this with water from Deceiver's frozen ice fields to create Black Lake. That in itself had taken two years due to the level of bio screening required. Instead of mechanised air purification they'd grown trees, and instead of transporting food for storage they'd grown every crop conceivable.

Then, when all interest in the challenge had subsided, the IMC had begun to decommission the outpost's status to that of reserve class.

Frank sat and scrutinised the tangible surface of the ceiling covering the basin. He couldn't even begin to contemplate how expensive the star lens had been to create. The IMC owned a lot of assets and a good number of planets. They'd erected a fully automated environmental field (ionosphere), around 30 per cent the size of Mars, and had completely covered Phobos, one of the small Martian moons which it owned outright. The star lens was now considered old technology but remained a pioneering and historical piece of engineering. The lens was an immense singular transparent plate; a layer of protection which contained the atmosphere within the basin from spewing into the vacuum of space above. It sat just below the basin's lip as a protective roof, where it carried out its other function – to manage solar rays into the required yields of both energy and light. *Such a waste of investment,* he thought once again as he regarded the outpost's slow decommission into the largest under-occupied green house in existence.

Black Ball at least still had its important uses, he knew. Apart from being a wealthy person's holiday destination, it was still utilized as a storage cache of various weapons, along with a far more central purpose of banking Earth's entire biological reserve.

Genetic samples of every species of animal and plant which had survived until this age had been carefully preserved for the IMC insurance protocol order 'Critical Presumption'.

Sharplin watched the only movement across the basin at this time of night. Way in the distance there were flickering lights moving rapidly above the landscape and which belonged to the sky trams that remained the basin's quickest form of transport. He listened to the echoes bouncing around the vast bowl as he stretched his arms above his head and yawned. Then, as if a lifelong ritual had been rudely interrupted, a communication box on his desk buzzed loudly.

He'd finished his duties three hours ago and sighed at the machine summoning his attention. He had thought he'd left everything to his first officer, Judith Gibson, unless of course this was her trying to contact him. He strolled over to the device to lazily operate its crude functions.

'Frank Sharplin here.'

He nodded a few times at some information until the look on his face stated that he had something to do without the possibility of evasion. *Where's Judith?* he asked himself, smacking the box in a tantrum. Frank's attention turned yet again when he heard a strange noise from the corner of his living room. *Is it that thing again?*

He was filled with utter dread at the thought. Over the past month Frank had repeatedly seen the largest insect in existence, he was sure. The black bug was at least fifteen inches long with sleek rhomboid-shaped wings which looked as though they could stab a man to death without difficulty.

He moved slowly over to the side table by the couch and turned the main light on. To his horror, what appeared to be the very same bug was now sitting on his lounge room table only five feet away from him. The thing appeared to acknowledge him, flexed its solid wings, then scuttled around the wooden surface of the table on six-inch-long thick black legs like that of a tall bird's. He wasn't sure what to do except analyse the creature as he did every other thing with some compulsive disorder. He noticed, for instance, that it had no head, except for a formation at the front of its body which wasn't too dissimilar to the nib on his antique fountain pen.

He also noticed that it had a back end not too different to an ant's rear, with a bulbous tip hanging off a much more slender mid junction near to where its wings were attached. His most shocking observation was that it had the same marble sheen as the shard the outpost had been built within. Frank's mind rushed with speculation. He'd seen this thing in the forest and while fishing on the lake. Now it was in his apartment, which was just too close for comfort. He had guessed it was two feet long in some crazy exaggeration. To see it close up as a confirmed monster bug left him with one option: grab his jacket and run away to address the call he'd just received.

Version

~

Black Ball's forest areas were dense, covering 60 per cent of the basin floor; a joyful and decent trek for any rambling enthusiast, except for those who were dropped off via transport buggy and abandoned, as had happened with one long-running IMC marine drinking gag.

Commander Judith Gibson had already been dropped at random as forfeit to the occasional party game three times this year due to her insatiable appetite for heavy drinking bets. *The air feels warm as if I'm outside,* she thought before opening her eyes. A feeling of stiffness rushed through her body as she twigged that her night of drinking games had left her on a park bench somewhere in the basin's wilderness. She gradually sat up straight and held the back of her neck to let out a groan of overwhelming realisation. *A hangover before a twelve-hour shift won't kill me,* she thought, although it felt close.

Judith delicately stood up to stretch and wandered a few steps to figure out where the next forest clearing could be. *At least I still have my clothes on, not like last time,* she mused. Without thinking, she accessed her server chip to call for a lift then quickly deactivated it. *Don't you get caught again!*

After an hour spent staggering, she came to an opening in the forest canopy and found herself in a small field with long unkempt grass. She fought her way through the brush to brave a look towards the star lens so that she could identify the webbed construction of the sky tram. This means of high-speed transport utilized a network of cables hanging from a webbed scaffold of thick girders hung only fifty feet below the star lens. Hangover or not, she would have to stare into the light and adjust her focus until the cables came in to view. She gazed hard while desperately trying to ignore her eye stems crying in pain for darkness. She also tried to gauge the time of day from the spectrum output of the false sky; as if it mattered at this point.

She continued to stare at the sky, grinning to herself over Sharplin's level of knowledge of the star-lens spectrum that accurately emulated Earth's sun. He would know instantly what time of year it was imitating or, more often, what time of day it was to the hour. Judith put this down to the length of time he'd spent at the outpost, then again he knew more than anyone else about such things; even those who'd been at the basin for thirty years of service. Frank was either ultra-clever or just a social diluter, perhaps both, when she came to think of the nerdy qualities he had.

Still with no idea of the time, Judith stopped to consider which game she'd lost her watch in. *Of all the things to lose!*

The server chip could be utilized for its internal clock, except that she'd drunk too much and its bio-circuitry didn't take too kindly to high levels of alcohol; it always needed a few days to recuperate. She checked the device's version of the time.

01:00 A.M. – 25-12-1989.

She groaned. *I've broken it for good this time!*

At least it wasn't too difficult to figure out that it was late morning and that she was basically somewhere near the science village and on the wrong side of the lake to her office. She flinched with fright as a small vehicle pounced on her location from the wall of trees to her left.

It was an IMC marine in one of the outpost's runabout buggies. 'Captain Sharplin wants you at facilities, sir.'

The man smirked at Judith and she stared back at him with a dead expression before climbing into the small four-wheeled cart and sitting next to the man without bothering to reply. *At least that's sorted,* she thought, hitting a lever to fully recline her seat.

The headache Judith was suffering had almost subsided by the time she arrived to meet Sharplin at the facilities zone. The zone, located to the south-east of the basin's lake, comprised of a small science building with research labs which had once been used to create concept weapons and vehicle technologies. In a way this was ironic as the hospital unit Opus Reflection had been erected next door.

At the far end of the open driveway to the buildings, Judith saw Sharplin having a conversation with Dennis Aginie, who was usually in Craft Design nearer the lake in his workshop. Judith had no real idea about the top-secret developments there. From what she'd gathered, the science team had once developed weapons and, a few months back, had created a component for a concept engine which had quickly been shipped off to Phobos as part of a test launch.

She made her way towards them along the gravel driveway then the large flagstones which led the way into the medical unit. The path actually came as a relief to her with its smooth and even surface. She took a deep breath and clenched her fists. The birds hadn't stopped singing from the minute she'd come to in the forest. *If only I'd had my rifle!*

'Sir.' She nodded to Frank. 'Dennis, I thought you were busy making a device for the tree games since the last time we raced and you broke a leg.'

Dennis nodded with an arrogant slit-eyed stare. The outdoor pursuit games held once a year had been an embarrassment when he'd fallen twenty feet to the forest canopy, only to bounce violently through the branches and snap his femur on hitting the floor. 'As I explained to the captain, I've been busy working on the new drift-mine drilling transports. It appears that the GSA has also decided to mine under our ice zone and have caused a complete disaster in collapsing a major part of our tunnel network.'

'What does that have to do with us?' Judith referred to Frank and herself, hoping to be excused.

'Our mining team found a small transport vessel in the ice. I've been up all night sorting the admin out with IMC command,' Frank added with a shake of his head at Judith's attitude.

Dennis checked his watch with raised eyebrows. 'I have things to be getting on with.' With this statement he walked off towards a buggy parked nearby.

'The ship have anything interesting on it, like treasure?' Judith continued to mock.

'Just a load of dead frozen passengers, as you can imagine,' Frank replied. A puzzled look on his face suggested he was deep in thought about his answer.

He took Judith to one side as though bearing a secret. 'The ship is GSA prison class, eighty two years old, to be exact.'

Judith felt her headache worsen as the captain continued. 'I informed the IMC regarding the find so they'd authorise its release to GSA hands.'

Judith shrugged at this and he carried on as though he had to make a point. 'They said we're to leave the ship on Deceiver and bring its deceased passengers here until things have been resolved with the GSA.'

Judith shrugged again at Sharplin's paranoid speculations. 'So what? GSA are dicks who always kidney swipe the private firms. Besides, who cares about that stuff? I just want to see the frozen dead people, I bet they're a mess.'

Frank could never tell what she was really thinking; her habitual sarcastic deadpan responses gave the impression she was continually bored. Still, he'd guessed the commander would react this way. She was only young after all and, even though a cleverer person than himself in many ways, Judith was what they referred to as slightly tweaked. The IMC had sent him potentially great officers like this for years now and he'd managed to build character into them until, that is, he was sent Judith. For a number of reasons, and by all accounts, he considered her to be slightly insane, perhaps even psychopathic.

THE GUEST

Frank crouched next to the cool concrete wall of the corridor just outside the mortuary lab. He felt both tired and dishevelled in the dimly lit atmosphere.

She must be nearly finished, he thought of the doctor who was examining the bodies after they'd been defrosted. If they were to be sent back to another colony they'd need to be quarantined like anyone else.

He wasn't sure if he could go in as it only served to remind him. It had been such a long time ago. Why, this week of all weeks, was there cause to visit such a place? At least these people hadn't died in the basin; that was a record he aimed to keep if possible. His train of thought broke off as Judith burst through the morgue's heavy doors with a look of bewilderment. He glanced at her and noted she seemed to be back to her radiant glow in comparison to the grey deathly look she'd worn earlier in the morning.

'Have fun ogling the bodies?' he asked in disapproval.

Judith nodded. 'You should see the state of some of them, they were in a seriously bad collision, plenty of blood gushing as they thawed too,' she said nonchalantly.

Judith noticed Sharplin seemed unsettled. 'Okay, I know I'm a bit twisted, but I can't help it, there's no need to look so depressed.'

'I saw that creature again. It's after me, I can tell. I can't even order the environmental crew to search for it again or they'll think I'm mad.' He regretted this confession immediately as Judith grinned without any empathy for him. 'I'm telling you, Judith, I'm the only one who's seen it. I think it wants something from me or worse.'

Judith did her best to be serious. 'Where was it this time?'

'In my living room on the table.'

'You make it a drink?' Judith asked, unable to maintain a serious tone.

'This is serious, it knows where I live.'

'Look, it hasn't hurt you so why worry? It's probably just a mutated mosquito or fly.'

'Just a mutation? It's two bloody feet long! You'll be sorry when I'm attacked and killed.'

'I told you to tell Leonard,' Judith replied as though she really had nothing more to offer.

Sharplin gave up his plea for sympathy. He'd already asked Leonard Pike, who was in charge of environmental safety, to keep an eye out. Leonard's response had been that the basin was so large he'd have more luck recovering a memory that had never happened.

Judith turned to the mortuary door, losing all patience with him. 'I'm going in again, you fancy a look?'

She was surprised when Frank nodded and made his way to the door. 'I'd prefer to be fishing or playing golf, but you paint such a lovely picture.'

'You mean you're too afraid to go outside in case the giant mosquito gets you,' Judith quipped.

They both entered the long, narrow brightly lit room to see Doctor Rita Siren looking over the bodies presented on a number of tables. She spoke to Frank without breaking her focus. 'Well now, Captain, I'm surprised you're here. Not your kind of scene, is it?'

Sharplin glanced around the room, scanning the clinical environment. *Such a drab place,* he thought as he regarded its reflective asaronite worktops and typical grey concrete walls and floor. There were robotic servant arms in abundance though, which remained the only proof that some imagination had been spared. 'I thought it would make a nice change from fishing. Care to give me the news?'

Frank had known Rita for over ten years and found her both weird and attractive. It was a shame he was so shy when it came to those he fancied or he'd have asked her for a drink long ago.

Rita glanced at Sharplin with a cheeky smirk before she got to the business at hand. 'There are ten bodies which have suffered from major trauma – the collision. You can see as much as I can. They have a variety of injuries, including severed limbs, a decapitation, and look at this poor sod with a crude robotic device of sorts straight through his chest.'

Captain Sharplin saw that Judith was enjoying every minute with the recently thawed bodies as she gave them all a second close inspection. He strolled around the room uncomfortably while observing a large robotic arm probe one of the bodies for any contamination. He hardly noticed that Doctor Siren continued to guide her guests through her findings. 'I've found a number of alien bacteria due to contact with the ocean water, but it's a greater exposure than I've encountered before. They couldn't have been there long before the planet froze, there's no decomposition at all. How's that for timing?'

'What?' Judith asked, looking closely at the different bodies still in strange positions.

A weird thudding sound emanated from one of the tables which drew their attention.

Doctor Siren looked on without interest and chewed her lip. 'There's sometimes movement from gasses,' she stated, referring to one of the bodies' moving limbs. 'Do you want me to do any autopsies or just put them straight in the containers?'

Sharplin thought for a moment. 'I'd box them, but take the bits out of them, poor souls.'

Judith was busy looking into the eyes of the man who had the robotic arm protruding from his chest. 'This one looks peaceful compared to the others, don't you think?'

The three of them gathered around to compare the man's facial expression to the faces of the others which, in comparison, were twisted in sheer terror. It was odd for sure. Here was a man who'd been skewered yet had a satisfied smirk on his face. It wasn't something any one of them would have deemed an appropriate expression considering how he'd died.

Rita began to drag quarantine tubs from under a tall worktop: basically airtight carbon containers which had replaced the standard coffin to seal a person for transport. 'So tell me why you both decided to spend your Sunday looking at dead people?' she asked as though they'd disturbed her solitude.

'The short of it is, the GSA have been busy mining through our company's plot for whatever and caused an IMC salvage team to find the ship with these corpses on board. The mining frigates have all left now and won't be back for weeks. It's pretty much messed up my day off. Judith's at work anyway.'

'None of the ships had freezers?' Siren asked, surprised. 'They could have decontaminated these corpses en route.'

'I don't know. IMC command ordered them to be dumped here. Maybe they think you don't work hard enough,' Frank said in jest as his best form of flirting.

Rita chuckled in a sarcastic tone and began pushing one of the bodies off the table in front of her into the tub she'd put in place to catch it.

Frank looked on with disdain at the procedure. 'Don't you get the bot arms to do this bit?' he asked.

Doctor Siren looked at him as though he were being rude. 'I enjoy my work, Captain, don't you? Actually none of this work has to be done by me, I was curious like you, Frank.'

Rita was a research doctor who sometimes treated people at the basin if she was in the mood. The robots were the real medical provision, which left Doctor Siren free – to do what, no one was quite sure.

A crash from the back end of the room turned the pair's attention towards Judith. Both Rita and Frank ignored her as she raised her arms as though innocent and perplexed. They moved on quickly to the next table where Rita shoved hard at the body of a headless male that in turn slipped over the edge, flapping wetly into the body bucket 'These people have been frozen for such a long time I wonder who would want them back now?' Rita asked under strained breath at the extra weight. 'Do we know who they were?'

Frank knew this question would consume the rest of his afternoon and rolled his eyes when he thought of the workload he now had to key in at the office. He glanced at Judith and considered getting her to do it in his stead. 'They're prisoners, I think. They used to be sent to work on the rigs before the ice age and I guess they were never missed.'

Version

Frank narrowed his eyes in suspicion. He could see the body that Judith was interfering with moving its limbs in small convulsions. 'I know you said that gasses cause movement, but that one seems to be having a fit.'

Rita looked over at the body. 'Judith, let him be.'

'I haven't touched it, it's full of wind.'

Again Frank witnessed a flicker of movement which appeared unusual. Rita and Judith also noticed it, which prompted them all to move closer around the table. They stayed silent in concentration as blood from the body's chest wound dripped on to the table – a central focal point for the three of them to fixate upon.

A gurgling sound filled the room, instilling Rita with a horror she refused to believe. 'I think . . .'

Before she could finish, the body jolted to sit upright, only to fall flat again in ferocious spasms as all three jumped back for cover.

'Assistance button now,' Rita shouted at anyone who hadn't yet gone into shock. She threw herself at the man who appeared to be fighting his way back to life, regardless of his fatal injuries.

'Shit, shit, press the auto on the emergency arm next to you, Frank!' Rita screamed as Frank idled in disbelief.

Judith leapt to the panic button and then to the robot arm before Frank could shake his stare. The robot arm in turn flickered to life with lightning reflexes, probed the room with a camera and swayed over to where Doctor Siren was trying to steady the man, who jolted so violently he was in danger of flicking off the table. The robot arm moved closer to the table on its treads and its main bulk split into several smaller limbs. It began multitasking at speed by first reaching over the body to use a large bulb-like object which scanned the body from head to toe in a mere second. It then placed one of its metal stumps on the man's body to hold him steady as other arms moved in and administered injections.

Frank couldn't help but grimace as the appliance forced a sponge airway tube down the man's throat to pump in oxygen. Seven thin and nimble mechanised arms worked quickly, making it difficult to watch the performance with any clear understanding as to what they were trying to achieve. The arms were strong too; the man's convulsions were easily suppressed by the weight of the appliance as it laboured on.

Frank could see Judith was thrilled as two more limbs removed the foreign object from the man's chest and quickly cut a larger opening through the sternum in order to operate. Crack. The sternum was brutally prised wide open to expose the patient's damaged heart and lungs. The machine's appendages, ready to operate in the confined space, twisted to release several smaller rods each a few inches long. They moved in all directions, freely allowing for easy, nimble access as they went to work within the chest cavity. One set of mechanical fingers held the heart, vacuuming excess blood from around its surface through a suction tube, while others cauterised a flat organic material on to the largest wounds with fine, hot soldering tips.

Another limb moved into position over the man's chest, rapidly adjusting moving parts with its own equivalent of a hand. Again, the very end of the metallic branch opened up just as the other two had and utilized its more accurate fingers to stitch various tissues with a very thin silky thread.

This is pointless, Frank decided, trying to keep up with the speed at which the machine worked. Judith meanwhile leaned in too close to the robot, which promptly pushed her away in a strange violating manner only a machine could achieve.

Incredulously the robot's audience waited for it to finish repairing the chest wound.

Dmmp. It finished its eighty-second human repair spectacle by zapping the man's chest with electricity from the very stump that held him in place. *Dmmp.* The body jolted slightly at another attempt. This time the robot arms retracted every utensil, seemingly satisfied.

The machine was one of the IMC's newer toys which could repair organs for transplant and, as on this occasion, remove embedded objects. As witnessed, it was also programmed to defibrillate and resuscitate while it continued stitching with what had become commonly referred to as therapy thread, and which enhanced wound recovery.

Version

Doctor Siren carefully watched the rise and fall of the man's chest. She couldn't be sure he was breathing independently as the robot continued to pump air into his lungs via the tube it had lodged down his throat. She couldn't be sure about anything as the new machine worked silently without the usual beep to the rhythm of a person's heart she was used to with older models. This new medical unit was a prototype field model designed to operate in combat zones and was classed as competent enough to do so alone, without the need to give any indications to those around it.

Rita crouched beneath the multiple arms of the machine to avoid being shoved in the same manner as Judith had, and looked for a pulse. She checked the wrist and neck, then stood back a few paces and turned to Sharplin. 'What the hell just happened?'

'Well,' Judith said, 'before he wakes up someone had better pull that big plug out of his arse, you know what I'm saying?

Evening fell as the star-lens spectrum adjusted. The man, who by all accounts had risen from the dead, had been taken to a recuperation hospital deep within the basin's farmlands ten miles to the north-east of the lake. The tall stand-alone building had once been used as an executive business retreat, and had many luxurious rooms all with balconies.

Frank stood on the balcony of the patient's room sipping a well-earned whisky while taking in another magnificent view of the landscape. He'd sent Judith to finish the admin regarding the other corpses and to find out more about the historical circumstances of the ship and its passengers. Eight hours had passed swiftly, and the man from the morgue – from Deceiver – lay very still and was unlikely to wake for days, yet Frank felt like waiting by his side, just in case.

He analysed the digital pad which held the list of injuries the man had sustained. The medical unit which had taken charge had sent a report that was hard to follow in many ways except for the most obvious of details. The robot had calculated that the organ recovery of the aorta, along with 30 per cent of the man's right lung, were non-salvageable. The report then listed its calculations regarding blood loss and the amount of synthetic solution used to replace it.

Sharplin knew little about the synthetic plasmatic enzymes used in hibernation-stasis journeys and which was also used for blood transfusions. If he'd read the digi-pad's information correctly, the amount of solution pumped into the man's body to compensate for blood loss had well exceeded the safe quantities recommended.

Sharplin let out an eye-watering yawn. He hadn't slept for nearly twenty four hours and felt as though his eyes had filled with grit, which only served to hinder his appreciation of the view. In the fields straight ahead of the hospital, a long row of large propellers fanned the surrounding area to create a breeze which moved across the grass until it gently rocked the forest a few miles away. He gazed further and across the top of the canopy into the distance where a holiday resort sat just at the north side of Black Lake's shore. People were still on the lake partaking in water sports and his own favourite hobby of fishing. He scratched his skin with agitation; before leaving the morgue his body had been blasted of all possible organisms from Deceiver within a decontamination chamber.

'Where am I?'

Frank spun around and was startled to see the patient standing next to him 'Holy . . . you should be a tax auditor sneaking around like that.' He frantically yanked his right hand out from where it was firmly embedded down his trousers to cure an itch. Luckily, the man standing by him hadn't noticed and simply stared like a zombie.

Frank quickly composed himself from his embarrassment to see an athletically built man over six feet tall with dark hair. It was strange to see him standing there alive; a person could look completely different in many ways if initially met as a lifeless mess compared to the physical presence now in its place.

A marine standing guard in the corridor popped his head in through the main entrance to the room at the sound of voices. 'Everything all right, sir?'

'Yes, yes. I'll call for assistance if I need it.'

The man peered out over the balcony at the basin's landscape. 'Where am I? This isn't anything like they said.' He looked at Sharplin as though drunk; his pupils completely dilated. 'Who are you?'

Version

'I'm sorry, my name is Captain Frank Sharplin.' He paused and waited for a response from the man standing scruffily in a peach hospital gown and with an intravenous drip attached to his arm. The man hadn't noticed the IV stand had fallen over and he'd dragged it along the floor on its side.

'Ologun Jowett.'

Frank shifted uneasily to grab the stand and rectify its position while being careful not to rip the syringe from Ologun's arm. He grabbed a chair for him and made a hand gesture to sit. 'I don't know how to start this conversation exactly . . . this isn't Deceiver, as you may have guessed, and you won't be going to any rig.'

Ologun peered out over the landscape as though he were not paying any attention to Frank's voice. He then looked directly at Frank, suddenly sober and switched on. 'Am I dead?'

Frank chortled for a moment nervously. 'No, no, you're quite alive. I mean you, and then . . .' He cleared his throat to continue. 'This place is an outpost not too far from Deceiver. It's sort of like a planet-sized flat piece of slate, we occupy a fair-sized area of this rock inside a convex bowl on its surface.'

Ologun's face looked blank at this information. 'So we are . . . what?'

Frank gulped his whisky to pour another. What does someone say to a man who had been pronounced dead and revived, and who then was not meant to be out of his slumber for days? *This is going to be a tough conversation which should have waited,* he thought with hindsight.

NATURE OF THE BEAST

'I have some strange information on our guest,' Judith said in greeting to Captain Sharplin when he entered her office.

He sat down opposite her at a large desk and made himself comfortable. The office was in a small concrete cabin sat at ground level. Its interior remained undecorated except for the desk, a computer station, and a few plants to break up the usual dullness of its grey walls. 'I don't think much will surprise me now, what have you found?' he said, adjusting the chair opposite Judith.

'His Flickr profile recognises him as the son of an Admiral Gavin Jowett, IMC fleet. That's only the half of it, though, listen to this. Sergeant Ologun Jowett, IMC security contract forces, was sentenced to life on Deceiver over eighty two years ago for the murder of twelve GEA soldiers. He killed them defending terrorists detained at the Mirage Six irrigation fields, eighty miles north-west of Casablanca.'

Sharplin nodded at this as Judith moved on with news more worthy of his attention.

'I got the doctor to do a genetic profile using the archive systems to confirm his identity. Something just doesn't add up here. He is Ologun, except that he isn't the blood relative of Admiral Jowett.'

Captain Sharplin sat and thought about this. 'The man at the recuperation centre isn't Ologun?'

'Yes, absolutely, I think,' Judith stated. 'I have identification from various Flickr files at many points in his life such as schools he attended, IMC records, GEA court logs. They all match. Here comes the real mystery. The DNA match system considered all the stored information over the past three hundred and fifty years and worked out that his parents were most likely to be Anoka Sykes and Sebastian Knowles.'

'He was adopted, nothing unusual there,' Frank argued.

'That's the real issue here. Anoka Sykes was a marine biologist sent on a mission for IMC aboard one of twelve ships trying to reach Deceiver. Doctor Knowles was sent on another of these ships as its physician.'

Frank rubbed his eyes as he listened.

'The ships were the very first to be launched and took over thirty years to reach us here.'

'Sent to us here, when?' he asked, somewhat lost.

Judith realised she'd jumbled what she meant. 'This frontier project was launched one hundred and ninety years ago when the IMC was just a rich company.'

'Still is,' Sharplin added.

'No, no.' Judith struggled with her own enthusiasm 'The IMC are massive now compared to then. They sent these ships which never came back. *They never came back!*'

Judith's office was located at the only remaining military compound still in operation and located east of the lake at the basin's wall. The faint sound of firing weapons echoed from the range only a mile away at one of the marine training centres.

Frank swivelled to one side in his chair. In the corner of the office stood a large vine of sorts which reached up from an elongated pot to seek light. The plant had flourished by wrapping throughout a large wire grid wedged into a window gap in the wall. He remembered that Judith had lost her temper over something a while ago and thrown a chair so hard it had shattered the window lens. The current unsightly grid had been fixed as a replacement.

He couldn't even begin to gather the fundamentals of the information she'd gathered and found no concentration by following the plant's success in weaving its way into the wire mesh guard. 'Just elaborate on that. What do you mean?'

'I mean that . . . what don't you get? Anoka and Sebastian go on a trip and never come back, they were missing on mission. There are no records that either donated the goods, you know sperm, eggs etc. Then, seventy-odd years after going missing they have a son who ends up in the custody of an IMC Admiral.'

Frank found her terminology a bit tasteless regarding specimen donations. 'Coincidence! Other genetic material was used. The IMC hold on to what they consider superior minds. The admiral had his own reasons for adopting. What's your point?'

'I don't have one yet. Here's the blinder, though. I checked Ologun's birth date. That year, Admiral Jowett was on the IMC ship *Zulu Surprise* out near Jupiter. I checked other history logs and came up with an incident that occurred near there on the same date. A rescue station known as the *Extended Pin* went missing: vanished without trace. Also a GSA ship, the *Granite of Wishes*, was out there and, at the very same time, pwwf, gone.'

'What else did you find on this?' Frank asked. 'Is there a connection between the three ships?'

'I can't find anything else. It's all classified, even now.'

'Let's not jump to any conclusions for the moment. I need time to think about this. And Commander, don't go breaking into any databases.'

'So how's the zombie?' Judith asked, changing the subject to avoid the avenue down which this conversation was potentially heading.

'He's in good condition, not the living dead,' Frank said, defending Ologun with some empathy. 'I let him tour the basin and gave him my old shed out near the Dark Zone. He can live there until I'm ready to tell IMC Command.'

'You did *what*?' Judith said, raising her voice in astonishment.

'I know it sounds crazy, but who the hell is he going to hurt miles away from anyone? Besides I had Doctor Siren tag him. Unless he can cut into his own rib cage and yank that out, we can keep tabs on him. It beats locking him up.'

Judith swung on her chair as though anxious. 'You put him near the Minx Machine, I bet. If he steps out of line I'll have his balls.'

'Actually he's about ten miles south of there and we both know that Whatshisface would kill him if he did anything!'

Judith agreed. The Minx Machine was her club; the place she went with the marines for a good night of mayhem. Ongdon Huya, the bar's owner, had a shady reputation and would regularly comment that he'd like nothing more than to poach himself a misfit.

She knew where Ologun had gone now. He was in the south-east of the Dark Zone in some orchards where Frank liked to go sometimes to enjoy the remoteness. The idea of Ologun getting hurt played on her mind. *How did he cheat such injuries, even death?*

'Could he be the result of some long-lost genetic programme by some crazy, I don't know . . . military terrorist outfit?' Judith suggested. 'He can't be normal.'

'Who would risk that? Besides, the penalty if caught would make it an insane risk. Starting such designs again would be reckless. It was even worse eighty years ago.'

Society had a strange way of moving attitudes for and against accepting new technologies, Frank had learned over the years. In the mid-twenty-first century, the trend for flawless designer babies had taken hold in a major way for those who could afford it. He'd studied this movement at university. His approach to the work had been lazy; it was a topic far too immersed in ethics and philosophy rather than science, and he found it difficult to ascertain the true nature of the beast. What he understood on the subject was that the general populace had taken the whole superhuman deal badly, with various detrimental consequences.

The universal outrage at enhancing a human's intellectual or physical attributes had been sustained through to the present and the consensus was that it devalued the very essence of being human.

'His recovery points to some form of engineering, I agree.' Frank took a moment to think hard about the situation as Judith waited for him to finish his sentence. 'If say, for military purposes, someone did make this guy able to heal, among other things we haven't yet seen, I think they'd have taken more care to hide him away rather than send him to prison. What do you think?'

Judith sighed and gave no indication that she knew anything about the subject. 'Well, at least he didn't need new organs. Siren doesn't have a licence for replication.' Although she realised that at Black Ball such laws made little difference. 'All I know is that we should keep him under close observation, preferably locked up.'

Sharplin really didn't want to delve into this topic; if Ologun had been some experiment, the last thing any of them, including Rita Siren, should do was uncover classified information. He feared only one thing from the IMC: obtaining knowledge they didn't wish anyone other than authorised personnel to have – even *those* personnel were on the containment list. In simple terms, the IMC was everyone's best friend until they thought you were a security risk. If that happened, even God would have trouble finding those who vanished.

'In my day I read of apathy and of food in abundance,' Frank mumbled.

'What?' Judith asked.

'You did history at the academy?' Frank asked, changing the subject. 'The two-thousand-mile irrigation and plantation lane stretching across North Africa began two hundred and fifty years ago, utilizing marine water processed to fresh then piped to massive farms. The Chinese division of the IMC instigated it as part of—'

'Don't patronize me over agricultural history, Frank,' Judith barked. 'What does that have to do with anything?'

Sharplin raised his hands in defence and got to the point. 'Okay, so you mentioned the reason Ologun was sentenced. He already told me. He wasn't protecting terrorists. I mean they don't teach you about the migration crises as it really happened. GEA estimated that thousands would try to tap the water lines and even show up to set up new lives around the newly built reservoirs. The whole thing was underestimated with tens of thousands turning up to try their chances at what they deemed as "water and crop theft" etc. Soon the IMC won a contract whereby they worked with the GEA to police the fields, shanty towns, and any other liable areas of conflict. Or was it the Moroccan government's change of tender that replaced the IMC?' he muttered, trying to remember the history. 'Anyway . . .'

Judith was intrigued as the general history files spoke of North Africa as part of the world's food salvation but never once mentioned conflict of any kind.

Sharplin continued, yet felt his knowledge of this era to be a little vague. 'Rebels began to arm themselves, became more organised with chaos breaking loose, hence the IMC stepping in to relieve pressure.'

'No, no, the IMC lost the contract with the Moroccan government to protect the plantations, you're thinking of the Algerian sand markets and reservoir developments . . . armed terrorists?' Judith corrected him, at the same time becoming confused at the mention of a rebellion.

'Yes, that's right,' he said, rubbing his chin. 'Our guest was an IMC soldier working at the forest plantation wall of the Western Sahara alongside GEA in a huge shanty town known as Demon's Crevice.'

Judith laughed. 'Really?'

'Actually the people who lived there called it Blessed Earth or something. I only know the GEA name for the place. A huge scandal erupted when GEA soldiers began killing and torturing the people living there, who by all accounts were just desperate to find a better life. At the time millions of people migrated for thousands of miles from the southern countries where poverty and other problems existed. Ologun caught a whole platoon of GEA troops abusing villagers on some wasteland and ended up, well, you know.'

'Well, the file doesn't say exactly how it happened, which is a shame really,' Judith added, leaning back in her chair in thought. She might have tried to come across as being concerned at allowing a strange man who'd been revealed to have killed GEA personnel go around relatively unsupervised. The reality was that she'd never met anyone who'd killed before. She was curious as, in principle, the story made him sound relatively heroic; a different kind of animal to the rest of the men at the basin. Judith decided to go along with the captain, although she couldn't figure out his agenda for not incarcerating Ologun.

'He told you this story and you believe him?' Her question was a mechanism to gauge his response as she was unsure of the level of Sharplin's sanity over the issue.

'I know what went on there. I know what the GEA soldiers did even if they do paint it in their favour,' Frank finally replied, staring deeply into the twisting vines. 'Besides, we're not a prison camp and he's been frozen for eighty years, don't you think he's done his time? He can do what he likes until he cocks up. Then and if he does, *I'll* have his balls, Okay?'

'Okay. I can believe the GEA would be monsters, even more so eighty years ago. So you think what he did was noble under the circumstances, I get it, though he's your responsibility if he does anything,' Judith stated, tiring of the whole debate. 'Did he really tell you?' she asked, wondering at Frank's vague account of the facts.

'Yes, of course,' he replied without looking at her. He suddenly had no recollection of any such conversation. He dismissed his lack of recollection and was relieved that Judith had submitted as she could have reported him to HQ in such circumstances. He was troubled by it all and just wanted to get Ologun far out of the way, out of sight; he really couldn't place the reason and believed it might be instinct. *Also*, he reasoned to himself, *if I lock Ologun up, there'll be endless administrative work and it would need to be reported to the IMC immediately.* He knew this to be poor ethics on his part, especially as an officer, but if he reported this they'd send a ship and interfere. *Maybe I can pretend this never happened.*

Sharplin's head buzzed with a message sent to his server chip.

Damn incarnation! He hadn't logged on to the server in a long while and absolutely hated the device. All systems required the use of a chip which everyone had connected to their nervous system and was implanted behind their right ear.

Frank excused himself from Judith and left her office to walk the long stone-paved driveway to the compound gates. He tried to remember how to switch it on. It had no button as such and needed to be done with a thought. The interface designers hadn't figured that some people had trouble tuning in if they loathed the thought. Frank finally accessed his domain as it flashed up in his vision. *It's peculiar, even dangerous,* he thought. *I can see the real world with my right eye and information from the network with my left.* 'How the hell do people have this bloody chip switched on all the time?' he mumbled as he tried to walk and control the system.

The captain stopped just yards from the compound at the bottom of a spiralling metal staircase leading to one of the sky-tram platforms. He never checked his messages as there were rarely any he considered important. Checking his account, Frank saw a message that would destroy his world.

IMC COMMAND – SECURITY STATUS REQUEST /\

SECURITY STATUS INCREASED . . . FIVE ENCOUNTER CLASS CRUISERS EN ROUTE . . . ETA SEVENTY TWO HOURS . . . PREP ALL DORMANT SYSTEMS . . . ACTIVATE ALL MILITARY ZONES . . . FORTRESS. ACKNOWLEDGE.

Frank wiped sweat from his forehead. Only the East Base was operational. The fortress, along with the original star-lens docking platform, needed to be re-booted in very little time. That wasn't really the issue though, as he realised his tranquil job of babysitting an almost defunct military outpost was about to be ruined. Something major must be going on back home that he was in no hurry to face.

Sharplin was so distraught that he hadn't noticed the man opposite talking to him. He looked up to see a completely naked dark-skinned man standing on the grass two feet away. *What the . . .?* 'What are you doing, son? Put some clothes on, for heaven's sake.'

The man seemed uninterested by Sharplin's instruction and glared, expressionless. 'I have come to advise you to leave this place in seven days. I suggest you leave sooner.'

Sharplin looked around him, thinking that a practical joke was being played on him. Then, before he could say another word, the very insect he feared arrived, hovered and landed on the man's right shoulder. 'Don't move, just stay still. I'll get help. Don't you panic, it might just go away.'

The man ignored Frank's concern and appeared completely relaxed as the creature flexed its wings and dug its pointed legs into the skin covering his deltoid. 'I say again for your own sake, be gone in seven days, I recommend it be thirty six, no, sixty eight hours.'

Sharplin's heart raced. He watched, paralysed in fear and complete confusion, as the strange man made his way to a tall hedgerow surrounding the military compound and passed through its thick foliage. He mulled over the incident for a few seconds then pursued the naked man. He pushed through the hedge and into a large field. Ahead he could see the firing-range bunkers way in the distance. He scanned the area left to right searching for the man and the creature; they had vanished without trace.

'Frank! Captain.'

Sharplin was stunned by the encounter and found himself a little detached from reality as he made his way back through the hedgerow.

Judith spotted him and sprinted towards his location. She reached him slightly out of breath where he immediately began jabbering frantically and incoherently. 'A man, a naked man. Judith, the insect landed on his shoulder like he was a pirate. A naked ghost pirate!'

Judith grabbed his collar and shook him forcefully. 'Frank, listen, we need to get to the Dark Zone now!'

The Dark Zone worked its way round the full circumference of the west side of the lake and had earned its name by being comprised of very tall trees which had been added for the purpose of air conditioning. The vegetation was of varieties mainly found growing throughout all rainforests on Earth and now thrived in the rich soil and pleasant conditions of the basin's environment.

This stretch of forest covered twelve thousand square miles in a crescent-shaped formation surrounding acres of farmland to its east and the old city to the north.

Such a development was minute in comparison to one of Earth's natural treasures, yet remained an ample quantity for the basin's purposes.

Frank and Judith arrived at the exterior north-west side of the jungle in a small buggy. Another larger vehicle with several armed IMC marines duly pulled up next to them and almost mowed through Doctor Siren in the process as she stood waiting patiently for them to arrive. The group organised themselves quickly and rallied in a small field leading away from the city's edge. In front of them the imposing wall of the jungle towered neatly as though a barrier had been measured across the entire landscape. Frank looked around at the surroundings. He felt trapped in this alleyway between the many tall buildings of the abandoned city and the peak of wild nature incarnate; as though two very different forces had gathered in confrontation.

The group watched as a machine unit Siren had brought made its way down the ramp from one of the vehicles, independent of human interference. The thick pole of the robot's body rocked back and forth as it came to rest on the grass and its treads gripped the more welcoming surface.

'Where to?' Frank asked.

Sergeant Thomas checked a digital pad for information and led the group towards the forest edge. 'This way. Here, you'd better have this, sir.'

Thomas handed Sharplin a digital pad which bleeped in accordance to a navigation marker. Frank handed it back. 'I have my own, here, see?'

'Okay, you take mine and I'll type the frequency into yours.'

Judith sighed loudly at the two men as they fumbled around with the devices. 'Just get on with it.'

The thick canopy high above kept the daylight emitted by the star lens at bay, and among the trunks the unusual gloom seemed inhospitable. Torches were switched on and the journey began. The search team remained silent as they moved deeper into the woods amongst a variety of vines which dominated any unused ground between the tree trunks. Rotting vegetation squelched underfoot where the humidity rose from the floor. Hordes of flying insects gave the impression the team had invaded their territory. They flew blindly, clumsily and in thick waves into the unwanted visitor's faces akin to kamikazes.

Sharplin had never been to this place before and realised it remained unsullied by any of the basin's occupants, in contrast to other, more pleasant, parkland where there were normally paths to be found cutting through and showing the way.

The ground remained flat yet unaccommodating as they all hiked along, half-slipping on the vegetation underfoot. From time to time the machine had to be picked up and lifted over thick exposed tree roots rising up and across the floor. This was an alien place; the odd one out in the basin's typical paradise. It would be too easy to get lost in the darkness and unrelenting features, and the navigation system on the digital pad was the only saving grace.

Twenty minutes in and the air was thick with the stench of stagnant decaying vegetation. They followed the marker on the digital pad left by an enthusiastic cross-country hiker who had found something Sharplin hoped was a mistake. This hiker had gone relatively deep, far enough to reach the mature specimens which had trunks measuring up to fifteen feet in diameter.

A rustling among the leaves startled the group as marines found their target with rifles. Infra-red beams accurately followed the sound: only rabbits.

They continued onward, listening to the sounds of birds as they sang, along with the whirring of one robot still lagging a few feet behind.

It's hot in here, Sharplin thought. He wasn't sure why he'd come. *Captains don't need to go places.* Then again, no one here was really meant for this hunt. No one in the basin was actually qualified to deal with what they might find.

If it was simply a case of police intervention, this situation had come too late. Along with many decommissioned components of this outpost, police forces and other investigators had re-located; order in this place relied on the military.

The marines suddenly spread out in a circle, indicating they were surrounding the beacon in a defensive formation. Captain Sharplin looked at the digital pad to register that it was ten yards ahead. Slowly he followed Judith with Doctor Siren closely behind. Judith scoured the area in a trained logical sequence, then stared ahead down the sight of her weapon. She stopped. Ahead of her the small sphere of the beacon pulsed with a low level of light amongst a carpet of dead leaves. It flashed bolts of illumination into the area of darkness which sent Frank's mind into a further state of panic.

Judith switched the beacon off with a solid stamp from the heel of her boot. She shone the torch fixed underneath her rifle's barrel around the area – her eyes and weapon as one. Across the ground, insects crawled among the leaves. Something smelled putrid.

Version

They all searched with torches until one of the beams came across a pale abnormality in the brown layer covering the ground. Doctor Siren moved in quickly and Judith unwrapped a pustule lamp from her shoulder sack and placed it on the floor.

Immediately the lamp spluttered on and transformed the creepy setting into an immensely lit cramped room with closely knit tree trunks as its partition from the rest of the jungle outside. There, amongst the leaves, a human body lay face down. Naked and bound with its arms behind its back, its skin was bleached and ravaged by the elements.

Frank began to shake with a kind of horror he'd never truly felt before, or at least not since before he'd come to Black Ball. He looked to Judith for support, but she remained firm with a watchful eye peering through a rifle scope into the darkness outside the area of pale-blue light.

It felt like hours since anyone had spoken; no one had any words.

Is this Ologun's doing?

'Not unless he did this, travelled to Deceiver and buried himself down under three miles of ice,' Doctor Siren blurted out, breaking the sound of a bird screeching blue murder in the distance.

'Did I say that out loud?' Sharplin asked. He was sure he'd only thought it.

'I read Ologun's file, you didn't have to say anything, I could tell what you were thinking. This person has been dead for nearly two weeks, I'd say.'

Fair enough, he thought. The circumstances surrounding the first possible victim to foul play ever to be found in the basin pointed towards Ologun in a stark way. 'Well? Is this what it looks like?' he asked.

'Well, they didn't tie themselves up did they? Just give me a chance to examine this for a moment.'

The robot moved in to begin some investigative work by turning the dead body on to its back. It was the corpse of a female.

There was hardly any need to answer Frank's question when, aside from the damage caused by the woodland's inhabitants, it was

51

clear someone had used a sharp tool to cut her open vertically from her pelvis to the top of her sternum.

Doctor Siren examined the corpse more closely and used a long metal tool with a flat lip at its end to lift the flap of skin of the long incision. 'Well, whoever did this has done a quality job of removing her internal organs.'

The seriousness of this affected Sharplin's vision and he felt far away from everything. Reality shrank and he felt sick. He suddenly felt the pressure of the universe on his skin.

Siren read information from the machine still scanning the woman's body. 'According to her implant she is – was – Karlitta Surpris, twenty seven years of age. She worked as a holiday rep, but she also has a second implant, she's in the sales business if you know what I mean. I think she'd have been found earlier, but both implants have failed. Very unusual.'

'No, sales, I don't know what you mean. What's the second implant for?'

Siren continued to work despite her astonishment at Frank's lack of awareness.

'She was moonlighting as a prostitute. The second implant is an illegal add in, a pimp chip. You know, so they can keep an eye on them.'

Frank was baffled. *How long has this been going on?* He looked to Judith for her input as his mind raced. The fortress, the docking platform, the IMC's arrival and the man Ologun back from the frozen dead. *The naked pirate and his pet! What had he said? 'Be gone in seven days, I recommend it be thirty six, no, sixty eight hours.'*

He'd woken in the seventh circle of hell, and the home he'd come to know had vanished in only a couple of days to be replaced by madness. He began to feel that he wasn't cut out to be captain in these circumstances and, to be fair, he'd been chosen by the IMC as steward to this place under certain parameters. His aptitude was for routine and relatively low levels of decision making. Recent events seemed to be perfect tests created to push his mind to the brink.

Version

Judith looked directly at him in deep concentration, rifle pointed into the gloom in the other direction.

Say something to them. Sharplin thought hard for an answer. *Nothing!*

Minutes passed until his mind unravelled to utter words that he hoped mimicked a command: 'Bag her up. Let's get out of here.'

'Shouldn't we investigate the scene for more evidence?' Doctor Siren asked.

'Leave the machine to continue, it can send anything it finds to you. Take the body back to the morgue and do whatever it is you need to . . . no one here on the base can deal with this.

'Commander, you can assemble a team to investigate this until qualified IMC personnel can get here.'

Captain Sharplin then felt his lungs stop working. *Five days until the anniversary.* Seeing this body hurt him with a tangible, excruciating pain which hadn't been caused by physical trauma. He turned to hurry back through the darkness. He desperately needed to drink, to forget, to be anaesthetised.

After a few days to regain his bearings, Ologun insisted on earning his keep. Doctor Siren had checked him over and given him a clean bill of health. In fact even the scar tissue on his chest had almost healed over, prompting the doctor to study him by extracting tissue samples, blood samples, and even the alien bacteria extracted from his skin when he'd arrived in his lesser state. She'd study anything which may give a plausible explanation to this phenomenon. Who could blame the doctor for being desperate to unlock the mystery of his rise from the dead?

Ologun had much to thank Captain Sharplin for, as he'd overruled Doctor Siren's wishes to quarantine him. It wasn't just his freedom that prompted him to be grateful. Earning his keep entailed farming of sorts, which in all truth was his chance to do something useful with his time. The trust Sharplin had shown him was remarkable as a few days to tour the basin had been granted him before he went to work.

Craig Jenkins

Ologun had been given a digital pad displaying a map of the basin layout and told to do as he liked, within reason. The map of the basin was peculiar to say the least as its overall view of Black Ball resembled a target. There was a blue circle at the centre representing the lake, surrounded by a green ring for the forests and farming areas. Finally, at its perimeter, a further grey half-circle represented the old city to the north. He felt a strange sensation as he wandered the old city along the basin's north wall which had once been home to the vast number of ice miners, and was now empty due to faster transport capability to and from other colonies. He just couldn't comprehend that a city of over five hundred miles in length – despite it being only a few miles in width – could be abandoned, leaving not a single person living there. There were, at times, the odd group of tourists and their guide who moved around like cattle being driven by a cowherd. Other than that, the whole place had become infested with wild flowers, vines, ivy, birds and rabbits, which had taken to roaming and flocking in astonishing numbers.

He hiked across the vast forests and farmland which led around the lake, then rode the sky tram in order to take in the magnitude that was the rest of this mostly deserted dreamworld. There were of course areas restricted to him in the form of a fortress which appeared to be slightly derelict and mostly abandoned. He also purposefully avoided the holiday resorts to avoid contact, simply because he wanted solitude for now.

Yet, despite this, Ologun was free, far more so than back on Earth, and could simply wander around by himself unhindered.

The square plasma-concrete block he'd been given as accommodation was also a nice touch. It was a crude little shack amongst vast fields which apparently no one else wanted because it was too small and too remote, but to Ologun it was terrific. His first day in the fields was strange, though: waking up in the future hadn't felt as alien as trying to learn how to use the crazy tools. A day of fruit picking from an orchard used to entail the use of a ladder, but now he had a self-guided pistol that fired twenty sophisticated gel strings with mechanical pincers which recoiled when they obtained a fruit. It was better than another device which emitted directed sonic vibrations from a large self-powered box. The ripest of fruit would fall easily enough, although Ologun suspected the device was bad for his health.

The most remarkable element in his exploration had to be the number of different fruit trees located in close proximity to each other. His understanding was limited when it came to species of plant life, but he was sure that rows of banana trees didn't usually grow next to hazelnuts, pears, oranges, olives and coconuts. In fact, every type of fruit tree grew across orchards stretching over many miles.

This strange sight created systematically by human hands reminded Ologun of the other woodland he'd explored over the past two days. Forests nurtured in this place were rife with all kinds of life which couldn't be taken for granted. Anything from bees to termites had been left to get on with themselves in the slightly ordered chaos of the mild nature within the basin. Some small animals were present too, with the odd squirrel scurrying around from time to time among many birds that included some sort of parrot, if Ologun guessed correctly. The few creatures he'd seen were no doubt there to complement each other, although he thought a few of them had become too successful when he considered the city of rabbits. At least he knew what to hunt for as there appeared to be no large animals present, unless there was some kind of deer occupying the land, and which he had yet to see.

Ologun was still trying to absorb it all, from the tiniest of details to the colossal achievements. Everything he'd seen in this place had at one time been transported from Earth and put here to function, to grow. *Impossible!*

Ologun soon realised that his new occupation had mainly become the purview of machines as there were no other people to be found. Robots planted, grew and harvested the fields with a delicate efficiency that certainly hadn't existed in his time. After watching them for a while, they confirmed his suspicion that the instrument which hurt his head was specifically for their use. The machines dropped the sonic boxes throughout the orchard as an aid to their inability to climb ladders or reach up high. *Genius! But why not make the machines taller?*

Craig Jenkins

Towards the end of his first day, Ologun sat in the blazing heat watching the robots with their pipe-shaped bodies elegantly wheeling around the dirt when he heard what he thought to be a loud scream.

A large intimidating crow sat high above him on one of the trees and released a terrible sound until a few equally-sized, bright-blue birds with colourful red tails encouraged it to leave. The bird wasn't the source of the shriek, however, as another scream emanated from a place much further away and where Ologun had yet to venture. The noise could be heard across the orchard and originated from a short distance away across a field separating the ideal from something far more overpowering.

He was both curious and concerned, and made his way towards the place. In no time, he'd managed to escape the domesticated coppice to arrive in the middle of the field which led up to a vast barricade of trees, hundreds of feet tall.

He stopped for a moment to assess what was clearly a jungle in comparison to the meek forests he'd become accustomed to.

It was dark among the tree trunks, a place more forbidding than other places in the basin. An unkempt monstrous force of nature spat out another loud cry, which he hoped belonged to a bird; the largest green ones were already expert at copying the whirring noise of the robot farmers.

Walking steadily towards the treeline, Ologun felt something was happening, an instinct he recognised from many years of patrolling locations where people did the most unexpected and horrible things.

He could see little amongst the trees. Loud rustling noises drew him in under the blanket of darkness as he sought out the sound's point of origin.

Birds sang loudly, distorting his ability to focus. He looked up as his eyes quickly adjusted to something unusual which he may never have noticed without the star lens being blotted out by thick foliage. Where light did find its way by piercing in sharp needles above, the light pulsed across in slow regulated bursts from side to side in one direction. This wave of light created shadows through the landscape in swathes to briefly invite the way ahead, only to snatch it back in an instant.

Version

Ologun continued on towards another terrible howl. His mind kept the memory of the briefly captured scenery as the light continued to move in radar fashion over and over again.

Bushes, ferns and other large leafed plants made use of these emissions in places, making it hard to negotiate the way. Areas of the ground had been littered with mounds of dry pine needles from evergreens which grew competitively next to more tropical varieties, which in turn rubbished their surroundings with leaves that had become damp and slippery underfoot.

Only mankind could throw these things together for such a strange effect. *If trees were sentient would they mind each other?* Ologun mused over such a superficial and idiotic thought. It was a sign he was definitely heading towards something *wrong*. His mind only went to such a place when he was under a certain stress, the calm before a storm which continued to keep him focused when all hell broke loose. He knew that something was across the way as surely as he knew his head was attached to his neck.

One element to this place, which differed to the other forest parkland, was how the vegetation strangled the space. In the other woods a person could look down long corridors where the trees gave each other a courteous berth.

Ologun climbed over vines, and slipped and struggled through twisted tree roots.

The screams had stopped a good five minutes ago, leaving him slightly lost until an unexpected clearing of shrubbery presented itself. Thick grass grew very tall amongst other mutated green plants on a patch of land where the canopy broke and trees refused to grow. Strong levels of light shone down from the star lens to create an overexposed heat bowl. He picked up a long stick and moved on through, making little noise and unable to see above the dense amalgam of the yellowing strands of sward.

He thought the screams had come from just ahead, unless whatever had caused the obscene noise had already moved on. The heat among the exposed vegetation caused him to sweat and the salty droplets ran from his forehead, burning his eyes. His whole mind lay ahead against the treeline ten yards away where darkness resumed in more jungle. The light faded the further he stepped into a boggy area, the smell of rotting plants filling his senses; the foliage grew shorter and thinner allowing him to see unhindered.

Sometimes cats make a noise like a crying baby. He once again hoped it was some deranged bird.

He stopped and crouched to probe the treeline only a few yards ahead. *Movement!* With lightning reflexes, he hit the floor before his mind caught up to register what he'd seen. Someone lay on the ground straight ahead in the dimness. It was a woman, naked, lying on her front with her hands bound.

He froze and his heart missed a beat as she lifted her head to look straight at him, making eye contact. *Shit!* Her mouth had been gagged, which at least helped him retain his position of cover. The woman's eyes said it all. Pleading and frantic, she strained to scream.

Ologun thought over the situation and was fully aware that whoever had done this had either been disturbed and had already fled; or they were still here waiting for another victim. Ologun wished he had the communication device Sharplin had given him; he certainly couldn't risk going back to his cabin for it now.

Keeping up his surveillance of his surroundings, he kept low while making his way to the woman's side. He knelt down and began to work on the woman's bindings, risking the distraction from possible danger only for a split second when a searing pain erupted in the back of his neck. His vision blurred and twisted and his eyes felt as though they might explode. Then relief came, followed by blackness. He lay still, listening to the sound of laughter. A terrible shriek like that of a hyena, high pitched and sadistic in its warbling impious tone. His hearing faded and he was gone.

CHANGER

'Go help at the fortress. I'll let you know when you're needed.'

Sergeant Thomas nodded and went, leaving Commander Judith Gibson alone to enter the morgue. *Twice in one week,* she thought on entering the room.

It was now early evening and Captain Sharplin had left Judith alone in charge of the investigation – to a certain extent. She wasn't entirely sure where to start and began to feel the effects of everything that had happened over the past few days; the things that were still happening. She'd been taken aback by Sharplin's response to her suggestion that she talk to the other holiday reps and even find the people who'd organised for this woman to take up such a lurid business. The captain hadn't just said, 'No,' he'd said, 'Hell no'.

She now felt that she wasn't trusted, and was unfit to deal with the civilians in the outpost. She walked along the row of empty table slabs until she was greeted by the sight of Doctor Siren hunched over the body.

'Found anything yet?'

Siren glanced at her. 'Not yet, I'm running a few tests to see where she's been. It's all I can think of for the moment.' Rita felt uncomfortable around Judith; she didn't know her very well and her reputation hardly merited her to lead a murder investigation. *Who knows how she'll fare?*

Judith wandered over to a large screen hanging on the wall directly behind the doctor. It displayed a digital overview of the entire basin floor. 'What's this for?'

'It's a map with information gathered by environmental operations,' Siren replied as she continued to work on the corpse. 'If I find anything unusual on her, this map may direct us to her last movements, you never know.'

Judith stared at the body of the murder victim for a moment. She'd been fascinated by the corpses from the shuttle crash. That had been her first ever experience of such things, but the initial buzz was gone now and had been replaced by something else.

She meddled with the controls to the large schematic of the basin until she found out how to manoeuvre around its detailed interpretation. She zoomed into the location where the woman had been found at the outskirts of the Dark Zone, not too deep within the jungle. Due to the Dark Zone's crescent shape, the area she'd been dumped in was only fifty miles in depth at the thinnest part before it led to the orchards on the other side.

Her finger moved over the screen to find locations she recognised. Her favourite bar sat ten miles from the zone, and further east again there was a large village and holiday resort. Her attention moved to the orchards another ten miles south-west to where Ologun was staying. Frank had a real soft spot for him after their initial discussion at the recuperation unit and had her wondering what they'd talked about. Siren had said Ologun couldn't possibly have any involvement with this murder and yet he was staying close to where the woman had been found.

Judith felt nervous for a change, perhaps mystified that she was actually concerned. Her entire career was riddled with reprimands and last chances over seeking entertainment instead of being a responsible officer. She often wondered why the IMC insisted she become an officer when being a marine was her preferred role.

She'd hated the basin when she'd first arrived and had been put on her very last warning for breaking the wrist of a flight lieutenant.

Slowly, over the years since her arrival, Judith had calmed down. There were the odd incidents at times, but she'd developed a fondness for the close-knit community which had been established at the outpost. Still, such a fondness remained in conflict with her insatiable need to be rash at times; well, maybe most of the time.

This new development stopped her dead in her tracks as it was sinister. Whatever she'd done in her life, it had never had connotations as serious as this.

Her mind mulled things over. Frank would be very upset; she knew these events would surely test a man of his nature for he was a peaceful man with a strict routine. Judith thought of the new orders for the IMC's arrival which really hadn't bothered her in the slightest. In contrast Sharplin would be going out of his mind by now. Whatever the reason for them coming, it was just something to speculate about. Then there was the issue of Ologun. She glanced around the morgue for a moment. He'd done the impossible here.

The commander brushed this set of thoughts aside as they were unfathomable. This murder was something she wanted to think about and she wouldn't let go that easily. Such acts were as old as the human race. This was a primitive and sadistic force which could be found on any colony; and now it had arrived to ruin the peaceful reality of the outpost. She was invested in this riddle in particular, and was drawn to the surreal nature of the murder which in turn had sparked her own aggressive nature.

Judith allowed a sly grin to twist upon her lips. She knew she lacked empathy at times and found it hard to muster sympathy for the woman who now lay on the cold metal surface of the mortuary slab. There could be only one true reason in all of this as to why she was motivated in such a way. She would find this person and feed them some of their own medicine.

Doctor Siren moved to a computer terminal to open a large drawer and placed a flat rectangular slate of glass on a shelf. She closed the compartment and waited.

'What's this?' Judith asked.

'I took some matter from under her fingernails, along with other samples found on her skin.'

They both waited. Siren didn't make small talk as the two of them had nothing in common. The machine bleeped and the basin schematic on the wall automatically moved to show a location.

'Here we go,' Siren said. 'According to the ecology system there's a large pool of water just east of the Dark Zone. Fungal spores were found on the body and they came from this area of the basin. Due to fungus in each location having its own distinct DNA, the match is conclusive and dispels any chance that she picked up this organic material elsewhere.'

Judith looked at the map to study the location. She'd once been to this particular area seven miles east of where Ologun had been allocated a living space.

'I'll check it out now,' Judith exclaimed.

'Leave it till the morning, your marine friends won't be there for well over an hour if you go by yourself now. Shouldn't you wait for backup?'

Judith began checking each magazine held in her uniform's webbing and didn't see the significance in Siren's advice. 'I'll call them on the way. I can look after myself until they arrive.'

The doctor slammed down an instrument in anger at Judith's constant poor judgement in all matters. 'What's wrong with you? You're totally bored with life is all I can think of.'

'Excuse me?' Judith replied, cocking the chamber of her rifle and becoming agitated at the outburst.

'Judith. Commander,' Siren said, waving an arm theatrically. 'What are you going to do? Solve this thing all by yourself? You don't know what to do out there. It's typical of you. You treat this place like a playground, drinking every – single – night. Doing anything that takes your fancy. The last time you were here you acted like a child ogling the corpses. It was disrespectful and I think you should grow up.'

'You should watch your tongue, Doctor, or—'

'Or what, Judith, you'll beat me to a pulp? Everyone avoids disagreeing with you in case you do something. You're meant to be a commander! The only reason the IMC gave you the position was because your aptitude test scores were so high. Frank needs you to be responsible and help him. You need to start being a commander, especially under these circumstances. Did you know that the IMC are on their way and have upped the alert status of the basin?'

Judith was stunned, even hurt. 'Of course.'

Siren calmed down from her rant. 'Go home and leave this until the morning. It'll be lens-out in three hours and there are a lot of things going on here that need to be sorted. If I were you, I'd think about helping your captain through this mess. You go out there by yourself tonight and you could end up like this woman.'

'I can take care of myself!' Judith said with a newfound wave of calmness and certainty. Doctor Siren turned her back on her and returned to her work to illustrate that she was washing her hands of the situation. She knew from experience that the universe had a way of teaching arrogant and aggressive people a lesson; the phrase 'famous last words' sprang to mind.

Judith took the sky tram to the nearest junction on the interior side of the Dark Zone. She borrowed a buggy parked nearby to complete her journey south-west of the lake to the coordinates on the digital map.

The Dark Zone was a fair distance from the Opus Hospital and it had taken nearly an hour to reach. Judith was hell-bent on resolving this situation and ignored the fact that the star lens was nearly ready to power down.

The buggy bumped around as it made its way over large fields leading to the orchards. Rough grassy knolls, which had been left to grow undisturbed, slowed her progress until eventually the ground became marshland. Judith couldn't work out how the landscape had managed to re-sculpt itself into such contours. The small vehicle continued to jolt as it manoeuvred over mounds and slipped into dips of saturated shrubbery which had replaced what had begun existence as a completely level and measured surface. In places the odd tree grew by itself at random and birds perched on the branches. She could only figure that this moor had come into existence due to water from the artificially controlled downpours accumulating in a slightly dipped level of the basin floor.

A further subsidence in the earth along a stretch of land within this plane had created a large pond that was narrow, around fifteen metres wide, and stretched on for two thousand metres. The pond was deep and sank to fifteen feet in some parts, which was remarkable for a defect in the once carefully constructed landscape.

This pool had been identified as the location Karlitta had been before she'd been found mutilated in the Dark Zone. Judith drove up to it, checking for any signs of disturbance. She then sat looking up to the sky-tram system way above and at the skeletal structure which held its cables in place. This was where the rain fell from. Large pumping stations drew water from the lake and sent it to the basin's exterior wall, up vast structural pipework, and across the sky-tram network to spray the land when required.

She never paid attention to such things unless they malfunctioned. The regular watering of the land had certainly had an impact here. Reeds from the shallow parts of the basin's lake had found their way to this marshland and taken hold. The pool ahead was completely covered in them, cleaning the water to a crystal clear quality where insects gathered to swarm in abundance in the warm humid air.

The landscape was by now coloured a deep pink in the late evening spectrum. An almost blood-red light crept in slowly as the star lens adjusted the light in minute increments towards night mode.

Judith made her way to a muddy bank through thick grass. With every step she sank into the flooded ground and water soaked through the fabric of her boots. She took in the sight, noticing fish darting amongst the reeds in response to her presence and even spotted a number of turtles obliviously swimming around.

The pond had a ledge along one of its sides which dropped to a beach comprised of thick mud a few feet wide. Sitting on the mud was a small object, bright in colour and unnatural in comparison to its surroundings. Judith trudged closer for a better view. She jumped down, sinking a little into the soft sludge where the pond's surface had receded to reveal the muddy patch. As she approached, it became clear that someone had left a shoe: silver in colour and clearly feminine, depending on one's taste.

Without picking it up, Judith examined the abandoned – *what is it, a stiletto?* – the kind she disliked at the best of times, never mind out here.

Without time to react, Judith was dragged backwards. She instinctively raised her rifle hanging on a strap over her shoulder. She was losing balance and whoever it was grabbed her weapon and twisted the rifle's strap tightly around her neck. She panicked, couldn't breathe and elbowed frantically, finding contact behind her.

She was then pushed forward and forced to land awkwardly in the water a few feet ahead, face down. Frantically Judith reached for her rifle again. It was gone! She turned to face a man rushing towards her.

Judith felt heavy, soaked through in water up to her waist; not the easiest place to defend herself. The man waded towards her, thrusting a long blade in his right hand.

'Back off,' she commanded.

The man lurched and thrust the dagger at her. She quickly slapped both sides of his wrist, sending the weapon into the water. She stepped back, putting distance between them while trying to edge her way to the bank. The man lunged again, grabbing her, then pushed her under the water. She smacked his nose hard with her right palm and swam away, then turned to face her attacker once again. His nose was bleeding, yet he was undeterred.

Judith waded sideways towards the shore without taking her eyes off him. As she left the restriction of the water she turned for an instant to find the rifle. The man lunged and tackled her to the ground and she ended up with a twisted torso, face down in mud. *This fool's asking for it.* She swung her head backwards, finding contact with his mouth. He screamed then laughed loudly in a muffled cry of pain and joy through a mouth pouring with blood after having been smacked shut. She thought that one should have hurt him.

For a moment Judith watched the man stagger backwards across the mud. He was of a smallish build with bright blond hair and unremarkable features; hardly someone to consider intimidating if seen in any normal circumstance.

She quickly glanced around the beach and saw the rifle on the mud a few feet ahead. *Why did he leave it?* Leaping for the rifle, she rolled on to her back and took aim. Her assailant tried to jump on top, only to be pushed away with force as she kicked hard at his chest with both legs. She leapt to her feet and moved forward, in control, then pointed the rifle at the man's head as he lay flat on his back, and stamped hard into his groin. *'You move, you die!'*

~

Craig Jenkins

The cracked land, tinged with red, was flat to the horizon. Dead shrubbery rustled in the hot wind and small clouds rushed across the electric-blue sky. All was empty with little life except for birds circling thermals in the distance. He couldn't move his head and he couldn't feel his body. His eyes swivelled erratically in their sockets, trying to gather more information. Reaching away from him on the ground, the shadow was of a long thin rod with something plump on top. He looked again and strained his eyes to the right to see a severed head on a pole with the whites of its eyes rolled upwards and glistening in the bright daylight. His eyes moved down only to see the bottom of another pole directly beneath him. His eyes moved up to something heading his way: a dog, no, hyena. It laughed in a high-pitched titter, sniggering, gurgling and chortling with malice. It moved closer until he could see into its eyes; until he could see a reflection. A line of poles with a line of skewered heads.

The hyena walked away and he caught sight of people in the distance kneeling down in the crimson dirt. His perception of things changed as though floating up and over and closer to them. There were many of them; all ages knelt in single file with their faces hanging down as they looked to the floor. Behind them were others in uniform: combats in a light-desert shade. They pressed rifles hard into the backs of the prisoner's necks as another man with his face masked walked back and forth. These uniformed men were not men at all; they were skeletons, ghouls with eyes which matched the fractured land. The long line of prisoners knelt in silence. Directly in front of them were baskets of food and jugs of water. The executioner stood directly in front of them and lifted his arm. The demons primed the chambers of their rifles and waited.

Ologun's eyes flickered open and he struggled with a racing heart. He sat up, breathing heavily, and sighed. He was in a bed and covered in light-purple sheets which were soaked through. Around him the room was small with grey concrete walls and no other features except for the intravenous drip standing to his left and attached to his arm. The door to the room opened. Frank Sharplin entered with someone else: a young woman; slim, with thick black hair and unusually dark-blue eyes. She moved to stand at the bottom of the bed, nodded and held a rifle pointed towards the floor.

'You're awake. How do you feel, Ologun?'

'What's going on?'

'What were you up to in the Dark Zone?' Sharplin asked.

'Dark Zone?'

'Don't act stupid, the jungle where the sun don't shine. Dark Zone,' the woman fired back.

Captain Sharplin raised an arm to her chest; an order for restraint.

Ologun thought hard for a moment. 'I – I was in the orchard, I heard screams. I went looking and ended up in the woods. There was a woman. She was in danger, what happened to her? Did you find her?'

'What do you remember about her, what happened?' Sharplin asked. His voice was slow and polite, helping to relax the situation.

'I don't know, I just blacked out . . . What's going on, did I do something?'

'Excuse us for a moment,' Captain Sharplin said and made a hand gesture to the woman to leave the room. They both exited into a small corridor, closing the door behind them.

'What do you think?' Judith asked the captain.

'I think he has no idea what's going on.'

Doctor Siren emerged from a room further down the corridor where shrieks of laughter echoed down the narrow concrete corridor. She closed the door to silence the heinous sound and made her way to Frank and Judith.

'Well?' Sharplin asked.

Doctor Siren exhaled as though releasing a great deal of pressure. 'No implant, no Flickr file. It's a real shame we don't have any stasis units to put him in. That man is . . .' She blinked a few times and her eyes widened with her loss for words.

'Where did he come from?' Sharplin asked, almost rhetorically.

'I don't know. I'll have to run another profile and see. It's going to take several hours.'

'There's no record of his arrival, he couldn't just arrive without checking in.' Judith added.

Siren shrugged. 'So far, it's as though he appeared out of thin air. I take it there's no way he could have stowed away on one of the tourist vessels?'

Sharplin looked at Judith. Her eyes confirmed the absurdity of the question.

The commander leaned against the corridor wall and flicked her head towards Ologun's room. 'What about him?'

'Nothing, he didn't do anything as far as I can detect,' Doctor Siren said. 'He probably saved that girl's life. The most insane way to go about it, but . . .' She paused as though avoiding something. 'The intruder down the hall, however, has remnants of the victims in his teeth and gut. He's like nothing I've ever seen, I just don't know.'

Sharplin looked pale and he felt a cold sweat on his skin. 'Do your best to find his details. What do you think about Ologun? I'm inclined to send him back to his shed until the IMC arrive tomorrow.'

'Once is a fluke, twice is, well, I don't know,' Judith stated. 'I think we should keep him under close supervision. He's got to be some genetic experiment or some kind of freak. I can interrogate him and find out what he knows.'

The captain looked concerned and frowned at the commander's suggestion. 'What do you think, Doctor?'

'I'd prefer to keep him here.'

Frank wiped his hands over his thick silver hair and made a squeaking sound with his mouth. 'I knew from the start that he was something else. I don't like the idea of investigating him. The IMC are your best friend until you uncover information above your station. I don't want any of us to mysteriously disappear if we discover anything tangible, if you know what I mean. That's my worst fear in all this and it should be yours too. None of the marines know anything, so let's just send him to the orchard and wait for the ships.'

'That's some fear going on in your head, Frank,' Judith said.

'I don't want either of you to pursue this any further,' Sharplin snapped, losing his temper. 'Find out who that psycho is and leave him under guard. Send Ologun back to his shack and keep him under curfew, within a mile of his digs should do it, and let him be. You both have to trust me on this.'

Captain Sharplin wanted to keep things simple and bury his head in the sand. He was now feeling desperate for the fleet to arrive and to relieve him of command. Judith wasn't helping either. He'd left this mess for her to gather some information and in turn she'd blown him away with her insane stunt. In fact, Judith and Ologun were both as crazy as each other in his eyes and all he wanted was for the next fourteen hours to pass without any more foolish behaviour. 'The fleet will be here tomorrow afternoon. Commander, why don't you take the night off, better still, look after Ologun tonight, have a night in and play some of that crap you call music or whatever. Yes, that's it, you babysit him at your place.'

'Okay, I can handle that,' Judith confirmed. 'What about the docking platform?'

'I'll take care of it, just take some time out and look after Ologun. That's an order.'

Judith excused herself and made her way down the corridor leaving the captain and the doctor alone.

'I'm ordering a dozen marines to remain here with you. If you need to see that man, don't go in there alone.' Frank placed a hand on Rita's shoulder, even though he was more disturbed by everything than she was. 'Doctor, be careful how much you learn about Ologun.' The doctor in return shrugged his hand away as she began to walk towards a room at the end of the corridor. 'What do you mean? The man's a miracle of science or nature or, I don't know, I'd like to present Command with something when they arrive,' Rita said, and as he caught up to her at the entrance to the room, Frank noticed that she looked concerned about something when discussing Ologun. 'I'd like to think I'm not scared and ignorant of the unknown in this instance.'

'That's not what I'm talking about. Like I said, the IMC are funny about this kind of stuff. Who else do you think could pull off such a thing as Ologun? You learn too much about something you shouldn't, and who knows what will happen to you?'

Rita kept watching Frank as she entered the room, dismissing what he had just said. 'Is there something wrong with your eye, Frank?'

Frank Sharplin shrugged and placed a palm over his left eye. 'It's been aching this past day. I think I'm tired that's all.

'You think she's okay?' he asked Rita, changing the subject. He sat down upon a couch in the corner of the room next to a small window lens and turned the gain down in order to dim the room a touch.

Rita meanwhile began rummaging through various apparatus on a table as though looking for something. 'Who, Judith? I think she's a tough nut. I don't know exactly what happened, but it's shaken her. Probably less so than if it had been either of us, I'm sure.'

Frank thought about this for a moment. He knew enough about Judith to realise that she became impossibly aggressive when she was afraid, which concerned him a great deal.

'What about you?' Doctor Siren asked.

'I'm okay,' Frank replied, quite astonished Rita had asked him the question.

Rita brushed this answer aside. 'I mean you, under this stress, especially now at this time.'

'What do you mean?'

Doctor Siren smiled a little. 'At this time of year, every year, you go to that horrible little cabin for a week and shut yourself away. I know about your daughter if you want to talk about it. It's been sixteen years hasn't it?'

Frank sat deeper into the couch and exhaled as though annoyed. 'How long have you known?'

'The IMC briefed me and asked me to keep an eye on you when I started here. I know that you drink too much, that you call your ex-wife at the same time every year, and that you find it hard to hold it together around this time. This mess must be taking its toll.'

'It's affecting everyone. I'm okay, really.' He kept a watchful eye out of the small window. He felt more confident than a few days ago, or was it just that he hadn't the time to think about it?

'How old would she be now?' Rita asked.

'Thirty three in December. Look, I appreciate the concern, but I should get going, I have too many things to do.'

'Why is Ologun with Judith tonight, I mean why haven't you kept him under observation?' Rita asked.

Captain Sharplin sat playing with his eye as the pain seemed to be increasing. 'I'm sorry?' he said.

'We recover bodies from Deceiver. A man comes back to life,' Rita said and threw a crystal blue transparent dagger onto the table. 'He is a genetically altered human being and all that the two of you, you and Judith, have done is completely ignore everything about him. Is there something going on between the two of you. Something classified?'

'Being involved in murky business is your and Dennis's department, Doctor. I told you that I want no part of or involvement in who or what he is,' Frank said, raising his voice.

'You have no idea what this thing might do . . .'

'Thing?' Frank raised his voice and stood up, moved to the door in order to leave the room. 'I make the decisions and the decision has been made. That's it.'

'I need you to know something,' Rita raised her voice back at him. 'There's something un-human about him, Frank. I mean I saw it with my own eyes, Ologun's not . . . I don't know. I need you to keep him here. I need to run more tests.'

Frank folded his arms and looked out the window again. 'You're ambushing me here and I'm not impressed, Doctor. What do you mean by un-human?'

Rita sat down and placed a computer pad upon the table. 'I found nothing unusual at first, until I subjected Ologun's blood and tissue samples to a number of stresses to replicate a more severe physical injury or illness. I eventually subjected the blood to FUENG 8,' Doctor Siren stated with a tone more serious than Sharplin had heard from her before.

'F-ing what?' Frank asked, sitting down and finding himself unable to resist wanting to hear what Siren had to say.

Doctor Siren paused every few words as she spoke now as she began to explain with detail and with caution in her voice. 'We made viruses for the IMC command to last within a limited timeframe upon release, until at least every target or genetic group within a population had been eradicated. FUE is the source strain, full universal killer.'

'Shouldn't that be FU—? Never mind,' Frank interrupted. He returned to watching the window in thought.

'The virus has a unique ability to adapt against any countermeasure, and above all can work through a person's immune system very quickly or, in fact, take decades depending on . . .' Rita said and stopped on seeing the look on Frank Sharplin's face.

'So this is what you do,' he said in disgust. 'You said something about exposing blood, Ologun's samples. You may as well tell me the rest now.'

Rita cleared her throat to conclude her confession. 'The virus was designed with the capability to adapt on the remote off chance that people could, in fact, fight off one form or another, especially through cell reinforcement design or chemical frequency matching. The strongest version is deadly to all life forms . . . except Ologun.'

'Explain,' Frank ordered.

'The virus devoured the red and white blood cells on a number of levels, trying to eradicate any possible resistance. I'm not quite sure what I witnessed – I can only describe it as an alien response that made the virus look insignificant no matter how it adjusted. The virus was destroyed and absorbed into the sample in under a minute, an absolutely ferocious reaction like nothing I've ever seen. It's as though every cell in his body is designed to be deceptive, accepting injury only to recalibrate and adapt to the damage inflicted. Then, most bizarrely, every blood sample I took dissolved into a basic carbon compound as though it were designed to resist analysis.'

'Alien, as in other planets, species kind of alien?' Frank sat back in deep interest.

'I don't know, I couldn't say. All I can theorise is that there are no technologies in place to develop such a complex system. Even if the IMC has the technology now . . . I don't know, I'm speculating about something I don't know enough about.'

Version

Frank churned over this information for a moment, then wished she hadn't told him. 'I told you not to go too far with this. If I were you I'd plead ignorance when IMC command arrive.'

'There's more,' Rita added. 'The deep spectral body analysis taken of Ologun has given a data feedback that I can't even begin to understand.'

'I don't want to know,' Frank exclaimed.

Rita ignored him. 'Take a look at these two images.' She passed two pads across the desk to Sharplin, who still just couldn't resist and studied the images. 'What am I looking at?'

The one on the right is a typical human mitochondrion. Well, that one of many belongs to me and, as you know, the mitochondria are the powerbase of every living organism and exist in every living cell, – primarily there are more in the liver of a typical fauna—'

'What's your point, Doctor?' Frank interrupted.

The image on the left belongs to Ologun and has a configuration that . . . Well, the data bank analysis recognised the image and identified it as a perpetual P-type energy cascade.'

'Excuse me?'

Rita shrugged. 'A P-type cascade is classified information according to the IMC mainframe. Although I did find alternative references from various historical files on L- and K-type cascades that state it's the theory behind the manipulation of energy "to massage the fabric of, in a non-violent capacity, in order to quantify and identify inter-dimensional spaces".'

'Well, that's it then,' Frank stated. 'You and I are done for no matter which way you look at it.'

'Frank, listen.'

'No, it's okay, really, I mean accessing the IMC mainframe to investigate spaces that cascade. I mean what does it really matter? Ologun has an extra space in him that cascades, I'm glad it's the reason I'll disappear without a trace . . .'

'Frank! Frank!' Rita fought for his attention. 'Ologun doesn't have *one* of these, he has hundreds of millions of them, just like anyone's mitochondria except that they're . . . I don't know. Look, we have things to do and I'm sorry to have put you in this position, really. You need to get him back here now.'

Doctor Siren collected her pad from the table and stood up.

Frank stood up automatically as though sensing this conversation was nearly over. 'I can't do that.'

'I am asking you to see sense, Frank.'

'You and I are going to act like nothing happened and that neither of us knows a damned thing.'

'You're wrong about this.'

'We know nothing, it was just a miracle him surviving.'

'I need to know . . .'

'No! This isn't something you mess around with here. I'm not about to lock up and allow you to experiment on what might come back on us and get us deleted. Life is cheap and you above all should know that. We play dumb and let command have him. Ologun leaves this place peacefully and happy that we were nice courteous hosts.'

'This is greater than any work I have ever done, Frank . . .'

'I know this is important to you,' Frank said, trying to reason with her. He looked at the floor for a moment and then said, 'I want all of us here to have a future when this, whatever it is, is over. I want Judith to sort out whatever it is that's going on in her head. I want, I wanted to spend more time with you perhaps. I wanted to stay here and retire here because there is nothing else for me now. I want IMC to come and go and perhaps they will just accept that we are not going to compromise whatever it is they . . .'

Frank paused. His body language pleading with Rita to see his point of view.

'All right, Frank. I can't agree but all right. I think you're worrying about the wrong thing. You know Judith is just selfish and spoilt. You shouldn't invest in her so much.'

'Judith is not who she, I mean that . . . there are several classified files on her that I do not have clearance for and trust me when I say that something has deeply affected her.'

'We should be going now,' Rita suggested.

'You will erase all data on Ologun?'

Version

Rita stood there in silence until she asked, 'You really wanted to spend time with me?'

'Absolutely,' Frank said and smiled a little.

'Fine then,' Rita said, 'but you owe me big time for this.'

DRINKS COMMANDER

Late evening left him feeling relaxed at last. Ologun sat in a field one mile from his cabin, enjoying the breeze originating from the huge fans pushing warm air over the tall grass and softly hitting his skin. He was weakened by its pleasantness, lacking motivation to exert himself in such a perfect moment. He was deep in thought, mulling over everything that had happened.

He remembered his first kill. He'd had an assignment for sniper detail on a tall building within a new environment dome on Phobos. The IMC's highest ranking staff had presented the grand opening of a new technology development centre and required heavy-duty protection for the executives present there.

Who had the lookout been again? Sonny Camden, of course!

There was crazy a man if ever he'd met one. He'd wanted to be an assassin. Sonny's only ambition had been to become an intelligence property protection agent. He'd wanted to kill; he'd been obsessed with killing. A new programme to invest in long-term assets had been created so that a skilled operative would be placed in a stasis chamber until called upon. A typical contract lasted between sixty and a hundred years, and Sonny had been just the right candidate. Wake him up, order him to take down a designated target, and return him to slumber. A hundred years later and he'd be wealthy and, more importantly, young enough to retire in great comfort, having only spent the first quarter of his life in service. Sonny had been the reason he'd made his first kill. Some poor guy had moved too close to the company CO and looked suspicious. Sonny had begun to shout, ordering the shot. Flustered, Ologun had fired. The target had been eight hundred yards distant; a precise shot with no wind factor in the enormous artificial environment. The man in question had turned out to be innocent. He had made a terrible mistake.

He watched as birds flocked and began a vicious skirmish near the edge of the orchard's treeline bordering the set of crop fields. A murder of crows had gathered to attack the large blue parrots which were picking at the waste of various fruits left behind by the robots. He observed with keen interest. The parrots were cleverer and much more dexterous when in flight. They picked at the crows with superior tactics by separating and herding them into vulnerable positions. Finally the ruckus died down as the crows fled. The altercation had simply been over food and yet there was plenty for all of them. The strange metaphor struck a chord with him and he shook his head. He couldn't understand people who enjoyed doing something that made him feel ill, even depressed, and felt bitter that his hand had been forced that day over what could only be considered mass greed and selfishness.

Random thoughts prevailed in Ologun's mind as he gazed towards a row of fans running at full capacity in the distance. His mind was still caught in his own time. The politics, the ideologies, the conflicts and things which by now would be or would seem insignificant, which in effect alienated him from the goings on in this alien land developed within a pocket found upon a large piece of floating rock. *Amazing! Deceiver*, he thought, remembering that they'd probably sent him on the basis that at some point, somewhere, he'd mentioned his love of deserts, mountains and enormous skies. *Did I fill in a form saying that oceans terrify me and the magnitude of them – their depths – petrify me?* Either way, someone knew, or perhaps by some irony or misfortune his punishment for his crimes had been perfect considering he'd been sent to a planet with a surface comprised entirely of deep water. Luckily he'd only found out the particulars of his sentence at the end of his trial. *If they'd told me earlier, when I was incarcerated for twelve months!* Ologun shuddered at the thought and his mind went back to his time, his homeland. He wondered if Morocco had sustained its agricultural investment through one of the companies and whether or not its northern provinces still had or should have a perfectly engineered rainforest. It took a long time to manufacture an eco-system to sustain itself; it needed an investment equal to that of running a country for decades in order to ensure it took hold. Egypt had managed it. They'd developed a class two eco-province, which was the equivalent in biodiversity and size to that of the Borneo rainforests. Still, back then the overall scheme, the plan, was larger and the Algerian government wanted to invest after re-inventing their economy via the commercial demand for the only real resource of value they had in abundance. If the houses of ecology for either the IMC or GEA could overcome the shear brutality of mid-Sahara's environment – the impossible levels of heat and the winds which rendered any level of irrigation next to impossible – then the most northern parts of Africa would by now have the second largest rainforest on Earth. Ologun realised that he'd forgotten to ask Sharplin and made a mental note for the next time he saw him, or to ask the next person he saw; surely everyone here would know.

He tried to remember what it had all been for: for that religion to develop, to re-programme nature. He looked around at his surroundings and realised then what had happened, what the mass shift in country and corporation investment had been for. Apart from Earth's population reaching absolute breaking point – Ologun found it strange that it had never really felt that way, not when compared to how the authorities had whipped up a frenzy of doom or at least the media had tried to instil the fear – the investment had been in ecosystems rather than facilities such as mass food production or creating new residential areas and even towns or cities. It was clear that the idea all along had been to use nature, to harness its power for colonising other worlds. Terra-forming a world was considered nearly impossible – it cost too much to develop an atmosphere – yet what would happen if a world could be found with enough mass to sustain its own atmosphere? Developing the desired landscape on a compatible world with Earth was the next ideal; to take that which was biologically compatible with the human species to an alien world was essential. Ologun realised that all along it had been about a future investment in real estate, albeit an incredibly enormous and extravagant quest for knowledge so that such worlds could be invaded with a solid agenda, a long-term investment and plan. That this basin he now sat in was large enough to be a moderate-sized country on Earth proved the point, had proved that there were great rewards for such remarkable labour.

Before Ologun had embarked upon what he considered a wasted life in the forces, he'd studied business: the culture of it and ways of forecasting future demands. One of his lecturers had said something to him once and he tried to remember. *Leaders of the world rarely create a culture or an ideology overnight and are often swept along upon the beasts they initially instigate* had been the gist of it. So to Ologun it was somehow clear that at some point in history the human psyche had become obsessed with Earth's environment and, with the passing of generations, this form of thinking had led to some expensive and stark changes to the world.

From the days of pollution and the use of fossil fuels through to the lack of fresh water and the destruction of ecosystems, conglomerates had found their niches via certain avenues. Transform ocean water and sell it as fresh; an odd result leading to the doubling of Earth's overall fresh water supply in less than thirty years. This alone sparked further ambitions through unexpected results, for nature was a hungry force and the rewards of feeding it were far more prosperous than simply raping it; why hadn't this been thought of before his time? Or rather, how had such a paradigm for sustaining humanity been ignored for so long? All of this grouped with a new race into the depths of space seemed less coincidental to Ologun; transforming inhospitable lands around the world into forests and farmlands had been practice, for nature was simply priceless and in the long term its running costs were simply free.

So many applications for just a few, even if complex, developments, Ologun surmised and wondered further as to whether or not a viable planet had been found to receive such a makeover. Yet more questions to ask someone – anybody.

He returned his thoughts back to the present and the basin. The marine who'd brought him back to his cabin had relentlessly asked questions the whole trip. Some of the outpost's holiday reps had reported a number of holiday makers missing, only to be told it was being investigated. He didn't really know anything except for the woman he'd found. The marine had speculated that someone had cannibalised a number of people from the holiday resorts and things were becoming heated between the tour operators and the marines. He sighed, realising that he was somewhere between being very concerned and not giving a damn, if that was at all possible; a sort of exhaustion from environmental and situation overload. He wanted to care, yet his mind wouldn't allow it at this moment.

He revealed nothing to the marine. *What can I say? I can't tell him I went into the wood and found a woman bound and gagged, only to wake in a hospital bed with no recollection of how I got there.*

He moved to sit on a pile of thick logs and watched the breeze as it swept across old spider webs between the gaps. He wiped them away as if to clear his mind. *Out with the old!* The spiders would make a new home now the old webs were gone.

He heard the faint whine of a vehicle's spin drivers in the distance, and raised his head to see a buggy moving towards his position along a dirt track amongst the potato fields. He followed its course until it eventually rolled up next to him. At the controls was the very attractive female from the hospital. 'Ologun, it's time for a few drinks if you fancy it,' she said without introduction.

He was taken aback by her forward approach, but felt a drink was definitely in order.

'Come on, it's nearly lens-out,' the woman prompted again.

'I'm under curfew. I'm supposed to stay within a mile of my hut.'

'Don't worry, I've cleared everything.'

Ologun thought briefly about the rest of his evening. *Too many reasons to be taken for a ride!* 'Okay.' He jumped in and the vehicle pulled away; its wheels skidding as though fleeing a robbery.

'I'm Judith by the way, first officer to the Colonial Marines for the IMC in this place. I saw you when you were dead, you know.'

Ologun listened above the blustering wind of the open-top cart as it sped along, and nodded without knowing how to reply to this statement. *She's a strange one,* he warned himself. 'How far is it to— where are we going exactly?' he asked as a last resort sort of response.

Version

'About twenty minutes, we're off to the Minx Machine bar, it's the only one that allows military to mix with tourists,' Judith shouted as the air blew her hair around her face.

'How did you find me?'

'You have an implant on you. Why else do you think you weren't locked up?'

Ologun thought about this and felt violated. *Of course they're keeping tabs.* At least it had given him his freedom.

They pulled up to a set of large rectangular concrete buildings with tall glass doors. A spacious garden lawn led away from a white paved driveway where an impressive circular fountain sat beside the main entrance. Ologun couldn't decide whether it was tacky or grand; he settled for a little of both.

'I hope you can handle your drink, oh and there's a fresh shirt on the back seat, you look like a tramp,' Judith said as she leapt from her seat and made her way to the entrance of the main building.

Ologun followed, only to be bombarded with what he could only regard as screeching on top of incoherent beats. Ignoring the sound he took in the scene of a very spacious room which he considered to be absurdly long – he couldn't quite see where it ended. Ologun wandered around, nodding to anyone who made eye contact. A few people smiled, but most were indifferent. He was quite relaxed, however, even though there were some fairly unusual activities going on: strange amusements that baffled him at first.

He made his way through the room and marvelled at people floating horizontally inside large glass tubes. He recognised it as a sky-diving experience, although these tubes were more elaborate in design. They were, in reality, slides which weaved in and out so that the occupants flew around, propelled at great velocity throughout the network that ran along the walls and ceiling of the entire room then into the distance and out of view. *Perhaps,* Ologun reasoned, *these tubes are also a form of transport to get around such a large place without being hindered by the dense crowds.* The place was busy enough to make him feel claustrophobic and was awkward to negotiate. He looked around for Judith and became interested in a game he could just see going on beyond the crowd. The sport entailed hopping from pillar to pillar within a rectangular formation of spires elevated several feet above the floor. The activity was both dangerous and challenging as the pillars would suddenly drop vertically into the ground, sometimes bringing the loser crashing with it.

At the mid-section of the room was a long bridge comprised entirely of bamboo sticks which overlooked one of the lower levels to another bar. Ologun moved to stand at its centre and stopped to lean over a rail to continue his search for Judith. He found it difficult to concentrate as the area below him flashed with brightly lit coloured strobes which shook and rotated. Through the centre of the room, the bar acted as a partition between a lounge area on one side and a dance floor of sorts on the other. There the dancers hardly needed a floor at all as they dangled from the ceiling like puppets on rubber strings and bounced around off various elevated surfaces and each other. Ologun followed one attractive woman serving drinks as she made her way above and over the serving bar on a long ramp towards the lounge. The scene here was somewhat less active as customers sat drinking and chatting, while others sat in a number of spherical transparent chambers allocated along the walls opposite the bar. The glass bubbles these people occupied had small transparent cylinders on top where staff serving poured in a thick dark-green liquid. The liquid then drained away to become a vapour inside the glass case where it appeared to intoxicate the occupant. As his observation of the strange activity continued, Ologun spotted a burly occupant stumble out of his chamber. The man took his time, swaying and staggering as he made his way. Clumsily he manoeuvred himself up the ramp and over the bar until, miraculously, he arrived at the dance floor without losing balance. The man warbled his way a few more feet, teetering precariously, then toppled over, grabbing the legs of a female aerial dancer. The woman screamed and panicked as the elasticised cords she hung from bounced erratically and dragged the two of them off the ground. Ologun laughed out loud as the deeply intoxicated man desperately held on while the woman almost hit her head on an elevated platform as they rebounded.

The spectacle was soon over when two men appeared from within the crowd to drag the drunkard away by his feet and out of sight. Ologun assumed they were bar security, but he couldn't be sure.

He continued his search and walked much further until finally he spotted Judith in another downstairs area where she was being served drinks. This bar was much brighter with a friendlier light where wooden tables and wicker chairs sat among leafy plants growing in enormous pots. The entire wall surrounding this area was made of glass and the view outside was pleasant with a particularly well-groomed lawn.

Ologun glanced again through the conservatory wall as though he'd seen something he'd mistaken. To his disbelief, the lawn was a firing range of around three hundred metres in length, and which appeared to be in use. On his descent of the stairs, he could then see that there was also a large assault course erected nearby. Its daunting height stunned him as he tried to follow its framework which worked its way off into the distance and over the canopy of many tall trees. In his mind there could be only one plausible explanation – the bar must be very close to a military training ground.

He made his way down to Judith, who was by now interacting with a group of men he recognised as the outpost's IMC marines. 'I see the rules of leisure have changed a bit, I mean drinking, guns and whatever else all under the same roof is a bit much compared to my day,' he blurted out before introducing himself.

'Everybody, this is Ologun. Ologun this is everyone,' Judith announced awkwardly, embarrassed at his remark.

The group nodded with little interest, only to turn their backs on him.

'Okay, we're going to play a game,' Judith told him before he could reply. 'It's called fire shot.'

Ologun was at first bemused at this announcement, then felt a little uncomfortable – his instincts told him he should have stayed near his cabin. 'What are the rules?' he asked.

'We down two shots. Then we have a go on the range. Whoever gets the best grouping has one shot and the rest of us have two. Of course the worst has three.'

Ologun was beside himself at this. 'The range belongs to the bar?'

'Of course,' Judith answered as though it were obvious.

'The assault course too?' he quizzed, even though he knew the answer by now. 'Do people often get killed here?'

'Lose the chat-up lines, macho, I've got work in the morning,' she replied, then darted off through doors leading outside.

Ologun followed her on to the firing range along with the others, who erupted in chants of enthusiasm as they went. *Judith's the leader of this demented gang,* he decided as the men chanted:

'FI ER SHOT . . . FI ER SHOT . . .'

They downed two shots of what they called Ongdon vapour and Ologun was prompted to visit the man to whom Judith appropriately gave the title of weapons dealer.

'What will it be?' the man asked. He was a tall man with a large mop of red hair, wearing fancy shades and an overly colourful shirt.

'What can I have?' Ologun asked in further amazement at the racks of rifles and other impressive guns on display like drinks behind a bar.

'Anything you want, but don't be a smartarse and ask for an RPG or sniper.'

'Just give me a standard rifle,' Ologun ordered as the drink began to kick in.

'Automatic or single?' came the next question.

Ologun gave a deep expressionless stare, prompting the man to grab a nice-looking chrome rifle with a black carbon butt.

'Come on,' he heard Judith shout in the background.

Ologun had second thoughts about this whole thing. 'Are you sure I should be doing this? I'm a convicted felon if you hadn't heard.'

Judith moved behind him and pushed him closer to the range. 'It's therapeutic. Look, if it makes you feel better, I'll shoot you if you do anything wrong, how does that sound?'

'Fantastic,' he replied.

He walked over to a sand-covered patch before a small wall of sand bags and quickly moved to assume position, lying chest down on the ground. The target they'd chosen was two hundred yards away in the shape of a large eyeball.

He zoned out the noises around him as Judith and her gang continued to extract urine from his every move. He took a controlled breath before eventually pulling the trigger to feel quite a punch into his right shoulder. Again and again he squeezed the trigger until his six rounds were spent.

'Shit the deck!' one of the marines blurted out. The result of his attempt flashed on a large monitor for everyone to see. The computer had logged six rounds, achieving their target, yet only revealed one puncture mark. Either the computer had malfunctioned or Ologun had just made each round go through the same hole perfectly every time.

'Impossible,' a guy named Trent spat in disbelief.

'My turn,' Judith stated in a competitive tone.

She knelt down on one knee to aim a pistol. Within moments she emptied the clip to receive an impressive result.

'See, I got all six in, maybe you can get more than one in next time,' Judith taunted him. She walked over to sit next to him on a small bench overlooking the range.

'Oh, I love this track,' she said of the music playing loudly from large speakers positioned high up on the building's walls. 'It's Jungle Rape with Pet Shop on Fire,' she added, nodding her head to the beat.

'Obviously,' Ologun quickly replied, both amused and bemused. He couldn't tell if she'd named the genre, the track title, or the name of the band. All these titles were fitting as he found the sound of what he thought were incredibly distressed or squabbling monkeys screaming within this not-so-melodic sound could be whichever.

Judith studied Ologun for a while, but she couldn't resist moving the conversation to something less casual. 'The captain seems to think you're okay. I don't see how he can tell. I'll take his word for it as he usually judges people pretty well. I was there when you were frozen, you know.'

Ologun thought about this for a moment as Sharplin had only vaguely explained things. 'I'm not sure what to say, it's beyond me. Lucky for me, I guess.'

Judith stared at him as if he'd revealed the hint of a lie. What he'd done when they'd found him in the Dark Zone was even more absurd. She would press him on that one later as Doctor Siren hadn't been sure if he'd even remember anything, and had said that he should now be a vegetable. 'You had a metal arm in your chest. We were all . . . er, surprised to see you recover.'

Ologun knew where this conversation was leading. He was aware his body healed quickly and left no scars. It wasn't something he ever liked to discuss, except that having people witnessing him go one step further and rise from the dead was an entirely new perspective on his condition. 'I don't know what happened there. The doctor said it could have been the unusual bacteria she found on my skin. Why do you think Frank allowed me to leave his custody like this?'

'Probably because you can't escape and he felt that you being so far away from anyone was just as good as anything else. I think he's in denial, at least scared that you're something, I don't know. He likes to see the best in people, but don't let that fool you, he'd do his duty and deal you out if you did anything wrong.'

'What – what about that woman?' Ologun asked, finding it slightly difficult to follow her way of speaking.

Judith was suddenly reminded of the past few days. She'd come here to forget about it all for the night before the IMC's arrival. 'I don't want to go into that. No one is to know what's going on until the IMC fleet get here. Frank thought you coming for a quiet drink at mine would be a good idea for us to just forget it – everything – for the night.'

'Yours?' he asked, looking around, then caught sight of two men pushing and shoving in a disagreement over something. The only thing quiet about this place were the weapons which were all fitted with silencers. Risk hardly seemed a concern to any of these people. He too had felt differently since being here. There was something very odd about the whole place; the basin. Drinking and guns didn't mix. How was it that a bar could have its own range with such lax rules?

'How is it you have a bar with a firing range that also allows people to jump around the forest canopy in an obviously advanced assault course? I just don't get it.'

Judith sank another drink. 'This is a special bar with permission to do some exciting stuff. It draws in a lot of business by not having the same rules as in other colonies.'

Ologun didn't see this as a real answer. 'Who'd allow a gun range at a bar?'

'Me. I'm the outpost's senior officer in charge of these things. Anyway, I can tell you're ancient by the fact you had to ask. It's not that dangerous. The rounds used here are dissolvable. If a person gets in the way, the bullets turn to dust. Don't ask me how the rounds can detect living objects, but they're quick to detect heat, a pulse, whatever. You know I went hunting with Frank a few months back and swapped his ammo? It took him hours to find something and . . . his face was priceless. Now, drink up and shoot, I thought you'd be more fun than this, Grandpa,'

Ologun glanced at the assault course where movement had caught his peripheral vision. A man climbing around on top of the tallest section of framework had lost his grip and fallen, to be caught by a superfast crane which simply plucked him from mid-air. The crane delicately lowered him to the ground unharmed, then deactivated by coiling up in a striking resemblance to a giant cobra. The man hadn't seemed to notice he'd been saved and walked a few yards before falling heavily on his face.

Ologun watched Judith down more shots, then observed the rest of the firing range as all kinds of people took turns firing many types of weapon. He was trying to place a word for the feeling he had which made him wash away his concerns at Judith's attitude. She was already sounding impaired with slightly slurred words as she bawled all kinds of nonsense at her comrades; he supposed he would soon join them.

The evening continued with more drinking and Ologun witnessed Judith fire off an automatic rifle across the entire spread of the range while staggering into a table full of other people's drinks. Soon, the range's conductor sent them all off, especially when Trent swung a rifle around his head before throwing it towards one of the targets, then ran across the path of everyone else still firing down the other lanes. As proclaimed earlier by Judith, the rounds self-destructed in small clouds of smoke before hitting the man.

By now they were all drunk. Ologun couldn't remember having been so drunk in his life before and was ready to go back to his small hut to collapse. He waited for his ride and was glad the night had ended with little drama. A large crowd had gathered indoors to the downstairs bar for yet another spectacle. Ologun, half-interested in his inebriated state, observed a game they called paranoia where two people entered a glass dome and stood ten feet apart opposite each other on spinning discs.

Ologun peered over from his position to see Judith having a heated discussion with Trent. He was a big man who towered over her, posturing and waving his arms aggressively. Judith wasn't backing down and mirrored him in his agitation, perhaps seeming more edgy as though she would do something at any moment.

Ologun returned his attention to the contestants, who had got themselves ready and put on helmets so that all they could see was an inverted view to their rear in the heads-up display. He shook his head in amazement as the contestants fought to stay upright on the platforms which spun quite slowly. They were clearly disorientated and somehow had to fire electrically charged darts at each other from small pistols.

Ologun was relatively amused on the odd occasion when they miraculously hit each other despite these obstacles. The darts must have been quite powerful too, as each time a person was hit they were knocked off the disk and sent into spasms on the floor. In time the paranoia aspect of the game became more apparent as whenever a pistol was fired it gave out a purposefully loud hiss that caused the competitors to flinch or lose their balance. At times the sound alone caused contestants to completely lose their nerve and sent them diving for cover. Ologun laughed hysterically as one of the competitors fired a dart which ricocheted off the glass dome, straight back at him, sending him to the floor in a fit. A noise then drew his attention and he saw that Trent had pushed Judith against the bar. He quickly rose to intervene. Before he had the chance to make his way over, Judith had pushed Trent back and headbutted him in the face. Ologun lowered his head in embarrassment when she quickly stormed over to him.

'We're leaving.'

The buggy jolted as Judith, still drunk, pushed hard at the gears in aggression.

She sped round corners, swerving, and on occasion drove at trees before yanking hard at the steering wheel to avoid them.

'So you're taking me back to my cabin now?'

Judith shoved another gear, causing a loud grinding sound. 'You're staying with me,' she hissed. Ologun felt nervous and shrank a little in his seat as Judith nearly missed a corner that would have had them fly off down an embankment and into a nearby field. He didn't dare oppose her decision. He thought she was a maniac and began to wonder what she'd do with him when they arrived at her place.

One white-knuckle ride later and the buggy skidded along a gravelled driveway to a building with one large pane of glass as its front wall. Judith leapt out of the vehicle.

'Come on, I'll make you a drink.'

Ologun made his way up the driveway surrounded by tall trees and lit from either side by spotlights embedded in the floor. Judith typed something into a pad on the glass next to a digital-lens doorway which quickly dispersed, allowing them to enter.

A wall of cooled air hit his body as he walked into the room as lights flickered on at a comfortably low level. Judith walked off through the living room area and to a kitchen at the rear of the long room.

'Nice place,' Ologun complimented.

'Thanks, what do you want to drink?'

Craig Jenkins

To Ologun's relief, Judith appeared to have calmed down. 'What have you got?'

'Any form of alcohol you can think of, tea, coffee, oh and yaepalm.'

'Yaepalm?'

'You know. You'll love the smell of yaepalm in the morning . . . du de de der de,' Judith hummed some old tune he recognised from somewhere. 'Oh, I forgot you missed a few decades. It's this herbal drink with iron, zinc and pretassium. It'll make you feel a bit better,' Judith said as she moved around the kitchen gathering containers and two mugs.

'Yeah, why not?' Ologun agreed and wandered around her apartment. It was open plan in design with painted white walls and thick black fabric tiles covering the entire floor. The living room included a particularly long deep-purple couch, and an equally long table stood before it. Hanging behind the couch were paintings of abstract shapes which dripped and somehow moved. Opposite the couch to his right and against the wall, a tall cylindrical machine flashed and winked in its metal casing. The tower had thick cables running into large stone pillars standing on either side. He walked over to take a closer look. The stone pillars were embedded with a thin strip of fabric which ran the full length down their fronts. He couldn't resist and began pressing buttons on the metal tower. Suddenly, a loud hammering of electric guitars and drums blasted the room and startled him into standing up.

'Play something nice – quiet,' Judith shouted, and the noise changed to a much quieter pitch of saxophones and serene bass. 'You like jazz?'

'This machine understands nice?'

'Of course, it's a decent system. It has tempered asaronite components in the player and amplifier. The cables are klenethium copper cord alloy and the speakers have organic bass pulse emancipation directors.'

Ologun's eyebrows lifted. He hadn't a clue what she was talking about. Asaronite and klenethium were the metals extracted from Deceiver which had replaced most of Earth's terrestrial equivalents for industrial use. In his day they'd led the way to create superior starships and had for the best part replaced steel, copper and gold. He had the idea that klenethium was a superior conductor of electricity, better than copper and gold, and that asaronite when tempered was far more robust than any steel alloy. It was strange to think of these metals in a home appliance for they'd been considered priceless in his day.

'Expensive?'

'Not so much,' Judith said casually as she prepared the drinks. 'Ghost metals have come down in price over the years so they're in most appliances now.'

'Ghost metals?' Ologun asked as he sat down on the couch. He watched as Judith filled a long glass cylinder with water and placed it on a stand of sorts. The water instantly came to the boil.

'Yeah, you know how all the elements on the periodic table have nothing to do with Deceiver?' Judith added as matter-of-factly, as if Ologun should know.

'What? No, not really.'

Judith stopped what she was doing and leaned over the counter to face him. 'Ghost metals, as in they shouldn't exist.' She glanced at him sideways and realised he had no idea what she meant. 'Look, Deceiver has an equivalent of most mineral forms found across the universe, except that whichever star created the elements on Deceiver is from somewhere else in the multiverse, see?'

Ologun gawped at her and shook his head. 'I'm not sure that I do.'

'I'll start from the beginning,' Judith offered, amazed at how uneducated Ologun was considering the fact that he'd been around long after the planet's discovery. 'Deceiver has a core similar to Earth's. You know, an iron nickel centre. Except that its crust, approximately several miles in depth, is made up of minerals that by all accounts shouldn't exist, sort of adding an extra thirty seven elements to the periodic table. Hence the scientists began more work to prove this old theory that there are definitely other universes similar to our own, but different enough to produce or be made of other substances.'

'Uh huh.' Ologun nodded dumbly and wondered whether Judith was still drunk or, worse still, that he hadn't been paying attention in science class at school. He knew his lack of knowledge was sadly due to the latter.

'They think the planet at some point moved through this other universe and for long enough to pick up elements from this universe through meteor showers and so on. So, for the past hundred years or maybe longer, I can't remember, there's been a lot of work into creating portals in order to, I don't know, twist or bend the fabric in order to travel through, no inside—' Judith paused for thought while she completed making the drinks, '—to travel to that or any another universe, anyway.'

Ologun sat in silence and thought hard for a reasonable reply. 'You think that'll happen?'

'Well,' Judith pondered for a moment. 'They said we'd never settle on Mars or get to Jupiter and past the failed binary, or past the Kuiper Belt and to the next solar system. Either way there's been no progress in over eighty years on how fast ships can go even with reverse-mass driver fields and so on. It has to be the next step, regardless of breaking the binds of this universe and going to another.'

'You'd think there'd be an effort to get to the next galaxy let alone another . . .' Ologun said, then tailed off realising he was about to comment on something he knew very little about.

'So, regardless,' Judith continued as though she hadn't heard him, 'it's a whole new world. I mean, without pretassium the forests in this place would never have matured in just over sixty years and our starships wouldn't be proofed against radiation without strong magnetic fields made possible through klenethium.' She leaned over the counter and narrowed her eyes at Ologun. 'You're so boring bringing all this up, you know that?'

'Don't look at me, I can only just about manage to tie my boot laces, let alone discuss whatever it is you're talking about.'

'Yip,' Judith replied, grinning thoughtfully. 'I've met scientists like that too. You want to drink these outside in the dome?'

'Back garden?'

'Come on, it's nice,' Judith said, leading the way through the kitchen.

Ologun made his way behind her and outside and was hit immediately by an invisible wall of hot air. He was disinterested in the conservatory with its large chairs and cushions aplenty, and made his way across a flag-stoned patio to a large swimming pool.

If I hadn't known such riches, Ologun thought when he compared Judith's place to his humble shed. The patio was lit up with more spotlights facing upwards from the ground where the partitions between flagstones had been invaded by the odd intruding vine. Other potted plants led the way in decoration towards the aqua marine glow emanating from the surface of the pool.

He sat on the floor by the water, legs crossed, and Judith sat on a small stool to hand him a mug.

He took a sip. 'Sweet.'

'Yeah, it normally tastes crap so I put some ants' honey in it.'

'Really, what's that?'

'Some environmental guy made a sand pit south of the lake and brought these Australian ants. Some of them have these huge backsides with syrup in them, it's quite nice.'

Ologun took another sip and nodded. 'So what was all that about in the bar?'

'I used to go out with Trent a while ago. He's a bit of a dead head. All brawn and nothing else.'

'So you headbutted him? Are you all brawn and nothing else too?'

Judith cringed. 'I'm trying to turn over a new leaf since . . . sometimes I'm not sure the IMC should have made me a commander with my temper the way it is.'

Ologun leaned over the pool to fish out a large bug which was drowning. He lifted it up to his mouth and began blowing it dry. 'How old are you?'

Judith watched Ologun doing his charitable bit for the insect in fascination. 'Twenty three, why?'

'You know, the one thing I assume is still the same about the IMC? I mean I can't believe they're still around after all this time –

is that they have a strange way of dealing with people. They used to have an ideal that if they chose a person for a role, that no matter how bad they seemed at first, they would wait until the candidate came around and was empowered into doing their absolute best.'

'Empowered?' Judith asked as though this was the only part of Ologun's statement that was odd.

'I was unemployed and just out of court for decking my next door neighbour when IMC recruitment approached me one day. Fortunately I got off with a caution, went to the IMC, took one of their tests and then they interviewed me. By the end of it I thought that becoming one of their intelligence protection agents was my own idea. I couldn't wait to start.'

'Intelligence protection, what's that?'

Ologun's tone changed a little, almost sounding ashamed. 'Well, if a person from the IMC tried to leave the company for say, the GEA, and they had a lot of sensitive information, they'd deploy people like me to delete them from existence. I mean kill them and dispose of them.'

Judith was very interested; Sharplin might not be so paranoid after all. 'So you were an assassin?'

'No. I made one kill on a protection assignment on Phobos while I was in training and dropped out. The psychologists said I suffered from excessive introspective morality dysfunction, so they posted me to admin until eventually I went on to do low-level security patrols for about twelve years.'

'What does morality dysfunction mean?' Judith quizzed, screwing her face up. 'Sounds made up to me.'

'It means that I don't like killing people. That's that. Nothing dysfunctional about wanting to see people live, is there? My point is that even with the IMC's despicable side they still do the most amazing things and do their best to get hold of and keep the people they want.'

Judith found it hard to believe that Ologun was against killing, yet chose not to pursue the subject. Either way the GEA files she'd downloaded from the archives suggested he was dangerous. That word alone made her feel oddly competitive towards and drawn to him at the same time. 'The IMC are okay, I suppose, I took the test and my parents virtually signed me over before I finished school.'

'You resent that?'

'Yes, I do,' Judith said, realising she'd never told anyone before. On top of everything else and how she felt around him, she was beginning to feel at ease with this man. He was easy to talk to and in hindsight she couldn't remember if she'd ever talked to anyone else in this way. The confusing mixture of feelings Judith was experiencing was intoxicating; then, out of nowhere, she was distracted by another agenda.

'The IMC have clever people at the helm,' Ologun said in obvious awe of the company. 'But in my day they wanted to do the best for mankind. They tried to change the world with their irrigation policies by making a deal with the GEA to turn unused wastelands into much more.' He paused. 'And they were duped by politics and greed. As you know, there was enough food and water to go around and the GEA made it a policy to sell the goods to those who could afford it and left out the very people IMC were trying to help, I think.'

'The immigrants?' Judith risked broaching the subject. 'You killed those soldiers because you pitied them, the thieves I mean.'

Ologun realised he had wound himself into this question and felt the anger well up inside. 'There was enough to go around. The GEA spent more money policing the Sahara parklands than they would have if they'd just handed the food out. I just never understood why the people in these countries were left with nothing, no matter how far technology had gone to cure the problem.'

'If it's any consolation, no one goes hungry any more,' Judith said.

Ologun smiled. 'Those people who stole food were breaking the law, but then who has the right to judge people for wanting to survive? Those soldiers only had to show some kindness, whatever happened to that?' He tried to remember the questions he'd thought of earlier, but went blank as he studied Judith in detail.

'Like that bug clinging to your thumb, I think it likes you.'

Ologun laughed. He studied Judith's face as though suddenly obsessed; as though he hadn't seen her before. She was slim but strong looking, almost fierce in some way. He couldn't help but be attracted to her right now, and she was also intelligent. He liked that. He had some principles, though. He was forty one and she was almost half his age. When she'd almost given him no choice but to stay with her earlier, he'd been stunned; now he was keen.

Ologun finished his drink and looked behind him to her typical concrete block, the same as many of the other outpost's buildings. The conservatory now seemed more welcoming with its big comfortable-looking sofa and chairs. He then noticed the wall the glass dome was built on to. 'What are those?' he asked and got up to head for the display.

'Oh, I made them a few years ago.'

Ologun approached the various swords and cleavers hanging on the wall, all facing in the same horizontal direction: 'You made these? They look deadly. In fact I'm a bit worried.'

Judith grinned and grabbed a large cleaver with an odd cut-off angle at the end of the blade. 'I used to make them from various steel alloys, then titanium. The asaronite ones were harder to craft, but they're lighter to handle and they'll never suffer from rust or fatigue. I folded most of them so they can cut through flesh like water. Here, try it out.'

Ologun took the cleaver and swung it around a few times. He looked at Judith with growing curiosity. 'Flesh like water. You're definitely an oddball. I hope you don't have deep aspirations to use these on anyone.'

'Na, I just like the way they look. I'm not psychotic or anything.'

Ologun placed the weapon back in its place on screws which had been driven into the concrete. He gazed at her again and noticed her tilt her head then flick her thick black hair in a way he found provocative. Her eyes seemed very blue, astonishingly beautiful to him. 'Wow, this handle looks so shiny,' he said of one of the blades, then panicked that what he'd said sounded utterly stupid.

'Oh,' Judith replied, smiling. 'It's PM33, another ghost metal similar to silver, and has all the same attributes within clinical applications. You know they use it in the compound for hibernation flights in space travel and in thread used to stitch wounds. In fact, you have some of it in you now, it's therapeutic and, er, shiny,' she added with another smile, then flicked her eyebrows, which excited Ologun. He was reassured that she was thinking what he was thinking.

'What's going on with this place?' Ologun said without any thought then, with an idiotic compulsion, added, 'Someone said you had a cannibal on the loose.' His heart leapt and he cursed himself for having temporarily been possessed by some demon which wanted him to blow his chances with this woman.

Judith stayed silent for a while and was displeased to be reminded of such things. 'I may as well tell you, seeing as you're involved. We found the body of a woman in the Dark Zone, I won't go into details. Then I went to a place to retrace her last steps, which wasn't that far from where you're staying, and had a scrap with this guy – killer.'

'What about the woman I found? I heard she's okay.'

There it is, Judith thought, *there's no avoiding this conversation now.* She was ready to get some answers. 'You were found near some killing frenzy. Eight men and women were in some dug-out pit of sorts. I wasn't there to see it.' Judith folded her arms and looked directly into his eyes. 'You were found with a strange kind of a crystal knife dug into the back of your skull. You were dead again, then Doctor Siren took the knife out and your brain knitted back together and your skull fused solid in little under an hour. You began to breathe of your own accord and here you are as though nothing happened.'

Ologun felt numb. *Is she accusing me? And if so, why am I here and not in some experimental lab?* 'Look, I don't know what to tell you, I really didn't know. I swear I have no idea what's going on. I'd like to know what's happening, too, although I'm fairly pleased I'm not dead. Wouldn't you be?'

'You don't ever remember being some sort of experiment or anything unusual like losing a limb and it growing back or . . .? What about your father? He used to be an IMC admiral, he ever say anything?'

Ologun felt uncomfortable and defensive. She knew an awful lot about him. 'Okay, I'll say this and only because I have no idea why this is happening and because I'm not a liar. When I was young, my father used to joke that I should be careful around deep water because he didn't want me to drown again.'

Judith held back. *Does he know he was adopted?* She decided it would be inappropriate to go there. 'That's it? No other revelation about . . . anything, except that you may or may not have drowned?'

'You and I both know that whatever it is, the IMC will be along to poke and prod me until they find out and neither of us will be privy to what they may find, so why don't we drop it? I was actually beginning to enjoy myself and you go and spoil it with this crap.'

'I hardly call cheating death crap. Anyway, if you don't know you don't know . . . do you know?' Judith said in agitation.

'No I don't, and if I did I'd hardly tell you now, would I, with that impeccable charm of yours?'

They stood looking at each other for a moment then burst into a laughter brought on by some sort of nervous stress – that and the fact that neither wanted to let anything get in the way of what was really going on between them.

'So, you got your man, huh? How many did it take to bring him down?'

Judith nodded. 'Just me. He lost his front teeth in the process!'

Ologun couldn't believe this woman. She was the prettiest, craziest hooligan he'd ever come across. 'Somehow, I can believe that's true. I hope I never get on your bad side. How did you feel? Excited, what?'

'Scared to death, actually,' Judith said to his surprise.

'And now?'

'I'm okay, but that guy is . . . evil, you know? I asked him why he'd done it and he said practice. We had to use a translator pad to figure out what he kept saying.'

'Broken teeth?'

'No, I mean this loon said it over and over in every language, even Latin. Who on earth knows Latin any more?'

Ologun could see her concern and felt a cold shiver run down his spine. 'You know there's no point in trying to understand some of the things nature spits out. No matter how far we go, there's always going to be the primitive crazies who go around spoiling things.'

'Spoiling things.' Judith said, trying to hold back a wry smile. 'Primitives don't speak Latin.'

'Well, of course they do, they were the people who came before us, that makes them old school,' he quipped.

'So you don't mind the IMC prodding around at you?'

Ologun paused and then shrugged. 'If someone has something the IMC wants, then they'll be treated like a king. It's better than the GEA. What am I going to do exactly? The IMC always wanted to have their own empire, and why not? Maybe I can contribute.'

'You really like the company that much, eh?'

'Take a look at this place. They could have made a dull cityscape full of machines and rubbish. They could have done anything at all, but chose to create this. They're preparing to terra-form worlds, I bet, and I can't help but admire them for that. No more overpopulation, famine, war or want for anything under their design, I'm sure.'

'You think they can achieve that?'

Ologun looked at the swords. *Beauty in weapons and the thrill of war.*

'Not a chance. Everything goes around in waves. Civilisations reach up high and crash over and over. To be honest, I'm amazed we've made it so far.'

'Grim outlook,' Judith replied.

'Realistic.'

He realised he was standing close to her and could smell her fragrance: a mixture of vodka and something quite nice. Her eyes had a strange, dull look to them, which he saw as a sign to finally move in closer, to make a move before he said anything else that was stupid. She raised her face to his.

DZZZZ . . . DZZZZ.

'Excuse me.' Judith sighed, paused as if she might ignore it, then hurried into her living room to deal with the ill-timed noise. She returned a few moments later. 'I'm sorry, Ologun, I have to go to

Facilities. Look, just make yourself at home and I'll be back as soon as I can, okay?'

Ologun nodded and waved as she left him alone in her backyard. He was disappointed to say the least. It wasn't the eighty two years that bothered him, it was the lack of any action during the twelve months before he was sentenced that he remembered.

He sat for another hour by the swimming pool, watching the insects darting around each other creating a distinct vortex like some minute tornado above the water. *Probably mating* he thought. *Lucky them.*

He gazed at the sky to look at the strange dull plate that was the star lens. He'd studied it a few times at night when it remained in complete blackout, except that this time, and unlike before, he could see a purple disk of what he assumed was the sun glowing angrily at its centre. He could swear he felt the energy particles desperately escaping the sun's immense gravitational pull. Something within him felt different, something felt wrong.

ESCALATION

The star lens activated, allowing tremendous amounts of light into the basin. Captain Sharplin continued working on the docking platform which sat only fifty feet beneath the false sky. It had been a long night of frustration trying to upgrade the control room interface systems, and the austere pink dawn only served to further aggravate him.

The star-lens docking centre sat way above the basin along the north wall on the same vast metallic framework which linked many of the basin's systems, including the main power hub of the sky-tram network. In comparison to Frank's apartment, the tower upon which the control room sat was a far more elaborate construction of just under a thousand feet in height, making it the tallest edifice in the entire outpost.

It had previously been the main docking station portal for all large ships before being decommissioned over a decade ago, only to be replaced by a much smaller tourist shuttle alternative further east.

Frank threw his digital pad down and moved on to a wire-mesh walkway outside the control room. He looked up at the technicians who were busy re-booting the hydraulic docking mechanisms. The docking crane sat on one large piston which manoeuvred within an asaronite air-lock membrane and upwards to extend through a large circular gap of eighty metres in diameter and which had been carved out of the twenty-metre-thick star-lens plate. The gantry would then protrude through the lens and magnetically fasten up to at least two large craft at a time.

'How long?' the captain asked one worker dangling from a winch way above.

'How long until the ships arrive?' the technician hollered back.

'About eight hours.' Frank strained his voice for volume.

'It'll be ready in eight hours then.'

101

Captain Sharplin was anxious. It had taken over two days to re-establish the fortress's running systems, leaving them little time to establish the platform systems.

He left the technicians to their work and took a break in one of the control room's small offices. He had forgotten just how high up this place was situated: the tubular scaffolding and wire-mesh walkways lent themselves to the illusion that the platform was in a precarious position and ready to topple over at the slightest disruption. In reality the vast amount of open framework had been embedded securely into the plasma concrete which levelled off the basin floor, ensuring it would never falter. It would have been better if this rock they occupied wasn't indestructible and the engineers could have attached the frame to the basin wall with a better means than sealant, but it was secure nonetheless. The star lens also sat in the very same fibrous adhesive. *Which should be of more concern than a thousand-foot scaffold tower,* he supposed.

The captain found that he soon got used to sitting at this height and was pleased that he'd spared Judith from coming here due to her tremendous fear of heights.

He returned to his work and tinkered with a control panel for the environmental controls. The whole area had become blindingly bright pink due to the malfunction of its digital window lenses, which in turn had let the full blast of the star lens enter the room unfiltered.

Dennis Aginie knocked and entered the office.

'The windows aren't working yet,' Frank said with frustration. 'The ships will arrive later this evening. We tried to contact them but they're not responding.'

Dennis narrowed his eyes, trying to cope with the light. 'I heard about the murders, terrible business. I bet you're glad the IMC are nearly here, eh? Any news on why they're coming?'

'Not a clue. Like I said, they aren't responding to hails.'

'These systems are still in good order. I can't offer any sound reasons for the ships going dark,' Dennis said, lifting his hand over his brow.

Frank began flicking switches on a console inside the office and looked to a screen at the far end of the room. 'We sent a message from the tourist portal dock, but I don't know why they're not responding. I can't tell if they're even our ships at this point as no one from any of the IMC networks have responded for the past twelve hours.'

He could see Dennis was hardly paying attention to the importance of the situation and decided to brief him properly. 'I told you the ships may be coming as standard drill for an exercise. What I didn't mention is that they're also coming as a precaution to protect the cache.'

Dennis relaxed his eyes as they got used to the glare. 'Of course.'

Frank's mind began to wander as Dennis twittered on about the fleet coming and how they should have let him know why above anyone else. He let his mind rest after the night's mundane slog. He was feeling tired and run down, and thought about the naked man and the insect on his shoulder. He checked his server chip for the exact time that particular incident had occurred. Sixty six hours had passed since the encounter.

Frank was caught between being on the cusp of relief for the arrival of the IMC and utter dread from some newfound superstition. *Insanity everywhere,* he thought. Judith had turned into some ultra-soldier, decking probably the most sadistic, psychotic man he'd ever come across, and then there was Ologun. Where could he even begin to start with such a man? The IMC would deal with it all soon enough. He liked Ologun though; he'd been such a pleasant person on every encounter he'd had with him.

Frank quickly checked Ologun's tracker and found he was eight miles from his shed. He continued to watch the pad's screen, getting ready to order the marines to pick him up. Ologun at least appeared to be heading in the right direction towards the shed.

One of the officers knocked and entered the office. 'We have contact, sir.'

Sharplin looked up from the pad and rushed to join the IMC crew in the main control room. He quickly walked over to a monitoring station which continued to track movement in the area. All personnel in the room flinched as the control room sirens activated with a deafening sound.

PROXIMITY ALERT. WARNING. PROXIMITY ALERT.

Sharplin shouted at the nearest officer for information. The officer in turn sat bewildered with his mouth open in surprise. Dennis launched himself over to take his place and accessed the control room systems computer. 'It's a ship, a big ship too. The computer states she's the *IMC Hollywood.*'

Captain Sharplin tried to think if he knew this one. Dennis and the captain then both ran to a control panel to access the large monitor at the front of the room. As the system warmed up, the image of a large vessel approaching their position was revealed. The large ship had all the correct security coding and clearance to be acknowledged as IMC Fleet, bombardment class.

'How does a ship appear from nowhere?' Frank asked, working away at the computer terminal.

The initial scan read it to be a good eight thousand metres long. *It must be the largest ship in existence, surely,* Sharplin reasoned. Dennis scrolled through the available angles transmitted by the floating security probes. The lettering on the side of the fleet ship read: IMC HOLLYWOOD.

The captain paced the room in anxiety. 'How the hell did we not see that coming? Where did she come from? Anyone made contact with any of the other ships out there?'

Dennis ran the files as quickly as he could. 'No prior information about the ship.' A small grin of fascination formed briefly on the man's face and was quickly hidden as his eyes shifted back and forth across the room.

'What are you grinning at, Dennis?' Sharplin asked, then returned his attention to other matters. 'Keep trying to get through, Ensign Gillot, let's say hello to them at least. Will someone turn that bloody alarm off?'

Dennis continued to work on the console, angry that he'd let himself slip for just a moment. *That was close!*

Ensign Gillot coolly relayed information as the monitor revealed five more ships, which quickly slowed near the *Hollywood's* position. Simultaneously, the five ships opened fire at the *Hollywood's* port bow. The proximity alarm died down and everyone in the control room looked on silently as the *Hollywood* was engulfed in a blanket of explosions. They continued to watch as the inferno slowly dissipated, expecting a display of total destruction.

Amazingly, where the *Hollywood* should have suffered vast amounts of devastation across its hull, there was only a patch of white-hot metal. The enormous ship continued to drift, then slowly adjusted her position until she faced her aggressors. Two large cannons unfolded from underneath elongated shelves which ran the length of the *Hollywood's* port and starboard sides. The two massive barrels then extended further on giant piston slides. With lightning speed, the extended parts of both cannons recoiled back to their original positions as large projectiles were released.

The huge missiles hit one of the ships through the centre, puncturing her through the bow and ejecting from the stern. The *Hollywood* had effectively destroyed an IMC patrol and destroy class vessel named *Paradox Volley*. The destroyed ship imploded within seconds, leaving the four remaining ships to regroup for a second attack.

'Communication band silence maintained between all ships,' Dennis informed everyone.

Sharplin thought about the strange warning he'd been given sixty six hours and seven minutes earlier; he felt sick, terrified. He searched the faces of everyone in the room. Dennis seemed concerned, one of the officers was shaking as his hands bounced uncontrollably upon a console and the rest of the crew looked to him in muted shock.

All eyes returned their focus to the main monitor. The four remaining ships spread out to attack once again. They were smaller and more manoeuvrable than the colossal beast *Hollywood,* which gave them a chance. They released another volley of over a hundred missiles, which exploded ferociously against the *Hollywood's* hull.

Again the *Hollywood* brushed off the attack with little sign she'd taken damage except for another small patch on her hull that glowed bright white with heat. The enormous ship then manoeuvred to fire her giant cannons once again and the resulting projectiles ripped through the sides of two more of the opposing fleet ships: the *Dobranoc* and the *Tainted Light,* which held position parallel to each other. After claiming their first two victims, the large missiles carried on at great velocity and tore straight alongside the hull of a third ship, *IMC Deep Vanquish.*

Dobranoc and *Tainted Light* immediately withdrew from the fight and accelerated sluggishly to a safe distance away, crippled with extensive damage.

In retaliation, the two remaining ships split up to flank the *Hollywood* and draw her fire away from the others. The *Deep Vanquish,* along with *Authentic Resilience,* fired her stampede guns along with another volley of missiles. This time the *Hollywood* suffered her first damaging blow as the projectiles impacted directly on the firing mechanism for the *Hollywood's* cannons.

The explosion was impressive with a large ball of fire, and was quickly followed by a tornado of flame spiralling off into space. The *Hollywood's* wounds were revealed to be superficial, however, as the flames were simply cut off at the source. The *Hollywood* now had a large hull breach sixty metres across with twisted metal jutting out in every direction where the missiles had hit. This time the *Hollywood* fired her stampede guns. She had twice as many rail guns which were new in design and fired with tremendous ferocity at her aggressors. The *Deep Vanquish* was the first to take hits and her hull shredded under the merciless bombardment. Gas, flames and twisted metal erupted as the stampede rounds penetrated her starboard hull at such an angle that the volley found its way through to its stern. *Authentic Resilience* accelerated as the *Hollywood's* stampede barrels took aim. Again the rounds found a target with vicious consequences and the *Authentic Resilience* drifted out of control, spewing her contents into the zero atmosphere of the vacuum. The two remaining ships had by now fled the combat zone, managing to escape the range of the *Hollywood's* might. The *Hollywood* in turn came to a halt just above the star lens, dismissing the chance to pursue her wounded prey.

~

Version

Captain Sharplin stared deeply at the monitor showing the three destroyed IMC ships as their deflated hulls drifted in a lifeless mess.

He lifted his head to address the room which remained silent and deeply disturbed by the events. Even Dennis appeared speechless for once and Sharplin realised that something tangible needed to happen immediately. He spoke with more authority than ever before, 'Evacuate everyone to the fortress, do it now!'

Judith yawned deeply as she parked the buggy just outside the main entrance to the Opus Hospital. She was tired but also anxious as the doctor had summoned her with a matter of great urgency. The commander made her way through the empty vast reception area to the building with its large glass windows allowing the full volley of pink morning light to blitz the room. She took two steps at a time up the stairs leading to the upper levels and ran down a long narrow corridor to Doctor Siren's main laboratory. After using her ID key and undergoing a retinal scan, the reinforced doors opened into a vast complex of processing towers, with endless tables of various equipment and row after row of live animals. Birds, lizards, monkeys, rats, cats and dogs, along with many more kinds of test subjects, all of which erupted with noise as she ran past them and towards the doctor's office. Judith hated such an endeavour for testing animals; whatever Siren did in this place was surely unnecessary in this day and age.

Inside a large cage to her left she spotted a gorilla which was obviously depressed and almost seemed as though it had given up as it sat rocking backwards and forwards in its deprived state. She was saddened to think that there were no monkeys at all within the forests in the basin and the only ones at the outpost were merely a few feet away from possibly the best habitat to suit their needs. Instead they were caged in a place that was clinical, dark and frightening with no consideration for their happiness or sanity. Judith forced herself to ignore the sight and knew this was one of the reasons she and Siren didn't get along and why at times she even had thoughts of physical violence towards the doctor.

Judith arrived at the door to the doctor's office. Hanging from a hook to her right was a skin bag, which was frequently used by the military for target practice when trying out new weapons or new and improved ammunition. Simply put, this repulsive organism was a human being grown to adulthood without the inclusion of a brain. Technically it was just a bag of flesh and bones without the engine of sentience. Judith saw that this one was dead and whatever had caused its heart to stop beating was more than likely disease-orientated as its skin was covered in strange blots, and blood and mucus oozed from its eyes, mouth and nose.

She nearly barged in on the doctor, then realised it was her usual way of being insolent and stopped to knock on the door. At a muffled, 'Come in,' Judith entered to see Doctor Siren sitting behind a desk in a particularly cramped room.

'What's going on? The marines reported the prisoner as secure.'

Doctor Siren broke away from the terminal screen and deactivated her server chip. 'It's regarding a breach at one of the fortress caches. You'd better sit down.'

Judith took a seat then placed her rifle butt down on the floor and leaned the weapon upright against the table. 'You inform the captain?'

'No, he's busy, so its procedure to inform the next highest ranking officer available. That would be you.'

Judith leant back in her chair. 'Anything missing? Weapons, what?'

Rita looked pale, almost as though she'd seen something awful. 'Nothing like that. Look, the fortress has a large biological reserve. Many high-ranking IMC members have deposits there for preservation. I don't know how to explain this precisely . . .'

Judith listened to the doctor and placed a tracking pad on the table. The pad bleeped every few seconds, satisfying her that the prisoner was still under lock and key.

'The prisoner – killer – is, according to the database, likely to be, or rather, with certainty, *is* the son of Vincent Taggert and Vargen Schmitvelle.'

Version

Judith sat patiently and listened to the reassuring beep of the tracking pad. 'I don't know who these people are!'

'You're not likely to know them. They died over seventy years ago. If the system database is correct it means someone has stolen their DNA samples and . . . I don't understand what's going on. He shouldn't exist, unless someone else here knows how to or even wants to incubate and process human life.'

Judith immediately thought of Ologun and his inconceivable parenting. 'Could the machine be mistaken?'

'I hope to God it is,' Siren replied.

'Well, you have the gear to grow a skin bag so why not a fully formed person?' Judith offered, recognising the doctor's obvious lie in regard to the technology.

'Okay,' Siren replied with a clear tone of defiance. 'That means someone has breached this lab's security or you or the captain have been neglecting security protocols and someone used your keys. Either that or one of you let someone in.'

Judith ignored the preposterous accusation and quickly tried to piece together exactly what Rita meant, then noticed the beeping sound had vanished. 'Shh.'

The pad remained silent and the illuminated blip had disappeared. Judith instinctively grabbed her rifle.

A loud crash from somewhere in the building startled them both. Judith made her way to the office door and peered out into the laboratory where the animals were now going completely berserk. Another loud crash, mixed with the sound of a blood-curdling scream, rose above the bedlam.

The doctor moved to open a small cabinet on the wall and pressed a large red button within it. Valves placed within each of the animal cages released a grey-coloured gas that soon rendered all the test subjects unconscious. Judith glared at Doctor Siren and felt like beating her with the butt of her rifle. She thought quickly about the situation and regained her composure. 'Stay here and lock the door,' she ordered and headed through the lab and out into the corridor. The building filled with the noise of gunfire and more screams as Judith led the way with her rifle aimed ahead. The sound of an altercation on the next level above escalated – then, silence.

Judith negotiated the stairs, crouching in caution. She tuned her comms in to the marine guard's frequency. 'Sergeant Wice, come in, over. Kamal, come in, over.'

Judith listened for any feedback from the squad of twelve assigned to guard the prisoner. The line hissed with no response.

She sent a request for backup and moved from the stairwell to the landing, scouring the area for any activity, then headed down the corridor to her left.

Moving with a long, rapid stride, she felt exposed under the powerful glare of strip lights embedded centrally along the ceiling, until a dark patch on the floor at the end of the narrow concrete passageway drew her attention.

She moved closer until it became apparent that the dark blemish was a puddle of red liquid which spread out across the smooth cream tiled floor. She hugged the wall and aimed her rifle. Her heart pounded until her senses were filled with her pulse thumping in her head. Judith then glanced around the corner to her left, then right to where the prisoner was being held. She retracted her head and stared at the corridor wall opposite. Breathing hard, almost wheezing, she moved into the corridor to face the horror once more and knelt on one knee in the wet, her rifle still brought to bear. The narrow passageway ahead flashed under the broken light, while the floor beneath was flooded with blood and strewn with body parts.

Judith couldn't move. Shock had set in and her mind was numb. *Keep moving!*

She stood up. Her eyes switched this way and that as though electrodes had been attached to their stems. Slowly, and with deliberate steps, she crept along and through the thick liquid on the floor. The doorways along the passage alternated opposite each other. She turned to her left and slowly turned the handle to open the nearest door, then flinched back, directing her rifle into the room. A desk with chairs stood undisturbed. The commander resumed her search and accidentally kicked a detached head across the floor. She stopped and didn't even attempt to identify the face. She opened the door on the other side of the corridor and was presented by another virtually empty small room.

Judith took a deep breath as the next room had been used to incarcerate the prisoner. She leaned back slightly to see the door was missing: it had been torn off its hinges. Stepping to her left to avoid an appendage-less torso at her feet, Judith peeked around the corner.

Inside the room there was a large metal chair at its centre with thick framework. Solid metal restraints hung off its arms and legs. The bracelet restraints had been broken and twisted by some major force. The walls, floor and ceiling had red matter splattered all over them.

Judith checked her surroundings quickly, aiming her rifle in each direction down the corridor before peering into the room again to see that several bodies lay in an entangled mess behind the chair. She recoiled with fright and slipped heavily on to her side next to a torso, then scrambled frantically on the saturated floor.

Eventually she found herself sitting against the corridor wall opposite the room and hyperventilating. Her mind had shut down for a moment and one arm hung limply in the blood, her rifle sitting in the open palm of her hand. Her sight seemed to be delayed by a few seconds so that each time her eyes moved, the scene lagged then quickly played catch up. *Snap out of it!*

The ordeal had lasted for only a few minutes but it already felt as though an hour had passed. A shriek of laughter struck Judith's senses and she stood up. Her heart pounded once again as she made her way through several corridors on autopilot until she entered an open-plan landing overlooking the hospital's reception thirty feet below. She hadn't registered the set of bloody footprints she'd followed to a large stairwell leading to the ground floor. The reception area glowed with the yellow of morning sunshine which sparkled off the polished floor tiles and the varnished reception desk. More sticky footprints glistened with fresh moisture and worked their way to the reception's entrance doorway.

The commander headed for the entrance, checking every possible space for one hidden assailant. She checked behind the desk and in the cupboards to the rear of it, then walked straight across to exit the building. Immediately she began sweating in the moist, hot air outside the hospital, yet felt cold; pins and needles prickled her hands and feet. The footprints continued along the brown flagstone driveway leading out of the facility's compound. Judith followed, moving along the path for a few moments before stopping. The bloody prints had faded and vanished halfway down the path, and she finally lost any remaining nerve to continue.

Large bushes and decorative palm trees either side of the wide path remained eerily still. Judith thought for a moment. This man had crept up on her once before and she realised he could do the same again, except this time she was absolutely terrified. The sounds of birds and the wind-inducing fans in the distance obscured her concentration as she probed the foliage from her position. She felt vulnerable and backed off towards the hospital while pointing the rifle back and forth to either side of the driveway.

'Judith.'

She leapt to the floor as her heart strained, feeling as though it had missed several beats, then lay for a few moments on her back in a daze.

'Judith, its Captain Sharplin. Come in.'

Judith had left her comms system on open-speaker mode and cursed her own stupidity.

'You fool! Couldn't you just this once use your server chip?' she blasted.

'No, this is an emergency, you know the drill.'

Judith aimed her rifle through the gap between her knees at the pathway. 'Rita contacted you, right? Listen, I lost him, I'm sorry.'

'No, what do you mean?' His voice was slightly distorted over the frequency.

'The prisoner's gone, he killed the marines. It's a complete mess here, I'll organise a search party and . . .'

'Commander, listen to me. Forget the prisoner, I've ordered the entire basin to evacuate to the fortress immediately. The block's been dropped. Get there fast for a briefing.'

Judith sat up straight; the aim of her rifle unwavering. 'Affirmative on that, what's going on exactly?'

Version

'Just get to the base, I don't have time to explain. Grab the doctor and go now!'

Judith remained still for a moment. Her head pounded and her nose began to bleed. She wiped it to little effect as it dripped more rapidly. Without taking any further notice of it, she sprinted off into the building to collect Doctor Siren.

EVACUATION

The basin was almost uncomfortably hot by mid-afternoon. The star lens let in more sunlight to maximise the temperature for a digitally run summer to allow the crops to gain some serious yield. Ologun felt it was too dry, regardless of the giant air circulators at the end of the field blowing a little cool air his way. He wiped the sweat from his face then watched in fascination as a number of piped objects rose from the ground. He looked closer at one of the thin cylindrical objects to see a digital display read: PRECIPITATION LOW. Within moments a heavy tropical downpour fell, giving the air a sweet smell of freshly wet soil.

'Hello.'

The voice startled him as he'd been too preoccupied to notice that a small scruffily dressed man had crept up on his position. 'Hello yourself,' Ologun replied, feeling a shiver run through him at his soaking.

'I'm Nelson. I grow things in the next field. Do you know where everyone went?'

'I'm Ologun, pleased to meet you. No, I haven't seen anyone all morning.' Nelson spoke in a slow manner which made Ologun think he was mentally impaired in some way. 'You think everyone's gone, is that unusual?'

Nelson stood in the rain, thinking about the question. 'My father runs the hotel, everyone's gone today. You want to see my plants?'

Nelson change of subject caused Ologun to pay less attention to the initial question and he followed the short, skinny man enthusiastically summoning him. He was bored anyway, and really didn't want to refuse an invite which would give him a change of scenery.

'How does it rain here, Nelson?' Ologun quizzed as they walked in the downpour.

'From the sky.'

'No, I mean it's a fake sky, so it must drop from pipe work of some kind directly above, don't you think?' Ologun speculated, even though all he could ever see above him was the distant framework of the sky tram. Logically it would have made sense if water could be routed via this framework and released from there.

Nelson took his time before answering. 'Rains from the sky.'

Never mind, Ologun thought. He could think of no other conversation and hoped that perhaps Nelson would chat about his plants and just allow him to listen. They passed through some woodland of tall trees to enter the next field. Before them a row of green plants around ten feet high stood in a neatly knit row. They gave off a particularly strong aroma amongst the smells of fresh wet soil and other vegetation that Ologun recognised.

'My father showed me how to grow these and when to do them,' Nelson explained as he skipped towards them.

Ologun had another eye-opening realisation about the strange rules of this place. Nelson had been growing large hemp plants. 'Are they for making rope or something?' he asked, although he expected the more obvious answer.

'Rope?' Nelson looked puzzled. 'My father takes the fruit before they can make seeds. I have to get to the males and take them to my shed and take a few girls and let them mix there.'

Ologun followed this explanation without the faintest idea of what Nelson was talking about. The only thing obvious was that either it was legal to do such things here or no one had noticed.

'Town's empty too,' Nelson mentioned, jumping in a large puddle and splashing mud all over Ologun's clothes and face. The downpour stopped as abruptly as it had begun to let the warmth return. It was stranger still to see the heat build to form a fog-like vapour across the ground in moments.

Ologun thought about Nelson's twittering on. *What's he saying?* For a simple mind which seemed to mind little, he was concerned about this difference to his life.

'Is the town ever empty, Nelson?'

Nelson skipped through the vapour. 'No, I've never seen it empty. I've never seen the hotel empty either. You want to come to the hotel?'

Ologun looked at the white-tinted sky. *What to make of this?* He hadn't seen anyone since leaving Judith's place in the early hours. 'I'll go to my cabin and contact someone. I can't go too far, I'm under a radius curfew.'

'Curf what?'

Ologun sighed. 'You know grounded?'

'Yes.'

'Well, I'm grounded,'

'You been bad, eh?'

Ologun nodded as he scoured the treeline to see a path leading back to his cabin. 'Yeah, I've been bad.'

'What did you do, Ologun? That's a strange name, is it real?'

'You don't want to know and yes it's a real name.'

The pair strolled down a road that gave a clear view of the basin's central lake many miles away. The star lens had reached full output to mimic an afternoon sun moving across the sky and the air had grown muggy. The rain had turned the soil to a slippery congealed muck that stuck to the bottom of Ologun's boots like an additional sole. He kicked and flicked his legs one at a time in agitation and felt uncomfortable in the smothering atmosphere of heat and thick mist.

Ologun continued to walk in a peculiar distracted fashion, stopping on occasion to pick the clay from his boots as he listened to Nelson who was wittering on about some strange childhood stories. 'My mother used to do the gardening, you know. She said I had to lift the slabs to kill the ants with alcohol because they were too close to the house. I used to leave some of the nests alone, you know, because they only want to spread out and find new places. Just like us.'

Then Nelson said something of profound interest to Ologun. 'Do you think they'll kill us when we've gone too far like the ants under the paving stones, Ologun?'

He hadn't the chance to contemplate the strange question as movement above caught his peripheral view. Against the glare of the star lens he could just make out a black shadow moving at speed. Nelson shrieked as five men dropped next to him from what appeared to be impossibly thin wire to hold their weight. They were well armed and wore strange smooth armour with mushroom-shaped helmets of a similar cast, with masks that hid their faces from view.

One of the armed men immediately struck Nelson in the face to stop him in his tracks and sent him flying backwards across the muddy floor.

'It's okay, I'll come quietly,' Ologun said to stop them hitting Nelson.

The soldier who had hit Nelson walked over to again smash the butt of his rifle into Nelson's face.

'Wait. I said I'll come with you, it's me you want,' Ologun shouted in panic.

Ologun was struck on the back of his head and dropped to his knees and watched, impaired. He could hear faint chatter from within the soldiers' helmets:

'No witnesses.'

'Execution confirmed.'

Nelson lay on his back whimpering as the soldier moved closer and raised his rifle to his face.

No way! Ologun moved in reflex and leapt aggressively, landing on the right knee of the soldier. The man cried out in agony as his leg snapped under Ologun's weight, then lost consciousness as Ologun punched him hard in the throat. These were soldiers of a kind he hadn't seen before and he was slightly dazed from the shockwave sent back through his body from the ruptured leg armour.

Ologun moved too quickly for them to find their mark as he pounced on the nearest soldier, clearing a space of six feet without touching the floor. The two men hit the water-logged mud of the field and slid uncontrollably along its surface.

Ologun, aware that he may be shot by the other soldiers, quickly pulled his downed assailant on top of him. The soldier straddled him, choking Ologun with the length of his rifle. Unfazed by his predicament, Ologun knocked the inside right elbow of the soldier's arm, causing the man to collapse on to his chest, then he grabbed the man's helmet and twisted hard, snapping his neck.

The other three soldiers backed off and spread out in a flanking formation to surround Ologun. He took the dead soldier's rifle and fired at the nearest target. To his dismay the soldier's armour took the rounds with little effect as the bullets ricocheted in all directions.

The soldier now took his turn, lunging down on to one knee to return fire, just missing Ologun as he hid under the body for cover. *Not this again!*

Two of the soldiers fired in short bursts at the dead soldier, perhaps hoping for a lucky shot through the tough armour as their comrade moved in closer.

Ologun was now at a loss for his next move. He looked around and noticed the soldier he was using for cover had a large machete strapped to his right thigh. He unhooked the weapon, thinking hard about his next course of action.

He peeked to his left to see one of the soldiers had crept up right next to him. He panicked, pushed the body aside, and launched himself at the soldier. The soldier fired his rifle with one short accurate burst, hitting Ologun fully in the centre of his chest. He froze and fell on to his back, then slid towards the soldier in the slurry and realised it was all over. His thoughts slowed, his ears rang loudly, and his vision faded then, unexpectedly, everything snapped back into focus.

Ologun looked at the soldier as he continued to slide towards him. The soldier was alarmed at the sight and quickly backed away, still firing.

He was moving too quickly for the soldier, who lost his footing and was distracted enough for Ologun to slide straight between his legs and hack him in the groin with the blade. The soldier gave out a muffled scream from behind his mask as he fell to his knees with blood pouring from under his armour.

His power slide ended with him being too far from his remaining two opponents. Frantically, Ologun scrambled to stand, sliding in the thick mud to escape being shot. One soldier raised his jackhammer towards him but was shot before he had a chance to fire. It was

Nelson. He'd taken the rifle off the dead soldier and fired the weapon erratically at the remaining soldiers.

Ologun could only see one outcome. One of the soldiers fired two shots into Nelson's chest, throwing him violently to land on his back.

Ologun felt his body move more quickly than he thought possible and he wasted no time in disarming the soldier and dropping him to the floor. The fury Ologun felt had him seething uncontrollably inside and he smashed the butt of the soldier's rifle into his face shield over and over. He only let up when the remaining soldier fired the jackhammer straight into his left shoulder.

Ologun erupted with vicious intent in response to the pain, rapidly launching himself at the man and taking another explosive shotgun shell to the chest. This time Ologun felt sharp penetrations from the tiny chips of shrapnel which tore his flesh. He grabbed the soldier by the head, lifting his feet off the floor. The soldier panicked, frantically trying to release Ologun's grip by hammer-punching the top of his skull. Ologun held him firmly by the ridges of his helmet and gave a small twist to snap the soldier's neck and render the man lifeless.

He dropped the soldier to the floor and absorbed the aftermath of his terrible deeds for a moment in disgust before regaining composure. He looked to Nelson, who was lying on his back a few yards away. He ran across and knelt at Nelson's side; the poor soul was barely alive.

Nelson opened his eyes and choked up blood as he spoke. 'They don't want these ants under their slabs.' He gargled deeply and went limp.

Ologun stared at the man as he lay dead in the pool of mud. The sound of more activity worked its way across the fields and he looked up and around in every direction to regain his bearings. In the distance he could see more soldiers moving in on his position from across the field. Some were on foot, but his main concern were the ones travelling at great speed on multi-terrain trucks. He only had moments to get away, and felt even more urgency when he saw more soldiers descending from the sky on their drop wires.

Ologun snatched the rifle lying next to Nelson and scrambled through the mud towards the jackhammer. He decided to make a dash for it. *Why not?* he thought, *there's no point in surrendering now.*

Ologun ran as fast as he could across the muddy field towards the cover of forest. He was going to make it as hard as he could for them to capture or kill him and even take a few down with him for satisfaction. Something about these soldiers told him to keep going at any cost. He felt the pain from the wounds in his chest and couldn't understand his ability to sprint with so many holes in his lungs that his chest was making a gurgling noise with every breath. *Never mind, no time to contemplate that now,* he rationalized, spotting one of the soldiers landing ten yards directly in front of him. He raised the automated shotgun as he approached the newly delivered assailant. *He should have opened fire when in descent,* Ologun thought as he dropped to slide along the mud, firing the shotgun upwards as he passed. The soldier received a close-range blast to the face and was killed instantly. *The neck!* He made a mental note of the weakest point in their armour as the rounds seemed to have little effect elsewhere; unless he counted the joint seams at the groin.

Ologun spotted the treeline only fifty yards away and pushed on as best he could. He watched yet more soldiers drop from the sky near the forest and took a chance at shooting them down with the rifle. One of the rounds knocked one of the soldiers off his wire, sending him through the last twenty feet of his journey in freefall. The other soldier managed to reach the ground and took cover behind one of the trees. Ologun had no choice but to continue down the same path as the sound of the vehicles to his rear grew louder. The soldier in front of him poked his rifle around the side of the trunk and fired at Ologun, who was now within reach. He took multiple hits to his chest and stomach and fell backwards, hitting the floor with force. He slid along the mud again, except this time his perception of reality slowed almost to a halt. As he looked up to the white sky, his vision followed what appeared to be a small rocket of some description skimming past his face.

He snapped back to real time as the missile hit one of the trees, exploded, and shook the ground. He sat up and tried to move, only to feel a pulse of wretched agony consume his legs. Braving a look, he saw that his shins and thighs had received deep lacerations as a consequence of the blast.

He stood up, stumbled forward, then finally made it into the cover of the forest and checked his surroundings. He surveyed the mess of smoke and ash left by the missile, which had destroyed a number of trees, and realised it had killed the soldier in the process. He turned to peer into the forest gloom where the sunlight was slightly diffused by the thick canopy. He realised the Dark Zone would have been a much better place for cover. *Too bad.* It was twelve miles in the other direction.

There were no signs of anyone ahead of him. The pain in his legs and chest was excruciating and prompted him to gag, although he produced no vomit. Again he got himself together and began tabbing through the forest at the sound of vehicles coming to a halt. He kept a steady pace for twenty minutes as he looked around for any pursuers deep within the forest cover, only to be greeted with an almost tranquil, dimly lit place of beauty. The trees were evenly spaced and rigidly straight so he could see in all directions down long passageways. The air was laden with mist, and blades of light illuminated its motionless formation. The ground across the entire woodland floor was covered in short grass with tiny white flowers poking through and which added a certain brightness to the place. *Where's the picnic basket?*

He knelt down on his knees to check the rifle and jackhammer for ammunition and threw the shotgun away when he found it empty. He badly wanted to lie down on the mixture of moss and flowers and enjoy the view, overcome the pain, and maybe sleep for a while.

The scenery didn't help. Nothing helped ease the pain coursing through his body, and which left him wanting to just give up. *My injuries should have killed me,* he thought over and over. *What the hell's going on?* The other thought which pulled at his desires was to make this manhunt as hard as possible; he was utterly pissed off with the whole situation. He remembered the sentencing and torture which he'd taken continuously out of some sense of guilt that it had all been deserved. *What have I done wrong this time?* He suspected something else was at hand here. It didn't make sense for Sharplin to do this and if it was the IMC coming to collect him, they'd gone about it in the wrong way.

Ologun sprinted through the soft undergrowth, only stopping to catch his breath and check his wounds. The pain of his injuries had subsided for now and they appeared to have stopped bleeding. He held his breath to listen to the sound of more vehicles approaching from his left in the distance, which prompted him to raise his rifle in caution. Like clockwork to his long-forgotten experience of these situations, a small quad bike broke on to the path a few yards ahead of him; its driver taking aim. He dived in reflex behind a thick tree to avoid the gun fire, then quickly peeked around the side of the trunk to see a dozen miniature darts grouped in the bark. *Close call,* he thought, only to turn to face the end of a gun barrel. One of his pursuers had flanked him.

Ologun didn't hesitate to tilt his head while simultaneously booting the man in the side of the face. Grabbing the gun, he twisted hard enough to flip the soldier on to the ground then rendered him unconscious with a swift strike to the throat. The quietness resumed with only the distant sound of chirping birds. He looked at his grounded foe before leaning against the large tree trunk behind him. His second attacker had abandoned his bike and was somewhere nearby.

The soldier had more than likely called in his position by now. He would have to continue the sprint, but where to? The only place he could think of was the lake. It didn't make much sense to aim for such an open place, yet his mind fixated upon the location as a last resort of escape. He ran at impressive speed as he began to think of the plantation incident. *I surrendered then, should I do the same now? These soldiers had orders to kill. 'No witnesses,' they'd said. Why?*

He kept going until the anterior edge of the forest came into view. He peered through and out into a bright clearing of fields which led to some buildings he recognised as being situated near the lake. What he'd thought was a forest was actually a small cluster of trees of roughly five square miles south of the resort where the Minx Machine stood and, with any luck, he'd stumbled across a small holiday resort near the lake. Once again he felt compelled to reach it. An itching sensation moved across his skin where he'd been wounded. He opened his shirt and took a quick glance to see the wounds had started to heal over.

He used to speculate that he just had a good ability to block out pain and use adrenaline to keep going regardless of injury, yet he'd always had to go to hospital for serious wounds and couldn't understand this strange phenomenon. He thought about Sharplin and Judith. They'd told him . . . they'd said things he refused to fully believe and he now realised they'd been telling the truth. *The basin!*

This rate of recovery scared him into thinking the outpost was having a profound effect on him, that it must be mutating him in some way.

He scoured the fields ahead near the buildings. Hopefully his pursuers were trying to cover the vast amounts of ground behind him and were nowhere near his position. This fact made Ologun think of another strange outcome. Not only had he managed to escape with such terrible wounds, the ground he'd covered was positively elite athletic and his pace was that of someone in top condition. He took a deep breath, felt strong again, and went for it. Within minutes he'd cleared the distance of the field and carried on through a small space between two large buildings where he could see the lake a few hundred yards ahead. He crouched behind a hedgerow leading to a large patio littered with loungers, tables and chairs with large wicker umbrellas surrounding a swimming pool.

He moved from his position of cover and ran across the patio, almost slipping into the pool as he aimed for a small bar. A number of glasses were stood on the bar's worktop and looked to be abandoned as some of them were still full. The tables surrounding the pool were the same with half-eaten meals and more drinks left untouched.

Ologun took one of the beakers and downed it quickly, then coughed against his will, creating a loud racket that echoed between the buildings and deserted terrace.

He negotiated concrete steps down to a lower level until he emerged under the cover of more buildings. He crouched down in the shade next to a row of olive trees. Sweat poured from his face and body and he wiped his face with his hand. He peered around a corner only to be greeted by more masked soldiers fifty yards either side of him. The feeling of anticipation engulfed him and his pace once more increased. He made his way down a sloping path to a large drop to the lake's bank. He glanced sideways to see the soldiers had made his position and were moving in quickly from every direction except the lake itself. The only route now would be over the ledge a few feet in front, dropping ten feet on to the concrete path, then sprinting another hundred yards to the pier.

Ologun grinned to himself at the absurdity of the situation. If he could make it to the end of the pier, which was at least two thousand yards in length, he'd be satisfied for some reason well beyond rational thought.

He took a few more strides towards the ledge when a large sledgehammer of pain violently struck his back. His perception blurred as he saw his chest explode in a vapour of blood in front of him. He staggered a few more paces before stumbling over the ledge and falling the ten feet to the concrete path. He landed with full force on his left shoulder, snapping his collar bone.

He wailed at the pain and shook with a sickness he'd never felt before. Could he risk the shock of finding out the extent of his injuries this time? With little sense of self control he looked down to see a five-inch-wide hole in his chest where his heart had been ripped to shreds. *Sniper!*

Ologun couldn't ignore this any more. How was he still alive? What was the need for this excessive force being used against him?

He realised he wouldn't get anywhere if he allowed his thoughts to distract him. Heart beating or not, he would at least have a go at reaching the pier. He stood up and made a huge effort to run. The movement of his body was both wretched and slow. Finally, and with relief, the tremendous pain which had engulfed him frittered away as he moved, so there was only the preoccupation of watching his own feet as he staggered along, half-crippled. *One foot in front of the other,* he kept thinking as the only rhythm in his mind that would get him to the pier. The long metal-grid walkway reaching out over the lake sparked with fury as rifle rounds ricocheted under his feet. He had no idea that many of the bullets were hitting his body; even his skull. The rounds tore into him, hit and bounced off bones; ripping through him at devastating angles, yet he felt nothing.

Ologun's world ground to a halt yet again as he saw blood vapour spray out above and ahead of him. His journey to the end of the pier was in real jeopardy of failing. The sledgehammer blow which hit the back of his head caused him to finally lose his balance. He could no longer hear the sound of rifle fire and could only just make out the surface of the lake rushing towards him. He realised that the game was over as his perception of all reality steadily drifted away. With one last glimpse he made out that he was under the lake's surface that bobbed and rippled above him. Sunlight penetrated with sharp beams of light which reached down into the green-tinged darkness. He sank and everything faded to black.

11

BASTION

Captain Sharplin waited and used a powerful telescope to peer through a narrow window to monitor the forest treeline only half a mile away. This place was the only way to fend off a substantial attack from any aggressor insane enough to try their luck. The unknown force had been in the basin for hours and appeared far more prepared than anything he could have imagined.

Remote cameras had scanned the area near the docking platform three hundred miles away and had transmitted images that the intruders were assembling a large transport, the likes of which he'd never seen before. Whatever the large vehicle was, the intruders had rigged it straight on to the sky-tram cable system then loaded a multitude of vehicles and other unknown devices. This transmission had been received three hours ago before all communication with the devices had been lost; presumably they'd been destroyed.

In principle, the sky-tram cable network could accommodate movements of up to three hundred miles per hour and all trams near the docking platform had been shut down as part of the emergency operating procedures. The enemy should have been forced to travel the most time-consuming route across the basin floor and around the lake. Now they had the possible advantage of full-line speed directly to within a mile of the fortress, which in turn had possibly diminished the amount of time left available to evacuate the basin. His team hadn't found time to sabotage the line, and even sending a tram for collision seemed pointless as the IMC trams were flimsy with paper-thin carbon-fibre chassis. The heavy-duty tram the invaders had constructed seemed a far more solid block in order to accommodate the weight of the vehicles it was being laden with. *Such a machine would surely push the tram cable system to its very limit and smash right through a sky tram like a hammer through thin ice,* he theorised.

'How many more?' he asked.

'Around fifty.'

'Commander, why don't you go help organise them in the main hall?'

Judith was unusually quiet and looked ill. 'I left Ologun alone. He's still out there, I'm sorry.'

'Don't worry about it. Something tells me he might be all right. In fact I'm beginning to wonder what will happen if whoever these people are come across him.'

'Spanner in the works,' Judith said smiling.

Captain Sharplin nodded. 'Are we fully operational?'

'I'm finalising,' Judith said. 'Completion in the next ten minutes.'

'Good. Get going, I'll be down shortly.'

Judith nodded and left the Captain alone while he scrolled through schematics of the fortress on a touch screen embedded within a long conference table at the centre of the room. He made a few mental notes regarding his next set of priorities and made his way to follow Judith just as Dr Siren walked in. 'I need the new access codes to the medical wing. I brought several medical bots.'

'Judith,' Frank voiced over the comm. 'Give the doctor access to the medical wing.'

'Affirmative,' Judith's voice came back. 'Weapons cache C is also playing up. Quantum code timers on some doors have gone to crap.'

Captain Sharplin moved to a narrow window lens upon hearing a commotion outside. The last of the evacuees were still dawdling, and even the buggies seemed to have slowed to a grinding pace. He lifted the comms device to his mouth. 'Sergeant Thomas, are you at the entrance?'

'Yes, Captain.'

'Can you speed this up a bit? We need to raise the blanket field pronto . . . can you do that? Oh and find the commander – she'll help you if there's any trouble.'

'Yes, Captain.'

Doctor Siren turned to leave the room. 'I'll set up the medical wing and then help organise the tourists – I expect the holiday reps will need help sorting them out. Frank, I got a report back from the lab about the maniac we captured, who escaped.'

'He's like Ologun isn't he?' the captain said.

'How did . . .'

A popping sound erupted into the room from the digital glass window, prompting Sharplin to duck. Doctor Siren flew backwards and landed on the floor. He crawled under the table to her side. 'What happened?'

'What does it look like? I've been shot!' Rita screeched.

He looked at her left shoulder, which oozed blood through her white blouse. 'What should I do?'

'Go, I've used my server chip to summon the medical unit from downstairs, I'll be fine.'

He took off his jacket and applied pressure over the wound. 'It's passed through.'

The sound of shouting and gunfire erupted outside, and he crawled over to the window and risked a glance out of the now vacant hole to see advancing soldiers chasing the remaining civilians across the field. Another quick glance through the scope revealed the large armoured tram had stopped at the last network platform and was now lowering more vehicles to the ground at great speed on slip wires.

His attention then shifted down and across the field where he saw two buggies being fired upon by three enemy trucks with stampede turrets mounted on their rear compartments. All three fired mercilessly, causing the buggies to shred, and instantly killing all on board.

He ran to the stairs that led down to the fortress's entrance as quickly as he could. As he entered a hallway he spotted Judith and six other marines run outside to take cover behind a concrete wall one hundred feet away from the entrance. Judith immediately took aim with a sniper rifle and fired a devastatingly accurate round that went straight through the skull of the driver of an enemy vehicle. Taking aim once more with the powerful weapon, she then eliminated the turret's operative as the vehicle sped on out of control and sideways across the field.

Sharplin ran to the entrance, fighting his way through a frantic crowd of civilians now desperately making for cover in the courtyard fifty feet behind him. He looked out across the field to see that a large number of people had been mown down by eight vehicles which continued onwards and towards his position. The vehicles manoeuvred slightly to reveal a large armoured tank making its way behind them. The monstrous vehicle travelled slowly under the bulk of its own armour, which hadn't been coloured for any particular terrain, suggesting it was being used for the first time. Such was the metallic sheen of the tank that it reflected the late afternoon sunlight, blinding the captain for a moment before his eyes adjusted, only to then see its cannon fire in his direction.

He dove for cover just as the shell shot straight above him and down the entrance corridor to explode within the courtyard behind. The noise was deafening and vast levels of confusion took hold as a thick wave of dust swept the entrance hallway. The detonation had caused plasma concrete to explode in large chunks all over the courtyard and the civilians who cowered in terror. The place was now in complete chaos with the crowd pushing and shoving to find cover within another large hall to the rear of the spacious quad.

'Judith!' he shouted. He needed everyone inside before he could activate the main defences.

IMC marines rushed to man the fortress stampede guns and pulse launchers, whilst more ran up stairwells to the roof to fire any weapons they had to hand. Within moments, the fortress stampede guns were being fired in all forward directions at the numerous trucks as they sped quickly across the last three hundred yards to the entrance. Five of these lighter vehicles were shredded immediately, but the tank brushed away the rounds. They had little effect on its asaronite fibre plating which contracted as though muscles on a large beast.

A cluster of marines operating one of the pulse launchers thirty feet up in one of the fortress defence towers quickly discussed the tank's armour while choosing ammunition. Aiming the launcher at its treads, they released missiles of a varying skill set. The two magma-class missiles hit the tank first as the supercharged matter exploded on to the side of the tank. The impact had no effect as the fibre metal plating was simply too thick and too modern, causing the molten liquid to drip off its sides and leaving the tank undamaged.

They chose to launch a set of missiles classed as coordinate chill shakers. Liquid nitrogen exploded from one missile, freezing a large area on top of the tank's surface. It was then bombarded with high frequency sound waves from another missile as it passed by. Part of the tank's amour shattered and fell inwards. The second chill-shake attack then succeeded in its objective by smashing the front section of the tank's treads and rendering it immobile.

Three more trucks sped in from the edge of the field, avoiding the stampede fire. The missiles were useless against the faster vehicles as heat-seeking guidance systems were distorted in the basin's environment, making the trucks the worst threat.

The sound of the stampede fire escalated as both sides opened up with everything they had. Hidden long-range stampede turrets from within the forest were now in play, giving off a ferocious racket which echoed off the basin's dense wall situated directly behind the fortress. The exchange of red-hot projectiles began to destroy both camps. The enemy cover at the forest wall splintered as trunks exploded and trees fell. In contrast, the fortress wall was blasted and chipped away in an eruption of minute impacts across its face with large segments of plasma concrete dropping down and releasing clouds of grey powder.

One marine, who had taken cover alongside Judith, stood up to fire an RPG at one of the trucks which had made it through the fortress's crossfire defence, and sent it careering in a ball of flames. Sharplin followed the progress of one vehicle that fired its turret directly towards Judith and six other marines who remained behind the protection of the wall. The truck pushed on and avoided the fortress guns as it made a bold dash to come within yards of the entrance.

Judith saw the breach and risked her cover to sprint along the wall as the truck passed her. She quickly grabbed on to the side of the enemy vehicle, pulling herself on to the turret platform at its rear. The truck was now at the entrance to the fortress and she efficiently unsheathed a knife from her belt and stabbed it into the neck of the soldier operating the stampede turret. Judith then leapt over to the front and bashed the driver's head against the control panel.

By now it was too late and once again Sharplin dove for cover as the front end of the vehicle clipped the left side of the entrance wall and careered down the corridor at great velocity. The vehicle then violently flipped over and landed on its side at the entrance to the courtyard.

He got back to his feet and ran towards the carnage within the courtyard, where the truck had finally collided with the rear wall. His state of confusion was immense as he realised that he still needed to initiate the blanket field to cover the entire building.

Sharplin stopped and looked back to see the marines had left their position of cover from behind the wall and had nearly made it to the entrance. 'Hit the switch to the shield when you're all in!' he yelled, resuming his awkwardly slow sprint towards the courtyard. He stopped for a moment to address them again. 'And flip the other one as well.'

One marine was shot to shreds and the other five stumbled as they avoided another shell from the partly destroyed tank which still had functioning weapons. The shell found its mark, hitting the corridor roof which collapsed in another cloud of plasma concrete. Two more enemy trucks got within range of the entrance before they exploded under the fierce thunder of the fortress stampede turrets.

One of the marines frantically climbed to her feet and darted into a room to the side of the passage to operate a control panel. The first input triggered a loud whining noise as thick metal struts sprang up from the ground outside the fortress entrance.

These pillars were each fifty feet in height and spaced evenly at intervals across the grassy ground a few feet further out from the wall. A large blanket of blue shimmering energy quickly erupted between each of the posts. The vehicles were stopped dead in their tracks. Their bonnets crumpled, pointing downwards with the back end of both trucks tilting upwards so that their occupants were thrown forward at force and fried instantly upon the shield.

The second input into the panel released thousands of spikes that shot up through the grass surrounding the fortress perimeter. The sharp spears slid across each other in tight patterns at seventy degree angles to skewer everything on this stretch of land.

The marine looked to a monitor in the room and was relieved to see that the tank had been impaled on the many seven-foot-long spikes. She then quickly flicked through the numerous camera angles to see that many other soldiers and trucks had succumbed to the same fate in their mad sprint to reach the entrance. She continued to monitor transmissions sent by camera units which hung from the blanket field's struts. One by one the cameras were destroyed by snipers, leaving everyone inside behind the cloudy protective shroud of the fortress shield both deaf and blind to the world outside.

The large courtyard of the fortress was a disaster zone with people still fighting their way into the main hall. Sharplin made his way through the thick smog of dust and over chunks of concrete strewn across the floor. A number of dead civilians lay in contorted positions on the thick debris.

Silence made way for the thumping sound of a pulse raging through his ears as he walked towards the truck Judith had tried to commandeer. It lay silently in the courtyard and upside down in the rubble with steam pouring off its bodywork and one of its wheels spinning.

He jogged around the side of the truck and through the smoke to see the commander had been thrown against a large flat shard of concrete. She lay completely still as a lifeless mess on the ground with her face pressed against the large grey slab and her arms pushed out behind her.

He ran to kneel at her side. 'Judith.' He leaned over to feel her pulse. Sharplin couldn't help but feel his own pulse distort every other sensation as he gasped for breath. In deep concentration he placed his index finger on her carotid artery. He took a deep breath to calm down, to make sure.

~

The field shimmered with an electric neon blue as the struts pushed charged particles out through a set of transformers, then dragged the spikes of energy back in again through earth chambers along each pillar. If these earthing mechanisms failed at any point it would cause a massive fork of electricity to escape the slender face of the field and inevitably kill those within its range.

He thought about this possibility and remembered he'd had the same thoughts when they'd been installed to replace the old asaronite plate system of shielding. He stared at it in wonder through the broken window lens of the officer's conference room. He found its power soothing and helped him put things in perspective. Amusement crept over him; an almost sick comparison as he remembered issuing simple orders: *Make sure the rain pumps are working, fell those trees out near the Diamond Resort.*

His commands now seemed to be in a strange new foreign language which he was growing accustomed to. He was saying other things like, 'Stockpile the ammo, strip those dead soldiers of their armour and move the dead civilians to the rearmost compartments of the bastion.'

The civilians had calmed, Judith had seen to that and had surprised him with her capabilities in a crisis – *and on more than one occasion,* he noted.

He was still none the wiser in identifying the enemy, even though they'd scavenged two suits of armour from the men who'd penetrated the fortress defences. Advanced body armour, dull grey in colour, it had micro-fibre plating laced with a power field for extra defence. The helmets they wore were bizarre and reminded him of those ancient straw hats the Orientals used to wear. He couldn't remember what those people did. *Rice farmers maybe?*

The armour had no echelons nor ID logos, and the fearsome faceplate heads-up display had been inactive; someone had pulled the plug.

That was it: *Samurai warriors!*

Not exactly, he reasoned. The hats were more Chinese than Japanese, a mix of designs for reasons well beyond any logic he could figure.

He turned away from the neon blue light of the shield which blocked the outside world from view to stare deeply into the blood-stained matted floor where Rita had lain. *Why such brutality?* he asked himself. When this was over his life would never be the same. *If I survive this ordeal my retirement plans at the basin are over for sure,* he told himself. Sharplin leaned out of the hole in the wall to check that the blanket field was still complete and fully operational. More klenethium struts jutted out from the fortress roof so that the shield covered the entire building in a protective bubble. He could only hope the fleet would arrive before these people found a way in, for up until now this unidentified enemy had been well prepared and they may have a countermeasure to such a defence.

He held his jacket, which was now stained the colour of dried blood. He decided he would visit Rita and made his way to the conference room door, just as it opened. 'May I come in, Frank?'

'Sure, sit down, drink?' Sharplin asked, sitting at the conference table to greet Dennis Aginie.

'No thanks.' Dennis got straight to the point. 'It seems our luck is in as the *Hollywood* has so much damage it needs to dock for repairs rather than blast the star lens to dust and pick up what they came for as it drifts out.'

Sharplin remained silent for a moment as luck seemed an inappropriate word for what had just occurred. He pondered his next move.

'What's likely to happen next?' he asked. His role as captain had so far been that of caretaker rather than commander of war. This whole scenario with the fortress was simply way beyond his knowledge and experience.

'Well, we don't have to do anything. The blanket field gathers enough energy from the star lens to allow it to run perpetually if needed, and it's impervious to any form of breach. As I was saying, the lens will stay intact as long as their ship needs repairs. I've re-run footage of the ships' battle and can say there is enough damage for them to need time for repairs before the possibility of them deciding to compromise the star lens.'

'What if they destroy the lens?' Captain Sharplin asked, needing to know the worst case scenario.

Dennis thought for a moment to work through the possible results.

'I would say that the weight of the plasma-concrete grid would hold us firmly here in the basin floor as the basin has some of its own gravity if our cells fail.'

Sharplin digested this information, amazed that he didn't know that. 'Natural gravity.'

'Enough to stay put perhaps, I'm not entirely sure. Our worst case scenario is that we'll only have a couple of days under the protection of the blanket field in zero atmospheric conditions with the backup cells beneath the fortress. Our chances against the *Hollywood's* main cannons, however, is another concern.'

Captain Sharplin rocked in his chair as he listened. 'We'd better hope someone comes before that happens, then.'

He didn't believe that these people would be in any way unprepared. 'Is there any other way into this shield? People like this wouldn't be able to steal a ship of *Hollywood's* magnitude without a plan. What would you do?'

Dennis had once been part of the IMC weapons research group on Phobos. He knew everything regarding the offence or defence of most technologies.

'The only way in here, I would say, would be to break into the blanket with a power-drain transfer rig. To put it simply, you have a specially designed drill which has the dual ability to confound the shield while it siphons off its power to another source requiring the same levels of power. Unless you can disperse the power somehow, even store it if you can.'

Sharplin sat up, his interest piqued. 'You think these people may have something like that?'

'No,' Dennis replied with certainty. 'Such a platform would need a ballast or a balancer larger than the docking portal. Even if that weren't the case, no one could get such a device to the ground and across the hundreds of miles in the time required before our backup arrives.'

'Could they have brought one on that armoured tram they brought the vehicles on?' Frank asked, remembering the strange devices the enemy had unloaded.

'No, too heavy. That's a specialist tool that, as I recall, has never been used for disabling a fortress blanket field.'

'Then what's it for?' Captain Sharplin asked, baffled.

'That's classified, Frank. I've told you a lot which is classified, but I draw the line at that.'

Sharplin grew agitated. 'Look, you're right. I don't know much about defence management, tactics or what's going on. I need your help to figure out what's likely to happen in the event the field malfunctions or is breached. If we lose this place I think we're all in for the big push.'

Dennis chewed the inside of his cheek while he decided what to say. 'I'd like to know how you knew to evacuate to here. I didn't have the Intel to assume we needed a full evac. How did you know?'

Sharplin thought briefly about the naked man and the insect. 'I have my reasons and that's all I'm saying.'

'Okay, Frank, here's what I do know, and I'll let you know, but you really shouldn't be allowed to know. Some well-organised group stole the *Hollywood* a month ago. The directors at IMC headquarters are going ape shit because their new prototype engine allowing faster travel with the added ability of stealth, dubbed as position processing, had been installed. Now it's here and I think you made the best call under the circumstances.'

'You mean my brilliant guesswork, because no one respects me enough to tell me jack shit!' Frank vented angrily. '*Now* what do we do?'

'I don't think there's any plausible way in here that I can see. I think those IMC ships were a scouting party ready to back us up just in case the *Hollywood* came this way. Now a whole fleet with the capacity to take her out should be here within twenty hours, I would say.'

'Can we last that long?' Sharplin quizzed in paranoia.

Version

'We can hold out here for months if need be but, judging by their persistence and firepower, I think they may go as far as blowing the star lens.' Dennis gave a shrug as though there were no more avenues to explore, then added, 'Besides, this is a weapons cache. We have enough firepower to at least keep those ground forces at bay.'

'I think I should switch the Keeper on just to see what it thinks strategically,' Frank suggested.

Dennis couldn't protest quickly enough. 'That's the worst thing we could do! It would instantly initiate final protocols. These people have a foothold. The AI would be ready to detonate a nuke under most circumstances, let alone the certainty of this one. We don't need the AI – they're stupid at the best of times. Besides, you don't really know what the Keeper is, do you?' Dennis then put his hand over his mouth as though something had slipped out against his will. Dennis watched Sharplin and hoped that these explanations were enough. The conversation had gone too close to the bone for him and yet, just as everyone else here, Dennis had found his superior level of security clearance stood for nothing and that he was just as vulnerable as anyone else. He at least hoped that what he had told Frank was vague enough to avoid either of them getting into trouble, if of course either of them survived.

The comms box on the desk flashed, interrupting the conversation. 'I think you should see this. Meet me at the main entrance.'

Sharplin was surprised to hear Judith's voice. He'd ordered her to rest and hadn't expected her to resume command of the marines for hours, if not days.

Sharplin and Dennis made their way to the fortress entrance to see the IMC marines and a vast number of the other occupants of the basin helping themselves to food and drink presented on long tables. The crowds moved slowly through the large concrete corridor to the courtyard, to and from the hallway where a large camping space had been organised. The civilians appeared to be suffering a mix of emotions. Some were distraught and huddled together, while others seemed relaxed and could even be described as enjoying themselves. Sharplin found it easy to ignore the rumble of the crowd, and only the occasional high-pitched cry of grief in the background touched him. *At least it's better than stampede fire and missile explosions,* Frank decided, *but only just.*

They exited the passage and passed through the mob to reach the main entrance. Frank peered outside through the tall archway to see Judith standing directly in front of the blanket field. She was very close to the shield's shimmering plane, her face almost touching it.

The two men joined her. 'Be careful, you'll burn your face off if you get any closer,' Dennis said.

'What is it?' Sharplin asked, trying to peer through the dense electric-blue of the shield.

Dennis squinted alongside him, then backed away from the field, looking ghostly white and afraid.

Sharplin glanced away and his stomach knotted as his fears about the attackers being fully prepared solidified. The enemy had built a large scaffold ramp above the stretch of land leading to the fortress, enabling them to avoid the field of spikes. They were manoeuvring ten miniature siphon drills into position around the front of the blanket field.

CHARIOTS

A dream took hold as Ologun dozed. He had a view of the basin but it was bare of trees or the sky trams. The sky was black with winking stars and the white naked sun. Where the lake had been was now an incredibly large dipped circle within the black marble floor, which appeared spherical rather than flat. His vision gradually floated over the dipped circle to its very centre which seemed to have opened up into a further, deeper chasm glowing with the same orange light as in some of his other dreams. He could see something emerging from this opening on to the basin floor; it looked like a giant snake or maybe some kind of transparent worm which had its own electric white glow pulsating through its body. It crawled along the floor inside the dipped circle of the basin and flexed in pain as though stabbed.

The sensation of movement urged him into some level of consciousness and away from the nightmare. He could feel himself floating horizontally and moving backward at pace. His eyes opened at last to see a strange orange glow emanating beneath him. He could move his head a little in some directions, although the rest of his body remained paralysed. As his vision improved he could see a black marble ceiling above him which was curved and reflected the orange light at angles.

This surface was only a few feet above his face and its marble pattern at first moved above him, matching his own speed, then changed so that it appeared to pulsate in a snake-like and repulsive fashion. The orange glow from beneath him also seemed very familiar. He may have lost all control over his body, but he felt as if he was floating in a warm, dense liquid far too viscous to be water.

He drifted along for hours in this state. He floated in and out of some strange state of consciousness as he travelled for miles in what he imagined to be a river of sorts. His memories from the past washed over him in clear detail as he relived the plantation atrocities, the trip to Deceiver and the ocean-sky horizon spinning towards him.

Then, without warning, the journey abruptly ended when his body flipped in a lifeless somersault and he caught sight of a glowing liquid falling into an incandescent pool. He landed violently and was submersed in the liquid long enough for panic to set in. He still couldn't move and was convinced he would drown. Underneath the surface he found his vision was perfect as the transparency allowed him to see just as well as in open air. *Is this a form of gas rather than liquid?* He tried to discern the answer before his body was dragged down through a large funnel in the black marble bottom of the pool. He was thrown into a tunnel which pulled him along at incredible speed along a steep incline which twisted and turned, making it difficult for him to keep his bearings as he bounced off its walls.

The panic he felt grew as being flung against the tunnel walls inflicted great pain, and he was unable to breathe through the vast amount of liquid being forced into his airway. His body became weightless yet again for a moment until he came crashing down into another passage, landing hard on his coccyx. This was physically the worst time he'd ever endured, unless he considered his experiences of being tortured, hungry, thirsty, or even shot at with a sniper rifle. The pain from hitting his backside made him unaware of the tunnel's gradient increasing until he was once again in freefall.

He looked down to see what he could only comprehend as an ocean. The orange liquid had accumulated into a sea so vast he couldn't make out where it ended in any direction. He struggled to grasp the enormity of the place and his perception couldn't quite understand how high above a sea of deep orange light he was.

He felt as though hours had passed in this state of flight and he'd reached maximum velocity a while ago. Relaxing into this far more tranquil state, he stared mindlessly into the acute levels of brightness below. At first the ocean had blinded him until his eyes adjusted and he could now see the soft waves lapping tranquilly as he approached from above. *Shit!* He suddenly snapped into full awareness when he noticed large snake-like creatures darting about near the surface, almost like transparent eels with large gaping mouths. For the first time in his life he felt true fear and he released an involuntary long shriek of despair. The ocean approached and he screamed all the way down, crashing head first into the glowing waters.

He hadn't known that hitting water could split skin. Due to the length of his fall he dove to depths he was sure were impossible for any human to withstand, yet these were just perceptions caused by his escalating panic to the nightmare journey that was so outside of his control. He frantically fought to swim in a semi-crippled state towards where he thought the surface of the ocean was. He fought and swam and finally burst through after an alarming amount of time spent submerged.

The light blinded him and he breathed and splashed around, then took a few moments to simply float as the sensation in his head made his skull feel as though it would explode from pain and disorientation. Full command of his body returned as he began to tread the orange liquid and he scoured his surroundings for any sign of normality. He dipped his face into the surface of the liquid out of fear when he remembered the creatures. Again he could see for some distance, and was shocked to witness the very creatures he'd hoped were imaginary swimming around and below him. He couldn't quite make out how deep down they were; some of them could have been a hundred metres down, or as deep as a thousand judging from the scale of the things. He decided there was no choice but to avoid his instinctive fears for now and return his attention towards the ocean's surface. This in itself proved difficult as the light emitted from the liquid was far brighter now that he was in it. He tried to compose himself as best he could until his eyesight adjusted to absorb the whole surface of the sea and its distant horizon. *Breathtaking,* he thought as he took in the magnitude of it all. The orange ocean of liquid light simply disappeared into the horizon underneath a jet black sky in every direction. There didn't seem to be any real indication as to where he could swim to find any form of land, if land existed here at all.

~

He decided to start swimming regardless of the overwhelming nature of the place. *What choice do I have?* He swam physically through the liquid's thinly gelatinous impedance while his mind swam in erratic thoughts. *Am I dead or alive? Up or down?* He still had no idea where or what was going on. There was leaving your comfort zone and then there was, well whatever category this scenario happened to fall under.

He swam for a long time until he looked up to see what appeared to be land a few hundred feet away. He thrashed towards it with a childish excitement to eventually wash up on a black marble beach which provided a much welcome, if not exaggerated, level of relief.

He eventually staggered from the ocean and along the slight incline of the smooth slippery ground. He made his way up the shore, sliding and struggling on the hard surface until he reached its crest. He took a moment to peer around in confusion, for beyond this slight summit there was an immense marble landscape with hundreds of various-sized pools of glowing orange which lit the way in all directions. His eyes adjusted to the contrast between pillars of light firing up from the pools and the surrounding blackness. Eventually he made out a number of large objects standing in the distance and considered them for a while before taking his next step.

It was impossible to identify what they were, except that the constructions were of a paler shade of black and reflected the orange light, shimmering and large.

He stepped forward and fell down a long banking incline until he came to rest a few hundred feet below where the floor levelled off. He stood up and began to walk, fixated on the objects which grew larger and clearer as he approached. He trudged through and around the numerous pools of light, which were of varying depths that on occasions caused him to stumble and fall. Still dazed he approached what he at first thought were large creatures, until it became obvious they were ships of some kind.

Eleven enormous craft sat as though they had congregated here only to die. He moved closer to one of the ships, checking its outer layer to see a more conventional structure of dark panelling which showed signs of wear from scorching and other forms of impact.

Version

Whatever they were it was apparent they'd come from a reality he recognised far more than any of the other elements he'd witnessed in this place.

He continued to walk for some time through an almost pitch darkness which was lit only by the orange light at his feet. He was now underneath one of the ships and looked upwards along its hull for any further indications of its origins when he came across the first sign that it was of human construction. He raced quickly to a large stilt that held the behemoth vessel off the ground and knew he had seen other ships using the same extensions to land in quadruped fashion.

Relief swept over him at such a find. He reached out to feel the metal of the landing pad under his fingertips and studied the ship's hull fifteen feet above him and which stretched to form an endless ceiling in all directions. He suddenly felt claustrophobic underneath the enormous ship and quickly made his way forward to find out more. *At least this is something, a way back to normality,* he thought.

He emerged to be greeted by an even more peculiar vista and realised all eleven ships were facing bow on to a long narrow lake of the orange liquid which stretched into the far distance. It also appeared that the ships had all unhinged their front halves downwards on to the lake's surface. All he could think was how small he felt at the sights he'd seen since arriving here. If he hadn't recognised one of the components to the ship he'd have started to think he'd shrunk to the size of an insect.

There was more confirmation on the lake that the craft were human in origin as all of the vessels had released smaller ships. These vessels were liners built to navigate oceans and had all been lowered from a large section of the spaceships' bows to facilitate their release. He became excited at this sight of the floating vessels which were more in scale to his own tastes. His father had once taken him on a large cruiser on the Indian Ocean back on Earth when he'd been younger and he found that the design of the ones presented here were not that different. Whatever their purpose, they were still large and measured a good eight hundred metres in length.

He ran to the lake shore, checking for any sign of the eel creatures before he waded and swam across to the nearest ship. He moved to the cruiser's aft section and managed to climb up on to a ledge, presumably used for diving expeditions.

He negotiated the stairs to the main deck, where he soon felt an eerie quietness. There were no signs of life or any indication that the ship had ever been used. He wandered around the deserted cabins containing unused bunk beds, empty laboratories, empty kitchens and an empty gymnasium. Whoever this ship was meant for hadn't even disturbed the frozen food lockers which remained fully stocked with every essential ingredient he could think of.

He finally made his way to the bridge where he fiddled with controls, lazily trying to relax and, above all, to think more clearly. *What do I do now?* he asked himself. The chair he sat in was very comfortable as it tilted backwards slightly, taking the weight of his body. The view through large front-facing windows complimented the glowing lake, which looked more like a watering hole for large cumbersome creatures from this perspective with the large vessels half in and half out of the lake on both sides.

I'm dry. It suddenly occurred to him out of the blue that whatever substance he'd just been immersed in hadn't soaked into his hair or clothes. He rubbed his eyes and his thoughts turned back to where he was and what he was doing.

Hitting all manner of buttons in what was almost boredom, he thought logically about his next course of action. So far everything he'd done had been born out of a primitive urge to survive and his rise and fall of emotions hadn't entailed any plan of action. He knew there were many people who would have handled the situation differently. Some would still be in the ocean panicking right now. Others may be further along in understanding where they were through pure deduction. He was less dazed now and realised that he was still on the shard somewhere. It was his only real conclusion as the black marble surfaces of the basin walls were identical to the ground here. The giant ships and orange transparent liquid were another issue he had yet to figure out. *Are they the ships the basin's occupants had arrived on?* It didn't seem likely from the lack of human presence in this place.

He thought about his next best move. He wasn't able to figure out how to sail the ship he was aboard. He was no good with that sort of thing. *Where would I go anyway? Cruise the lake for a while and eat from the frozen food stores?*

He examined the controls displayed across large panels throughout the bridge in search of any apparent communication device. He hadn't thought of this at first and was surprised he'd thought of it last. He intently flipped switches using the trial and error method, until he activated a small monitor to his left and which was embedded in the control panel. The screen slowly lit up to reveal the face of a woman.

'Hello!' he shouted in a desperation which made him cringe the moment he'd said it.

The woman was middle aged with dark skin and greying hair, and wore a uniform he didn't recognise. 'Hello, can you hear me?' he asked again with more restraint.

The woman began to speak over him. It was a recording.

'Welcome. My name is Doctor Rajendra. For those of you who are unfamiliar with me, I am the chief navigational calculations officer entrusted to ensure the success of the journey you have now completed. By listening to this you have successfully transcended many years of travel and have arrived safely at the correct solar system co-ordinates. If the journey you have undertaken is a success and our ability to reverse mass with no ill effects on living matter over such a distance . . .'

His mind wandered and he stopped listening as she continued to babble on; he had no idea what this woman was referring to. Dr Rajendra said farewell and good luck, and the screen went blank.

A chill ran down his spine at the creepy recording. He'd never needed much company before, yet now he wanted to see another person more than anything else. He needed to clear his head, and made his way to the main deck which was littered with numerous machines and other smaller boats.

Crouching down he looked out over the lake and at the ships around him. *What to think of this whole affair?* he wondered. This was the stuff fuelled by feverish dreams. He closed his eyes for a moment to try and find some kind of way to curb the level of shock he was experiencing. A voice startled him and he misheard what was said as his eyes opened and darted to see a totally naked dark-skinned man standing at his side.

'Are you listening?' the man enquired.

He leapt up, hugging his back against the deck's outer rail. 'Who are you? And where in the shit fire are we?' he asked in panic.

The man moved closer and wiped a wet transparent substance on his neck. Ologun recoiled and lifted his arm.

'It's time to remember Ologun Jowett,' the man said.

Ologun stared for a moment, and then he knew. His eyes grew dull and calm and his mind divided between who he used to be and what he really was.

'Ray,' Ologun said. 'You named yourself Ray?' He looked at Ray for a moment. 'Aren't you going to put some clothes on?'

Admiral Novex sat on the ship's bridge and surveyed the operations being executed on the basin floor. He was tall and thin with pale skin and bright white hair. His sunken, almost totally black eyes revealed him to be someone who very rarely saw daylight; preferring instead to remain aboard the vessel he commanded.

His career from off-world anti-terrorist agent to GSA officer had been a strange ascent and he'd succeeded in every mission pushed his way. *Politics,* he thought once again. GSA Command had had no doubt he'd accept the mission, for they knew he believed in the quest.

It hadn't taken long for his meeting with senior executives in command to convince him that the GSA's future was at stake. It had transpired that the IMC had spotted yet another planet compatible to Earth's own environment, causing a shift in the low-level standoff between the two corporations. GSA were many years from succeeding in producing a ship fast enough to reach the find. They'd learned that the IMC had developed the *Hollywood* and would beat them to it, which was unacceptable. It meant they would own another planet which in turn meant another vast power boost to the most powerful competition Earth's leaders faced.

This was where the mission had come into effect. He'd taken eight hundred men and women he'd personally handpicked for their capabilities, commandeered the *Hollywood* and then picked the best possible means of acquiring arms for the journey to the distant planet.

So far the mission had been handled with care. All knowledge of the plot could be denied by GSA command, while the IMC were still wondering who'd had the sheer audacity to take out an entire construction centre and steal the most priceless asset they owned. It had been a mission of extreme difficulty as the construction centre on Phobos boasted an armed division with thousands of well-trained soldiers for security. The theft had been more of a silent burglary than an all-out assault, which had been the complete opposite of his usual style. Stealing the ship had been a great success which GSA Command would revel in for some time. Still, over a hundred of his men had been killed in the process, which was hard for any commander to take.

Once again he found himself on a mission to steal IMC property. The Black Ball outpost had been chosen for its lax security after being constantly decommissioned and transformed into more of a holiday village than a military outpost. He hadn't accounted for a caretaker to be vigilant enough to fire up the fortress in time to lock them out.

He watched a transmission on a large monitor at the front of the bridge. An image of the fortress was being relayed from a camera positioned half a mile away from within the cover of the forest. *Such a strange design,* he thought. The fortress could only be compared to a volcano which had been cut in half and pressed up against the dense basin wall. The image showed that its electric blue defence shield was still in operation and he grew impatient.

Novex got up and paced the bridge floor. The *Hollywood* was an exceptional ship with long-range detectors which suggested they had twenty hours to complete the mission before more IMC ships arrived.

It was a small and dangerous window of time to reach the weapons cache, although the worst outcome would be for the *Hollywood* to continue her journey empty handed with no chance of any other ships being able to catch her.

'I think you should see this, Admiral Novex, *sir.*' Sergeant Jackson entered the bridge and saluted. He held a digital pad which he handed to the admiral. He was in charge of relaying the power conduits for the siphon drills, and had not been expected to return to the ship so soon.

'How long do you estimate, Sergeant?' the admiral demanded.

'The shield will be down in eight hours.'

Novex looked at the pad with increasing interest.

'The cannons will be ready in a few hours I heard?' Jackson added, browsing for information.

'Ten,' Novex replied. 'What is this?' he continued, intrigued.

'V squad were on the initial scouting mission on the south-west side of the lake trying out the IMC prototype armour and equipment, and decided to jump from the tram structure. They scoped a target and pursued him. Our men were taken apart by this man, *sir.*'

Novex looked at the footage taken in first-person view from within the soldiers' helmets as a man with inhuman capabilities attacked them. The footage then cut to the same man running across various landscapes and taking multiple hits from gunfire to his body. Fascinated, Novex watched the man's final moments as he fell into the lake.

'What do you think, Sergeant Jackson?'

'No armour, close-range impacts. The guy's a freak. Could be an IMC experiment, who knows? If there are any more locked away in here we could be in trouble. He took out six, left one critical, *sir.*'

'Relax, Sergeant, Where's his body?' Novex quizzed.

Jackson paused before answering. 'We looked, no sign, *sir.*'

'Dismissed,' Novex ordered.

'Yes, Admiral, *sir.*'

'Sergeant, you don't have to shout sir after every sentence, take it easy.'

Version

'Yes, Admiral . . .' Jackson paused as he almost shouted it again, then saluted before turning on his heels to leave the bridge in a disciplined march.

Novex's gut feeling about the operation was changing. This was meant to be the simple part, yet somehow it had become complicated. He could understand the caretaker's retreat to the fortress as they were bound to have been spooked by the altercation between the ships. Now there were elements at hand here he didn't understand. He evaluated the digital pad again. *Are the IMC producing super-soldiers here?* Such a thing was illegal – *but then again who am I to judge?*

Novex then turned his attention to the biggest problem of all. They had stolen the ship because it had an engine that produced what was called an energy cascade. Novex still hadn't come to grips between the types of cascades and what the differences were, yet the simple understanding was that a cascade was a portal linking vast distances that was less destructive and less permanent than say a singularity and the still unobserved theory of wormholes. None of this was his domain of expertise and it was alarming to now have a ship that was built and designed to create and travel through cascade portals but was unable to do so. The first jump had worked even though a number of so-called capable scientists and engineers assumed that the six series quantum computer was the machine that powered the cascade engines. The ship had what they called position-processed all the way to the shard, only to find upon arrival and during battle that the quad of quantum computer towers had burned out. It was unlike IMC to build anything that didn't work and Novex thought about the reasons why such a thing would happen. *Sabotage perhaps, something that was missed?* Now, on top of everything else, Novex was worried that a replacement system wouldn't be found and that the *Hollywood* was stranded.

Novex returned his thoughts once again to the basin. It felt as if everything had been jinxed since their arrival. The intelligence received about this outpost from GSA Command was supposed to be more accurate than this. All of a sudden there were super soldiers and a captain with great resolve. It appeared that the resident force here was more prepared than he'd been led to believe.

Admiral Novex's second in command, Captain Adams, had taken the opportunity to eavesdrop from the other side of the bridge where he was helping the other bridge officers with the unusual computer interface system the *Hollywood* provided, and now made his way over to Novex. 'We should blow the lens and grab what we can in the next six hours, Admiral,' he said, sensing Novex was uncertain.

'No, we stick to the plan.'

'The backup plan is dangerous,' Adams insisted.

'I'm not risking the time it takes to scour the debris for the odd warhead and we still haven't replaced the computer system for the engines. We stay precise and take the ambush class. I'm positive they still have twelve here,' Novex concluded.

Captain Adams gave a nod to acknowledge this comment as the admiral's final word on the matter and returned to his duties, leaving Novex alone to think.

Novex's main concern was that his men had been allowed to use deadly force, which might even tip the caretaker into implementing last protocol by detonating a weapon. He didn't like to gamble and was beginning to feel that the mission had become a game of chance. He leaned over to activate a comms system on the control panel next to him.

'Get me Professor Houseman.'

Ologun regarded Ray as more memories came back to him in steady revelations, then punched him hard in the face. 'You let him do those things!'

Ray fell backwards and over the railing into the ship's loading quad thirty feet below, and Ologun rushed over to see Ray flat on his back. Ray got up and ran up a set of stairs as Ologun waited for the next bout. When Ray reached the main deck, he rushed at Ologun and pushed his right forearm into his throat to restrain him against the rail.

'Get your testicles off my knee, Ray.'

Ray backed off and calmed down.

'I'm going back up there to jettison his arse out into space,' Ologun declared.

'Why? He's done as much as you would.'

Ologun stared in disgust at Ray for allowing such a thing. 'What *is* he doing?'

Ray sat on a bench, his legs spread, so that Ologun had no choice but to look away towards the bizarre landscape of the orange lake and docked spaceships. 'He had things to do. I mean if you access the information, you'll find that all those people were actually double agents intent on espionage and sabotage. Of course some of them took their cover quite seriously, I mean selling sex for cash is a bit distasteful, don't you think?'

Ologun looked out and over the lake of light and caught sight of three flying objects in the distance. 'He ate their innards, Ray . . . Well, anyway, moving on, it's nice to see that someone came for me eventually.'

'We need to leave soon,' Ray said after a while. 'Learn more before you take action, you'll understand in a while.'

Ologun realised the information he was now able to access was too much to take on board and he'd already begun to feel confused once again. He said nothing of this and considered Ray's advice.

Three craft circled and landed on the ship's rail on long stalk legs. They looked strange with rhomboid-shaped wings in two sections which slid back and forth akin to scissor blades.

'I dreamt they were larger, I thought they'd be able to carry us around,' Ologun stated.

Ray looked surprised and curious. 'You couldn't have dreamt anything, they were designed and incubated long after you crashed and were frozen.'

'I envisioned this black one as being much larger. How long before they grow to full size?'

'They'll reach maturity in five years. The black one directly in front of you is yours. You might find it hard to grasp this but it's related to you . . . like a brother or . . . I'm not sure. Either way, it's amazing what you can grow by re-writing the genetic code.'

'You,' Ologun said to the one apparently related to him, 'can you communicate?'

The creature made some odd noises that were long and flatly pitched.

'Creed's a strange name,' Ologun replied. 'Any chance you can fetch me some weapons – fast?'

The craft calling itself Creed made some more noises and Ologun turned to Ray in disbelief. 'There are no weapons, Ray! What have they been doing for the past hundred years?'

Ray sighed, beginning to lose patience. 'What exactly do you think is going on here? We go to Prospect then Veil, and continue on with our designation. Nothing more.'

'What about Vanguard?' Ologun quizzed. It was still all a bit hazy to him and he had no idea what he was supposed to be doing on any of these worlds he suddenly knew existed. He decided to bluff the conversation anyway.

'You're quick at taking in information, I'll give you that,' Ray offered. 'But there are no real plans, besides, there's a great deal going on and I can't encourage you to chase ghosts.'

'What's going on, who killed me?' Ologun asked, remembering something else.

'That's taken care of, a small glitch in the overall plan,' Ray said.

'The new state of independence shall be,' Ologun muttered. 'I really need a weapon.'

'We don't have any,' Ray replied.

'Really? No guns or cannons, no nothing?'

'Ask a third time if you like. Why do you think we're off to war?'

'Vanguard.'

'Bad situation.'

'I have the idea that we were made for one thing and you're telling me we're not.'

Take your time and have a think, it'll come to you, oh, and if you really must do something in the meantime there are some cudgels here somewhere, Creed knows where.'

Ologun thought about this for a moment. 'Who do they belong to?'

'Who else?'

Ologun turned to Creed. 'Go get me those weapons.'

The creature shot off at speed towards the great ocean. The other two remained still perched on the ship's rail. One of them was dark brown in colour with a skinny body and had a particularly long nib as its head. Ologun looked closely at a ghostly white and grey craft which he was sure was staring at him and stretching out its nib towards him. This creature was larger than the other two and bulkier. Its wings bore strange patterns in an interesting design and glowing white light broke through the pale marble skin of its bulbous back end.

'You're no better than he is, you know,' Ray said.

'I don't eat people,' Ologun replied. 'He's crazy.'

'Kettle black and pot spring to mind,' Ray finally said and shook his head before walking off down the steps to the lower decks of the ship.

'How long do we have before we leave, Ray?'

'Around twenty hours,' he shouted back.

'Hey, Ray?'

'Yes?'

'Put some clothes on!'

ANOTHER WAY

'How long do we have?' Sharplin asked again.

'Seven hours judging by the sapped look of the blanket field,' Dennis estimated.

Judith had left the two of them to talk shop while she ensured all weapons systems were fully charged and loaded to go. She had even spent time offering the civilians, including tourists, if they wanted to help themselves to arms when the time came. For the time being Judith had organised for the civilians to be given basic weapons training.

'I'm switching the Keeper on,' Frank declared. His options were running out.

'The fleet will be here in a few hours, we don't need a thirty-year-old demented construct to tell us the obvious,' Dennis insisted.

'We have hundreds of tourists and sixty two soldiers waiting to fight far too many well-armed troops out there. We need advice,' Sharplin argued.

'That's easy for you to say, but I think we can fend them off. This is a class seven system. Stampede turrets, pulse launchers. Full rotational defence towers. What can we be told that would be any different?'

'These are people who were fully prepared to get in here. You didn't see the drills coming. Dennis, you didn't even know they existed, for damn sake. What else have we missed?'

Dennis grew angry at the accusation. 'The drill is a concept, it's something for future skirmishes on off-world colonies, where bases with blanket fields are the main source of defence. I was throwing a wild idea out there. The *Hollywood* must be carrying them as a standard part of future protocol, and there's been talk of finding a power source ample enough to run a defence field around a ship too, so I'm guessing the smaller ones are for inter-ship combat purposes.

So you can see why the IMC have a good reason to keep much of its data a secret, I'm sorry.'

Captain Sharplin nodded and accepted the apology. 'It might know a way that you're not aware of. We have to try.'

Dennis thought for a moment and wondered how much information he could divulge. *Perhaps,* Dennis considered, *I should trust Frank Sharplin.* The man had made some sound decisions over the past twenty four hours and it seemed that keeping some secrets at this stage was counter-productive.

'I know more than a machine, Frank. Okay, if you insist on turning it on we should at least seclude it from the rest of the systems or I promise the people out there will be the least of our worries. You want to see the Keeper, Frank, let's go.'

The two men made their way to the Keeper hidden away deep within the fortress, way below ground level near the genetic library and arms cache. Down steps, along dusty passageways with a multitude of locked security doorways, until eventually the two men entered a large rectangular room with aluminium walls surrounding a large square pool of water at its centre.

Hanging above the water on eight thick deep-red cables was a strange being of the same burgundy tint. Its torso was almost human with cables embedded in its rib cage as if limbs and which were tautly stretched up and along the walls on both sides. It had a skull connected to its neck, which had no eyes, nose or mouth, yet held the traits of a head with a jaw, cheekbones and brows above eye sockets and was covered with deep-red skin. Cobwebs hung down from the cables and had collected thick dust so that the suspended creature appeared before them as a human-sized butterfly which had been caught and pinned out by its wings.

'What's this?' Sharplin asked in horror and disbelief.

'The Keeper.'

Frank looked away. *Nightmarish,* he thought. 'Is it alive?' He wished Dennis had explained this bit before entering the room. It was a truly unnerving sight and wrong on so many levels.

'It's organic. I mean it has a synthetic silicone genetic structure where cells divide and grow to eventually form this,' Dennis explained, waving his arm towards the thing. 'It has a uniquely designed functioning brain for superfast processing, and has an excellent capacity for memory yet, most importantly, it can perceive things that we mere humans cannot.'

The abomination hung, elevated over the pool. It jolted a little and Frank sought cover behind Dennis. It released some sort of pale excrement from its anus which plopped into the pool below.

'It craps? Does it drink and eat too?'

'It needs sustenance, definitely. It's fed through one of the cables with a high pH level compound. The pool below breaks down the used-up matter it discharges with ultra-violet rays.'

Sharplin was horrified and unsatisfied with Dennis's reply to the most important question: 'Is it happy hung there like that? Surely it feels and thinks? It looks so . . .'

'Look, Frank, it's a thing. It may look like some live puppet, but it's an advanced piece of kit designed to think in strict forms of logic. It doesn't feel happy or sad or desire a better life in the tropics drinking cocktails and getting laid. It just calculates and runs things. This is a highly classified piece of hardware.'

'If you say so.'

Dennis placed a hand on Frank's shoulder 'They use these on starships. That's how the IMC have the edge. This is one of the first ones grown, a test that proved very successful. It's over thirty years old, as a matter of fact.'

'There are more of these things out there?' Sharplin was disgusted. *If they could grow such things why was there a need to make it look so much like a person who'd been experimented upon?*

'The only reason it was housed here is because of the biological cache. In reality it's too powerful for the rudimentary functions of the fortress, a great waste in many ways. Anyway, I took it offline when I arrived here, I just don't trust it. Let's take all weapons systems from its control and push on, shall we?'

They turned to a workstation behind them and covered in thick dust. Frank wiped the fluff away and switched the power on. Piece by piece they disconnected the Keeper from tangible control of any fortress systems before bringing it back online. Dennis then made the final adjustments in order to wake the Keeper. 'Hey, Frank, you know what this model's called? Dennis asked before hitting the final switch.

'No, I don't know what any of them are called,' he replied, thinking how much he hated most technologies let alone this thing.

'They named this model TESTI. Total Evaluation Strategic & Tactical Indicator.'

The two men laughed out loud, breaking the intensity of the situation.

'Testi Keeper,' Frank added causing them to giggle like children.

Dennis was sure the machine had no remote access to the nuclear devices, yet he was beginning to doubt his level of knowledge after seeing the miniature siphons.

'Here goes.' He sighed then pressed the word ACTIVATE on the monitor screen.

'It's a good job these systems don't run off the server chips, I have a knack of accidentally turning things on with a stray thought,' Dennis revealed.

'Like your pleasure bot,' Frank replied, grinning.

The Keeper's torso flexed and its head moved. It swung slightly on the cables over the pool as it was released from its long coma.

The two men waited until the AI voice fuzzed an unexpected welcome over speakers mounted along the walls. 'All connections to physical systems malfunction.'

Dennis rolled his eyes at the abrupt announcement. 'I always turn the sound off my lab assistant.'

Frank couldn't relate to Dennis's relationship with technology at all. Accidentally turning things on with the interface chip was the complete opposite problem to his.

He also doubted that his machine assistant was anything like the organism in this room and felt a mixture of fear and pity for the abomination; there was no way of knowing if it was sentient in any way.

His mind wandered for a moment. He hadn't been able to contact his ex-wife and had usually done that by now. Once a year on this day, every year. It usually ended in an argument with intense anger and tears before she cut him off. *Life's too short for this all of a sudden.*

'You have an AI assistant?' he asked.

Dennis ignored the question and swallowed his sarcastic answer in order to address the machine. 'Okay, we have a situation. An unknown terrorist group has managed to get a foothold in the base. The fortress is up and running at full capacity. The primary attack at present is a machine that's about to drain our shield. What do we do?'

'Protocol one. Detonate warhead immediately.'

Frank decided to intervene and rephrased the question: 'We'd like to survive and gain more strategic information. Can you help us in any way?'

'Yes. Protocol one. Detonate warhead immediately.'

Dennis folded his arms and shook his head in frustration. 'I told you this was all it would do, stupid thing!'

Frank had an idea. 'The base has been decommissioned and there are no longer any weapons here. How do we defend ourselves now? Can we do something to save ourselves?'

The AI took its time to respond. The two men waited as the Keeper's head flicked around as though following an invisible fly from where its eyes should be. 'Escape is recommended.'

'Nice try, Frank. It's a different answer at least,' Dennis mused.

'How do we escape when the fortress is surrounded?' Frank asked in frustration at the stupidity of the thing.

'Warhead tunnel route transport to platform is recommended.'

The two men looked at each other in bafflement. Dennis shrugged his shoulders. 'Show us a visual representation of supposed tunnel,' he said, convinced the AI was fabricating ideas.

The monitor on the workstation revealed a schematic of the basin floor with its plasma-concrete foundations running underneath the entire outpost.

Dennis analysed the diagram. 'There's the fortress and there's the platform at the opposite side of the basin. It thinks there's a tunnel between the two points.'

'I never knew there was a tunnel, did you?' Frank asked.

Version

'Would I be sat here doing this if I did?' Dennis was super-intelligent and typically used a supercilious tone which Frank had learned to ignore.

'I thought you would know about this stuff?'

'Well, *you* didn't know.'

'I *don't* know. I don't know anything!'

Dennis thought about the new information. 'The schematic indicates a tunnel ten feet in height and twenty feet wide. My educated guess would be that it's a transport conduit for the weapons which the basin used many years ago. It even runs through the middle of the lake thirty feet down.'

Frank stood to address the Keeper. 'If you're alive and can understand this, thank you very much, I owe you one.'

The Keeper hung motionless.

'Crying out loud, Frank, come on!'

They restored the Keeper's control over the stampede turret and pulse launchers before rushing off to find this apparent means of escape. Sharplin instructed Judith to meet them at a large cargo lift which went to the lowest levels of the fortress, deep underground, to another chamber where the WMDs were stored.

Sharplin did his best to keep up with Dennis as they rushed back the way they'd come. They continued through a disused firing range, sheltered living quarters, and via several large weapon lockers stacked with serious levels of artillery. Dennis emerged into an empty, open-air courtyard, shaded a brilliant blue by the force field above. At the far end of the yard he saw Judith talking to several marines standing next to a tunnel entrance which was void of any light. He hurried towards them.

'I take it we're about to prime a warhead?' Judith asked nonchalantly.

Dennis leaned on his knees to catch his breath. 'Would I really be running only to blow myself up?'

Frank shimmied towards them with legs which would hardly bend at the knees and ankles.

The marines laughed at the sight, prompting Judith to lose her cool. 'Next one who laughs at the captain takes a nosedive into the shield, get it?'

The marines piped down and carefully backed away from their commander.

Sharplin caught up to them and automatically adopted the same position as Dennis to rest. 'You're not going to believe this.'

The three of them made their way along the tunnel towards a row of elevator cages where Dennis began flicking switches to power up the machines. They crammed inside one of the cargo lifts with the marines and began the slow descent. They moved downwards and at an angle for a few minutes until the lift eventually shunted on to three large springs and the cage doors opened.

'Where's the light switch?'

'Hang on a moment.'

'Watch where you're putting your hands, Dennis.'

'That wasn't me, I'm over here.'

The room lit up to show a cold and very long empty hall. The floor, covered in thick dust, paved the way to a large steel door at the far end. The warheads were behind this steel door, where they remained under guard and surrounded by more concrete walls fifteen feet thick and laced with asaronite plates every two feet.

'Captain, Commander, you have to key in your codes,' Dennis instructed.

'Where do we do that?' Judith asked looking around for some sort of terminal.

Dennis shook his head in disbelief. 'Don't they train you people, or at least give you a tour before you start work? It's that panel next to the lift controls.'

The pair of them did as they were instructed and deactivated the hidden turrets along with a few other nasty surprises, including a spike mechanism in the floor similar to the one surrounding the fortress.

Version

When a green light on the lift panel indicated the defences were disabled, they disembarked. The marines spread out in caution before allowing the others to search for the location of the tunnel.

Dennis wandered off to the right-hand side of the hall and down a large passageway ten feet in width. He hardly lifted his head from scrutinizing his digital pad until forced to when he came to a dead end fifty yards in.

Sharplin ordered the marines to stay near the lift, while he and Judith followed.

'What have you found?'

Dennis checked his surroundings and compared them to the map upon the pad. 'This is where the tunnel is meant to be.'

Judith scanned the wall in front of them. 'Maybe we're already in the tunnel, and this is where it ends.'

With this statement she lifted her rifle and fired it across the wall, narrowly missing Dennis. The rounds bounced off its surface sending pinging sounds around them, and Frank and Dennis dove to the floor for cover.

'Are you insane? You want to prove how stupid caretaker officers are, is that it?' Dennis fumed. Sharplin intervened as best he could.

'Is everything all right, sir?' one of the marines shouted down the passage in response to the ruckus.

'It's okay, we're doing fine,' Sharplin shouted, giving Judith a look as though she were merely embarrassing him. 'Please, Judith,' he said in an attempt to curb her insanity. It was yet more proof that Judith wasn't quite firing on all cylinders – her arm was still fused together with a static gel cast and was surely too painful for such antics. She seemed to be detached from the proceedings and her unpredictable tendencies were on overdrive.

Dennis placed his hand on the wall before thumping it a few times in various places. He knelt down to assess one of the grooves created by Judith's spray of rounds. The concrete wall was chipped, revealing some sort of metal socket.

'It could be behind the wall, or maybe the wall retracts to access it.'

'How do we get through or operate it or whatever you said?' Sharplin asked, growing impatient.

'We blow it up,' Judith suggested, sending Dennis into an immediate rant about drawing attention to themselves and collapsing the entire place.

He rushed over to a number of boxes hanging off the wall to his left and proceeded to open each one for a clue. 'Here, I think we have something.'

The three of them gathered around a small set of switches inside one of the wall-mounted cases but none gave any indication as to their purpose.

'One of these may remove the wall,' Dennis insisted, about to try one out.

Sharplin grabbed his arm before he went any further. 'What if you do something that gets us killed?'

'What, like firing a rifle in close quarters at a solid wall?' Dennis replied, offended and yanking his arm free. 'If I'm right, these are just power switches to an automated system that will get rid of the wall,' he continued. 'We may as well try.'

They loitered there for a moment until Judith launched at the controls, switching them all on at once. Immediately, the wall dropped into the floor with a loud crash, leaving a dark and empty void in its place. The three of them covered their faces against the wave of dust, stinking of decay, which engulfed them.

Dennis was the first to move forward, shining a torch as he went.

The thin powerful beam of light pierced the dark, reflecting off the dust particles and illuminating something beyond. They moved closer and Dennis played the torch over small segments of a large room fitted with a concrete platform. On further inspection, they could make out a docking area of sorts, complete with various small cabins sitting above and to their left on an elevated scaffold structure.

'I think it's some sort of rail line,' Dennis muttered to the others.

He made his way on to the structure's main dais and searched for a power source. A few moments later the entire area lit up under powerful strip lighting hanging from the ceiling and illuminating a large tunnel leading far into the distance.

Version

On the tunnel's floor next to the concrete loading area, a single thick girder was elevated a few feet and ran the whole length through the subway until it was obscured by a train a short distance away.

'It's an old style rail line and relatively quick,' Dennis concluded when he saw that the train rested on the magnetic beam. 'This is it,' he added to the other two, who were exploring the old dust-ridden room of derelict equipment. 'I'll have this thing running in no time. It's immaculate and built to last.'

Frank took a moment to survey the place and saw that the marines had joined them to stand at the entrance to the corridor. They seemed impressed at the sight and talked excitedly amongst themselves. He too was relieved to an extent, and reminded himself that this would only extend their survival for a few more hours. The blanket field would be compromised in the next half hour and then the game of cat and mouse would resume. 'Commander, let's get everyone down here. It's time we left.'

KILL SWITCH

The place was dark with the sound of fan propellers and moving water. Low levels of light shimmered off the lake's surface several metres away. The air was warm and insects darted around in the pleasant fragrance.

Dank stood guard and waited for the rest of his division to return from patrol; they had marched off further away around the lake's circumference and were beyond visual range. He took off his helmet to avoid using the comms system.

'Day Job, Day Job, have you finished yet?' he whispered towards a row of palm trees behind him next to a decking area with a barbecue stand. A number of metallic tables and chairs reflected the low levels of bright blue light emitted from their tubular framework.

'Shut up, fool, I'm laying a cable back here, give me a minute, okay?'

Dank took to probing the area, his eyes adjusting from having the visual aid of the thermal imaging in his helmet taken away. He moved to place his helmet back on, unnerved to be without the technology to assist him in the dark. He lifted the flat-shaped cap and adjusted the mask, then paused.

'Psst. Day Job.'

'Dank, if you don't leave me alone to shit in peace I swear I'll—'

'Shut up a minute, there's someone stood on the shore.'

He turned back to look. They'd gone. He froze as a blade came to rest under his chin. He followed the edge of the strange weapon until he was faced with a tall man, almost shadow like, standing next to him. The man raised his index finger to his lips. 'Shh.'

Day Job appeared from behind the palm trees and walked around the set of tables and chairs, adjusting his armour's leg plating as he moved. He looked up and immediately raised his weapon to fire.

Version

Before he could pull the trigger, he suddenly flew backwards and was forcefully lifted off the ground by a long, thin object which pinned him to a nearby tree.

The man turned calmly back to Dank, still holding his blade pressed against the soldier's throat. He then swung the blade around and sliced the back of his knee, cutting all tendons. Dank screamed in pain and fell, clutching his leg and trying to stem the spurting blood.

The man knelt down, picked up the soldier's helmet, and walked across to retrieve the weapon pierced through Day Job's chest. He grabbed the handle and yanked it hard, knowing from the resistance that it was embedded in the tree. Day Job flopped heavily to the ground.

The man stood patiently and admired both cleavers as he swung them around at his sides, then held them up. They were made of a strange material: transparent like glass but with a slight tint of neon blue. He sheathed the weapons behind his back and once more picked up the helmet.

'You'll be sorry, damn you!'

He looked at Dank, still lying on the ground and rocking in pain as he clutched his wound with both hands. He walked over and decapitated him in one swift move, then replaced the blade upon his back. He resumed his examination of the helmet, then placed it on his head, adjusting the face mask as he did so.

The heads-up display glowed bright green with its thermal imaging. He didn't need such an aid as he could see perfectly in the dark without it. A small pad inside the helmet pressed against his forehead. He thought carefully so that the helmet's interface received exact neural commands. He worked his way through the heads-up display options until it offered a number of comms frequencies, which he scrolled through.

1 ... A SQUAD
2 ... FORWARD ASSUALT COMMAND
3 ... B SQUAD
4 ... DEFENSIVE PERIMETER COMMAND

He made his choice.

~

'It's a ghost town, Admiral, everyone's gone.'

Admiral Novex sat in thought. 'What's the status of the package?'

'Defences should be down in a moment, package will be aboard the tram in the next half hour, sir.' There was a pause. 'Sir, there's what looks to be a subway station down here, I think they escaped to somewhere in the basement. Hold on, we just located the systems control room, the AI may shed some light on this.'

Another long pause ensued as the Admiral waited anxiously for a report. 'I think I should patch you through on visual, sir, you should see this.'

'Do it.'

The monitor on the *Hollywood's* bridge switched from the IMC logo to a helmet camera feed as Private Mason searched other chambers within the fortress. Novex watched as the soldier provided coverage of a room containing a large pool of water over which something had been elevated. His eyes narrowed when he recognised there was a similar room aboard the *Hollywood*, except that one was empty with large sockets up and along two of the walls in vertical formation.

'What do you make of it, Private Mason?'

'It's some kind of AI. It's dead now or deactivated, I don't know exactly, should we bring it along?'

'Yes, but do it quickly.'

'What the hell was that?' Captain Adams asked, horrified. He was sitting at the front of the bridge and observing proceedings.

Version

Novex shook his head as he thought, then turned to Adams. 'Why don't you go to the defence perimeter and find out where that rail tunnel leads? It more than likely runs directly here and must have some sort of access point on the basin floor. It shouldn't be too hard to find, seeing as it's large and should be routed in a relatively straight line.'

Captain Adams said nothing and made his way outside to the basin, glad to finally have something constructive to do. Novex rewound the footage just taken by the soldier and paused it to look at the thing hung over the pool of water. It appeared that whatever it was, Novex would bet that this creature was the very thing they were looking for and needed to replace the burned out computer.

'Admiral, there's a Private Williams on the comms.'

The admiral turned to his communications officer sitting to his right. 'Is it urgent?'

'Sir, the voice recognition states that it's not Williams.'

Novex took his time before answering, 'Put him through.'

The admiral waited to be addressed, his suspicions growing. 'Who is this?'

There was a long pause.

'I'm here to ask that you leave the basin and that you leave the residents here unharmed.'

'Really, well I'm afraid I don't do requests. Where's Private Williams?'

'B squad is . . . gone.'

Novex quickly assessed the situation. 'Perhaps we can come to some arrangement regarding the outpost's residents. We need to meet and discuss this.'

'I'm not here to negotiate. Leave.'

'That sounds like an order. What exactly do you think it is you can do?'

'You don't want to know.'

'I wish you luck.'

'Sir.'

'If it's the last thing I do I'll . . .'

'Sir.'

'*What*?' Novex screamed at the comms officer.

'He's gone.'

Novex paced up and down the bridge. His face had gone from pale white to a more colourful pink. He held a digital pad and watched re-runs of the man who had been chased earlier that day, up to the point where he fell into the lake and a cloud of red filled the water. He threw the pad down:

'Listen up . . . there's been a change of plan.'

He turned to the comms officer again. 'Get me Professor Houseman, now!'

The carriage moved with a relaxing cadence. Sharplin's face was hot and he was so tired his eyelids slowly closed in this much welcomed respite. He thought about Judith as he watched her cleaning her rifle. She carefully detached each mechanism of the rifle's housing and placed them on the long leather seat next to her. She scrubbed and oiled them before replacing them.

He was glad she was here, and at last he understood her. They'd had a long talk and she'd opened up, leaving him in no doubt that she was capable and level headed to some odd degree. He wondered what he would have done without her, knowing now that she was very good with the marines and had done an exceptional job in getting the civilians aboard this train to oblivion.

Dennis sat next to him with his head resting on the window, snoring loudly in deep sleep. The train's engine rumbled underfoot, which Sharplin found soothing. Working out the controls of the driver's cab had been far easier than cramming the civilians into the limited space of the few carriages. In the end he'd made a choice, a decision that had needed little thought. They could have used the carriages to carry any number of heavy-duty weapons from the ample supply within the fortress and in turn protect themselves, ensuring a greater chance of survival. He'd chosen to bring the tourists, naturally, except he couldn't help but wonder what another captain would have chosen to do.

Version

They were due to terminate their journey in just under twenty minutes, and he felt a mixture of relief that the star lens was still intact, and dread of what would come next.

Dennis had explained their options. The tunnel stopped exactly five miles from the docking platform tower. The stretch of land between the tunnel access and the platform meant traversing three miles of forest with the final leg of the journey through the old city. He leaned forward to cure the feeling he had in the pit of his stomach, and checked his server chip. It had stopped reporting information from his domain a long time ago, although its internal clock was still functioning.

He checked the time. *I'm sorry, Sam.* He wondered what she would think of him failing to send his regards and thought about what he would do if he got through this. He had an idea that it would be best to visit Earth, go and see her, and visit the memorial for all those who'd been lost. He'd never seen the sense in visiting the plaque with a thousand names in place of a thousand graves. Just this once, he'd visit and gaze upon his daughter's name.

Judith cocked and aimed her rifle, then dry-fired its empty chamber. 'Good,' she declared with satisfaction.

Frank smiled at this and Dennis stirred. 'Ducks, ducks, I never wanted to join the navy!' he said, still deep in sleep, then recommenced snoring.

'You ready for this, Commander?'

She nodded and began sharpening her knife on a small stone. 'I don't think you should come on the scouting run. You should stay with the civilians along with the rest of the marines.'

'If we're going to leave this life, I'd rather it be among people I know, if it's all the same.' Frank replied.

'You've been on the front line up until now, so why not?' Judith shrugged. 'It would be my honour to bow out next to you, sir,' she said.

Sharplin was taken aback at her words. In all his time of knowing her, she'd never called him that.

Sharplin nodded, then crossed his legs and leaned back to look through the compartment's window into the next carriage. One of the marines was trying to suppress an argument between a group of tourists. He couldn't hear what was happening through the soundproofing, but all the same he would rather not have to deal with them face to face. He continued to observe the silenced ruckus in the next carriage, and spotted Doctor Siren enter from the far end. She negotiated her way around the arguing group and clutched at the sling that held her left arm in place as she made her way towards him.

'Acquired one target, negative on all other signs of personnel. Orders received.'

The soldiers waited for the vehicles to arrive. Their dull grey armour glistened in the lens-light as they prepared the defences. It was now 3:00 a.m. Designated Outpost Time and the star lens had been overridden and activated for an early sunrise. An entire division had gathered ten miles north of the lake and listened in for feedback regarding the man running towards their position through the woods and open grassland.

'Confirm barricade established at coordinates.'

'Copy that. Barricade set and operational.'

Trucks emerged from the forest behind the makeshift garrison and tore up the field as they moved. They swung around and parked a few feet behind sand bags, which in turn had been placed behind thick asaronite-plated barriers in an additional defensive measure. The tanks arrived a few minutes later and moved into position in front of the barricade, facing the tightly knit treeline a few hundred metres away. Soldiers behind the defensive front adjusted the stampede turrets whilst checking large ammunition boxes which were to be placed next to them. Mortars were pegged down and set.

The valley of grass was sandwiched between two large forests north of the basin's lake and which stretched both ways beyond view. The platoon had rallied under orders from Admiral Novex to capture the man headed their way. At first the order had been treated as some sort of joke and the soldiers had been perplexed. That was until a scouting party had spotted the target. They'd kept their distance while monitoring the target using telescopes from high up on the sky-tram scaffold until he'd slipped into the cover of the forest. Other scouting parties deep within the parkland had then taken over and had confirmed that he was most likely headed towards the docking platform.

Novex had clearly stated not to engage the man until he'd reached open ground. This in itself was a bizarre order; especially with the availability of so much firepower. Intercom chatter continued between the soldiers, who were taking bets on the outcome of this strange situation. Novex had said to bring the body back to the ship, which the soldiers took to mean dead or alive. It wasn't clear why he hadn't been taken out by forces further south, and so they waited.

Another truck sped across the field from behind their position. It pulled up and Captain Adams stepped out next to a group of soldiers. 'Where's Commander Howe?'

One of the soldiers pointed and he walked across the length of the defensive wall towards another soldier with blue echelons on his shoulders.

'What's your status?'

Howe removed his helmet and mask out of respect and saluted. 'Everything's set, Captain. May I ask what exactly we're doing here? It's just one man. Is there any need for all this?'

Adams looked across to the treeline upon which all the weapons were aimed.

'I'm sure the admiral knows what he's doing.'

The silhouette of something shot across the ground. He looked up to see that the armoured tram was headed back to the ship.

'Shouldn't we be leaving now?'

Captain Adams silently agreed and couldn't grasp what the admiral was up to.

'No witnesses,' he replied.

Commander Howe replaced his helmet and made a comment over closed comms, addressing the whole battalion.

'You heard, people, no witnesses.'

Due north had led to this one tiny location. With a slight change in course north-east or north-west he could have bypassed this confrontation altogether. That, however, was beside the point and his adversary knew it.

Ologun held back and watched before making a move. They were waiting patiently, which made him curious. His senses were more acute than before, allowing him to see much further and enabling him to quickly assess his surroundings. It only took a split second for him to count how many soldiers there were on the battlefield, for instance: sixty. The cleavers hung in his hands at his sides and he regarded them. They were primitive, less efficient and more barbaric perhaps than a rifle. They did, however, add one great difference to proceedings: using them made sure he would get up close and personal.

He went to cure an itch, only to feel the layer of his second-skin suit. It had the same capabilities as he had, as it was, in essence, his skin. Now that had been an absurd argument for him to navigate:

'Why do you want clothes?'

'Because I don't wish to be naked.'

'Why?'

'Because I wish to compose myself with more dignity.'

'We don't have any clothes.'

'Then what happens if mine are burned off in the heat of battle?'

'You'll be naked.'

'There's no way I'm going around with my bits hanging out.'

'Why?'

'Because if they catch on anything it'll hurt, and trust me, you don't want that at all.'

'Then don't fight, there's no need.'

In the end they'd taken his genetic information and fashioned a sort of leather that fitted perfectly. In essence he was now covered in his own skin, on top of his skin: a second skin. He mused over the thought. They'd even asked him what colour he wanted. *The vanity.* He'd settled for black with a tinge of purple. He now had a black-skinned body and a white-skinned head.

The rain began to pour in its controlled yet exceptionally heavy mode. He still had to catch up with his senses, with his mind. He could feel the energy from the moisture as it hit the radiated soil and could see millions of insects throughout the forest as they swam through the air for cover. *Is that right?* He'd never realised the air was so viscous to them, so that in fact insects swam rather than flew. Spiders took the opportunity to catch their prey as they fled the enormous droplets of water. His mind returned from its scrutiny and he thought for a moment.

He'd killed twelve men at the lakeside. It was too easy, almost accidental and without any consideration. He couldn't decide if it had been vengeance or necessity, excitement or mindlessness. Sometimes they all meant the same, and he knew he had to be careful. At this moment in time he felt no pity or remorse and found it hard to feel any of the emotions he'd once taken for granted. With a conscious effort he made a quick and fast rule, a logical choice, just in case and until something more human returned.

He left the cover of the forest to face the long line of troops behind a low-level wall of metal which had been erected into a curved barricade fifty meters wide.

Surveyed the tanks in front of the wall, he cricked his neck from side to side with a loud crunching sound, then swung his cleavers around a few times as though warming up for the physical exertion ahead.

Killing is killing in any context. He didn't believe this and knew that even though these people had families and that they'd be all loving and caring in one reality, they were also murderers in this one. He didn't want to be judge and executioner, and yet knew that his hand would be forced. *Warrior against warriors,* he thought, but found no real justification for what he may be about to do.

His cue finally came with the eruption of the tank's cannons. Shells exploded into the tree trunks next to him, their shockwaves flinging him backwards to the ground. He stood up and checked his body to see the deep-red of would-be fatal injuries healing over and leaving no trace.

He sprinted diagonally across the field against turret fire; the white-hot projectiles traced his every move and ricocheted off his body. More shells were fired at the ground directly in front of him and he jumped towards the tank. His mind raced – he hadn't taken the time to get used to his body's newly unleashed potential, and was now in mid-air and around fifty feet up. He noticed the dotted lines of stampede gunfire glowing with white-hot energy as they followed his every move. The rounds hit and just bounced off him.

He landed on the roof of one of the tanks with ultra-finesse and cleaved its large barrel in two. He then sliced into the thick armour which seemed to be made of metallic muscle fibres that twanged as his blade cut through them. He could still feel pain; an annoyance as the stampede rounds hit his head, back and legs – the ones impacting behind his ears causing him a tremendous amount of grief.

He cut the tank's treads and then the mounted weapons with ease. Satisfied that the tank was disabled he turned his attention towards the turrets and leapt over the defensive wall. He moved more quickly as time passed; a spectre which had the soldiers firing in all directions as they lost sight of him. One by one he destroyed the turrets and mortars then worked his way among the soldiers who were now spreading out in retreat. From their perspective, they could only see the turrets falling to bits and looked on in dismay as their rifles succumbed to the same fate as they attempted to fire them at the invisible enemy.

He began to push them around to instil fear. He wanted to be a ghost; striking a soldier to the ground here and another one a few yards further away there. He grabbed one of the soldiers, intending to throw him. *Crack.* He stopped dead in the middle of the entire battalion, which was now mostly empty handed. The commotion had halted as he held the soldier like a rag doll after accidentally breaking his neck.

The soldiers ran. They abandoned everything and sprinted towards the forest treeline without looking back.

A tremendous pain hit his face. *Snipers again!* Another sniper round hit his skull with little impact, only blinding his vision for a moment, then he was hit full force by one of the trucks. His body left the ground and he was flung against the sand bags. He looked as the same truck came back at him for another swipe. This time the truck crashed into his body, crushing him against the defensive wall, and left him motionless under its weight.

Version

'Subject is down! Yahoo!'

His body needed time to adjust to this new level of stress inflicted upon it and he tried to find a way to move from under the truck pinning him in place. A terrible pain seethed through his shoulders, chest and limbs, which had been crushed on impact. He was surprised at the slight levels of adjustments his body made; bullet-proof for now, truck-proof in moments. He felt his body re-calibrate to overcome the twisted mess of his legs and shattered ribs, and became nauseous.

He peaked timidly at his limbs underneath the vehicle's body to see both legs bent at right angles at the thigh. Then a new mechanism to his abilities became apparent as the muscles in his legs pulled in strange ways to straighten the bones. His chest and shoulders then did the same, causing yet another horrendous wave of pain. Within moments, the relief of his body once again righting itself caused him to sigh with pleasure. He just hoped that, along with being renewed, he could move a two-tonne truck off himself.

There was no need to perform any test of power or strength, though. A large explosion threw the vehicle up and over the sandbags. He stood up and scanned the forest ahead. Within seconds he spotted two snipers and one other soldier holding an RPG.

He threw one of his blades at full force. It spun, making a hollow whistling noise as it flew, spinning a remarkable distance until it hit one of the snipers perched in the trees a few hundred metres away. He slumped then fell, hitting almost every branch on the way down, before finally smashing his face on a large tree stump.

He listened in the aftermath and could pick out the frantic levels of comms chatter between soldiers.

'Barricade has been compromised! Retreat to the next defence perimeter.'

The remaining sniper abseiled down to the forest floor as the other soldier again fired the RPG. The propelled grenade flew towards him and he stepped to one side, allowing it to pass by. There was another large explosion behind him and the soldier ran off to join the others.

He glanced at a still-intact truck; there was no way of getting to the basin's north wall in good time, even running at his speed.

Where are they? Gazing at the bright sky above the field, He spotted three craft moving towards his position. They landed, scurrying and hopping around as they flexed their wings.

'Where have you three been? It's bad enough Ray sits on his arse and refuses to help. You were supposed to carry me to the north wall!'

Creed whined and honked for a short time.

He chased the three craft, which in turn scurried away, both flying and leaping about on their long legs that had bulbous joints at the middle. 'You have to take me! It's Ray, isn't it? He's forbidden you to help.'

Creed made more noises and he listened as the craft gathered closer to him on the grass.

'Okay, I get it, I'll take the truck.'

Creed communicated further and he crouched down closer to listen.

'Go. Find Sharplin and protect them, can you do that?'

Creed blasted something that sounded like okay and the three craft launched off and away towards the basin's north wall. He ran to the truck and fired up its motor, then sped towards the forest and down the track upon which the soldiers had retreated. He then stopped the truck and raced over to the dead sniper to retrieve his cleaver. He ran back to the truck and continued down the muddy road.

'There, it fits okay.'

Sharplin moved around as though wading through dense air. The armour was heavy and felt cumbersome. Dennis moved in to operate a small set of buttons on its collar. The suit silently powered up and removed much of the weight.

'Feels okay . . . it's a shame the boots and gloves don't fit.'

'Try the helmet,' Dennis insisted.

He looked at the fearsome mask and the mushroom-shaped cap. 'I'll be okay without it.'

'All right, Frank, it's your call.'

Sharplin sat down on the concrete platform opposite one of the train's front carriages. People were moving around up and down the platform's lengthy ledge where weapons were now being handed out. Tourists, mainly the men, marched around with their newly acquired rifles; cradling them and playing around with the weapons' moving parts.

Judith walked over and sat next to him 'That's it, the revolution begins.'

'What have you given them?' Sharplin asked.

'Standard TZ nineteens, two clips each.'

'I hope they don't start shooting each other.'

Judith punched his chest plate. 'At least you'll be okay all wrapped up in foil.'

Sergeant Thomas came over to them. He wore the other set of armour and looked guiltily at Judith. 'Are you sure you won't have this, Commander?'

'How tall am I, Sergeant?'

'I'd say about five eight, five nine.'

She stood up next to him. The top of her head came up to just beneath his chin. 'For six footers and above. Keep the suit, you look dashing.'

'Are we doing this today?' Dennis hollered from some distance away in the tunnel.

The trio made their way down the tunnel, following the carriages until they reached his position. They were now at the very end of the tunnel, which ended abruptly with a concave wall behind large safety buffers and the train's engine unit sat a few feet in front. A group of eight marines had gathered around to prepare for the scouting mission.

Sharplin looked to Judith and took a deep breath. He'd hardly ever commanded anything from these men and felt uncomfortable ordering them to their possible demise.

'Listen up. We avoid the enemy and look for a safe path out of here. This is a scouting mission only. Defend yourselves by all means, but let's keep this on the QT, okay people?'

Judith nudged him in support. 'I already told them that bit. On the QT? She laughed and he pulled a face in embarrassment.

'Does the fact you're wearing that suit mean you're coming with us?' one of the marines asked Sharplin.

'It certainly does, son,' he answered.

'You'd wanna leave this place too with all those crazy sightseers flashing their T-Zeds like they own the place. There's more chance of being shot down here.'

'Hold your brain together, Private Hong, the tourists aren't deaf,' Judith ordered.

Dennis stroked his chin, then pressed a few buttons on a large control panel on the convex wall behind the large impact buffer. A flat circular area grooved into the subway ceiling creaked and shunted apart in two large flaps, which fell against the tunnel walls on either side. In their place was a deep cylindrical hole which gave off the dull surface gleam of a digital lens. They could see something resting on the lens through its transparent field.

Sergeant Thomas immediately climbed a ladder leading to the circular access hatch which measured fifteen feet in diameter.

'Where do you think you're going?' Dennis shouted after him.

'I'm leading the way, it looks blocked.'

Dennis shook his head at Thomas's stupidity. 'No wonder you ended up posted in this place. Look again, Sergeant. Tell me what you see.'

Thomas looked closer at the lens and peered through its transparent field. 'I think it's soil and roots.'

Sharplin intervened. 'Come on down, Sergeant, we need to deactivate the lens to see what happens and you don't want to be crushed under a ton of dirt and a few trees, I'm sure.'

Dennis made some alterations to the control panel, then ran for cover and joined the others twenty feet into the tunnel. The train was then backed up so the driver unit now sat parallel to them.

'Any moment now,' Dennis relayed to the squad.

A few tourists had gathered behind them with the expectation of some sort of show. The control panel blinked a few times and the digital lens deactivated. Small amounts of soil rained down on to the concrete floor and collected on the thick metal girder of the magnetic rail.

Sharplin ran a hand through his hair. 'Obviously the soil has knitted together well, it may hold indefinitely. We'll have to dig an access hole through to the surface.'

Immediately, the hatch imploded and soil rained down with a loud, staggered thump. Dirt exploded into the tunnel with a dense, thick wall of dust; blinding everyone in complete darkness and even the subway's lights couldn't penetrate the haze. The air took its time to clear against a soundtrack of coughing and spluttering. An impressive mound of soil sat on the subway floor in a miniature mountain which reached as far as the tunnel roof and was topped by a few tall trees with thick trunks which stood upright and poked through the circular hatch above. Strong beams of light now flooded down from the large hole, illuminating the swirls of movement in the thick atmosphere.

'Or we could duck for cover,' Judith said with perfect comedy timing.

The group laughed before focusing on the task at hand.

'Uh oh.' Dennis frowned. 'Daylight at 3.30 a.m. Should we wait?'

Sharplin stopped himself portraying any emotion in front of the marines as he assessed this development. 'They must be keen to find us if they've overridden the sky's control centre. We don't have time to wait, everyone be ready in ten minutes.'

He activated the comms tag on his suit collar which had been re-programmed to communicate with the marines.

'Sergeant Grey. How does the defence field look?

'It's up and running, Captain. It's drawing power from the rail through the transformer Dennis fashioned. Should hold, could even take a few hits from missiles.'

Sergeant Grey had taken command of the marines who'd been ordered to protect the civilians. He was now a few hundred yards further into the tunnel behind the train where technicians had erected a makeshift force field. Sharplin had no idea such a portable ensemble even existed. Ten equally spaced block sockets had been fused into the tunnel's interior walls and drew power from the rail to form the makeshift shield.

'Get everyone behind and power it up when you're done, Sergeant.'

'Will do, Captain.'

He watched as Judith took charge of the marines. They were checking their weapons along with other essentials. *Is this how it all works?* He thought back to this time last year when he'd locked himself away for a week and drunk himself into a stupor every night, and compared that sorry state to his situation now. He felt better, even under these circumstances; *especially* because of these circumstances. It had been extraordinary how these people had come together with little conflict in order to survive. Survival in itself wasn't always the main catalyst for such an achievement and it really depended upon a number of factors he had yet to ascertain.

He thought back to when the IMC had interviewed him. "Why do you think you would suit this position? What do you think creates good teamwork?"

He'd given the same old bullshit answers everyone did to those questions. As soon as he'd arrived at the basin he'd alienated himself from the troops and everyone had formed their own little cliques. He had an inkling that real teamwork or comradeship existed at its best potential in the military for obvious reasons. Now he felt its reality, the tangible achievements of worth which brightened his once exhausted soul.

He chuckled and decided his thoughts were just nonsense, or at least didn't want to admit that this whole predicament had empowered him to be an actual captain; one who had made good decisions and saved lives. He couldn't deny that people had shown their true colours and had become such good assets. Dennis had been a man he'd avoided for being so anal, pompous and annoying – even unbearably supercilious. The man had now become the very definition of a problem solver throughout this crisis and possibly someone he may later call friend. The good Doctor Siren had also been isolated, but had now been drawn from her own world of solitude. She hadn't seemed to like anyone up until a few days ago, and used to have a bedside manner that could only be compared to a punch to the face. She had asked him how he was, which in itself was bizarre. Even now she roamed the platform with her wounded shoulder, helping the operation run smoothly; a real human being had emerged. He gazed at her for a while and imagined what he would do with her if ever the chance emerged.

'We're ready, Captain, you still up for this?' Judith's voice came over the suit's comms speaker and above the tunnel's ambient level of noise, breaking him away from his rude thoughts.

'One minute, Commander.'

Commander Gibson. Sharplin looked across at her. She was a force of nature that he'd never got to grips with. He'd been ready to send a report to IMC Command that would have finished her career, and now felt ashamed in many ways. An uncontrollable whirlwind who started bar brawls, disobeyed orders and had the relentless energy of a newborn sun. She had worn him down for years, only to rejuvenate him in just a few days. She reminded him of someone else all of a sudden, and he quickly banished the memory.

The squad moved out and climbed the ladder in single file to the access hatch and towards daylight. He took a deep breath as he was flooded with fear and followed.

Craig Jenkins

REASON

The ship had endless walkways, lifts and open plan areas which were large enough for a combat truck to traverse through. Admiral Novex stopped from time to time to access screen terminals to remind himself where he was and where he was headed. He toured through corridors of shining pristine metal, down stairwells and across vast hallways fitted with firing ranges, assault courses and gymnasium halls; perhaps inadvertently taking the long route in order to think things through.

Control could be considered an elusive entity. With the smallest of changes it could sway either way between sides. He had known this to be something that needed mastering and on many levels a long time ago. The master of strategy; a prodigy of tactics who analysed every option thoroughly, without emotion and with few regrets that had made him one of the most feared GSA officers to have ever taken command. There was always that moment he dreaded, the time he met his match and even a scenario which would stretch his ability to make a good choice. Doubt was a disease he had never suffered throughout his entire life and now it had found him and injected itself deep into his very being. *Can't back down, never back down!*

The stairwell presented itself and led to the lowest deck of the ship. He made his way into the dark to then be surrounded by many vehicles. He walked the rows of tanks of many shapes and sizes parked along the vast hanger bay; the best and most up to date, courtesy of the IMC. Trucks with various battlements were situated further along in single file against the wall. Some had wheels with reinforced tyres where others had treads for other, more difficult terrains. An automated spray unit for camouflaging the vehicles before deployment sat quietly in the distance. The vehicles themselves presently stood naked in a flawless silver sheen straight from the factories' production lines.

Version

The hanger stretched for thousands of metres in an otherwise empty space which was just as wide. In the distance he could see a deep orange glow rising from the floor. He made his way to a small transport cart and drove towards the light.

The motor whined and echoed with the high-pitched sound of the mechanised components within its drivers. He pulled up next to a large rectangular hatch in the hanger floor which was currently open except for the still-activated digital window-lens surface. Where trucks and tanks had been parked in allotted bays either side of the hanger, here stood combat jet planes and helicopters, also silver in colour and just as pristine. It was a shame that the basin's depth didn't allow for them to be utilized in combat and that the very nature of the place would distort their navigational equipment to the degree that they'd be dangerous to use.

He parked the cart and exited next to the massive rectangular window in the floor. Ahead of him, other aircraft exits remained closed; and above him, thick armoured doors stretched away in single file across the very centre of the hanger bay's surface.

He looked at the man standing at the centre of the window. His long robes were navy, yet shone a green colour from the powerful light coming from beneath. The man's features were partly in shadow so that his eyes and forehead couldn't be seen, whereby his chin and cheekbones created the same ghoulish illusion that could be achieved from shining a torch upwards under a face. Novex made his way to a row of desks beside the window lens and sat down. The man watched as though interested.

'Do you believe in God, Christopher?' the man asked. His voice carried within the enormous hanger and became hollow, almost theatrical in its enhancement.

'That's Admiral to you, Professor, and no, I never give it any thought.'

Novex reclined in his chair as the Professor turned to marvel at the magnitude of the basin's star lens only fifty metres below.

'My father was a mathematician, my mother a physicist and my sister is one of the GSA's foremost genetic engineers. My brother is an accomplished philosopher and I myself am somewhat gifted in all these fields, and yet such achievements mean nothing at all when you draw your focus towards the larger scale of things.'

'Well I'm sure you had a riveting time around the dinner table, Professor, but I don't have time to listen to you blow your own trumpet.'

Professor Houseman paced along the surface of the window. Its fabric dipped slightly with rings of condensed light surrounding his feet. 'My point is, that in all their accomplishments, they all agreed that the universe was made by design and there was the strongest possibility that God, whichever way you imagine him to be, does exist.'

'I never took you to be religious, Professor. What can you tell me about the man headed our way?'

'Religion is merely a way to show our appreciation of the awe, the entity that has made existence possible. I choose to value God's gifts in my own way. Has it ever occurred to you that if there are eyes of truth watching, they may have tipped the balance against you for your actions?'

The admiral dismissed this so-called philosophical conversation and lost his patience with the man the GEA considered to be a prized asset; one of the most perceptive men in existence assigned to offer counsel to him when things went beyond his own capacity for reasoning, or so it was suggested. He didn't agree with Command that such a man would be of any use and preferred instead to make decisions on tangible information along with good old-fashioned facts. 'I hope you have some useful information, Professor. You are capable of providing me with that I hope? Rather than the guff you're hiding behind at the moment.'

The Professor had spent some time analysing the digital pad which held footage of a man who had earlier been hunted and apparently killed. He'd been given less of a chance to absorb the second spectacle, when possibly the same man had risen as though a phoenix seeking retribution. 'Did you have to kill so many? Did you have to cremate the bodies in such a systematic and heartless way?'

'You'll be joining them unless you provide me with some answers. Your file states you have a high-level rating in genetic modification, genome alteration, and immune system enhancement. It doesn't say anywhere that you specialise in lectures on morality or the pathetic inducement of guilt trips.'

'Quite,' the Professor said. 'Although I can't quite explain my thoughts on this without creating a context for you to understand the enormity of this. You're a simpler man than you think, Admiral, and I suggest you pay attention before making another move.'

He paused for a moment and the admiral remained silent out of interest.

'You stay because you want to know how such a thing could be achieved. In your eyes the new world can wait and you figure that bringing such a find to command would be of more benefit. After all, what use is claiming a second Earth only to lose it to a legion of bullet-proof soldiers who can disarm an entire battalion in seconds, destroy tanks, and who knows what else? What if you can't detain him, what if he's something else entirely?'

Novex stood and walked across the lens towards the Professor. He looked down to see the landscape of the basin tinted with orange through the star lens, and then glanced for a split second at the ship's hull directly below. The hanger bay exit doors had slid sideways into grooves to reveal the *Hollywood's* outer skin as being twenty metres thick. A further vacuum lens remained operational at this outer level of thickness so that between the two fields a chamber had been established for aircraft to disembark without having to decompress the hanger bay.

'I don't have time for this, so how about you use your superior intellect in order to articulate a decent theory in double time?'

Professor Houseman backed away from Admiral Novex, who was now invading his personal space. He decided that he would rather risk proposing his conclusions, regardless of the fact that, even though logical, they were both absurd and, to a great extent, non-provable.

'At present we can modify a human subject to eradicate genetic defects, prolong life and, as you know, extend life well beyond its natural cycle. It's even possible to modify the immune system in order to regenerate, to grow new limbs and to heal efficiently.' He walked around, looking through the floor while he gathered his thoughts.

'It takes time to heal and, even with modified subjects which are immune to all natural diseases, this doesn't make them immortal. A subject can't be developed to overcome great physical trauma and the genome can't be programmed to become that much more robust – certainly not bullet proof. Simply put, the man is an impossible feat beyond our means of technology. It's just impossible . . . at the very least he defies the laws of thermodynamics. That is, he regenerates tissue from seemingly nowhere and at little calorific, or rather cost of, energy. Also, he continues to function when key systems are destroyed. It's either a very good mechanical or biological machine disguised as human or . . . sorcery.'

'I hope you're not going to suggest that he doesn't exist or that he's some sort of illusion, Professor. At least tell me he's a clone of the one killed earlier or, better still, come up with a way to stop him so that he can be taken and studied. I won't allow the IMC to have the edge on this, and unfortunately you're my best chance of understanding how such a weapon could work.'

The Professor laughed nervously and continued to pace. 'The abomination you retrieved, the new means of AI, is IMC. That is our next form of progression, Admiral, for someday we will upload our thoughts into one of those creatures and become a far more robust species in our own right, surpassing evolution and perhaps even becoming immortals based on the genetics found within that primarily silicone AI. And yet we have a long way to go in order to reach the levels of adaptation as witnessed with that man.'

'So he's a machine, synthetic. Now we're getting somewhere, Professor.'

'I don't think so. You're bypassing and merging the two definitions between machines grown from one material with that of another. He *is* a machine. We're all machines in a sense. But consider this. If the IMC created a silicone machine without eyes to see and ears to listen, why create such a complete perfect solider? Better still, why doesn't he kill when we both know the IMC would programme such a thing without mercy to destroy us without hesitation?'

'It malfunctioned! You talk of this man as though he belongs to something else, Professor, what?'

The professor made his way to the row of desks and sat down. His head hurt at the prospect of his conclusions on this subject. 'How old are you?'

'One hundred and twenty,' Novex answered.

'And your licence?'

'Full span as of yet.'

Professor Houseman folded his arms and crossed his ankles underneath his thick robes. 'Isn't it strange how we don't question having a licence for life? Depending on one's skill and heritage, we're given anything between eighty and two hundred years and why? Because a few hundred years ago, genetic engineering allowed us to live too long and therefore created the necessity for deletion. So many ways we could go, and yet I don't think it's this, this man you're so eager to find. Do you consider any of us are natural human beings any more?'

'We are what we are, Professor. I would calm down, you're starting to rant. I get the impression you're scared of something. Just spit it out and we'll deal with it.'

He pushed back on his chair and propelled himself along the edge of desk to reach for a glass jug. He poured himself a glass of water and drank it all in one go.

'The GSA had to shield my entire family from persecution because my parents were developed in a test tube. I'm an illegal, living my life hidden away and for what?

'Yet the harm that would be caused by creating such a powerful human being would have repercussions well beyond the limits of my imagination. But think carefully about what you've seen thus far. Here is a man that has rapid cellular adaptive capabilities. His skin is able to polarise to the extent that he can deflect stampede rounds, even two-inch calibre sniper rounds with armour-piercing magma tips. I hope I'm speaking in your kind of language, Admiral?'

'What then, you think this is something metaphysical extra-terrestrial?'

'Absolutely, and my advice is that we should take that which we came for and go right away.'

Admiral Novex laughed in a deep long drawn-out tone at the Professor's paranoia. 'Right away . . .? I'm not convinced there's any need to run away, Professor. I'll give it three hours. The IMC will be just about with us around then, and if I don't have him by the time they arrive, we'll leave. How strong do you estimate a blanket field is?'

'It all depends on the level of power it draws on. Why?' Professor Houseman asked.

Novex looked calculatingly at the star lens and across its vast plane. 'Can you help the technicians develop a transformer to increase its density for, say, an atomic detonation? Something modest of course.'

Professor Houseman gave a small nod while trying to work out the particulars. 'I see. The field would be destroyed in the process, but hopefully it would contain much of the blast. Much of the field's components are susceptible to an EMP wave, especially from an internal level of force.'

'None of that matters. Ramp up the *Hollywood* transfer lines. Better still, take the backup components and create a new pathway and set the field against, say, one kiloton,' Novex ordered.

Professor Houseman stood and turned to make his way out. 'I sincerely hope this doesn't backfire in any way, Admiral.'

Judith made hand gestures; commands Sharplin found easy to understand and yet found her ability to position the marines with such decisive knowledge a complete surprise.

She made a fist and held it up and they stopped. Then she looked to one of the marines, pointed two fingers at her eyes, and then away towards the next pathway through the trees. The marines made their way in this direction and took up new positions a hundred feet away. He looked again and they'd gone, hidden amongst the thick brush next to the path.

Version

He found it similar to hunting, although that was less intense and extended periods of rest were an option. The marines moved, scoped the area, and signalled for them to advance. His legs ached and the armour was stifling. The birds were curious and watched them as they made slow progress through the moderately lit forest.

It dawned on him that his being here put them at risk. He was slow and cumbersome and unfit in many ways. He had another goal to achieve if he managed to survive this mess. Go to the therapists and get himself seen to. They could iron out his joints and mend his muscles and tendons so that he could begin a fitness regime. If it all went wrong now, he'd be left standing, whereas in contrast, the others could sprint away. If in fact that's what they did in such situations.

He wasn't sure what to think. *What are the others thinking right now?* All focused on doing what they'd been trained to do. His thoughts were random and he was out of his depth. Another thought he'd had a few days earlier returned to him: c*aptains don't need to go places.* He held a powerful assault rifle and felt its weight burn his shoulders and biceps. They'd only travelled a few miles; he was already exhausted and was considering offering to return back to the tunnel alone.

Judith crouched and typed in a code on her digital pad, which she now wore on her left sleeve. *How does she know this stuff?* He realised she was sending reports back to the marines at the subway every ten minutes so that they'd know if something had gone wrong if a check call failed.

Judith looked to him and made a gesture she hadn't taught him. He wasn't sure what she meant at first as all she did was point her finger to the sky. He shrugged and she rolled her eyes. She then began to climb the tree with impressive speed so that a few moments later she was gone and out of sight. Sharplin looked on in amazement. *When did she conquer her fear of heights? What's happened to her?*

She took a position on a thick branch which gave her a clear view across the top of the forest. The tree she'd picked was an oak tree that just pipped the height of those around it; she could survey above and beyond towards the basin's north wall. She pulled a digital telescope from her satchel and used it to scan the area.

The device adjusted and began measuring multiple objects on its display. Thermal imaging registered flocks of birds sitting a few miles away high up within the canopy of the trees. The scope's sight moved upwards and higher, then zoomed in towards the sky-tram network where the reddened heat signature of two soldiers came into view. They were camped on one of the cable's junction boxes, keeping surveillance below and around them through the scopes of their sniper rifles.

She adjusted her scope's setting and zoomed further in towards the old city. The enhanced view panned across and above the buildings and further behind to see halfway up the basin's wall. Her heart sank at the scene. The tower leading up to the docking platform was now enclosed behind a blanket field of a light-green colour which resonated with charged particles. She then tilted the scope upwards to see the rectangular silhouette of the *Hollywood* above the star lens.

She began the long climb down from her position and hoped that the enemy hadn't made her position with their own thermal imaging equipment. *It's all been a waste of time,* she thought, and they now had no choice but to sit this out in the tunnel and hope for the best. Carefully she completed her climb and leapt on to the lawn of thick moss covering the forest floor without making a sound. *Click.* She felt the end of the barrel press hard into her temple and then a blunt impact to the back of her head.

A forceful slap woke him. Blurred visions of grey surrounded by greens and whites adjusted slowly until the enemy soldier came into focus. Sharplin seethed in pain. *They chopped my hands off!* Then he felt his fingers moving behind him. His wrists were bound so tightly his hands were swollen and numb. He breathed deeply and his nose throbbed immensely, refusing to allow air to pass. His nostrils made a strange wheezing noise every time he inhaled.

'Ah, you're awake, Steward. Can you understand what I'm saying? Nod if you like.'

Version

Captain Sharplin knelt before an armoured soldier who was holding a digital pad close to his face. On the screen was a man with bright white hair, very pale skin and darkened eyes.

'I have questions for you, Steward.'

The man's voice frightened him. It was both charismatic and confident, yet it was also cold and menacing.

'What do you want?'

'There's a man, a soldier within the basin. I want the files on him. Where do you hold such information?'

Frank looked around for a moment to see that in front of him and to his left the other marines were also kneeling and facing in his direction. They'd been bound with their arms behind their backs and blindfolded. Beyond them he could see they were all in a clearing somewhere within the forest and the trees ahead encircled them in a concave formation.

'I don't know what you mean.'

'Captain Jux.'

One of the soldiers standing opposite the captive marines raised his arm then quickly dropped it. Three of the enemy soldiers standing behind the marines raised their weapons and fired.

He couldn't think. His mind swirled as though it was floating up and away from his head. Another slap from the soldier's gauntlet brought him back.

'Don't be rude, Steward. I need you to pay attention.'

Sharplin leant forward to vomit then lifted his head to face his surroundings. His eyes were streaming and he could barely see through the glaze.

'You do such a good job acting all innocent, playing the part of a caretaker. Such a cunning strategy that I can only applaud. Deceit plays a major part in winning wars, don't you think?'

At that moment Sharplin felt they were all done for. He looked at the five remaining marines, then to the ones who had been executed and were now lying face down in the tall grass.

'I'll jog your memory, using simple terminology for you. You released a soldier on our arrival who has some interesting attributes. Does genetic re-coding and modification ring any bells?'

Ologun! Time had stretched to the point that Ologun was now a distant memory. His mind fought hard for the information and he was flustered. 'The files are at the fortress, in the genetic cache.'

'Captain Jux.'

The soldiers executed the rest of the marines.

'Deceit only works if the other party is unaware of the facts, Steward. Try again.'

Sharplin laughed painfully, hysterically, and in shear despair. 'The thief and the liar, we are both sinners, sir! His name is Ologun and he was discovered buried under six miles of ice on Deceiver. He has a habit of coming back from the dead and has a long history of killing bastards like you, and I hope he—'

Frank gasped, feeling faint again and leaned forward to collapse, only to be held in place by the soldier standing behind him. His chest wouldn't allow him to exhale and he was sure he would die from heart failure at any moment.

'There are no files or reports on this anywhere in your database, Steward. You're a professional, I can see that, and such unwillingness to compromise and submit sensitive information deserves kudos. Captain Jux, encourage the steward to reconsider.'

Sharplin's binds were cut and one of his hands placed on a wooden block in front of him. One of the soldiers took his rifle and smashed its butt into his knuckles.

His scream echoed around the enclosure and a distant bird mimicked the sound.

'I don't know anything about him, why don't you—'

Another blow to the hand silenced him and he began to hyperventilate.

One of the soldiers placed a mask on his face and turned the oxygen down low.

'If you don't know, then you don't know. I'm sure your second in command will be more helpful. Let's see now . . . a Commander Judith Gibson.'

Frank began to breathe less erratically and looked towards movement coming from his right. He immediately saw Judith slumped forwards over a thick log. She was unconscious and had her hands bound behind her. Two more soldiers moved in so that one stood behind and the other in front of her.

'Wake her.'

One of the soldiers placed a small pencil-shaped device into one of her nostrils and it released a small electrical charge. Her eyes opened instantly and she shot up, only to be pressed back down on to the log by the weight of the soldier's foot between her shoulder blades.

Her eyes moved to see the marines lying on their fronts, and then the bloody mess that was Sharplin with the oxygen mask pressed against his face. She immediately began to struggle and her face contorted in rage. The soldier's boot pressed down harder.

'Commander Gibson, I'll get to the point. I'm looking for information on the one called Ologun, if that truly is his name. You have been developing a programme here for advanced biological weaponry. I want the programme files, now.'

Judith swore and cursed and shouted for some time until the soldier holding her in position fired a round into her left calf. She made a small controlled grunt of pain and then held silent.

'I'm pressed for time, so I'll make either one of you a deal. The first one who gives me what I need can live.'

The minutes passed with neither of them willing to respond. Sharplin could see that Judith's wound must be hurting and couldn't understand how her face looked so unaffected and emotionless. She was far more cast iron than he could ever have imagined.

'I can see I'm wasting my time. Captain Jux, you decide.'

Sharplin's heart pounded with fear at this new command and he watched the soldier with blue markings on his shoulders point his finger. *No, don't you do it!*

The soldier lifted his rifle and fired one shot.

Reality moved to another realm. Sharplin's ears rang so that no other sounds could penetrate the bubble. He could see and yet had no thoughts other than to pray. He hadn't been to this place before, even back then. A prayer entered his mind and expanded. He pushed forth the currency in the form of his soul to the highest bidder in exchange for the most vicious retribution conceivable. If he could detonate every atom in his body he would, and if he was asked to serve the Devil for eternity, then so be it.

His gaze fell on the tip of the barrel pointed at his forehead and he felt calm. The finger fell over the trigger and squeezed.

Viiiiiiiiiiiiiiiip.

The barrel disappeared and the soldier had gone with it. He watched calmly as though relaxing in front of an old black and white movie, dozing with eyelids half closed. The soldiers ran around. Flashes of gunfire erupted in slow motion without sound. One soldier flew into the distance and hit a tree. Another walked around headless until he fell to the ground.

Viiiiiiiiiiiip. Viiip. Viiiiiiiiiiiiiiiip.

The sounds and movement he was aware of were beyond recognition. Flickers and shadows of movement high above swooped and rose. A soldier to his left fired his rifle; then his chest exploded, leaving a large hole in its place. Sharplin felt the spatter of liquid on his face and his eyes fluttered in an automated reaction.

Another soldier slid across the grass in front of him with both arms and legs missing. He stared at the body, detached from the grotesque spectacle of it.

A noise filtered through: a toot followed by a grumble and a tinkle. Sharplin looked down to the floor in front of his lap. On the grass stood the very same large black insect he'd come to recognise over the past few months. Two more creatures landed to either side of it and hopped around, flapping their wings and flicking specks of blood on to the grass as they did so. He'd been correct in his analysis that those daggers could stab a man to death. *I'll tell Judith.* Then reality returned to him and an awful feeling shot through him in a terrible pulse.

He knelt without fear of them, without even acknowledging that they were patiently waiting with him. There was a pale one which was almost the shade of bone in colour, except for the splashes of red upon its body and wings. It regarded him and nudged him with its nib-like head. The brown one kept its distance and the black one made a noise as though crooning at him in sympathy. He ignored them.

Version

He crawled towards the log to his right; slow and cumbersome under the weight of his suit of armour. His injured hand was closed and he held it close to his chest out of instinct to protect it. With his good hand he grabbed Judith's collar and pulled so that she fell into his lap. He looked away from the terrible wound and his face contorted in pain. The three craft gathered in close behind him, curious about his movements. They watched and scanned.

He hung his head and remained still for a while. The craft grew interested as his body heaved up and down erratically. They listened as he made a curious sound which they couldn't translate into any language known to them. They were concerned that his vital signs had erupted into tremendous levels of trauma and they could find no identifiable reasons. He knelt like this for a long time with his body heaving and making the strange noise. They just couldn't understand that he was utterly broken.

CORRUPTOR

'Detach the docking rig, we're leaving.'

'Prep for launch confirmed, Admiral.'

The bridge personnel continued to relay information regarding the launch sequence.

'Engines one through five engaged.'

'Reverse-mass generators primed and ready.'

'Engines five though ten operational, new AI is functioning, position processing available in five minutes . . . mark.'

'Mark confirmed.'

The commander stood next to him. His blue epaulettes turned purple in the red glow flashing on the bridge.

'Excuse me, Admiral, sir, we still have men down there, surely we can wait for them to evacuate?'

Admiral Novex ignored him. 'Time to launch?'

'Two minutes, sir.'

Laughter filled the room. A continuous cackling and gurgling came from the bridge access way and echoed down the corridor behind. Novex looked up from the activity of the bridge to see Captain Adams standing in the doorway.

'Ah, you made it, Captain. I fail to see what you find so humorous.'

The lack of reply prompted him to look more closely at Captain Adams. His head twitched and his eyes looked to be staring to one side at nothing. Novex scanned him quickly from head to foot and saw that his feet were elevated a few inches off the floor. His body then flew across the room and into a control panel, just missing one of the officers sitting near the console. She stood up and ran to the other side of the room. 'Sir?'

All eyes were now fixated on the doorway from where Captain Adams had been thrown. Novex glared and struggled to recognise the man standing there and who wore a grey suit of armour without the helmet.

'I don't recognise you, Private, what's your name?'

'Oh, I'm a new recruit.'

The man walked across the floor of the bridge and down its coliseum formation towards the control stations.

Novex grew nervous. 'All positions are filled, I'm afraid.'

'Well, I disagree. You lost so many men today I thought I'd help take up the slack.'

The man had bright blond hair and held a transparent crystal staff with a blue tint and a large flat blade at one end.

One of the officers risked informing the admiral of an update. 'Ready for launch, sir.'

'Do it,' Novex ordered.

She went to access the console where the man immediately swung his staff and decapitated her in one forceful swipe. 'Delay that order, there's been a change of plan.'

The man spoke in a strange tone that was both theatrical and absurd. His voice lifted and fell in odd places so that he was whiny and camp one moment and aggressively gruff the next.

Novex grabbed the rifle hanging from the shoulder of the commander standing next to him and emptied the entire clip. The rounds hit the man directly in the face and blood sprayed over the console behind. Novex then looked on in horror as every wound across the man's destroyed face healed within seconds. The man pranced around with an agility that defied the weight of the armour he wore.

'See, Admiral, I'm in need of your assistance, you know what I mean? There's a man heading our way, a very powerful individual that has taken a disliking to us both. You could say that you and I are teammates, brothers in arms so to speak.'

Novex rushed to the comms unit and was thrown backwards into the bridge's command seat. He looked up to see that the bridge officers had all been slain and the strange man was holding the commander by his neck. He then rendered the commander lifeless with a flick of his wrist.

'Alone at last, eh, Admiral? You see, you and I have so much in common.'

Novex surveyed the carnage in the room. He hadn't even seen the man attack them; it had been achieved in the blink of an eye. 'I very much doubt that . . . you're an abomination.'

The man suddenly disappeared; seemingly teleporting from where he'd been a few yards away to stand over Novex, crushing his chest with one knee. He then leaned in so that their noses were almost touching.

'He presses the button and orders the kill, yet never is he present to witness the thrill. I think you suffer from hypocrisy, Admiral. So many motives for murder and yet all murderers scramble to defend their actions,' he whined mockingly. 'God made me do it, I did it for God. I have mental issues. I did it for my country. It was my duty. It was an accident. They deserved it, 'cause they killed my pet fish.' His voice changed to a low bark. 'I did it because I can and feel its necessity to achieve my own deep pleasure and satisfaction.'

'What do you want from me? You're just like that man headed here, surely you can deal with him yourself?'

The man pranced around, pressing buttons and flicking dials on various consoles as he went. 'It's a little bit more complicated than that, because unfortunately our nemesis is a tougher model, a sort of entry unit if you like.'

Novex felt it. He'd been confused by this alien emotion at first, but finally he felt the fear. He launched at a control panel next to him and pressed a metal key into the console. Within a split second he was held aloft by his arm with the key held high in his grip.

'What's this? I open my heart to you in full confidence and you betray me by trying to destroy the ship? How lovely.'

'How am I supposed to help you? I can't help you!' Novex shrieked.

The man dropped him to the floor and sat down into the command chair to lean towards Novex, who now sat at his feet. 'Human beings are so stupid. You have to think laterally, boy!' He sat back into the chair and surveyed the room '. . . mmm, I think I'd like to be an admiral or captain of a starship. Ordering the annihilation of an entire planet here, taking a country for myself by force there. You see, killing Ologun isn't really a possibility. We have to take charge of the two forces available to us . . . time and motion. Help me realise my plan and I'll make it worth your while, you can even serve me when I'm king of Earth. I may even let you have your own kingdom, how does having all of Mars sound? Now, I need you to gather your brightest minions together, so listen carefully.'

The truck skidded sideways and he managed to correct it back to a straight course. An explosion hit the rear wheels so that its bonnet dipped; the back end rose then dropped so that the vehicle bumped around out of control. It then sped up along the grass banking and crashed through a stone wall, careered along a flat terrace, and landed upside down in a swimming pool. Ologun fought and swam from underneath through thick blanket weed. The water was stagnant and foul, and stringy masses of algae wrapped around his limbs and torso. His head broke the surface of the water and he ripped the green web from his face.

Exiting the pool he thought about this new dilemma. It would have been easier to abandon the vehicle mid-collision and he realised he'd been reluctant to do so. The docking platform was now only twenty miles from his position and yet it remained too far without the vehicle. It wasn't stamina that caused him a problem: he could run for as long as he needed to. The real issue brought a clear weakness to light in a way that concerned him greatly. *Time and motion,* he thought.

The attributes he had were impressive in a great number of scenarios, specifically aggressive and destructive. His abilities, however, didn't allow for a speed that, in turn, diminished the amount of time he had to achieve an objective. 'They' had thought of a number of things, except those denied him by the laws of physics.

A sniper round hit his chest, sending him backwards a few steps; another hit his forehead, forcing his head to jerk violently backwards. He looked at the truck as it lay on its roof in the pool of putrid water. The soldiers had changed tactics since their encounter at the barricade, and they had now turned to setting up ambushes along with various traps throughout his route. He was surprised that the truck had made it this far, and he had pushed through in a straight line without altering course, risking the perils to the truck in exchange for more time.

He cursed his arrogance. The truck had taken a great deal of punishment and had finally been rendered useless. The terrace he stood on was derelict and overgrown with many weeds and vines. Tropical ivy had taken advantage of a particularly tall fun slide and grew through and around its transparent tubular structure. The buildings surrounding the terrace were concrete chalet apartments which had been decorated in half-cut logs giving the effect of real wooden cabins. They were derelict and run down with large gaps where the log slats had fallen off, revealing dull concrete. This small set of apartments had been abandoned long ago, allowing the strength of nature in the basin to take hold, both utilising and destroying that which had been constructed.

More sniper rounds hit Ologun's body and face; accurate shots in groups of three: one to the head and two to the chest on each occasion. *They're so dumb!*

He lost his temper and ran to the front of the pool. Reaching over, he grabbed one of the wheel's suspension branches and pulled. The truck moved closer and he took hold of another, more solid section of its body work. *Let's do a little experiment.*

The truck creaked as he attempted the lift. He pulled harder until he lost all patience and yanked with all his power. The pain caused him to scream in a deep grunt and sent him walking around the patio bent over and feeling completely idiotic. The muscles in his lower back and shoulders were torn at the tendons and ligaments. He had also slipped three discs which finally had him swearing and shouting as he waited for everything to correct itself. The injuries healed in seconds, and this time his rage helped him throw the vehicle a few hundred feet towards a few mature trees. The truck rolled a few times along the sward, flicking dirt and sludge as it went.

He moved behind one of the chalets and out of sight of the snipers. They were menacing him and he couldn't concentrate with them taking pot shots.

Version

'*Ologun*!''

His eyes moved from left to right at the sound.

'Ologun, can you hear me?'

The sound was a high-pitched whining in his head that he thought translated into his name.

'Don't be obtuse, it's me.'

'Creed?' he shouted.

'No, it's Ray, fool, and I can't hear you. You have to think your reply so the suit can transmit.'

Ologun thought his responses as instructed. *Where are you? And why do you sound like a badly tuned radio with no words, and how am I able to understand this rubbish?*

'I'm at the pool relaying thought waves to your extra skin and into your brain, and in turn you're doing the same to my mask.'

Ologun's imagination rushed with the image of Ray sitting naked by the swimming pool wearing a leather mask made of his own skin. The different colours and designs of the head mask rapidly changed as his mind went off on a blistering tangent: black, red, purple . . . pink.

Good Grief!

'What?' the suit whined into his head. He still wasn't convinced it was Ray communicating.

Erm, nothing, Ray. He peeked around the corner from his hiding place to look over the terrace and couldn't see Ray anywhere. *You invisible? I can't see you.*

'Not that pool, the vision one.'

Oh . . . all the way from down there? Not bad range, except you sound more annoying than usual. Can't you just talk to me with words rather than this screeching?

'No.'

Ray, listen. I'm running out of time, can you delay them at all? It never occurred to me that it would take so long to get there.

'This is your own little project and there's no point to it. You have two hours to . . . what are you trying to do exactly?'

I'm going to find him. I think he's up to something.

201

'No, he isn't, you're both idiots and I recommend you . . . never mind. The ships have come home. They got overly excited protecting that man you like so much.'

Sharplin, is he okay?

'He lives. The three craft ended up killing over a hundred soldiers. The rest have gone back to the north wall. Well, except the few following you, that is. I don't know why they bother. It's all quite amusing, though.'

I'm glad people's suffering tickles you, Ray. Where is he, anyway?

'He's on the ship, practising.'

Practising? Practising what . . . Ray, Ray? There was no reply. *Shit!*

Ologun felt the round hit the back of his head. Another two hit the back of his neck and sent him stumbling forward a few feet.

He turned to look at the wall he'd been leaning against to see two holes which had gone straight through. He peeped through one of the holes and another round hit him in the eye. The pain sent a shockwave through his skull and he suddenly had an idea.

The sniper lost sight of his target and lowered his rifle, then almost jumped off the branch with fright when he spotted Ologun perched a few branches above and in front.

Ologun leapt down and grabbed the sniper by the collar, then lifted him up to his face.

'We need to talk.'

He sliced the soldier's mask and helmet off to see a man of Oriental nationality with a curiously long white beard.

'What's your name?' he asked the soldier.

'Darren,' the soldier replied. The look on his face suggested he was somewhat confused as well as terrified.

'Just relax, Darren, I need a favour. You people have vehicles?'

'I don't think I should tell you, I mean you're the enemy.'

Ologun stared at the man. His accent and voice defied his appearance and wasn't what he'd expected. 'Where are you from?'

'I shouldn't tell you that either.' Darren paused. 'London, West End as it happens. American, ain't ya?'

'My father was, I grew up in Medina.'

'Thought there was summink weird going on, you sound Swiss.'

'You just asked me if I was . . . never mind. Listen, you people have to evacuate this place ASAP. You need to tell your commanding officer to leave for the docking rig now. Oh, and I want a truck.'

Radio chatter emitted from a small speaker within the soldier's collar. 'Position compromised and acknowledged, High-Chance. What exactly is your status, over?'

Darren pointed to the small button and made a face as though asking permission to respond. Ologun nodded in agreement.

'Yes, mate, I have the enemy sat opposite me advising us to evacuate to the platform and eh, can he borrow a truck?'

'Negative on that, High-Chance, there's fat chance of that happening.'

Darren laughed then withdrew his amusement at seeing Ologun's lack of humour.

'Sorry son, bit a of a pot conker that one.'

'Look, Darren, Fat-Chance—'

'It's High-Chance, mate.'

'Right. I know your team are camped only a couple of hundred metres away and you know I could just take what I want and by force if necessary. Tell whoever that was on the comms that I'm coming to take a truck and they're better off just giving it to me. Tell them to take my advice and evacuate this place before it leaves.'

'What do you mean, leave?'

'Leave, the present tense of left, i.e. is about to go somewhere you really don't want to go.'

The two men sat for a moment as Darren thought this through. 'Why should I trust you? What's going on?'

Ologun unsheathed one of his blades and lifted it to the man's chin. 'I'm trying to be nice and helpful. If I wanted to kill any of you I'd have done it long ago and with ease.'

'You've already destroyed six platoons. Why do this?'

'That wasn't me as I was here, as you know. Just make the call so we can avoid further bloodshed; you know it makes sense.'

Darren thought about things then made the call in his own quirky way. Eventually, after some heated debate, his squad appeared to agree.

'So what's England like? I've never been.'

'Bloody scorching these days, took the missus to Brighton a few summers ago, and do you know what? There was a flipping great white shark swimming about near our rowing boat one day. It's a shame fishing's illegal or I'd have had it – thirty foot long it was, like a great big white turd just bobbing along.'

Ologun hadn't the faintest idea what the man was trying to say and did his best to follow the short story, or whatever it was meant to be.

'I'm going to collect my truck now, Darren. You're not going to shoot me, are you?'

'I suppose not, doesn't work does it? What's up with you anyway?'

Ologun stood up to make his way and turned to Darren. 'You don't want to know.'

Still dazed and confused he found himself walking aimlessly through the woods where solders lay slain in large numbers. Frank Sharplin felt as though he'd entered the underworld, the basin's negative reality where bodies ran with blood and their body parts lay scattered. Many were high up in the trees like decorations; hanging upside down or folded over branches in various ways. They'd all died in such terrible ways and he was convinced his prayer had been answered in a way he'd not imagined possible.

Birds, mainly large crows, had already taken to scavenging in large numbers and picked at the corpses. They didn't even budge when he approached them. The feeling of sickness filled him as he scanned soldiers' faces which had no eyes; they were the first prize to have been taken by nature's opportunists. Ahead of him, and for some distance, the nightmare continued.

Version

His mind refused to work properly and simply functioned on autopilot. His hand bled at his side yet he felt no pain. He couldn't remember hitting the release clips to the upper part of his suit of armour and that it had fallen off some time ago. He now wore a white vest which was grubby with sweat and stained with large red blotches across the front. He still wore the armour's leggings. They were heavier now without power, making his mindless journey a difficult and cumbersome business. His feet dragged along the floor with every step and he regularly fell over bodies, tree roots and shrubbery, then took valuable effort and time to get back to his feet.

A large hole in the floor presented itself with several trees jutting out from deep within the ground. Without any particular thought he found a ladder and climbed down.

'Who goes there?'

He faced the direction from where the voice came and jumped down to the floor.

The light in the tunnel had an odd artificial luminosity as it mixed with the more perfected version of sunlight.

'Captain, sir, is that you?'

He said nothing.

The marine lowered his rifle, rushed over, then stopped when he got close enough to see the state Frank was in.

'What happened? We lost contact with you well over an hour ago, where are the others?'

Sharplin walked past the marine without acknowledging him and made his way along the carriages of the train. He walked towards the shimmer of blue light beyond the last carriage, then stopped just outside the protection field.

A few moments later the field lowered and he found himself surrounded by people. He couldn't understand them at first as they bombarded him with questions. The marines held back the crowd as someone placed their hands on his shoulders and pulled him close.

'Frank, what happened? Listen to my voice, please, Frank. Get out of the way, sit him down . . . quickly!'

He found himself sitting against the subway's platform with Doctor Siren crouched in front of him and shining a small torch into his eyes.

'Rita. You're here.'

'Yes, Frank, I'm right here. What happened out there, where are the others?'

She began examining him. A case was handed down to her from one of the marines. She opened it and took a number of bandages from within.

He sat there in a daze. He tried to remember and felt the emotions erupt, only to then force them back with all his might. 'They're gone. We were ambushed and they're all gone.'

The marines bombarded him with questions again. Some of the tourists standing further behind them began to shout questions, while others gasped and screamed at the revelation.

'Please, be quiet. All of you.' Doctor Siren shouted above the crowd.

Sergeant Grey continued to shout her order until relative quiet resumed. She began to wrap a bandage around his injured hand. 'Where's the commander, Sergeant Thomas and the other seven, Frank?'

He looked into her eyes as though she'd been told enough times already.

'They were killed! What are you finding so difficult to understand? They died and I prayed and the black angel came with others and they killed them all. Everyone's dead!'

The marines silenced at this outburst, although a number of hollers, screams and whimpers in the background continued from somewhere behind them. Sharplin stood up as if new energy had suddenly been injected into his battered body. He spoke with a verve that defied his personality; he seemed possessed and almost appeared intoxicated.

'Listen to me now. The path ahead is clear and the demons have agreed to take my soul so that you may escape and live.'

'Frank, sit down,' Doctor Siren insisted.

'We must leave now so that the Seraph of Death can complete its task. To the city and to the ship, it will ensure our safe passage.'

'Frank, please stop this now.'

He looked at the doctor and she could see that his eyes held a strange madness. She realised he'd been broken in some way and he wasn't the same man who had left only a few hours earlier. She struggled with him and finally managed to sit him back down.

'Where's Judith? Tell me what happened, Frank.' She was desperate to reach him and to distract him. She wanted to break this barrier of insanity and needed him to open up for everyone's sake, not just his own.

He looked away and was unwilling to budge.

The marines looked around them in silence and uncertainty; they seemed lost in the hopelessness of the news. The crowd held back behind them began to shout and holler in debate, realising that their military guides had failed them.

'Crazy fools supposed to lead us, we're all dead!'

'You brought us here to die! We should have stayed at the fort!'

'We should fight; we should go out there and show them we mean business and that we won't hide like cowards any more!'

'The man has seen the light, God will lead the way!'

'Shut your face, idiot! We don't need a bible basher preaching to us.'

The marines struggled to maintain control as the crowd grew hostile. The noise escalated into a loud roar with people pushing and shoving. The marines were very aware that most of the tourists had rifles and things were turning ugly. The squad spread out along the platform to distance themselves in a more secure and defensive formation. Doctor Siren struggled and pulled Frank to his feet then directed him further into the tunnel and away from the commotion.

'Wait . . . everyone stop!'

Dennis came running from deep within the tunnel. He'd been more interested in the state of affairs topside and had managed to convince some of the marines to go with him to the surface where he'd made a discovery of great importance. He climbed on to the rearmost carriage of the train and shouted again. The crowd continued their course towards a possible riot.

He lay down on to the carriage roof and grabbed the attention of one of the marines standing nearby at ground level. 'Give me that!'

A loud racket of automatic gunfire shocked the room into a sudden halt and complete silence. The crowd looked to the carriage and Dennis as the marines continued to maintain a defensive formation upon the concrete platform.

'I think you had all better take a look at this.'

VERSION

The chapel roof reached high with thick wooden beams hanging below a ceiling decorated with a number of lush and colourful paintings. A large chandelier made of red glass pipes had been suspended from the central joist and the hollow tubes chimed and rasped under the slight breeze working its way across the hall. Thick long drapes made of a glistening golden fabric had been tied back on to the partition walls between the tall windows on either side of the room. They reflected light and rustled at their creases whenever the large wooden doors at the front of the chapel opened and closed.

It was now late enough for the sun to blast its powerful summer rays through the stained windows and the room filled a bright mixture of blues, reds and greens. One of the windows had a decorative scene associated with that of Christianity: a man in blue robes kneeling with arms stretched out and a white halo encircling his head. Another window had a large golden Buddha sitting and smiling, and the window next to that had another figure sitting cross-legged with six arms raised at its sides. There was also a window stained red and portraying a black crescent moon with its sharp points facing to the left. The building had been restored with a few design alterations in order to accommodate many functions across many cultures and religions. Weddings, funerals and all manner of ceremonies were held in this place, and the local community also utilized it for their own relatively mundane purposes.

She skipped along without the faintest idea why she'd been brought here. Her Aunt Perdek held her hand and ushered her to the front of the hall and a long wooden bench with one long purple cushion running across its length. She leapt up and sat down but couldn't reach the floor with her feet.

'Look, my dress matches the carpet,' she said.

Her aunt faced the front of the room and moved her hand to the girl's shoulder without looking. 'The carpet is burgundy and your dress is ruby red, honey, don't you see?'

Wide-eyed, the girl took to watching the people of many colours and ages, both men and women, milling around the room. They shuffled around and moved to sit along the rows of benches which faced towards the front of the hall at matching intervals on either side of the carpeted walkway. Her aunt told her to face the front where a man in a black suit, blue shirt and bright yellow tie stood on a podium.

'Evening everyone, and thank you for coming to this event. As you know this quiz will help raise money for charity. Remember, the winner can choose the good cause of their choice, not themselves of course—'

The room filled with laughter.

'*And* the winner has the chance to win a number of prizes including a dinner for two at the Se La Ve restaurant at the Nevada Heights plaza resort.'

The man wasn't a preacher of any religion and acted more like a salesman or a game show host, although the girl was too young to know that sometimes religious figureheads acted in exactly the same way.

He looked at her and smiled. 'And who do we have here? What's your name, sweetie?'

The girl thought for a moment. 'Terror.'

The room erupted with more laughter.

'Well now, I'm sure that's not your real name now, is it?'

'That's what my mother mostly calls me.'

More laughter ensued and she blushed.

'Well now, Terror, how old are you?'

'Six.'

The room filled with oohs and aahs, indicating how cute she was.

'Are you going to do the quiz?' the man asked.

'Yes I am.' She beamed with confidence.

Terror listened as the man started the questions. Some were mathematical, others general. Some were to do with science and still others were ambiguous in order to catch people out. She was clever for her age and answered every question with confidence. The quiz finished and the answer papers were handed in.

The man quickly looked through them and marked them in only a few minutes. He looked over at the girl and at the paper he held, then quickly scribbled on the paper before shuffling it away.

'And we have a winner with fifteen correct answers. Mrs Lenhihan, you and one other have won a meal for two. I hear it's very nice there, beautiful food and has wonderful service.'

Later, after all the winners had been announced, the girl waited for the man next to the stage at the front of the chapel. He eventually saw her and knelt down. 'Can I help you?'

'I answered all the questions right. I want a prize.'

'You got most of them wrong I'm afraid, didn't your mother teach you to be a good loser?' His face was grinning, yet his eyes said something else.

She snatched the papers from his left hand and ran to the nearest bench. She sifted through them and found her answer sheet. The man jumped down from the stage and ran over to snatch them back. His face had turned red and he was both furious and nervous.

'How dare you?'

'You cheated!' she screamed.

'Now be quiet, young miss.'

Her aunt ran across and knelt down next to her: 'What's wrong, honey?'

'The man cheated.'

He looked at the woman and smiled awkwardly then looked for her paper to pull it out from among the pile.

'You answered too many wrong. Okay, question twenty. When two people barter a deal; they negotiate is the answer. You put the right answer, but spelled it with an eight, look, see? Question fifteen, if a plane carrying passengers crash lands between two countries in no-man's-land, where would you bury the survivors? The answer is that you don't bury survivors, not contact the appropriate people and have them airlifted to a more suitable place to be . . . be what exactly?' he sighed. 'Need I go on?'

The girl erupted in anger and punched him in his pelvis hard enough for him to fold over in surprise. She then ran through the chapel and into the garden outside. *Liar!*

Terror continued across the driveway until she found herself running through a country lane lined with tall hedgerows. She came across a gap in the bushes where a fence bordered a field and climbed over. On the other side she could see a herd of cows grazing at the far end. They stood out against the green backdrop with completely brown bodies, and to her they were giants. She made her way through the middle of them and was terrified. One of the animals flicked its tail and caught her on the chin. She screamed and ran as fast as she could to the nearest fence, then climbed over into the next field.

The sun still added heat to the day and had enough brightness to obscure her vision. She slowly walked forward into the new field. The ground was more of a dust bowl in comparison to the other field, and had dry dirt patches between mounds of dead, yellowing grass. Terror held her hand above her face to block the sun's glare. She could hear a rhythm of thumping noises moving closer to her along the ground. She strained her eyes across the dusty field. The last thing she remembered was something running towards her.

She would always associate this memory with the dream, and for the first six months spent in hospital, Terror dreamt of nothing else. At first there was the vision of a pool of water in which she stood up to her knees. The ground underneath the water was a bone-white stone which was smooth and slippery underfoot.

As she grew older, the dream continued so that where at first there had only been darkness surrounding the pool, now the landscape expanded. Eventually the water became an ocean or a vast lake and, as she became taller with age, the water became only ankle deep. With adolescence additional features added to the dream; everything became clearer and textures more detailed. She walked across the shallow waters for miles; the wind blew huge crescents across its otherwise still surface so that it rippled and frilled in energetic flurries. In the distance, an empty horizon surrounded her and the overcast light-dull-grey of the sky met with the dark blue of the water's surface. Terror couldn't remember when or how the dream changed as it sometimes did.

At some point, a huge mountain range of black stone came into existence to her right. It was the only feature to inhabit an endless layer of water and stood only a few miles away from where she walked. She would look at the large rock as she trudged through the shallows and could just see a large number of white birds flying across and up towards the mountains' highest points. The mountains were more of a damaged mass of standalone towers, covered in flat cliff faces and jagged peaks. In her vision, she always walked towards and around them, yet never managed to get near enough to touch them or pass by to the other side.

By the time she reached her late teens, the dreams became less frequent and changed every few months. Sometimes she would get close enough to almost see around the mountains' largest cliff face, which was both wide and flat. Sometimes there'd be an immense convex waterfall which dropped for thousands of feet cutting across the direction she walked. The water would fall over the edge at her feet and to the bottom in a powerful torrent; white vapour rising up level with the lake's surface.

The dreams went away for a couple of years and then returned with yet more detail. They were intrusive and relentless and came night after night. She went to a dream specialist who told her that to dream of water meant she feared loss and change, but she never told him of the other thing. Her walk across the shallows and to the mountain had ended a few times by her falling down the face of the waterfall and she'd wake up drenched and screaming. The sensation was so real that she shook with the actuality of it. That frightened her far less than the other, far more mesmerising part to the dream; the alternative version. At times she would walk and manage to work her way around the mountain range where the largest cliff face towered high against the grey sky behind. This was where it hugged the cliff face, hanging vertically on the wall. It was a monstrous creature of whites, creams and greys covering its smooth bone skin. Its multiple legs were folded underneath its long sharp wings which pointed forwards and upwards to the sky.

Sometimes the dream would end and other times the real nightmare would begin. She would stare for too long and it would see her or became aware of her. It would then release itself from the cliff face and hover before swooping with its wings stretched out forward as though a gigantic skeletal moth. It rushed at her, flying low across the shallows and parting the water as it went. It came closer and at speed. She was exposed in the water with nowhere to run and nowhere to hide. It was too fast and she would scream in panic.

She blinked. The white light ahead should have hurt her eyes and her pupils shrunk until they became minute dots. She lay there facing the sky and felt strange. The air had a metallic smell to it which mixed in with that of soil, perfumed flowers, oil and moisture. The sounds were hard to decipher. Birds chirped above the noise of many insects buzzing, scurrying and swimming through the air around her. There was something else. A rhythmic sound carried through the air, a sort of robotic whining, its frequency lost and incomplete underneath a rapid thwomping noise.

She sat up. Bodies lay mutilated around her. Some of the dead lay on the ground and others hung high up in the trees across branches – some of those branches pierced straight through them. Body parts were strewn all over the floor in front of her and the level of bloodshed had dyed the long grass a deep red. She tried to think and recall her last memory. This place she sat in looked familiar: a large circular clearing among the trees. To her right a fallen tree reached its branches up towards the light. The tree had been cut down at the base of its trunk, and yet remained alive having rooted from underneath and its new branches were lush with foliage, growing on top and across. On closer inspection, there appeared to be a bare area on the log stained a deep red.

Her gaze lifted towards the forest treeline to the sight of someone heading towards her. They walked among the corpses in a slow and relaxed fashion. It was a naked man with very dark skin and particularly brilliant white eyes. She couldn't help but focus on his genitalia and remembered that people seldom exposed themselves in such a way. He moved closer, unhurried, until he stood next to her.

'Hello, Judith.'

'Full stop, bring aft through thirty six degrees and hold position.'

'Aye, full stop, rotating now, Admiral.'

'Drop the pod. I need eyes on the blade.'

'Counting five enemy vessels, Admiral.'

Admiral Yevonichka paused to consider her options. 'Partial power down, let's wait for the feed.'

The bridge lights dipped to a virtual blackout, apart from the control consoles which remained painfully bright with focus.

She felt anxiety creep up on her at the thought of war and essentially being part of the process that would eventually lead to conflict. She held numerous questions in her mind and felt that many secrets and lies had been inadvertently exposed via the incestuous behaviour of the two great companies. With all their posturing and debating, the standoff was both confused and precarious. As things were, it would take a little while longer for both sides to cease their long-term cooperation and begin the process of becoming adversaries.

The console next to her winked and lit up in a bright beacon within the darkness of the bridge. She entered her code on the screen.

'IMC Update . . . Admiral Yevonichka, Captain Strauss . . . Proceed to co-ordinates instructed . . . abandon Class G prototype . . . seek assistance from Prospect Division immediately.'

Yevonichka had been given instructions to rendezvous at a place previously unknown to her or anyone else within the IMC standard fleet; or at least she had to classify one as standard now that the other had been revealed to her. The whole idea of the Prospect Division troubled her greatly as the whole façade of the IMC as one transparent entity had been rudely pulled from beneath her and left her reeling in confusion.

'Pod is in place and transmitting at optimum range, Admiral.'

Yevonichka nodded and waited. 'Keep an eye on the GSA ships, Commander.'

There was no reply and she looked towards the man standing over a large flat table keying in various commands on an interface screen.

'Commander Tarrick, are you listening?' she enquired.

His face lifted in the gloom and the light from the table partially lit his features. 'Sorry Admiral, I'm trying to figure out this image. It's meant to be the blade, yet its proportions have changed. Mass, length etc . . . all confirmed except . . .' He held his chin in thought then swept a hand through his hair as his mind finally processed the sight. 'My God,' he whispered.

Admiral Yevonichka moved to the table situated at the centre of the bridge. 'Bring that up on monitor, please.'

A large screen fixed high above and at the front of the room revealed a black shadow against the lighter shade of the system's sun. Its surfaces were featureless and appeared deceptive when trying to discern any texture on its exposed plane.

'Is that . . .?' Commander Tarrick asked, seeking an answer he already knew. He pulled himself together even though a deep-seated fear and awe rose within him.

'Quite a measured shape, a deft sleek rhomboid, perfect in all proportions. I'm not sure . . .' he continued and tailed off as he stared at the shape.

Yevonichka stood in thought for a moment, keying into her console for a comparison from historical data regarding God's Blade. There had at some point been a massive transformation from what had once been a rugged splinter to a now perfect and symmetrical shape. She reached to her left for another console. 'Captain, how go the preparations?'

'We should be able to begin the retrieval soon enough. The amalgam struts have been re-tested and are functional as intended,' Captain Strauss replied.

'Unfortunately I don't think there'll be a chance to test the combination,' Yevonichka stated. 'Run a diagnostic of the blanket systems, make sure the field is operational. We have a GSA shoal monitoring the system. Oh, and Captain, check the deck monitor, I want your opinion on this.'

There was a moment's silence as Yevonichka surveyed the bridge officers in the dim light. They were looking at her in silence, perhaps in anticipation of some revelation regarding the new find.

'My recommendation is that we head for Tumbolees now. We're not in a position to gawp at this, we're abysmally outgunned.'

'Agreed, Captain,' Yevonichka replied. 'Commander, return power to all systems, take us to the iron ball.'

'Admiral, I don't understand, why Tumbolees?'

Yevonichka couldn't really answer the question yet and remained silent. In all her years of service it had never crossed her mind that the IMC would split into two divisions and that the real power, the true fleet, existed near a large planetoid way above the solar system and beyond the knowledge of much of the company.

In many ways it made sense, after all the GSA and the IMC had become far more entwined on many levels over the past few decades and it had become difficult to know exactly how the two sides would become distinguishable from each other if the hammer should strike. She'd been assured that the Prospect Division was the uncorrupted true colour of the company, that which the real IMC had become.

Fanatical was the word Ologun chose to sum up the level of dedication these soldiers had to their cause. In one respect he'd have expected them to see sense as they'd been shown on enough occasions that they just couldn't win. His attempt at diplomacy when trying to acquire his new vehicle appeared to have worked at first and the soldiers held back from engaging in hostilities. He had walked over to their camp in the full expectation that these men would allow him to choose one of their trucks so that he could be on his way without incident. *Sneaky and defiant!*

Why not? he thought and smiled to himself over the incident. Their trap had catapulted him off his feet and thrown him into an ancient domestic grocery cart on wheels. He rolled at speed down an inclined path before being flipped on to his head and into a boggy ditch at the bottom.

The truck he'd taken from the soldiers had broken down a few miles short of the old city on yet another valley of thick sward. It had taken too many hits from various weapons which had ruined one of its main drivers. At least it had taken him a further eighteen miles and with much more speed than he was capable of. *Time and motion!*

The so-called enemy were not willing to cooperate and it concerned him more now that he'd finally made it to their strongest position. He was convinced they would execute an order which would force his hand with bloody consequence, and there would be no way to avoid it. He closed his eyes and listened. It was hard to focus with such acute sensory overload and needed time to concentrate. *Such energies!* The star lens above quivered with heat as it held back the full power of the sun's solar radiation. The surrounding noises were hard to single out and distinguish between. Insects such as crickets rubbed their hind legs. Some of the bugs cleaned their faces and bodies, while others chewed at the vegetation with the distinct resonance of continuous munching. Birds, deer, squirrels, lizards, hedgehogs, termites, cockroaches, ants and too many other life forms flooded his mind with activity. The sky-tram network above buzzed with power through cables and the various mechanised boxes which controlled the directions of the trams and transformed the levels of power throughout junctions. He could hear water being pumped along thick irrigation pipes hung lower down from the same framework and which leaked and dripped so that the droplets warbled strangely as they fell towards the ground.

He opened his eyes to return his senses to a preferred equilibrium as the mass of activity was far too difficult to absorb. The noise couldn't be visualised as a form of sonar as he wished and had to be identified through imagination – guesswork. His eyes scanned the city ahead as listening had given him no further information.

He moved in closer, lay down flat on the crest of a tall embankment, and used a sensible level of surveillance and deduction to decide his next course of action. The buildings closest to him were grand with an elaborate architecture, giving them the aesthetic of a subtle contemporary Gothic. They were still composed of concrete and were the same dull grey as other structures within the outpost, yet the surfaces had been sculpted with an artistic flair to their many decorations. The most flamboyant had magnificent designs with wide steps which led to large rows of wooden doors and where splendid canopies made of stone shaded their entrance. There were shelves beneath empty window frames between each level of the buildings where statues of animals and even sculptures of planets sat at intervals across the ledges. From his position, he saw the wide streets glistened with a thin layer of moisture. These avenues were a strange mixture of concrete slabs and an encroaching nursery ground for young tree saplings that led the way into the distance and towards the basin's north wall, and to something else of extreme interest. He stared at the scene of nature which had taken hold along the way and marvelled at how it had no consideration for anything manmade. In some ways it felt like some merciless invasion had filled him with an unusual sense of being somewhat exultant. The young sprouts had just managed to grow from the rubbish of vegetation which had collected in neat mounds on pavements and across boulevards. He studied and followed the complexity of roots which reached across and eventually became indistinguishable through the amalgam of green. *Humans,* he realised, *would never have been allowed to stay here if they hadn't offered such gifts to 'them'.* The riches of Earth, he assumed, would be allowed to grow and the chamber would eventually expand to accommodate one of the more complex levels of natural evolution in this galaxy. They would pay tribute to this one particular offering and they would extract and develop more life from the bio-library kept at the fortress; and, more importantly, they would have it all to marvel at in their own curious way. Plasma concrete was tough and just by acknowledging the power of nature as it grew directly out the tops of concrete walls and upwards across the faces of buildings, he felt that he knew what 'they' were trying to achieve. Given more time, the city would become lost within the invading force and would simply be utilized as a prop to reach the light. The more dead plant matter that collected upon the solid surfaces on the completion of each season, the more ground the city would lose from the invitation provided by the enriched compost. He was beginning to understand that his creators needed to understand that which was alien to them and needed to understand nature as a struggle; as a nonstop competition of use and conflict that they hadn't evolved against, or ever had to endure; until, that is, their existence took a dramatic change for the worse. For a moment he questioned what he really knew of it, and of them.

He ran across the last stretch of the basin's parkland and climbed one of the buildings towering amongst the city's outskirts and crouched down low. From the embankment where he'd just camped, the city looked like a dense wall of grey which bowed around in a concave row of tight-knit buildings. This new angle from above was peculiar: the depth of buildings stretched around the basin's northern wall in a long crescent which worked its way east and west for many miles. In the distance and at the centre of the city he could see movement: a shadow that could be blue or green. Whatever it was quickly disappeared under the cover of buildings. He scanned the area further to his left where, in between the gaps of taller buildings, a number of tall monuments came into view. It looked to be a marketplace where the street was much wider than many of the others. The enormous square patch of grassland at its centre, perhaps a lawn in its former state, was surrounded by decorative metal statues. In the middle of the lawn, a vast terrace made of stone was cluttered with the green impressions of benches, tables and chairs which had been overcome by the ever-present vines and ivy. The information came to him as quickly as his eyes moved; the signs, the street names. Haley's Square leading to Haley's Boulevard. A familiar name cropped up among the statues on an Ely Rajendra memorial plaque.

The scene was pleasant enough, perhaps a touch haunting if it weren't for the abundance of sauntering wildlife. He watched with yet more curiosity as a few deer grazed on shrubs growing through the concrete floor, while a variety of lizards ran a few yards, stopped, then darted off again across the streets and up walls. *They hold their breath to run!* He watched the larger ones with curiosity as they moved around the street. If there'd been more time he'd have been happy to sit and observe this strange unification of wildlife which truly didn't belong together in such a contrived environment. He continued to watch as a squirrel darted across the way and directly into the path of a particularly large reptile. The two creatures stopped just shy of collision so that a bizarre standoff ensued. The lizard held its ground while the squirrel, now both annoyed and inquisitive, bounced around for a moment, then continued on its journey up and on to one of the buildings.

His focus shifted towards a number of soldiers moving across the tops of buildings towards a junction at the end of Haley's Boulevard. The enemy soldiers looked like grey plastic toys at this distance as they hurried into position to face the row of buildings ahead of them. Their level of movement indicated that the soldiers had found something, prompting him to make his way towards them. He took a running jump to the next building, leaping with power and an inhuman agility. His acrobatics allowed for a quick journey over the flat tops of tall buildings, on to balcony ledges, then on to towers with tiled cone-shaped roofs where he swung on their spires before moving on. There was one building which the vegetation had taken a particular liking to; the thick green foliage had crept up its walls and along the roof and the building now wore a complete coat of green, patterned with the spotted whites of large flowers in full bloom.

He landed on its surface and hid in the cover provided. Immediately, a swarm of angry wasps badgered him and attempted to sting him in retribution for disturbing their nest. He crept across the roof through the entanglement and closer to the building's anterior ledge to spy on the soldiers now camped along the front row of some lower flat-roofed buildings ahead. They were mainly snipers and lookouts lying chest down, facing what appeared to be a town hall with a large clock above its entrance. The building was grand and very wide, with a long row of windows at ground level and double-glass doorways at its centre which were still intact and in fair condition, although derelict and grubby. His mind worked over the situation and he couldn't understand why they were still here when they'd already gathered that which they'd come for. Looking behind and through the full length of Haley's Boulevard, he appreciated the level of thought and ingenuity that had been invested into the street's design. Stone bridges led up and over dry canals, now filled with more thick vegetation which crept out and along the ground. Many walkways led through wild gardens and elevated platforms of concrete which combined into a bizarre pattern in the distance until he could see the north wall. He was mesmerised by that same something he saw earlier, and which continued to shimmer a brilliant neon green; *beautiful*. He'd never seen such a thing before in his life and studied its strange surface of highly charged energy, feeling its existence with even more bewilderment.

His vision zoomed in to scrutinize the next and hopefully final part of his journey. Against the towering black marble of the north wall and in front of the pillar of light, a long line of tanks sat at intervals amongst battlements on a very wide and quite tall barricade of dull metal. Turrets of varying kinds swivelled and probed the streets and buildings ahead. He grew anxious at the sight and began to work through options and scenarios. *Time and motion*, he thought over and over; something about the location was troubling and beyond the issue of this invading force.

The civilians he'd been trying to help could be taken to the colony without any need for him to bother with any of this; at least it was safer for them and he needn't risk killing anyone in the process. He returned his attention towards the soldiers and surveyed them as they kept watch and decided it was time to move.

The soldier kept his scope fixed against the tall hulk of a man, exhaled and slowly squeezed the trigger. His finger stopped when he lost sight through the scope as something moved in front, blocking the view. He felt the back of his armour being pulled, then quickly found himself held by the scruff of his collar and face to face with the man he'd met earlier. 'Hello Darren,' he said quietly. 'You beat me here after all!'

He ripped Darren's helmet and mask off and threw him on his backside.

'You! How'd ya know it was me?' he screeched in a strained whisper as though ready to have a panic attack. He glanced to his side to find his spotter laid out cold on the floor and began taking deep anxious breaths.

'I'd know that stench anywhere, Darren. What are you doing here exactly? I can only guess you're up to no good. At least you led me to them, they're in that building over there I take it?' he said, flicking his head towards the town hall buildings.

He looked around him in a deliberately slow fashion over towards the other soldiers who were targeting him across the full width of the surrounding buildings. Keeping a tight hold of Darren, he turned to observe the situation over and across the thin copse which used to be a wide street, and towards two men standing chatting outside the town hall's entrance. One he recognised from the Minx Machine bar as Judith's ex-boyfriend, Trent.

Darren sat and stared in silence as Ologun knelt close to him. 'You still have orders to eliminate all witnesses, Darren, is that why you were about to shoot them?'

'No, er,' Darren flustered, 'no orders mate, just game practice, er . . .' He hushed, realising he may have said the wrong thing.

Practice! Ologun scowled at Darren and swung one of his cleavers so that it rested under his chin. 'You're a nasty little man, Darren. You promised me you wouldn't shoot me and you shot at my arse. I spared you because I'm a nice person, Darren. Do you think I was too soft? Do you think I should gut you and your comrades here and now, all because I've been too soft, Darren?'

Darren crawled backwards a little, his eyes wide with terror. 'I, I don't know, we just follow orders, mate.'

Ologun jumped on him and pressed the blade to his throat. The other soldiers fired their silenced rifles with accuracy and the rounds hit his face and torso. 'You just said you were practising, that there are no orders, Darren. What's it to be, Darren, eh?'

The whining in Ologun's head began again and interrupted his train of thought. 'What do you want?'

'What do you mean?' Darren asked.

'Shut up. What? . . . Really? . . . Why, what is he? . . . Prospect?'

Darren thought Ologun was possessed as he ranted to himself; and, seeing the opportunity, he began to crawl away.

Ologun grabbed Darren by the collar. 'I think we should kill them all, Ray, they're all cowardly butchers. What? Oh that's low, Ray, really low.'

'Wait, wait. Bleeding nuggets of crust, mate.' Darren whispered as Ologun grabbed hold of him, held up his hand and waved it to signal his colleagues to hold their fire. 'What do ya want?' His voice was strained.

'I've been told, for whatever reason, that you're to go to your commanding officer. I want you to tell them that you're all to wait peacefully until you're disarmed. Congratulations, you're all to be forced into retirement and live out your days in paradise.'

Darren spat a whispering laugh. 'Yeah, whatever, mate.'

Ologun heard the defiance in the man's voice and gazed towards the defensive grid at the north wall. His eyes narrowed and he thought quickly about his next move. He imagined killing every one of them without mercy, regardless of Ray's intervention. He glared at Darren for a moment, then his eyes softened as he thought better of it. 'Just go and tell your commanders or captains or whoever, that I want to talk to them. Tell him or her that I have something to offer as sort of a compromise to your quest.'

Darren shrugged and grinned, mocking this generous offer, which triggered Ologun into grabbing his arm and crushing the armour with a grip that clearly hurt. Darren stared without listening to Ologun as he spoke with venom; he was entirely distracted by a wasp crawling out from under Ologun's thick black hair. The insect spread its wings then launched directly at him as though it had premeditated the attack, stinging him on his right eyelid. He tried to scream but was suppressed by Ologun's palm which clasped tightly across his mouth.

Ologun checked that the two men over the road were still oblivious to their presence. 'Just tell your commanding officer that they can do as they like when I arrive and I expect the courtesy of a chat, okay, Fat-Chance?'

Darren nodded. His face was pale and his eye was red and swollen and seeping quite a lot of fluid. He reached over and pressed a small button on his armour's collar. 'Checkpoint Tango, this is High-Chance.'

'Receiving. Go ahead.'

'I think we need to retreat, now,' Darren stated.

Ologun nodded and kept eye contact with him.

'Roger that. Hostile has been marked as a non-viable target. What is your status?'

'Said hostile wants to propose terms of surrender,' Darren replied, not quite able to believe what he was saying.

'Cease all activities and return to base.'

Darren gathered his kit and left without fuss, followed by the other soldiers, and they moved efficiently to the rear side of the building before clunking their way downwards to negotiate the metal grid work of the fire exit stairwell. *What is to be judged of such people?* The two realities smashed through his mind at a meteoric rate. Such a terrible thing overshadowed this scenario, which was so minute in comparison to that which lay further ahead; yet still the here and now weighed on him. It had been bad enough that the craft had been so vicious despite seeming so innocent at times. So many dead soldiers along the way but, amazingly, these men were still unwilling to see sense or even stop to imagine that possibly a far greater horror awaited them. Somehow he'd gathered that, to these soldiers, death and killing were like eating and sleeping; they had no concept of it being wrong at all.

The soldier, Darren, had shown some signs of fear, but had then switched into nonchalance without any regard that what he said and did may get him killed. Conditioned and well trained would be the only answer to such a brazen attitude; it had thus far kept them going against an obviously unstoppable force. *Have the soldiers even thought about the desperate hurt and sadness of killing and burning the bodies of innocent people?* Piles of them were smouldering around the northern shore of the lake right now. The thought of it was enough for him to seek a terrible vengeance; he was amazed that he'd managed to restrain himself at all.

He jumped down from the building to approach Trent and the other man. Ologun hadn't noticed before that the very dark-skinned man with Trent was humongous in stature: an intimidating seven feet of solid build. Ologun moved quickly and silently across the street checking his surroundings, until he stood next to the two men who were oblivious to his presence. 'You two must be the worst soldiers I ever did set eyes on.'

Trent and the other man lifted their rifles. 'Halt.'

'Take it easy, it's me, Ologun. Remember? From the bar?'

Trent lowered his weapon and the other man did the same. 'Emissary Jowett.' He nodded to Ologun. 'Colonel Aginie is waiting for you inside. This way.'

'The tourists and some marines have moved further north-west into the city, Logan,' the large man said in a very deep voice that carried and rumbled across the street. 'Can I just ask a question, if you beg my pardon?'

Ologun had no idea what these men were talking about and tilted his head in curiosity. *Emissary?* he wondered. 'What's your name?' he eventually asked the man.

'Buffer,' he replied.

'What's the question?'

'Has the Spectra left us to die? We haven't had any assistance at all, I don't understand.'

Ologun chose not to answer as any response would have been contrived. He had no knowledge of the Spectra at all. And then, as if the penny had dropped, he said, 'Take me to this colonel and we shall see what's at fault here.'

Trent nodded to Buffer, and Ologun entered the building. He walked into a reception area of wooden counters, then through more doors which emerged into a particularly wide and elongated hall with a high ceiling supporting a large and dirt-coated crystal chandelier at its centre. The wooden slat floors creaked underfoot as he approached a measly looking man who was relatively short and thin in stature.

Ologun passed by one of the side doors and noticed his own reflection in the glass. He hadn't realised how he looked to these men. His second skin of black hugged his torso and held his blades in place on his back. His hair stuck up on end in an elongated spiked mullet, and his eyes had turned an emerald green; he'd become positively feral. 'I'm looking for Captain Sharplin,' he declared.

Colonel Aginie's eyes narrowed at this. 'I'm at a loss as to what he has to do with this. Time is against us and we need the vessel in order to trespass. Do you have it?'

Ologun realised his lack of knowledge had in some part been his own fault. Searching for answers, he felt his second skin tighten as it became a conduit between something and himself that seemed to be waiting with the information. He began to drift from the present and towards the memory of the past, visions filling his mind.

He was already aware that there'd been an attack on the shard and that the mighty splinter, a small piece of something much larger, had drifted with the last remnants of life. The light had all but diminished when a large comet had collided into the great shard. Within this clump of rock and ice there existed an unusual and remarkable life form which had evolved in order to survive the vacuum. Against all odds, an opportunity had presented itself and, in both optimism and desperation, the Spectra set to work on the organisms. However, all attempts to hijack this life form's gift at survival proved difficult; something was missing.

More time passed and the light dimmed further. When all avenues to save themselves had been exhausted and the inevitable had been accepted, something else changed their fate. Across the void, a tiny shoal of unusual objects approached. They had assumed at first that the enemy had found them, yet upon closer inspection the twelve vessels belonged to something else entirely. With the sentient being close to death they took the shard and followed, eventually intercepting the craft, and found that the small shoal had led them to a planet rich with life. The values of risk, chance and that of reward were concepts which they'd never considered, except they would learn such traits from observing this species now under scrutiny. Disturbingly, there were many similarities between these creatures and the enemy, so much so it defied all probability to such a degree that all plausible reasons were explored; a connection could not be found.

Ologun realised he had leapt to a great conclusion; an assumption caused by his own ignorance. What he was and what his role in all of this had initially been were both far more important and yet, to him, strangely more mundane than he realised. He pushed for more information, realising that even though Ray had uploaded much information into his mind on their first meeting, much of it was either vague or distorted, almost as if he'd been purposefully led to fill in the blanks with assumptions. It now dawned on Ologun that it was like reading the horoscopes and applying meaning to utter nonsense. *But why?* It was time to wise up. His mind drifted and the dimness of the vast hall filled with static, then its walls fell away.

The city and the forests faded until he now existed within the vast emptiness of the basin. To his left the blackness of the north wall towered high, and above its lip the constellation of stars shone down into the naked chasm. The basin's floor was smooth and concave, yet had an unnatural texture which refused to reflect the gleam of the universe above. His mind searched and his vision drifted quickly towards the centre of the basin, and the motionless ship above it.

Sitting on the basin's floor before him was a small waiting vessel, and people nearby wandered and explored the area. They bounded here and there in the low gravity and appeared cumbersome in their puffy suits and airtight helmets which protected them from the vacuum. Movement caught Ologun's mind, and in turn the men in spacesuits gazed at the light. It moved directly before them, up through the floor and from a small cavity until it became similar to a human form; a creature of liquid light which rippled and flickered.

The humans ran to their craft and immediately evacuated; the obvious reaction for those with any wit about them. An unusual set of events followed. The great ship above repeatedly launched its most terrible weapons and the vast basin filled to the brim with nuclear fire. Ologun's mind flinched at the brightness, the power, and looked to move on beyond this savage reaction. Later, when the basin had returned to black, someone returned to the basin alone. The figure of light returned. 'Thank you,' it said. Contact began in a slow and drawn-out mode. The being of light, the Spectra, as the humans had by now called it, asked for more fire. Yet humanity is seldom altruistic at the best of times and was cautious of any being which could drink the flames from one of their most destructive weapons. The Spectra offered terms knowing that humanity could transform the minerals found buried deep within a planet's crust.

'The planet in this system is of little use to you unless you wish to devolve many millennia and back to that which you once were,' it said.

The Spectra realised it wasn't enough to simply offer up the metal ore alone, for humans were in their element in extracting such a find. However, the Spectra knew it could barter with something else. 'If you trespass you will die, and you do not have the time nor ability to immunise yourself against the life that has earned its right through evolution to be there. If compatible planets to your own make-up are your desire, more can be located. We can find them for you.'

Ologun stood in this virtual memory and walked forward to take a closer look at the one sent alone to act as ambassador for humanity. His mind swam with more realisations when he found that behind the glass of the visor there was a face he recognised. He was younger and his eyes were brighter than he remembered, but there was no doubt that it was definitely the face of his father.

He processed this as best he could and concluded a number of things. The negotiations continued and all was done in great haste. He was to be the vessel sent with the data; the immunisation against all biological threats, specifically the alien bacterial and viral elements that would surely kill any human invasion. Ologun had been developed with extensive use of the human specimens found within that original shoal and eventually he had been sent to Earth. In secret he was to be received by the newly formed Prospect Division of the IMC, yet the Spectra wasn't interested in the nature of humans as they kept their secrets and began to horde the spoils of their find from the rest of humankind. With the speedy and miraculous capability of developing inoculations against Deceiver's micro-organisms, the IMC grew ever more powerful. They built their technology and mined the planet for its valuable resources, history casting some light on this whole saga. Yet the more he learned, the more questions he had; there had been some unexpected developments along the way, not least regarding his role in this: was it now over or yet to begin?

His mind returned to the hall and its dank dimness. He crouched against a wall and found that Colonel Dennis Aginie had been talking to him this whole time.

'Where's Sharplin?' Ologun asked, ignoring Dennis's constant barrage of words.

'We need the one assigned for Prospect now,' Dennis insisted. 'We may not need it yet, but it was part of the deal.'

'That which has been promised will be delivered,' Ologun offered and took one more glimpse into memory, deep within a mind of some kind, and began to realise something else was here in the basin acting as some avatar for the Spectra. It appeared that more negotiations had taken place in recent times and all that had happened since his re-animation from the deep freeze had occurred because of it.

The Rising! Ologun needed to see Sharplin, a more domestic issue perhaps, and yet he felt that one more kind deed was in order before returning to the business at hand. He paused, wondering what the hell he was doing running around the basin like this in the first place. *Ray,* Ologun mused. He was serving hard lessons. Hina and also someone else, he couldn't tell who had planned and served a hard lesson; the simplest lesson Ologun had never grasped his whole life and one his father had also grown tired of trying to instil. *A test!* Ologun remembered that he'd failed a test before. *Christ!* Memories lost, and even taken from him, were coming back in waves and he trembled at the knowledge of just what a wasted mess of a life he had lived.

Okay, Ologun thought, *I get it now. Take your time and look before you leap. You came back again this time and the epiphany is that you're an arsehole, a narcissistic selfish arsehole. So then,* Ologun concluded, *there appears to be no urgent need to worry about the safety of the tourists at the hands of the hostile force at the basin's north wall.* 'Take me to Sharplin now,' he ordered Aginie.

'If you insist,' Dennis said and led the way through the hall to a rear passage which opened into the rear of the building. They took the stairs to the next level and on to a landing with corridors leading off in opposite directions.

'This way,' Dennis offered with a hand gesture as they reached the landing. Ologun nodded courteously then turned to see that Trent was close behind him as he emerged from the top of the stairwell. 'You don't have to molest me, Trent.'

A sheepish look washed over Trent's face and Dennis hurried to midway down the corridor and knocked on one of the wooden doors.

The corridor had an even stronger smell of damp and dust, and the floor was covered in a cerulean blue carpet stained with dark oily patches. The walls dripped with moisture from underneath a mass of cobwebs on the sheen of glossy grey concrete. The door opened and Doctor Siren stepped out. 'Ologun! Well, I can't say I'm that surprised to see you alive, where have you been?'

'Doctor.' Ologun nodded majestically. 'I need to see Sharplin if I may.'

Doctor Siren looked pale and very tired, but her eyes lit up with energy when she scanned Ologun from head to foot. 'You'd better come in,' she said unable to find the question that would provide answers to what he was wearing, and she felt even more perturbed as he entered the room with his back to her. His cleavers were bound by small straps to his suit of skin so that the crystal handles jutted up and above each shoulder and the blades themselves faced inwards, crossing over between his shoulder blades. The doctor glanced at Dennis and he shrugged, offering no explanation.

Ologun scanned the dimly lit room then looked at the frail man sitting on a grotty camp bed to his right. He was hunched over the side of the bed with his face in his hands and his elbows resting on his knees. He looked up, brushing his hands through thick silver hair.

'Ologun! Ologun!' He jumped up and launched at Ologun, grabbing his arm. 'We have to mobilise, the angels are waiting to take us, they're going to save us.' His eyes were wild and bloodshot and he appeared fragile in his dirty vest with his thin arms and torso trembling as though a dog standing in cold rain.

Ologun stood still, half listening. He understood what Sharplin meant by angels and could see the confusion that had occurred. He was, however, more interested in something else; a level of activity in Frank's brain which became a vivid display of energy that only he was aware of. He could see the thoughts and commands as eruptions of chaotic bursts whilst everyone else in the room had a more streamlined rhythm of structured waves and pulses sustaining the mental loop of mostly subconscious processing.

'What's wrong, Frank?' he asked.

'He's in some sort of deep shock, suffering from a nervous breakdown. I'm not sure yet,' Doctor Siren intervened, placing a blanket around Frank's shoulders.

Trent and Buffer stood at the doorway. 'Still mad I see,' Trent scoffed.

Buffer nudged him in the ribs with an elbow that clearly hurt. 'Show some respect, man.'

Ologun thought he knew what was wrong with Sharplin and quickly grabbed him by the top of his skull. A few threads on the sleeves of his second skin untangled like silk, barely visible to the naked eye. These threads then snaked the distance between Ologun and Sharplin and penetrated the skin on Sharplin's neck. Ologun then found himself linked to Sharplin, perhaps interfacing in some fashion; his own mind adrift in the chaos of the other man's bizarre thoughts.

'What are you doing?' Rita asked. She felt protective and placed a hand on Ologun's shoulder.

'I'm helping him,' Ologun stated and looked to Rita's hand to be removed. 'Give me some space, please,' he said softly.

Ologun returned his focus and fought to rein it all in. He soon found within Sharplin's mind the seeds which had caused the problem and looked at Dennis in disgust. The memories passed by quickly and with intensity. He saw a young, headstrong girl with long, thick black hair and bright blue eyes. She was in the midst of a party; she would leave the next day. The next image was of her departure, a happy time full of excitement and she was full of pride; she was setting off for the ship, the *IMC Rising*. Ologun felt the emotion, a deep and terrible despair which reminded him of something, except Ologun was more selfish and bitter about his own not too dissimilar experiences. Love, selfless and pure, was an alien concept to Ologun, who became overwhelmed to the point he had to steady himself at such a new and irrational concept. Grave and terrible were the next set of feelings as the memories moved on. Grief, despair, loss and guilt invaded Ologun's mind. Again these feelings were strange to him in that they were real and yet they were very deep and far more destructive, causing him to push on with difficulty. *Sharplin should be angry and bitter*, Ologun thought and wondered which out of the two of them was the better person. Arguments and blame and a time of ritual were pushed to the fore in Sharplin's mind, along with a more intrusive outside force.

Sharplin was now laid flat on the mattress and writhed in agony. He screamed aloud and violently convulsed.

'What are you doing to him? You're hurting him!' Doctor Siren cried. 'Someone stop this, please,' she said, looking at the others.

Dennis smirked at the proceedings and left the room in a hurry. *I can't stay for this!*

Buffer moved in and placed Ologun in a neck lock. He used all his strength to pull Ologun away from Sharplin. There was a look of complete surprise on his face as he struggled with the completely immovable object which appeared to be a man but was more akin to a statue of heavy stone.

Sharplin howled in agony and Trent lifted his rifle. 'Move.' Buffer leapt out of the way so that he could fire.

'Wait,' Doctor Siren shouted as Ologun released his hold on Sharplin and simply knelt in thought.

'Frank, can you hear me?' Doctor Siren asked. She readjusted the sling holding her left arm against her body and reached over to feel Sharplin's pulse.

At first the man was quiet and his eyes were closed. Then he stirred. He sat up straight and his eyes flickered open. The room held silent with bated breath to see what had happened; to see what Ologun had done. Then Sharplin's face contorted and his eyes flooded with tears which flowed heavily down his cheeks.

Buffer backed up against a wall and made the sign of a crucifix across his chest. 'Oh lord, the man's only gone and made him cry!'

'Talk to me, Frank,' Rita insisted and gripped his right arm firmly. He was oblivious to her presence and spoke to Ologun. 'She lives? You will take me to her . . . soon?' His face lit up in delight. 'I'm a grandfather!' Then his face became confused. 'Judith too? I don't understand how . . .'

'Rest now. In time you will see your daughter,' Ologun said.

'What about Judith?' Sharplin asked again.

'I'm sure you'll get the chance to see her as well. Don't worry about such things and rest if you can,' Ologun said, rising from his crouched position.

Frank appeared to be satisfied and lay back down on the bed. Doctor Siren covered him with a blanket then turned her attention to Ologun. 'What in God's name is going on here?' she asked forcefully, although careful with the volume of her voice.

Ologun stared at her for a moment as she waited for a reply. 'I have to go now, Doctor.'

He left the room to see Dennis still loitering in the corridor. 'Those soldiers who invaded this outpost are a little more void of emotion than even I would expect. Is it the same process, the same level of control you applied to Sharplin?'

'I don't know what you mean,' Dennis said in denial.

'Cut the crap, Dennis. You used that device, that server chip attached to his system against him. Why not let him do as he wanted? When you delivered me to this place, his every instinct told him to incarcerate me and yet you took away his free will, his ability to choose, however such things work. You brought him so much closer to breaking point, don't you see that?'

'Or what, have him alert the IMC to your existence? Besides, who is he to deal with the emissary to the Spectra?'

'You and I are the scum, aren't we Dennis? If I had half the capacity for love and affection that man has . . . well, I suppose it takes all sorts, and I learned something today, Dennis.'

'Is that so?' Dennis replied.

Version

'What's this about?' Doctor Siren interrupted. She stood in the doorway to the room with Trent and Buffer looking over her shoulders.

'I was just telling Dennis how twisted and evil he and I are, Doctor.' Ologun regarded Rita Siren as though he knew some other terrible secret. 'And you too.'

He gave Dennis and Doctor Siren one last look of contempt, then left them where they stood. They didn't see him leave; it was as though he simply vanished before their eyes.

DARK SEVEN

The ship searched for the Prospect fleet and continued its orbit above Tumbolees. Admiral Yevonichka sat in silence for a while, feeling her faith in the situation deteriorate. She leaned over to use an intercom system to her right. 'Captain Strauss, could you meet me in the conference room immediately?' Yevonichka turned her attention to Commander Tarrick, who was still deep in thought and dividing his time between searching for the Prospect fleet and studying God's Blade. 'Commander Tarrick, I'd also like to see you.'

Yevonichka sat on a long grey couch opposite the captain and commander. It was perhaps a little too relaxed for the discussion at hand, yet the conference room remained one of the most private locations aboard for what the admiral had to say.

'What I am about to tell you is classed as protected material issued by Director Styles of Command,' she said. Her face was grave and the two officers grew uncomfortable. 'This ship, the *Dark Seven*, as you know is a prototype for the new shield system. The *Hollywood*, her sister ship has the gravic drive system.' Admiral Yevonichka cleared her throat and looked at the face of Captain Strauss. It seemed to her that Strauss already had some idea of the situation. 'As you are aware, Captain, the *Hollywood* and the *Seven* were to be combined as one ship to be commissioned as the *Pariah*. However, in recent days, Styles saw fit to enclose a full dossier regarding the Prospect Division and it appears that these ships are not prototypes at all. The future launch of the *Pariah* after full testing of its two important separate components was, in fact, a ruse.'

The room fell silent for a few moments while Commander Tarrick looked out of a large rectangular digital lens to his left. The strange landscape of Tumbolees was reflected weakly in the distant light of the sun as the *Dark Seven* moved towards the planet's south pole. The planet was predominantly stark grey with ice and had many patches of black where rock formations jutted from its surface like billions of towering needles reaching for the sky. 'Prospect Division are the IMC in what form exactly?' he asked.

'The Division is a safeguard against any possible contamination,' Yevonichka confirmed.

'Interesting use of language,' Commander Tarrick said with a slight grin. 'All these years spent safeguarding against the GSA and it turns out we're being safeguarded against ourselves. You think the company is that far gone?'

'I think that IMC command is just as likely to be absorbed as it is to fight. This mission is meant for us to seek out the IMC's remaining assets and draw them back. According to Director Styles, the IMC has spent too much time and effort out here lately and its assistance is urgently required.'

'This con with the *Hollywood*, what exactly was it meant to achieve?' Captain Strauss asked. Tarrick turned his gaze away from the planet below and leaned back in his chair. 'Let me take a stab in the dark here,' he said cynically. 'There are more ships, many more I'm guessing, that have both blankets and G-drives for position process capabilities. The IMC have had them ready for some time and has decided to publicise its achievements at long last, only it needs to do so as if it's a remarkable breakthrough, negating the fact that it already has an armada ready.'

'That's a good theory, but it's incomplete,' Yevonichka said.

'Then where's the division fleet and why are we on the verge of war?' Captain Strauss asked.

Yevonichka nodded as though she shared Strauss's need for answers. 'All this new technology has been ready for over thirty years at the hands of the Prospect Division. I'm not sure why the push is on for the GSA to go as far as to take such technology by force, if in fact that's what happened. My own thoughts are that they have no idea that a fleet exists and may be desperate not to be left behind at the news of a ship able to further contort the fabric of space.'

'Can the ship really travel so far without the need to move that much at all?' Strauss asked. 'From this location, for example, I hear it can reach Earth's system in only a few days.'

'I don't know,' Yevonichka answered without offering any further speculation. 'If it *is* true, the GSA will be eager to stop the company claiming anything else of great value. A ship which can cover such distances in such time and without the need for conventional movement poses a serious threat.'

'That makes sense,' Tarrick added. 'The next find could potentially change our very existence. It wouldn't take much for the IMC to completely fall away from Earth's jurisdiction all together and the *Hollywood* would have greatly increased the chance of this, except that the IMC, or rather the Prospect Division, have already been using this new system for a long time you say.'

Captain Strauss stood and paced the room to help her think. 'That's provided there are many compatible planets out there at all,' she argued. 'If we're on the brink of war over the theft of technology, isn't it a little premature considering there may be nothing for the ships to find?'

'The prize isn't necessarily a new home world,' Yevonichka intervened. 'We can't rule out such an event in the long term, although there are many locations rich in resource materials.'

'I don't think so,' Tarrick said. 'Tumbolees is rich in minerals, yet it remains untouched. We've already decided there's enough junk floating around out here to warrant that much has taken place here over the years. I'm thinking that wherever the fleet has gone, they've abandoned the IMC for something it regards far more important.'

'Then we're left with only our secondary objective,' Captain Strauss insisted.

'No,' Yevonichka objected, noting a look of dread on Commander Tarrick's face. 'You saw the shard and its new dimensions. For the time being the *Hollywood* is lost. I'm going to send a message that the PD fleet is gone and not responding to the coded hails. I think we should pull anchor and return to Phobos.'

'I recommend we go to Sleet,' Tarrick interjected. Ships need to be dispatched to analyse the shard and I'm going to report that it is most definitely alien in its activity.'

Version

Fear was apparent in the admiral's eyes, and both Captain Strauss and Commander Tarrick recognised the same unnerving aspect to all of this.

'Alien activity,' Yevonichka repeated. 'You report what you see fit, Commander. I cannot comment on this matter without more data. Are we all agreed upon Sleet?' she asked.

'There's nothing here and we'd do better to report our find,' Strauss said.

'Fine,' Yevonichka confirmed. 'We head for Sleet and send word.'

A low whistling sound came from a desk to the left of the admiral. 'All officers to the bridge immediately, contact confirmed and on approach.'

'On our way,' Yevonichka replied.

They rushed to the bridge, seeking a status report. Commander Tarrick moved to the pod table and checked it for details.

'Ensign Frow, sit-rep now,' Captain Strauss ordered.

'The surveillance pod has relayed a positive contact, yet I'm not sure how it's come to that conclusion,' the man said as he continued working feverishly at his workstation.

'It's not what the pod sees, it's what it doesn't see,' Tarrick clarified. 'The machine thinks there's an unusual distortion in the fabric and that it's headed on a course with a trajectory which will pass us by and take it directly to the shard. It should pass us in approximately twelve minutes.'

'Cut all power, I mean everything.' Yevonichka ordered in an unusually stern tone of voice. 'Let's do it now. Strap in, masks on and switch to internal servers.' She clapped her hands then did as she herself had ordered and put on a protective suit which had been folded in a drawer under her seat. All seven bridge staff, the captain and the commander did the same before putting their masks in place. The order for power down was sent throughout the entire ship and repeated several times over speakers. A little over a minute later and the bridge staff were ready for the blackout. In many respects, such a procedure was in place for when the ship lost power for long periods of time and Yevonichka hoped they wouldn't be in this situation long enough to require the suits' independent sources of oxygen or their protective insulation.

'All personnel locked in and ready, Admiral,' Commander Tarrick communicated via his server chip.

The already dimly lit room became darker until even the workstations were diminished of all power. Yevonichka watched the thermal representation of the bridge through her mask's visor. Debris comprising of loose objects floated around freely and she too felt the weightlessness take hold.

'Be advised, we are now twenty minutes before P.O.N.E. orbit,' Strauss projected.

Yevonichka grew anxious as the ship's orbit had begun to deteriorate towards Tumbolees' immense gravitational pull. 'Ensign Frow, make sure you punch out in exactly sixteen minutes, regardless of what happens.'

'Understood.'

'Objective is Sleet, calculate route for immediate sprint.'

'Evacuation course to outpost Sleet confirmed.'

'Admiral,' Tarrick interrupted, 'we have a few problems brewing here. My server chip says the sensory pod is measuring said disturbance as an outline of three miles by two miles by two thousand metres. It has quite a distinctive shape. It doesn't seem to have noticed us either and I think we blacked out in good time, there are five GSA contacts heading to intercept our position.'

'How long?' Yevonichka asked.

'Six minutes. If said object continues it will pass near to us soon. GSA are now directly in its path,' he replied.

The situation was monitored and the surveillance pod's use of energy restricted; it floated three quarters of a mile from the *Dark Seven* without the use of any propulsion.

Slowly the distortion moved to within a few miles of the ship and passed without incident. Yevonichka's attention turned towards the shoal still headed their way. 'Ensign Frow, get ready to punch out.'

'Wait,' Tarrick insisted. 'There's something happening.'

Yevonichka looked at the pod's system to see for herself, risking the distraction from her duty. The shoal of GSA ships approached the distortion, which had by now moved a great distance beyond the *Seven*. The shoal appeared as tiny objects even at full magnification, although the clarity and resolution were still good enough to grasp the situation. Suddenly there was a flash, and a massive burst of energy shot from the direction of the transparent object, destroying one of the GSA ships. In response, the remaining four opened fire. One by one the ships were engulfed by a powerful barrage which was enough to melt each ship to a cinder within seconds.

'Engaging reverse-mass drivers in five, four, three . . .'

'Cancel that, Ensign,' Yevonichka ordered, unable to decide which was worst of the two dangers.

'Ship now entering P.O.N.E., Admiral,' Frow informed.

Her mind remained fixed on the pod as it monitored the gulf beyond, and it appeared the object had gone and was hopefully out of range. 'Power up,' she ordered.

The bridge lit up and all masks were thrown aside just as all floating matter dropped to the floor as artificial gravity was restored. All personnel on the bridge slumped and fell as they scrambled to the control terminals. Yevonichka sat quietly as the staff went to work saving the ship; the *Seven* was now on the precipice before being caught in the immense gravitational pull of the planet and beyond the point of escape.

Captain Strauss tore off her gloves and worked on one of the consoles. The ship shuddered and its hull made obvious sounds of stress as it creaked and groaned.

'We're too far in,' Strauss shouted above the increasing volume as the ship continued her struggle.

'Ship is now two minutes from surface,' Frow advised.

'Divert everything to engines,' Yevonichka ordered.

'Contact just appeared on the starboard aft. They've hailed us,' Tarrick said.

'Put it through, quickly,' Yevonichka shouted.

'This is Captain Hunt of the PD ship *Rising*. Extend your amalgam joists immediately.'

'Twenty thousand feet.'

'Do it,' Yevonichka ordered and Strauss began the procedure. Moments later, loud clanging noises could be heard throughout the ship. Tarrick continued to watch the pod, which was now monitoring the *Seven* as it began to lose its battle with gravity. A ship, much smaller in size, had manoeuvred itself directly underneath the *Seven* and was now interlocking with the very same mechanism designed for the *Hollywood*. Their descent continued for a short while as Tarrick stared at the logistics table in disbelief. *Suicidal*, he thought of the *Rising's* attempts.

'Ten thousand feet until impact, nine thousand . . . eight thousand . . .'

'Shut up, Ensign,' Yevonichka screamed. His countdown to doom had hit a nerve.

Suddenly all communication with the pod was lost and the noise created by the ship as it twisted and spun towards the planet had ceased.

'Admiral Yevonichka.'

Yevonichka listened, then moved to the comms system by her chair. 'Captain?'

'We have now processed to three systems away. We are quite safe,' Hunt said.

'Are you of Prospect Division?' she asked hopefully.

'Yes, Admiral. We'll begin the journey now, it's the only option left to you,' Captain Hunt suggested.

'What's the ETA for Earth's system with your ship's ability to pierce the fabric?' she asked.

'Sorry, Admiral, we're not going in that direction. Sit tight and enjoy, I'll transfer to you in a while and brief you.'

'Captain,' she said in a raised voice as though the volume would catch him before he left the conversation.

'Yes, Admiral?'

'That was one hell of a weapon you released on the GSA shoal, I thought it was headed towards us at first, I had no idea of the level of optics you have at your disposal.'

There was a long drawn-out silence as Yevonichka watched the comms unit for a reply. 'That wasn't us, Admiral,' Captain Hunt said. His tone of voice had changed, perhaps seeming more concerned. 'I shall be over to discuss shortly.'

Yevonichka sat down in her chair and felt a strange sensation, a sort of vertigo, and could only assume that the *Rising* had used its gravic drivers again.

'Admiral?'

'What is it, Tarrick?'

'There's a new set of information being relayed to our computers from, well something odd in terms of its use of the system.'

'What does it say?' Yevonichka asked.

'A device calling itself Version no. 746 states that we are now en route to Prospect.'

VANGUARD

'Open wide. That's it, Two.'

The boy designated as Two sat on the bench shivering; his body ached and he felt terrible sharp pains along his limbs. *The crawling!*

'Oh dear, these suckers are nasty little parasites, but don't worry, you have a handle on it as always.'

Two watched as the man shone a powerful narrow beam of light into his eyes and mouth. He finished his observations, switched off the torch and activated the main lights. The man wearing a thick hazmat suit then moved to stand behind a long rectangular bench where he performed tasks that Two had no understanding of. 'I'll give it three days and we'll see about specimen 6553650, how does that sound?'

Two nodded, recognising the significance of the number. It was how many invasions he'd survived and destroyed over the past three years. Two couldn't tell whether the man was paying attention to him as the light in the cabin reflected heavily off the glass plate covering his face. He didn't know his number or name and he hadn't known any of the ones who'd visited. They'd poked and prodded and injected. They'd cut him open, drilled into him and held him down so that things could attach themselves or burrow inside him.

It was no consolation that he always survived, and it was no victory to have destroyed so many invasions. Viruses were mostly inert and he could sense an incompatibility to the majority placed in him. Bacteria had a more active role in causing mayhem – some of them ate at him from the inside and, regardless of being the creator of cures, the pain was often too much to bear. And then there were the rest of the micro horrors. Parasites were the worst of the bunch as they hid and moved and deceived and fed and decimated.

'I'll be back at 08:00 hours, Two, so I'll see you then for some more tests. You know it's New Year's Eve, 22:17 tomorrow.

Version

Beginning of Year Four on Vanguard. What do you think about that, Two?'

There was no reply from Two as the man made his way to the airlock door and pressed a few buttons on the keypad. The door hissed loudly and opened. The man walked into a small chamber to be sprayed with a thick liquid from head to foot, creating a green gel gloop on top of his yellow rubber ensemble. A few more minutes passed then he exited through a second door and was gone.

'Energy saving protocol activated.'

The hollow voice always followed in the same way and he braced himself for the darkness. The lights went out and Two continued to sit on the bench rocking back and forth in agony as the invasion designated 6553649 continued in its bid to devour him. His eyes adjusted to the darkness and he could see once again. The small cabin had been his prison for so long that he knew every piece of equipment. The tools and devices neatly placed on shelves and in cupboards were of no curiosity and yet he knew nothing of their purpose. Like an animal that had become accustomed to inanimate objects made by humans, his perception of his environment was of both indifference and ignorance.

In the beginning, those that had come had been friendly and appreciative and they would say things such as, 'You're an amazing asset to us here, Two,' and, 'You'll be saving a lot of lives, not to mention the lives of countless indigenous species here.'

Over time they said less and less. They were now indifferent to him, even though they caused such pain and suffering. His eyes shifted to the robotic arms attached to the wall next to him. They were stronger versions put there after he'd broken the last ones, and were thicker and stronger metal monsters created to hold him down when he couldn't take the pain any longer, or when he didn't want to have anything else put inside him.

Lately he'd felt different inside. The loneliness and agony had been so terrible that he had to get away, had to escape. He knew the codes to the hissing door and he knew a large corridor was behind the second door. Beyond that there was always someone sat in an office behind a desk watching the second door to the corridor.

He concentrated and achieved what he wanted with the parasites writhing inside him. *Done!* He'd succeeded in killing them all as he always did. The pain raging through his limbs dissipated and he stood up. He moved to his left towards the pull-down lavatory and lifted his gown. He sat and let the waste empty from his bowels.

Two stood up and turned to see the results. His faeces were in part the usual waste but mostly the remnants of the parasites: pale tubular worms with long sinewy spindles protruding from ridges along their bodies.

Satisfied, Two moved to the door and pressed the code on the key pad. The door hissed and opened sideways to reveal the spray chamber. He stepped in and waited as the spray guns covered him with the gloopy substance that stung his eyes and burned his skin. Once this had finished he typed the code for the second door. His heart was racing now and he was both terrified and excited. The corridor lay ahead as a strange and alien world, and towards the end on the right side was the pane of glass where there would be someone watching. Suddenly the door at the end of the corridor opened, revealing an overweight man with black hair and a moustache.

'Now what are you doing, buddy? You know you can't leave here.' His tone was patronising and condescending. 'Now turn around and go back inside, there's a good boy.'

The security man stood there wearing boots, shirt and trousers with no hazmat suit and Two realised that the man was a simpleton – he hadn't heard him call for any assistance. 'Turn around please.' The fat man walked towards Two and held his hand above what Two knew to be a gun at his waist. 'You need to go inside, now.'

Two felt the usual emotions of fear and loneliness turn to excitement and then into something else entirely. He was unfamiliar with this strange energetic feeling that was in fact anger and hatred filling him to the point where he felt much better, even powerful. 'Get inside now,' the man repeated, his voice raised.

Two leapt at the man and grabbed him by the sides of his head. He bit into the man's nose and ripped it off. The taste exploded in his mouth and he bit again, tearing at more flesh and quickly swallowing a large chunk of neck tissue. A gurgling noise filled the corridor as blood sprayed the surrounding walls and Two howled loudly with exhilaration.

He rushed through the open doorway and through more corridors until he found himself outside. His senses were on fire as the alien smells of fresh air and so many other elements intoxicated him. He ran to some trees to his right and away from the buildings, up a hill and onwards until he reached its summit. He stood there dizzy and bewildered, breathing heavily and shaking at the world that had opened up before him.

He was on a cliff top overlooking a vast ocean with a deep-red sun setting over the horizon. He collapsed to his knees, forgetting that he was running away, and was awestruck with the sensory overload. Time passed as he watched the red disc fall into the ocean and his emotions welled up inside him.

Two wiped his eyes, surprised that he was crying and happy at the same time. The birds in the distance, the beaches, the waves crashing, the grass flowing in the breeze, the clouds, the insects, the smells, and the sensation of everything on his skin; he had never seen or heard of these things and felt the betrayal embed itself deeper.

A loud noise startled him and he saw the grass in front of him come rushing towards his face. Someone landed on him, wrapping their arms around his neck and pulling him backwards. Two then felt pain in his left shoulder, then more pain in the face as someone else hit him hard with a solid object.

There was a lot of commotion, shouting and movement all around him as he was dragged to the very place he had run away from. The buildings surrounding him reflected the last red embers of the day, making the camp a demonic red where people clad in a different type of environment suit gathered round. He felt suffocated among the buildings and the faceless people who were making such a noise.

'I can't breathe,' he screamed.

'Can't breathe!' a man shouted back at him. Two looked at this man's shoulders, at the marks there that were a different colour to those he usually saw, and it scared him. He couldn't see behind the masks and couldn't see any other difference in the environment suit, yet the bright purple shoulders seemed to be a warning.

'Winters, go get a towel from the stores.'

Two's gown was violently ripped off. His small body, thin and pale, bore a multitude of marks and scars from years of brutal research.

'Sir, wait . . . we can't kill him.'

'This is bad, very bad.'

'He's just a child.'

'Quiet!' the man with the purple epaulettes screamed. 'Make sure his wrists are secured.'

Two felt the strip holding his wrists together squeeze harder, cutting deep into the skin. 'Please,' he wailed, 'it hurts.'

The one who seemed to be the leader took a large knife attached to his leg and flipped it in his hands so that he held it by the blade. He then swung it hard, clubbing Two on the head with the handle. 'Silence, freak.'

Two screamed with pain and began to cry, wailing loudly.

'Give me the towel,' the man said, returning the knife to his leg sheath. He then took the towel and wrapped it over Two's head and face. Two then felt the towel being fastened to his neck by a cord which choked him. He was hysterical and grunting with sheer terror.

'Fetch me that water. You want to be an animal then be treated like one.'

Two felt the sharp cold of the liquid being poured over his head and realised he was drowning. Silence replaced the din of voices and an eternity of death crept over Two as he fought for every breath from inside the towel as it smothered his mouth and nose.

'More water.'

'Sir, we can't do this.'

'Shut your mouth, everyone keep quiet, that's an order!'

Two weakened as he panicked, trying to breathe. His rib cage heaved and his heart pounded. His mind flipped upside down with the horror of silence surrounding him and the redness hazily piercing the cloth now suffocating him to death.

Version

A high-pitched noise echoed across and above him. Then a burning sensation tore away at his chest. More noises came and went with the eruption of screams and movement all around him. Two felt the past three years rush through his mind as a violation; an unwanted lesson of pain and sadness. Then, as though happy it would all end at last, nothing.

Eight tanks sat lifeless and, behind them, the defensive barricade that the basin's intruders had assembled hugged against the docking platform's tower scaffold. The metal-plated wall spanned the width of two hundred feet and was twenty feet high. Along its top various battlements surveyed the ground ahead, seemingly automated as they panned and tilted; twitching and checking when any of the basin's wildlife moved too close. The docking platform's tower was shrouded by the shield that continued to shimmer a bright green and protected the structure all the way to the basin wall's summit. Apart from the automated systems mounted on the defences, there were no signs of life detected.

Ologun watched carefully before walking steadily across the street. He glanced again at the mosque's exterior then entered. Inside was a large room, its floor covered by a soft canvas. His bare feet left dirty tread marks over its dusty surface. At the end of the room someone kneeled, facing towards him. They had strikingly white-blond hair that even in the gloom seemed tawdry.

'I have a vision of someone I was headed for who looks like you, I think, but it isn't you is it?' Ologun said and knelt down several feet directly in front of the figure to face him.

A man's voice echoed across the room. 'How did you know I was here?'

'Some things told me.'

'The human construct, again . . . really? They call them Versions. You know they existed in your day? Your father took you around with him and on occasions you interacted with them.'

'I don't remember them.'

'You never saw them.'

'I don't understand.'

'Well,' the man replied, 'they're connected to the Spectra. They're the fourth part of the deal. A sword usually has two edges, though, and the Spectra used them to steal ideas and do . . . you know. The strangest idea of all came from you.'

'What ideas?'

'The craft,' the man stated. 'Eighty plus years of making, adjusting and testing. Some were derived from ocean mammals found on Deceiver and others from the cache sent from Earth and placed here. You see, it's all just code to be hijacked and refined.'

'This is crazy.'

'No,' the man said. 'A spacecraft made through forced mutation using the human genome, a tiger's, a killer whale's, or a shark's, or a gorilla's, or from any numerous living thing. Not a bad imagination for a ten-year-old.'

Ologun chose to move on from this as it wasn't what he came here for. 'Vanguard?'

'Yes, humans drove my brother to insanity there.'

'What happened? I mean the colony there was wiped off the face of the planet by something.'

'I don't know.'

'The Spectra knows.'

'No,' Hina's brother said. 'The Spectra could be a god if only it didn't have brain damage. Besides, the human race is about to go to war with itself and phantoms that may never appear again are the least of anyone's concern. You know we couldn't just give you all the information at once, and the same goes for Judith. I'm glad you got it out of your system, Ologun, but I wouldn't go after Hina.'

'I gave that one up hours ago.' Ologun sighed. 'Besides, he isn't really any worse than me, is he? And I'm not sure why I got so self-righteous.'

'Context is all we have left when the rules fly out the window.'

'Sure,' Ologun replied. 'So, do we have any further role in any of this?'

'They let you go a long time ago, this IMC and Prospect Division of the IMC. Some meddled for a while thinking we were demi-gods and then they sort of forgot about us except for Prospect. Apparently one of us has to go, and maybe we should all go. Hina likes meat, human meat, so I'm still not sure what to do . . . it's a problem.'

Hina's brother lay flat on his back, stretched his arms and legs, then breathed deeply several times. 'This whole thing has taken many, many years and it's tiring. You may think that by not knowing any of this information to do with planets and factions and what you are and why you were left in a grave of ice is a bad thing. The reality is that Ray and I have been watching and waiting and wondering why humans would kill vast numbers of themselves when they could just cooperate. This Prospect Division has been planning to attack Earth for so long it's almost a joke. It's a great irony that this human war is ten years early. Another ten years and you could have asked the Spectra to intervene, I suppose, but then the hundreds of thousands of craft below are for their own protection, and let's just see if those things are ready if something else does come out of the woodwork. Hershal, by the way,' he finally introduced himself and rested his head on his arms.

'Yes, sorry I didn't ask,' Ologun replied. 'So what do we do now?'

'Nothing. Ray and I had you extracted from the ice because you might be forgotten about in the coming fallout. It's all about bad timing. You and that planet and now this war. Makes me wonder what else can occur. You know running around across the basin like that and what you did, then going after Hina until you realised he'd been ordered to take out those spies, and then the *Hollywood* makes me think that you wouldn't be happy unless you're doing something . . . let's say, altruistic. If you take out the violence and do what you were designed to do you might just be happy for a change.'

'I can't cure a bullet wound or a nuclear bomb blast, what the hell can I do?'

'Who knows what we can do? No one ever tested us for that.' Hershal sat up to face Ologun. 'Doctor Rita Siren. You want to be useful, I suggest you have a snoop at what she's been up to. I'm sure the all-seeing and all-knowing Version will tell you, you make its life so much less lonely, Warrior Jowett.'

YEAR 2243
The Amazon

DEAD MAN'S BED

If Heaven and Hell could be amalgamated into one place then this is it. It feels like Hell and looks like Heaven, Ologun thought. The lumps on his face from insect bites had stopped seeping and the rot on his feet had somehow gone away. *This is a place you have to be insane to traverse alone,* he thought. He grinned to himself then frowned a few seconds later at the thought of being so alone.

He continued through the dense terrain, hacking at the foliage with a large machete. He stopped, took a digipad from his pocket, and checked the distance to the beacon; only a few miles now. The gradient grew steeper until he eventually found himself climbing a buttress leading to a waterfall which, after a while, led to the summit where a large pool surrounded by a gravel beach greeted him.

The Colombian government had put a lot of money into repairing this section of jungle and had invested heavily in surveillance to keep it from being harmed. They didn't like trespassers and technically he was trespassing. *That's the whole point,* he supposed. Escape and evade, except that if he failed, whoever found him would shoot before bothering to ask any questions, or so he'd been told. The noise of a drone came from somewhere overhead. In response he dove to the floor, grabbing his satchel and pulling a hybrid cloak from the top compartment. Thermal and standard optic distorters would confuse the machine, or so he'd also been told.

The drone passed at great speed and, he hoped, without spotting him. He sat up, removed the cloak and peered south over the jungle canopy and to the water cascade away from and beneath him on to rocks a few hundred feet below. A place like this made a person

252

think and he didn't want to think. Introspection and remembering were the very things he needed to avoid; thinking how nice it would have been to bring her . . . He shook the thought away.

'You're quick, I'll give you that.'

He turned to see a woman sitting on a rock a few yards away.

'Chief.' He stood and saluted her.

She whistled as though in exclamation at something. 'At ease, Jowett, come, have a seat.'

He moved towards the woman with the designated rank of master chief and sat down on an adjacent rock.

'Ologun Jowett,' the chief read from a pad she held. She shook her head as she did so before looking Ologun in the eyes. 'You're a fit bastard, for sure.' She paused, looked out over the jungle, then back at Ologun with curiosity. 'What are you doing here, son?'

'Training for the asset protection assignment, ma'am.'

'Cut the crap, Jowett, and don't ever call me, ma'am. Call me Graves, I don't really have a rank, that's for real armies. Ever been in a real army, son?'

'No.'

'Well, I served in the Marine Corps for fifteen years and Navy Seals for ten and I can tell you that this, what you're doing, is a joke.' Graves sighed deeply and read from her pad again as though referring to a speech. 'I've never seen this before. Of all the people who have come this way you're the first non-ex-military candidate. You know that?'

'No,' Ologun replied, wondering where this was heading.

'How was Nepal?'

'Good.'

'You started sixty miles outside the usual marker zone.'

'I thought I'd start closer to sea level, didn't want to get altitude sickness.'

'Your physical record shows you have a very high capillary count, almost as if you were born Nepalese, so not much chance of that. Interesting, though.'

Ologun sat and waited for the casual talk to end and the real point to be made.

'I knew your old man. I served under him for a while when he was a naval captain. Yeah, he was a real tough bastard. Managed the space entry programme at thirty five which is just absurd. The thing is, I know about you and what you've been through and I can't see how you passed the shrink evaluation.' Graves shook her head and whistled again. 'You know you'll only get a few jobs and you're finished either way, right?'

'Yes, I understand.'

'Eighteen months ago you had a sweet job in Damascus, nice city. I mean you were selling sand for the Arabs for Christ's sake.' Graves chortled and then her face changed to a very serious demeanour. 'None of this is going to help you,' she said, waving her hand around in small circles.

'Maybe,' Ologun said softly.

'All right, that's all I'm going to say, but your dad would have my head blown off if he were still around.' Graves reached into a long case she'd brought and pulled out a rather unique rifle. 'This is a new weapon which is being tested in certain fields. It's called a KL Trip One. It performs as a highly accurate mid- to long-range unit that fires rounds via a chamber powered by miniaturised rail-gun technology.'

'A stampede rifle,' Ologun interrupted.

'You could fire a hundred rounds from three clips in around five seconds on full auto, but the increments are designed to keep this thing firing slow and accurate. Don't waste this thing's capabilities. It has a power cell that lasts three weeks in the dark and a lens here for re-charge, but note the lens is a bit flashy, so keep it under its cover when in the field or you'll attract attention like flies round a bull's ass.

'Understood.'

Graves took out a number of magazines from the case and laid them out on the ground. 'Here we have armour piercing, magma and tampon rounds, so get used to the new colour-coding system because all these clips will be held simultaneously by the rifle so you can change in the heat of combat.'

Ologun nodded, making a mental note of the colour scheme. 'Tampon round?'

'Sure.' Graves smiled. 'You know what a tampon is, right?'

'Yes.'

'Well, these horrible little things are like vampires. They hit a target then draw blood from them into a fibrous material. One round can draw a quarter of a pint if a target is hit well enough. Officially they're called VM rounds as in vampire, but I like tampon, I'm sexist that way, reminds me of my ex who drained everything, including my bank account, dry. Guess you're luckier than you thought, eh?'

Ologun recoiled at the statement and Graves saw she'd hit a nerve.

'Okay,' Graves said, moving on. 'Armour, as in body armour.'

'Yes, I'm kitted out with sixth-generation custard armour.'

'Ooh, snazzy eh!' Graves spat and chuckled. 'No, no, you need to don this flex vest. It's a lightweight metallic fibre resembling the torso's own posterior and anterior muscular structure − back and front to the rest of us. When worn it'll mould to your shape and size and flex real hard like a muscle when hit, except of course that it's metal and very tough.'

Ologun changed body armour and swapped his rifle for the KL Trip. 'So what now?'

Graves stood up and briefly pointed over the canopy, then moved to illustrate something on the pad she held. 'You move south, following the river until you reach the sharp turn left where you need to cross a bridge. Ten miles south of that we've set something up for you, but I'm not saying what or why. Oh, and you'll have to use your eyes and ears on this one. No magic marker, just assess what you come across and figure it out.'

'Affirmative.'

Graves set off walking towards the treeline to the rear to the pool. 'Good luck.'

'Thanks.'

Ologun watched until Graves was out of sight then gathered his things. He looked at the rifle for a few moments and found the function to place it on silencer mode. Either side of and at the end of the barrel two small pieces of metal sprang out and moved to form a thicker cylinder encompassing the end. Ologun dropped to one knee and took aim. He selected non-auto fire and chose a target. He selected standard ammo for long range and breathed steadily. He exhaled and fired, then repeated the process a few times. The recoil was minimal, which led to good results. He zoomed in on maximum and checked the tree trunk he'd chosen as a target. He'd achieved a tight grouping of four splintered holes at a distance of eight hundred and fifty yards. Satisfied, Ologun slung the weapon over his shoulder and began his journey south.

Ten miles was a tough and elongated affair across such terrain. Ologun reached the river where it banked left; no bridge yet. He wandered along its bank for a few miles, but still no access across its wild torrent. He then remembered that the river must slip a little below ground further north and headed to where he thought he might cross. It wouldn't be easy, yet a crossing should be far more easily achieved and less likely to kill him in the process.

Two hours later he reached the location, feeling hot and tired. Evening had set in and it would soon be dark, which made him think about his next plan of action. Ologun climbed down towards the river where rocks seemed to present viable options to allow for a safe crossing.

At the river's edge he saw it was still deep and fast flowing, which made him wonder what would happen if he messed up here in the middle of the jungle with no backup: nothing good.

He stepped on to a moss-covered boulder, then stepped on to another then another with slow deliberation and well-placed feet. A gap appeared in front of him and he looked up across the way. The next boulder was a good leap away and it looked slippery. He thought maybe he should go back and construct a miniature bridge to go over the gap, for he could see the stones after this were close together again.

Ologun noted the rapids and the water's speed, then glanced at all the rocks the river snaked around. If he failed here he would be in serious trouble. *To hell with it!* He shrugged and leapt as hard as he could.

His foot hit the rock he aimed for, but he slipped, his trailing leg fell, and he was submerged up to his waist. He now had one foot on a rock and one leg in the river which pulled violently at him. Ologun grabbed the boulder and pulled hard, yet found he was at an impasse with the situation: his body was in too much of a contorted position to move.

Ologun was startled by a woman hopping towards him across the rocks. She moved quickly until she landed on the nearest rock before reaching over and grabbing at the satchel on his back. She heaved with effort and pulled him up and out of the river. 'Man you is one crazy mo fo!'

Ologun found his balance and jumped the rest of the rocks to the river's edge. Once there he sat down. He glanced up to see the tall, thin woman with buck teeth and bulbous eyes had come to join him. 'Thank you,' he said, trying to calm down.

'Name's Jean, Jean by the way.'

'Ologun,' he offered. 'What are you doing here?' He noticed her IMC insignia hidden fairly well in her forest-camouflage combat uniform. 'Jean Jean?' Ologun asked further in confusion.

The woman laughed but didn't answer. 'I'm collecting wood, and you?'

Ologun thought about this and wondered if it was part of the test. 'I'm here to assess the situation.'

'Oh, its bad news here . . . Ologun's a pretty weird name.' She took out a small pad and began typing something. 'Warrior,' she mused in an accent Ologun found hard to follow. 'Your name is Warrior, oh I see, it's a code name. 'So what's your real name?'

Ologun decided to tread carefully. 'That's all you need to know.'

'Oh, okay,' Jean said, winking.

'Come on, we need to go back to the village. It's a bad thing this outbreak, of course they say it's safe now, but I'd like the mask and full gear – you never know, right?'

Ologun agreed, with what he wasn't sure, and followed her up the river's embankment and over to a wide road among the trees. They followed the road until an opening cleared in the forest with a scattering of cabins and various tents. Ologun continued to follow Jean towards a group of what he considered to be more soldiers. It was then that the smell hit him. In the heat and humidity he clearly recognised death and freshly begun decay.

'This is Ologun, he's here to assess the situation,' Jean hollered to the group.

Ologun looked at the soldiers who were in a line paired off facing each other, and then to the floor. On it lay many bodies in a long row, each sheathed within thick black rubber contamination bags.

'What you think?' one of the men asked.

'It's not good,' Ologun said, being elusive.

'No, no it's not good at all . . . nope.'

Ologun watched as the man he was talking to and one other heaved a body into the back of a truck. Then, out of pure curiosity, Ologun reached into the truck, unzipped one of the bags and had a look. 'What you doing, man? You're gonna get us killed, chump.'

The group recoiled in horror, not sure what to do.

'No,' Ologun said. 'These people were killed by nanotechnology. Machines did this.' He zipped the bag back up.

'How do you know that?'

Ologun suddenly realised that he didn't know how, but just knew; he really knew and without a doubt. *But how, why?* He then thought this must be part of a test. 'It's classified and, well, you're all safe.'

'Where you from man, you Polish?'

'That's classified,' Ologun stated.

'Where you were born and raised is classified? Man, that's full on.'

'Don't mind Magic Fingers here,' one of the men said, 'this is Jean who you already met, this is Dumb Ass.'

'Hey,' a man protested.

'This is Snaith.'

A young blonde girl waved as though intimidated by Ologun's presence.

'And I'm Tongue.'

'Nice to see you all have real names,' Ologun quipped.

'You got a real good name too, Ologun,' Jean fired back.

'Halt.' A woman's voice shattered the pleasantries. Ologun found himself surrounded by other soldiers with rifles aimed directly at him. He turned to see a female officer standing a few feet away. 'What in the hell is wrong with you all? You're all on report for this!' she screamed.

'Ma'am?' Tongue replied.

'Who are you?' she demanded of Ologun, ignoring Tongue.

'I'm here from Operations to assess and assist,' Ologun said, trying his best to lie about his purpose, even though he wasn't sure what he was doing there at all.

The woman tilted her head in a fashion that prompted one of the soldiers accompanying her to take Ologun's rifle.

'Everyone continue and I'll deal with you later. You, come with me now.'

Ologun followed the woman across the village, taking in the scene of wooden huts, the odd car parked along the dirt track, and further rows of bodies wrapped in the black thick airtight sacks. Eventually the officer entered one of the wooden cabins and two soldiers followed close behind. Ologun entered, flanked by another two soldiers.

'What's your name?' she asked, sitting down to a table and offering him the chair opposite with a hand gesture.

'Ologun.'

A little pale for a Nigerian aren't you? Name's Harper by the way, now I think you should explain to me what in the hell you're doing walking in on my operation.'

'I'm here to assess the situation.'

'Yes of course, you said, but assess the situation means nothing at all, it's an empty sentence.'

'Nanotech,' Ologun replied quickly. 'My assessment is that it's not cost effective for the IMC to continue investment.'

Harper nodded in fascination. 'This is a classified mission, Ologun, you shouldn't be here. Then again, this is a strange company we work for and a little unconventional so I'll accommodate you for now and see if I can sort this out.'

Harper nodded to one of the soldiers, who in turn placed the Trip rifle on the table. Harper looked over the weapon without touching it and took a small tube from one of her jacket pockets. She squirted a small amount of cream on to her fingers, then rubbed it into her pale, thin face before wiping her hand through thick red hair.

'Nice to be in the shade of jungle,' she mused. 'You and I are too pale for Middle Eastern operations, right?' She chuckled.

'Sure,' Ologun agreed.

'This is one serious piece of kit. My, my, and that flex vest you have. You know that it's highly unlikely you're from anywhere but IMC? No one has equipment like this, it's a little over the top for a start.' Harper sat back in her chair as a flash of lightning outside lit the room. Thunder followed and a few moments later the sound of rain pelted the tin roof. 'About time,' she said. 'The heat was pissing me off. So, what are your orders?'

Ologun wiped the sweat from his eyes and was relieved to feel the change in air pressure. 'I'll assist with whatever you need until we exit, then I'll help the exit operations. I'm not privy to where these bodies are going, I'll just help in security.'

Harper scanned the man and wondered. She would check all of this over with Command but couldn't figure out why he was here at all. There was nothing to be gained even if he wasn't who he said he was, although that was very little. This was a clean-up operation of the most horrible, tedious type to train candidates fresh from initiation yet, out of literally nowhere, a man who seemed particularly capable and was carrying some serious hardware was sitting opposite. 'Okay, proceed as you think you should. What's your rank, soldier?'

'On this mission I'll continue on as Private.'

'Fine, carry on and assist the others. Tongue is in charge of the riff raff out there. Oh, and I assume you're experienced or at least sensible, so pull rank if you see anything idiotic going on.'

'Affirmative, ma'am.' With that, Ologun stood up and left the cabin to wander off into the heavy downpour.

'What do you think?'

Version

A man entered from another room located directly behind Harper. He was a hulk of a figure who took up all the space as he stood in the doorway. 'What I think is classified beyond your level. I've seen this before and it seems he's made a wrong turn somewhere.'

'What do you mean?'

'I'll keep an eye on him.'

'You seem concerned,' Harper suggested.

'Perhaps.'

'What is it?'

'I just received new orders.'

'What?'

'You remember Mexico City?'

'Good God,' Harper replied and sat deep into the wooden chair. She looked at the other two soldiers still waiting by the cabin's front door. 'Tell the others when they return from escorting that Ologun. We have a secondary clean-up to attend to.'

The soldiers nodded without any hint that the new orders bothered them. Harper, on the other hand, felt sick to the stomach and ashamed. *Why? Why do they keep doing this?*

The night was still hot with insects attending their business and avoiding the light drizzle of rain which had set in.

Ologun sat in the darkness next to Tongue and opposite another man they called Magic. The two men were the best of friends and had formed a long running joke to do with them being the duo, Magic Tongue. Apparently they'd conquered many female conquests leading from this joke and had already told ten or so anecdotes about them. Tongue sensed that Ologun was bored with the stories and looked to Magic to change subjects.

'So, where you from really?' Magic asked.

Ologun looked at Magic, trying to work out if he should tell him. 'I grew up in many places all over North Africa, spent a few months in Italy, and then settled in Libya before finally doing this.'

'What are you doing?' Tongue intervened.

'That I can't say,' Ologun replied and realised he had told two truths which had allowed everything to remain vague.

'I grew up all over America until I finally touched down in Detroit,' Magic offered. He was a darker shade of black than Tongue and his eyes and teeth seemed as though they would be spotted by a drone even without thermal imaging if one were to pass over. 'See, Tongue and I hit it off right away. All that moving from town to town made me feel like I was on a different wavelength to other people, everyone, like I was, what's the word?'

'Alienated,' Ologun answered.

'Yeah, that's right.'

'See, me and Magic know each other's thoughts we been together so long. Even our women back home find it hard to deal it with at times.'

Magic made a sound of agreement and Ologun nearly corrected Tongue on his grammar by saying Magic and I, but held off and pulled his hybrid cloak tighter around his chest. The other two had dark-green camouflage ponchos which seemed to keep the wet out far more efficiently.

'So, how do you know about what happened here?' Tongue asked Ologun.

'At first I didn't know how I knew,' Ologun said and followed this with a nervous hoot. 'Then I remembered the invasive species programme from years ago; I did it at school along with environmental sciences where they did . . . Anyway, in places where animals were introduced into eco systems, where they are both successful and destructive, there was a plan to return the habitats back to normal. The initial tests were performed in the Florida Everglades to destroy, I don't know, pythons and other animals which were killing the indigenous wildlife or destroying the habitats. Eventually some bright spark said that the nanotech used for heart surgery and other health applications could be programmed and used successfully and specifically on targeted species and restore habitats to how they were. Of course it's hardly used any more, everything is organic these days when it concerns microbiology.'

The two men listening seemed a little dumbfounded at this explanation and Ologun wondered whether he'd gone too far.

'So, what you are saying is that these people were killed on purpose,' Magic finally said.

'These men and women were cocaine farmers. Albeit it's a dying trade, but then that may not be due to demand,' Ologun quipped.

The rain fell harder and the light of dawn crept in through the canopy above.

'How do you know all this stuff?' Tongue asked suspiciously.

'I pay attention. It's time we got some sleep.'

Ologun wondered if the remark he'd made was a little condescending and quickly made his way to one of the empty cabins. Everyone else, including those already sleeping, had chosen to use tents. As Ologun walked along the wet soil he overheard the two men as they settled into their tent.

'Man, this is some crazy bullshit.'

'I hear ya. He's okay, don't you think?'

'Who, Ologun? He's creepy like, like a guy I once knew. He went Tonto and killed everyone at work.'

'Magic, Magic, shut up, man!'

Ologun entered the dark cabin and made his way until he found a bedroom towards the back. He lay down on the bed and stared at the wooden ceiling. Light was breaking through the dirty rag on the window, causing a dusty hue to be visible, and somehow enhancing the smell of body odour left behind by its prior occupants. He realised the others didn't sleep in the cabins because they were dirty and smelled. They slept in tents because no one wanted to sleep in a dead man's bed.

Two hours sleep, a swift packing up of all equipment and a quick check of all the body bags had the whole platoon on the road. Several soldiers had taken trucks and had paired up to go on alone. This was where Ologun noticed a stark segregation in the unit which unsettled him. He and the ones Harper had referred to as riff raff on several occasions were now sat in the back of an old-fashioned troop carrier. They were crammed in on two opposing benches under a thick canvas canopy and unable to see anything outside the truck. Most of the soldiers were snoozing in their snug and cramped positions.

Some chatted idly about this and that while Ologun thought carefully about the next part of the mission. A boat was to meet them at a disused harbour to the north-east shore somewhere on the Venezuelan coast. Ologun had checked his digipad and was sure they were headed for Pen. De Paria.

Days passed with Ologun watching the soldiers and the riff raff with some interest. The tour was long and tiresome, yet sometimes breath-taking as the convoy passed over, and at times under, the Pakaraima Mountains. Ologun thought on many occasions that he'd made a mistake and that this couldn't be part of the mission. Travelling over a thousand miles north and through various border checkpoints seemed to be the complete opposite of what he imagined the test to be.

Finally and towards the end of the third day of the journey the caravan of trucks arrived at an old port exactly where Ologun had guessed the main destination would be. There wasn't much to do at this point and Ologun admired the ocean as he wandered down the main pier to where the ship was to rendezvous.

It was a strange place and the whole area seemed abandoned, yet Ologun knew that whoever used to occupy this location had been paid off to move on and that it was all part of the rainforest restoration programme. Weathered empty buildings, mainly large hotels, and a few abandoned vehicles lined the road which ran the length of the beach and stretched beyond sight into the distance; a strange thing to behold considering the world's immense overpopulation. Land that was once owned by companies and where hotels blocked the way leading to idyllic beaches were now under new ownership and purposefully abandoned and left to nature undisturbed.

Out to sea and a quarter of a mile away, a great wall designed to create electricity through the power of the ocean had begun to break apart. Great parts of the wall had been smashed away and taken into and beneath the sea, yet the wall was substantial enough to protect the paradise beaches. Tongue and Magic hadn't said much to him all day and seemed to be avoiding him. Jean seemed tired and on another planet, and so Ologun had time to observe the goings-on between one set of soldiers who had things to do and the riff raff who were now lazing around and chatting near a building at the very end of the pier. Ologun noticed a large man regularly glancing his way and then retracting his gaze as soon as he was spotted. What the man's role was here Ologun couldn't tell, although he seemed to be observing or even assessing the situation which, when he thought about it, was ironic.

Ologun turned to the ocean and used the zoom on his rifle to scan the horizon. No ship as of yet and evening was setting in quickly. Above the din of waves, people chatting and trucks revving on the beach, Ologun could hear a quick form of beating almost like a machine gun in the distance. The sound drew his focus down the scope towards a black speck in the sky. 'Magic! Hey, Magic, Jean, Tongue, anyone, I thought you said a ship was coming for you?'

Magic stood and moved with hesitation towards Ologun. 'So we were told, that's right.'

'There's an aircraft inbound,' Ologun stated flatly.

'So?' Magic said.

'Go tell Harper and see what she says.'

The others cupped their hands over their brows, trying to see what Ologun was referring to. Ologun kept an eye on it as it came closer. His heart punched harder as he went to maximum zoom to see a helicopter with various armaments hanging from its undercarriage. Stampede guns, missiles and a side turret, probably operated by someone inside the aircraft's rear compartment.

Ologun turned round to see where the other soldiers were. Magic was walking back up the pier with raised hands. 'I don't know, man.'

Ologun looked at the others, realising something was very wrong here. With no time to run as the aircraft closed in he shouted at the riff raff, 'Get into the building, now!'

They ran just as the helicopter swooped overhead, firing its stampede guns. Wood splinters tore up the pier deck and cut down three, including Jean. Ologun ran in the opposite direction to a set of large crates to his rear. The craft lifted, did a large barrel roll in the air, then positioned itself sideways on so that the side turret could take aim. The rest of the riff raff made it to the pier building. *Good,*

Ologun thought. It was more than likely hurricane proof with thick brick walls and a solid concrete roof. The turret opened up, pounding the building, and plumes of dust and brick exploded in thick chunks out and over the decking.

Ologun surveyed his flank; still no one there. He clicked the rifle to magma rounds, adjusted the sights to mid-range and took aim. He fired a few rounds, hitting the side of the aircraft where the heat of the bullets ate into the metal body armour. He fired again, hitting the midsection of the helicopter's tail just in time before the turret fired on his position. He took cover, then realised the crates would be obliterated and ran for the building. The aircraft may have had the advantage of height and heavy guns but it had to remain steady to hit its mark. The turret ceased fire and the helicopter changed positions to fire its stampede guns. Ologun reached the building and dove as all hell broke loose.

The noise and carnage of the building being pounded drowned out the screams of those hiding inside. The stampede guns cut the building in two horizontally and its roof caved in. The force of this demolished its foundations and the building crashed into the shallows below. Ologun crawled behind a wave defence wall which surrounded the east perimeter of the pier. He checked his rifle, searching for ideas as the aircraft continued to pummel thousands of rounds in his direction.

They all died. There was a side to Ologun which had caused him more trouble in his life than might be thought possible. This, Ologun felt, was it. The end of the road and a certain kind of spite crept over him. He switched the rifle to full velocity and chose random on the firing mechanism. Chance would decide which round he fired and what that round would do; a one in four chance of firing something useful at just the right moment. Ologun took aim and fired on full auto, trying to keep control of the rifle's increasing recoil. The rounds flung out, finding various contact. The aircraft's cockpit window shattered, causing reinforced shutters to slam down. The helicopter then swung starboard, firing off target as the pilot flinched. This meant the side turret was on the wrong side of the aircraft, which was now exposed. Ologun switched to explosive rounds and took aim. Five shots and three hits ravaged the helicopter's tail but still it wasn't enough. He checked the ammo count. There were fifty standard rounds, only two magma and twelve VM rounds left.

Ologun flicked to the VM rounds and took aim once more. The helicopter moved sluggishly as Ologun fired into the gaping holes in the craft's tail. He took cover and listened. The tail propeller stuttered and struggled, and Ologun poked his head up to see. The helicopter spun back and forth like some animal shaking something off its back. A loud clang was followed by the craft spiralling round and round, losing height as it went. A moment later the helicopter hit the sea, its rotors snapping violently as it hit the waves and the craft sank sluggishly beneath the water.

Gunfire broke the triumph and he realised he was being shot at from the shore line. Crawling once again, Ologun just about reached the front end of the pier when he was shot in the back of the leg. He turned the corner and moved to lie in front of the pier's protective front wall. *What kind of test is this*? he thought. *Am I meant to side with the other soldiers in some grotesque moral scenario?* It made some sense in that they needed to know if he could do it and actually kill. Well, he had done that all right and it seemed they had trained him rather well, except he was beginning to realise they were probably right: he was liable to make bad decisions which would compromise missions. They had tested and he had failed, and the penalty would be death.

'What? Are you crazy? He just took down our ride with a rifle!'

Harper crouched behind a truck, straining to look up at the large man she knew as White. He was assigned now and again to these projects and only once before had this order been issued for reasons beyond her. Either way, for a second time Harper felt party to murder and couldn't help feel some form of – *what was it? Retribution? Justice perhaps? Even karma?*

'Keep firing,' White ordered the soldiers hunkering down behind the trucks.

'I think I got him,' one of them shouted.

White turned to Harper. 'I'm going to get him now so stay here.'
Harper shook her head in disbelief. 'Who the hell is he, White?'
'An idiot, that's who.'

Ologun sat looking out over the ocean; he hated the sea and didn't feel it would be the greatest way to bow out but, then again, it was all deserved. That poor riff-raff ensemble of disposable grunts didn't deserve this.

Ologun noticed a body floating in the waves below; a torso with no arms and no legs facedown, bobbing quietly. He reached into his satchel beside him and rummaged around its shredded compartments. He found a band of metal normally used to shrink tie his rifle to his chest. He improvised and slipped it over his boot and up past his knee. He felt for the wound and placed the large band above it before pressing a small button on the device. The band closed around his leg and tightened until it restricted the blood flow. They were known as python bands throughout the service. Not strong enough to constrict breathing, it might be enough to act as a tourniquet. Ologun grunted in pain as the band went as tight as it could. He picked up his rifle and, with an awkward shuffle, positioned himself to take aim towards the bay.

A row of trucks were parked a good eight hundred yards away by the pier. Continuous muzzle flash erupted, followed by the ping of bullets on the concrete wall he was hiding behind. The lens zoom gave a good indication of wind direction and a set of line arcs to help achieve long aim success. He fired a VM round towards one of the snipers, struggling to achieve his target in the bluster of sea breeze. *Crack.* The round hit the sniper in the top of the head and the round had by now probably sucked his head dry. A shadow caught Ologun's peripheral vision and he flinched. A forceful smack to the head knocked him on to his back and the rifle flew out of his hands into the water below. 'Good night, dickhead.'

Ologun received another smack to the face and was knocked out.

'This is Polar Three to Command. I need a sit rep on second pick up.'

'Roger that, Polar Three. Pick up en route. ETA is thirty minutes.'

White admired his catch, now laid out on the deck in front of the wall. He considered either shooting him or simply pushing him off the pier to drown.

'Polar Three, this is Command.'

'Polar Three receiving. Go ahead.'

'We have satellite feed over your position. Further instructions are to bring assailant back to base.

'Roger that, Command. Bringing the cargo home, orders understood.'

'Copy that, Polar Three.'

'Copy, over and out.' He looked at Ologun and retracted the rifle. 'You're dead either way. Better I did you quick than what's in store, unlucky prick.' White shook his head and wondered how this man had managed to take out the helicopter. It was beginning to sink in that Asset Protection was indeed a division to be wary of.

'This is an announcement for Colonel R Vosper, please report to sublevel sixteen.'

Colonel Vosper stood and made his way to the lift. At the lift doors he was patted down by a security guard whilst being carefully watched by another.

"This way, sir."

Vosper entered the lift which took him to the subterranean location where he was to meet Doctor Xue. Vosper walked the corridors, remembering this place from many years ago. Once this underground complex had been for research and development; high-end investment, not just nuts and bolts but real tech such as the likes of CERN or NASA used to put together. The lowest levels of this place had now been gutted. No more colliders or Planck energy drivers or STC reality fabric stressors, just an empty basement. The complex stretched fifty square miles underground and it was almost impossible to monitor the whole base; which he was counting on.

He came to the room he was searching for and knocked.

'Enter.' The voice was how he remembered it from past encounters and he prepared himself to deal with the obnoxious man on the other side of the door. Vosper entered a small room with whitewashed walls and where only a desk and a couple of chairs remained. Doctor Xue, or alternatively General Xue depending on whether you addressed him by his official rank, did not stand to greet Vosper and instead sat waiting, swaying from side to side on his chair as though agitated.

'I told Command I have no time for this,' Xue said.

Vosper sat down, thinking that the man was even rude enough to choose a decommissioned room for this meeting. 'How about a drink? It's been a long ride out here.'

Xue ignored the request and stroked a pen on an otherwise empty desk. 'What do you want, Vosper? Forced visits annoy me, even more so when they're from Asset Protection.'

'Okay, there's a dilemma, or crisis should I say.'

'Crisis? Crisis is a big word. Like the energy crisis or oil crisis. We've had a crisis of magnets, helium, food, meat, housing . . . crisis sounds awfully big, Vosper. Question is, why come to me when you know I'm not the helpful type?'

Vosper scanned the room for any indication of surveillance, but with any luck this fool would have brought him to a secure location. The room's walls were bare, with only remnants of old fixtures and fittings. Marked lines of picture frames and furniture could be seen as less grotty and a testament that the room had once been in use. No small dots on the walls or ceilings, nor any indications that the room was rigged for eavesdropping; still, there was no way to discreetly check for listening devices, and if there were any it was no real issue.

'You have an operative of ours, Xue. We need him back.'

Xue raised an eyebrow at this, grinning like a Cheshire cat. 'I have no idea what you mean.'

'We had our own satellites monitoring events in South America and we know you brought him here, so please cooperate on this one.'

Xue's face took on a more hostile, less fake smile, expression and he grabbed the pen as though Vosper would steal it. 'Still doesn't ring a bell.'

'Why are you deleting recruits, Xue? I know that's what you're doing. I know human life is dropping in value by the year, by the day, but seriously.'

'You can't have him,' Xue interrupted.

'You have to return him to us.'

'And who are you exactly, Vosper? I presumed you were Asset Protection and we all know the assassins' club doesn't care about the expendable riff raff.'

'Ologun Jowett. We need him back. Final warning.'

'Warning!' Xue laughed. 'We haven't finished with him, and between you and me I think someone's gone a little far in breaking the rules.'

Vosper had been in asset protection for over half his life and was now into something else far more important, yet his reactions remained frosty to certain phrases or trigger words. Xue had said something that put him straight into that old mode. Vosper lifted his right hand and pointed his index finger at Xue.

'No need to be so theatrical,' Xue protested. 'I suggest . . .

Vosper activated a mechanism within his false hand made of reinforced carbon tube-fibre and fired a bullet from the end of the finger into Xue's head. The force of the shot was enough for an entrance wound but did not exit. Xue slumped forward on to the desk, then slid backwards on to the floor. Vosper checked the man's pulse and saw thick bright blood ooze from the hole in his forehead.

Vosper activated a small device on the palm of his false hand. 'Operation Mexico is a go. I repeat, Operation Mexico is a go.'

He headed to the door and reached for the handle, then lifted his fake hand to inspect the index finger's missing tip. A set of explosions could be heard from somewhere in the distance followed by gunfire. *The clichés of a full intrusion,* Vosper decided, and on cue the base alarm sounded.

He waited a while then exited the room and activated his server chip. One day this device, as with all military applications, would become commonplace, but for now it was quite basic in its functions. It projected the information along the stem to his eyes where he could view a schematic of the base in his left eye's vision. He searched for the time-space continuum distortions created by a specific type of energy cascade which perforated the fabric of space/reality, and became disorientated. *Damn!* The basement still gave off a huge level of interference from the experiments that had taken place many years ago. It appeared that if you meddled with the ether it hung around for a long time like radiation from a nuclear bomb blast. Still, he knew what Xue would have been up to here and, if he was correct in his assumptions, Ologun would be emitting something quite unique even in comparison to this installation's basement.

Vosper locked in on what was classed as P-class energy cascades, and lots of them; all compressed and streamlined in cohesion. *The beauty of it!*

He tabbed though the corridors and came across a felled soldier. He picked up the dead man's rifle and slung it over his shoulder. He knew this place and knew he had a good fifteen minutes of double timing it before reaching his destination. Smoke and tear gas filled the narrow spaces as he ran and forced him to stop. He took off his hand and opened a small valve embedded in its palm. His eyes were streaming by now and he coughed and sputtered. Vosper placed the hand on his face, feeling the fingers grip his temples and cheek bones. He sucked on the valve and the hand was now an air-filtered gas mask. Although he could now breathe, his eyes were still exposed.

He continued to jog through the chaos where bodies were strewn across the corridors, and into open intersections filled with cafeterias and lounges. The remnants of intense firefights and the destructive force of the new division's laser scalpel precision was devastating. This was an insane conclusion to one man's mistaken change of direction in the Amazon jungle, or at least that was one major part of it among many others.

Vosper headed up the crème de la crème of forces recruited for something of a long-term venture and this man, or whatever he could be described as, was one issue that needed sorting out. Beneath the barren lands situated between the Mexico-Texas border in an old IMC research and development complex now run by arseholes and sadists in a world gone utterly mad, the newly formed Prospect Alliance was keeping secrets at any cost.

Version

Vosper kept a scan on all the dead and wounded bodies as he kept pace, whilst his server chip kept a tag on any friendlies who may have fallen in combat. So far he'd found no one and he realised just how good this team were. Turning a corner, Vosper ran into a blockade and dove to the floor for cover.

'Stand down, stand down,' one of the soldiers ordered and walked from behind a defence blockade to greet Vosper.

Vosper stood, took the false hand from his face then attached it to his wrist. 'Sit rep, Captain.'

'Area secure, Colonel, package is this way.'

'The base?' Vosper asked.

'Secure, no witnesses.'

Vosper followed the captain, dusting off his blazer jacket's shoulders in mindless reflex. He would have preferred to have full combat gear but then that was no way to arrive for a civil meeting. The thing was, he'd been ordered to learn just how much Xue knew before executing this extraction and he hadn't learned much at all. Vosper had also been ordered to find a passive way, to get Xue to hand Ologun over without bloodshed, as the clean-up operation if this failed would be immense. Vosper smiled in some satisfaction, for that's the man he was and he knew there was a big chance that everyone working in this place would have to be killed. The world was better off without any of them. After all, this place was a cesspit used for interrogation and torture amongst other sordid research projects. IMC brass would be livid and shaken to the core, and yet they were behind the curve of events to come and the Prospect Division, the IMC's most dedicated of the company, had only just begun.

'Through there.'

Vosper stopped outside a thick vault door. *Appropriate,* he mused.

'Where's Leigh?' he asked the captain.

The man in full black combat ensemble waved at the others, who kept tight surveillance of the area towards the end of this section of base that could only be described as a heavy-duty, state-of-the-art prison.

Four soldiers moved up, carrying a large case which appeared to be some sort of coffin. They placed the box on the floor, then one of the soldiers opened the seals running along one side before lifting the lid. Inside was a woman, who quickly sat up and exited. 'Where to?' she said.

Vosper nodded and two soldiers heaved the thick circular metal door open. Vosper and the woman he called Leigh entered a room with static protected walls. The pointed formation of this even covered the ceiling. Leigh moved to a console to her left and began working. Vosper told the captain to remain outside and close the vault door.

On the wall at the end of the room a round grey portal cover opened, eventually revealing a man lying down inside a tube. Leigh entered more commands into the console and the tube extended to reveal the man, who was pale-skinned with an athletic frame, had very black hair and quite bony facial features.

'So this is what we came for. It all seems a little excessive for one man, Colonel.'

'Leigh?' Vosper looked over at the woman.

'Yes, sir.'

'You've been handling my affairs and my memories for seven years now, right?'

'Ten, Colonel.'

'Maybe you want to know what it's all about,' Vosper offered.

'Not at my level of clearance, sir,' Leigh said as she took a small device from her webbing and attached it to her console. 'I'd like to know why you didn't bring him to me. Memory adjustments are tricky, you know that.' Still, Xue had been using the very same equipment she had at her own lab and so she wasn't too worried about the results of the procedure she was about to undertake.

'Libya and mundane job, correct?'

'Christ, no!' Vosper shouted. 'Morocco. I said Morocco.'

'Sorry,' Leigh said, 'give me a few minutes to re-programme this then.'

Vosper went and stood by the cot Ologun lay upon and watched him breathe in his deep state of unconsciousness.

'Oh,' Leigh said loudly, 'I don't think they were looking for memories here, sir.'

'Excuse me?' Vosper said, turning to look at her.

'They were eliminating short-term memories. I have files here, erm, Judas box sessions, record-breaking waterboard sessions, heat room sessions, stress position sessions, noise inducement sessions and . . . well this is a long list. What's a Judas box, sir?'

'Des,' Vosper replied and turned to look at Ologun. He nearly moved to touch his hand and abandoned the idea. 'Desmond.'

I'll be done in a while, er, Des sir.' Leigh knew his name and she knew the man, yet he was acting peculiar as though his personality had taken a turn since entering the room.

'I've known this man a long time, or known about him,' Vosper finally said. 'His father and I were good friends for a long time. Well, I say his father, you see Ologun isn't this man's name really. That was the name of a project which took place in Nigeria many years ago. The thing is, Jowett the idiot just kept the Ologun project, the warrior project name for the boy. He took the boy when they'd finished and took him around with him before he retired to Egypt.'

Vosper grabbed a chair and sat next to the cot as though he were visiting a patient in hospital. 'So time passes and Jowett rings me one day and . . . and Gavin calls me at home and says you have to come to my place it's important. I say no, I'm heading up a project in New Zealand, I can't come. He says to me that he needs me to see something that changes everything and he mentions Ologun and says you need to know where he came from. So I take a stratosphere transport to this Murton Dam complex a hundred miles west of Cairo to where he lives like some kind of nomad. I remember leaving the shuttle as it landed like it was some sort of drop-off mission in the middle of nowhere, and there was this storm that had been raging for several days. The country is on some flood alert and I head off . . . Anyway, I'm at his house standing in the dining room – we'd had words about the whole crazy call – and he presents me with this mound under a cloth on the table. I say to him, what the hell, Jowett? He pulls the cover back and I'm thinking there's this grey pulp of mess sat there. I'm thinking he's gone crazy or has dementia and that he had me fly halfway round the world to see some road kill. Then he tells me it's Ologun. Now I'm thinking he's killed the poor boy in some terrible way and I realise that the empty costume of a human being on the table is a young boy. I accuse him of God knows what, I mean I totally lose it and he tells me Ologun fell in Murton reservoir.'

Leigh had stopped working and horror formed on her face as she listened.

'The boy looked like some hideous thing,' Vosper continued. 'His innards had been pulled out and were all over the table, hanging out of his back end, and his eyes were gone with his brains or something coming out of his sockets, and I'm thinking shit, shit what the hell's Jowett doing? Jowett tells me he's okay and he's doing it . . . doing something. I lose the plot at this stage, grab him by the collar and start shaking him.' Vosper laughs out loud. 'We start fighting, good old-fashioned Jap slapping like professionals, and we end up knocking Ologun off the table. Then Gavin stops and scoops up the remains and I remember feeling numb with pity for him. Then the real terror begins.'

'I don't want to know,' Leigh said and returned to her work, ignoring him, then looked over at Ologun on the cot. 'Are you talking about this man?' she asked in confusion.

'Oh,' Vosper replied, 'Jowett tells me to look down the barrel of this huge bizarre-looking microscope he hangs from a hook on the ceiling over Ologun's body and . . . I remember seeing this thing like a, like a whirlpool of light particles flowing downwards into nowhere, nothing. Jowett then puts his own arm under the scope and says take a look, and I see something I think are cells, and the computer on the microscope says mitochondria, mammal, human, and he puts it back over Ologun and the thing says description subroutine error, unknown cell structure.

'And that's when he tells me about where they got him and what he was for and that he doesn't know what to do because this is far more than they ever bargained for . . . I mean literally bargained for.'

Leigh had by this point completely forgotten why she was even there. 'What the hell are you talking about, sir? We have another hour at most to get this done and I don't have time for this.'

'Seven days later,' Vosper said, 'he was as good as new like nothing had happened and the craziest thing is that he didn't even *remember* what happened.'

Leigh placed her hands on the console and leaned heavily against it. 'Why are you telling me this?'

'Because you're part of the Prospect Division now and my closest ally and aide. This is a dangerous and yet extraordinary time, and I need you to know what you're continuing with by being here.'

'Why?'

'Just think of the Prospect Division as a cult rather than a business and you'll be halfway there. You see, you have to make a choice here because everyone outside this room, those soldiers, know who Ologun is and what made him. With the IMC you can't afford to be naïve. With the PD you need to know what's at stake, the Integer Project.'

'The what?' Leigh asked, reeling at what she'd begun to think was a trap set just for her here in this soundproof vault.

'Gavin did the same to me that day, so please don't panic yet. If you refuse we wipe your memory here and now and simply transfer you back to the IMC, so please stay calm and listen to this because you're important to me, Leigh.'

Leigh found a chair and sat down. 'Okay.'

'Many years ago ships were sent to Deceiver and they vanished without trace. Fast forward and a starship sent to investigate reaches Deceiver's outer system's rock belt. The ship encountered a huge rock which appeared unusual, and on its side was a perfectly formed basin. Gavin Jowett was sent down, along with a few others, to investigate and came into contact with something Jowett described as liquid fire, Alien life, Leigh.'

Leigh's skin ran cold with disbelief. 'Ologun's an alien.'

'No, Leigh,' Vosper spat, grinning like a mad man. 'The entity was in trouble, but in some twist of fate we saved it by trying to kill it. It offered those on board the ship a way to start something, a better way. You see, this entity took . . . had intercepted those ships sent years before and took the people on board. God knows what it did with them but when it came to it, the Spectra, as it was eventually called, gave us a factory with the ability to cure almost any ailment.'

'Why would we need that?' Leigh asked sceptically.

'He's the reason we don't need such a thing any more. Do you recall the great crash thirty years back, when all the pharmaceutical giants suddenly went bankrupt and the IMC were accused of destroying a sector of business worth trillions? No more legal drug pushers.'

'Jesus,' Leigh blasphemed. 'Then this man is the reason for life-span limitations and the whole mess we're in with . . .'

'No, Leigh. The world population was always going to spin out of control, but that leads us to the next part of what I'm telling you and what I need you to do for us.'

Leigh felt fear at all of this. 'Aliens, Des?'

'We found two planets. The deal or offering from this entity wasn't for Earth, it was for one world twice Earth's mass we called Prospect and for another called Vanguard. What we're aiming for is big and maybe beyond immediate reach, and this plan that's been put in motion may take generations.' Vosper made his way back to Ologun's side. 'The thing that started all of this was the whirlpool of energy attached to each mitochondrion in Ologun's cells. This place we're in, this big old underground base, once led to the discovery of the ether that churns between what we imagine is another universe next to our own. Don't ask me, I don't know the physics. This whirlpool that we now dub an energy cascade is what we always thought a wormhole would or was supposed to be.' Vosper almost leapt towards a device standing on a desk which was used to synthesize any number of appliances. 'What's this exactly?'

'A 3D copy machine,' Leigh answered, frowning.

'We started with the ability to enter the realm where we could travel faster than light and, after the study of Ologun's cells, we're one step further. We're deeper and can travel vast distances in what would have taken us hundreds of years. We've kept this to ourselves and away from everyone because the IMC have forgotten the dream, the Integer Project, Leigh. Ologun exists in two places like that copy machine. Imagine that somewhere in another universe, for who knows what reason, the elaborate design that Ologun or everything that makes him is held in some construct. Now this construct creates trillions of cascades which penetrate into our universe, and on the other end of these strings of information is a man. Every time he's harmed and damaged, he's replenished, re-constructed: copied. Albeit one of the most insanely complex of things to achieve, but all the same the concept is remarkably simple and yet so effective.'

Leigh saw that the transformation of Vosper was complete; this assassin-made-officer who was now part of something that, if at all possible, might be worse than the company. 'What do you want from me?' Leigh asked.

'We don't want to kill those who may compromise our secrets. You are one of only a few gifted enough to change a person's memories with these machines, and I agree it would be better to alter and take away, say, any scientist's breakthrough than to kill them. One of a few, Leigh, for a world with no hunger and where everything is free, people are free, and where things are built to last, so that we can pursue better things away from commerce and greed.'

'The Integer Project,' Leigh said.

'Yes,' Vosper whispered.

'What about him?' Leigh gestured towards Ologun.

Vosper gazed at Ologun and rubbed his eyes, thinking. 'You know what the term loose cannon means or where it comes from?'

'It means you can't control something, I think.'

Vosper laughed at this definition. 'Well, it's from a time when archaic wooden galleons – ships – roamed the seas. Below decks these ships had these heavy cast-iron cannons attached to thick ropes. The canon fired with violent recoil and these ropes kept the cannon in place. If a rope should ever snap, the cannon would smash around the lower decks as the ship rolled through the waves, injuring or, more likely, killing everyone in its path. The thing is, Ologun has issues now. Some terrible things, or an accumulation of things in his life, are . . . well, I don't know what it is, but I'm told he might be prone to running amok.'

Excuse me?' Leigh exclaimed.

'You know . . .'

'Oh, I know what amok means,' Leigh cut in, offended that he was about to explain. 'So you have a man who doesn't die with psychological issues. Let me rephrase that, you mean someone who's likely to explode and go on a rampage?'

'Don't say explode,' Vosper said. 'Do you know how much energy is in a cascade? Makes antimatter look like a nasty cough, so what we're here to do is give him a false memory which leads to remorse. Give him a job, the one on Phobos that actually happened a few months back, as I ordered. Hopefully this false experience will put him back in the box until we can figure out what to do with him.'

'This may not work.'

'We have to try,' Vosper said. 'A mundane job in a mundane place, but interesting enough to hold him steady for a while and, with the memory of a mistake, the memory of an asset job gone wrong, he'll think it was wrong. In this context he'll see it as murder.'

'Give me twenty minutes,' Leigh suggested. 'Oh, and don't be wiping my memory, I'm in. Besides, if I refuse whoever you use to wipe my memory will likely botch the job and I'll end up a vegetable.'

'He's to go to Morocco not Libya,' Vosper ordered.

'If you insist.'

'Trust me. I think most of what's wrong with him was triggered in Libya.'

'What happened?'

'Something so very sad.'

Both Ray and Judith were just up ahead across the street. Judith walked towards him and dropped the satchel she was carrying to the floor where it made a clunking sound as though she'd brought crockery.

'Shall we? Judith asked.

'What?'

'Kill 'em all,' she replied.

'They're all going to die anyway,' Ologun suggested. He could see the anger and confusion in her eyes and felt a great deal of empathy for her.

'Well, I'm not going to that planet to be poked around anytime before I've had it out . . . they killed a lot of innocent people. They killed me,' Judith argued.

'That's true enough,' Ray said, following close behind Judith while Ologun held silent, seeing her hair still matted with dried blood and a dark stain covering most of her navy shirt.

Judith's eyes changed as she became preoccupied. She ran her eyes over Ologun and Ray in turn. 'What are you two wearing?'

'Second skin,' Ologun said.

'Combat suits,' Ray said simultaneously.

'You saw me wearing it earlier,' Ray added.

'You were naked earlier.'

'And you were offended, so I picked it up when we went below to the Spectra,' Ray said, wondering what was wrong with Judith.

Judith went silent for a moment, then walked over to Ologun. She appeared as though she would hug him, but instead she grabbed the cleavers and took them. 'I believe these are mine.'

'What?' Ologun spat in protest.

'Actually,' Ray intervened before an argument ensued, 'I made them for Judith in the hope of gaining sexual favour.'

Ologun was dumbfounded, although he couldn't be sure as to which part. 'Subtle, Ray, that's just how you woe the opposite sex.'

'Don't you mean woo?' Ray asked.

'I know what I meant,' Ologun said scornfully.

'They're just decorative pieces for Judith's collection,' Ray said in defence.

Ologun felt particularly wounded at this and added, 'I thought Hina made them.'

'Well,' Ray flustered. 'I gave him the design and . . .'

'Nice one, Ray,' Ologun said, tapping him on the shoulder. At least Ray was now covered in second skin which was a sort of deep copper colour that seemed more appropriate to his actual skin colour.

They then both turned to Judith who was stripping naked. 'What the hell are you doing?' Ologun shrieked.

She moved toward him and used one of the blades to cut her wrist. 'Come here,' she ordered Ologun.

'Ray, what's she doing?' Ologun asked, seeing that Ray was unhealthily amused and absorbed by the scene.

Judith grabbed Ologun by the arm and he pulled away. 'Judith, get off me; what the shit fire are you doing?'

The two of them struggled for a moment. 'Maybe I should leave you two alone,' Ray said, looking a touch disappointed.

'Don't you dare,' Ologun said, in plea as much as threat.

'Will you hold still? I can't concentrate on a colour,' Judith complained.

A thread from the sleeve of Ologun's skin wrapped itself around Judith's arm and broke off. It then spread out to engulf her torso until she was covered in a skin that was similar in colour to the uniform she had worn.

'Oh, I see,' Ologun stated and relaxed.

'We're not going into combat, Judith, you don't need such a thing yet,' Ray advised her.

'Are you kidding me? This is, this is something for me,' she said with a wicked smile, then looked down at her newly acquired garment. 'Shit, its navy! Well, I'm just going to have to make another.'

Ologun stepped back a few paces, believing that somehow it would involve him. 'Is that my skin?'

'No,' Ray said, then shook his head unable to find the effort to explain the process.

'I would have preferred purple or cyan,' Judith continued, running her fingers over her arm.

'So what are you saying, Judith?' Ologun asked in disbelief. 'Are you, what? Going to have a wardrobe full of skin?'

'Oh,' Judith said and knelt down to grab her satchel. 'I thought you'd be upset when I took back my ornamental gifts, so I found these in Hina's cave.'

Ologun looked utterly perplexed at this statement, but decided not to ask and watched as she pulled two weapons from the bag. They were made of a black marble and their strange surfaces appeared smooth yet elusive in texture. The first weapon, a cudgel, was instantly recognisable as a tonfa – commonly referred to as a nightstick. The second weapon was a long machete with a fearsome blade cut off at a forty degree angle at the end.

'I admit they won't look as good on your wall as two crossed blades,' Judith said. 'I get the impression that this level of work is like an upgrade – a stronger material so you can at least use the machete for work or something.'

Ologun stared at the weapons as Judith chatted away. Ray could see that Ologun had drifted and he grew anxious.

'What's going on?' Judith asked, sensing the rising tension which was way beyond the level she'd expected at retrieving her property.

'Nothing that concerns you,' Ray explained. Judith nodded and decided to press Ologun on the issue later. She at least realised he was acting peculiar and asking him further questions at present might be a waste of time.

'So, are we going to war?' she asked and swung the cleavers.

Ray began to answer when Judith cut him off. 'Ray, why don't you piss off for a while?'

Ray stood for a moment then finally slipped away, trying to be as dignified as possible.

'Dammit,' Judith blasphemed, holding her forehead with her left hand. 'This is all a bit much. It's like some animation, it's not real is it? I mean, I'm calm and I can think straight but the information I think I know is messed up somehow. What's with Vanguard?'

'I'm not sure,' Ologun offered. 'Could be something, I mean you and I need to take longer on that one, a suggested idea or thought bandying about doesn't make what happened on Vanguard . . . There are other things to think about right now.'

'Like what? I tell you something, though. Those GSA soldiers are going to be absorbed as information into the Spectra.'

'Just like our parents,' Ologun said, not sure what he felt about it.

'You ready for Prospect?' Judith asked. She was optimistic and trying to filter out the rest of the thoughts and information settling in her mind, which was at this point akin to a loud noise.

'I have to go to Earth.'

'What? Why? I don't understand.'

'You know the Prospect Division or Empire has just gone to war with Earth? A thousand ships have just processed around the planet and it's not so much a war as a slaughter.'

'That has nothing to do with us. We belong to the Division,' Judith pleaded.

Ologun's tone changed to anger at Judith's remark. 'Did you know the woman, Doctor Siren, made a weapons-grade virus here? And that this virus is to be used to kill off everyone who refuses or is unable to go to Prospect when this so-called war is over? Did you know that this strain will take the next two hundred years to cripple and destroy until no one is left? Judith, I can't even begin to grasp how evil this whole thing has become. I know the reasons for this revolution, and I know it's been in the making for a long time, but the whole independence thing is out of control.'

'There are twenty four billion people on Earth, Ologun. Too many to take to Prospect and too many for Earth to have a viable future. This has to happen.'

Ologun was stupefied and his eyes flashed a more vibrant colour.

'Shit, Ologun, calm down.'

'Who has the right to decide all this?' he shouted. 'I'm going back to Earth and doing what I was made for.'

'You can't,' Judith said.

'I'm going for a drink and wait for that clown hiding in that ship to come out, and then I'm taking the *Hollywood* home.'

'You know he can kill you,' Judith warned.

'I know. If he sends the ship to position process and detonates a bomb, the link to whatever keeps re-making us might be severed.'

'You know a lot more than you let on.'

Ologun turned and began to make his way south away from the city.

'Where are you going now?'

'To get drunk,' Ologun shouted back.

'I thought you were going for the *Hollywood*! Okay, I'm sorry, I know what the PD are doing is unspeakable . . .'

Something drew Ologun's attention away from Judith. His senses shifted towards the rushing movement of birds flocking away from the north side of the city. He peered down the long avenue ahead, past Judith and then beyond Ray, who was sitting on a pavement sulking and throwing stones across the street. Ologun focused his vision towards the barricade where he heard the sound of gunfire followed by a loud explosion.

'Oh dear,' Judith said smiling. 'They shot Hina.'

Ologun could see Hina flat out on the ground sixty feet away from the barricade and soldiers were running across the top of their defensive wall.

Then Ologun saw what he'd been searching for as it descended rapidly from the star lens and towards the basin floor. His heart raced at the sight. 'Judith, you need to hand Ray one of your blades now!'

YEAR 2255

Western Sahara Development Zone: Mirage Six

TWO WRONGS

'More bread, Ologun?' Feisal asked and offered the plate across the table. It was all he could offer the man who had brought most of the provisions for what he considered a bountiful meal. Feisal's wife Haelu kept both eyes on Ologun, and to him she appeared deep in thought, perhaps wondering at his level of kindness. She ate small amounts of food from her plate, yet her gaze never wavered.

'And so you think this waste food can be taken without raising suspicion?' Feisal asked once again. 'You say it's below standard, but quite good enough to eat, yes?'

'Don't bother him with such things while eating,' Haelu insisted.

'Let me think about things,' Ologun said and finished the remaining food from his plate. 'Very nice, thank you, Haelu, you're very good at making the best of very little.'

Haelu smiled. 'Shall we head outside and make a fire?'

'You're right,' Feisal offered. 'We shall discuss this later. Now it is time for coffee and sweeties, though I do not like coffee.'

'Then drink water,' Haelu said, taking offence and glaring at her husband in response to his rudeness.

They moved outside the large tent and sat on old plastic chairs. The evening was cool and the sun had almost set. A strong breeze had picked up across the camp and swept the fabric of the many tents which had been erected in a neat row.

Opposite the camp and half a mile to the north, the more permanent residential area for immigrants could be seen as a mishmash of square huts and other oddly fashioned buildings which formed the town its residents called Blessed Earth. Officially the camp had been coded Mirage Six, but the further moniker of Demon's Crevice had become popular among the security forces working there.

The caravan Feisal had travelled with consisted of many families who had set up camp with makeshift tents of cloth held aloft by various bits of scaffold and other pipe work. Some of the travellers had vehicles with trailers which were large and secure and, even though old and battered, they were safer places to sleep than the roughly constructed pergolas.

Ologun surveyed the shanty town across waste ground blown into swathes of fine dust clouds by the trade winds, which somehow created the illusion of a well-developed and vast city wreathed in dimness and shadow. Things were quiet in the town but had only become this way after the hand over from the GEA to the IMC in order to implement a strategy of old. The GEA had not welcomed the immigrants, and had made life very difficult with appalling conditions, which in turn had made the area dangerous for the people and themselves.

The first phase, which had begun with the old-fashioned and sensible 'hearts and minds campaign', had seen the IMC teams install plumbing as well as carrying out their usual peacekeeping duties. It was surprising to see how effectively offering a clean water supply free of charge had calmed the situation down. The next three phases were just as important and had sealed the deal so that the immigrants realised that the new occupying force had come to help. Ologun had hated the second phase where all excrement had to be cleaned from the muddy streets; they had set up a further engineering project to install sanitary blocks at intervals across the town: the human waste was classed as an extra commodity to enrich the soil.

The third phase, and one which was hard to establish, was that of law and order. The IMC had arrived to riots and bloodshed and it had been too dangerous to uphold any conventional laws. It had taken time to establish a civilised environment, and it continued to be a challenge. At least the IMC had gained much praise for cutting costs through such efforts. Investors were hardly concerned with the loss of life, yet such exploits had proved far more economical than

GEA's management style. Everyone knew that the most feasible way for the GEA to deal with the situation in the easiest, most stringent way would be the systematic and total eradication of the town's population, which would also enhance the discouragement of more immigration. Fortunately the world had not yet become desperate enough to sanction such ideals and had in turn left the GEA at a loss; they'd been left without the option of deadly force and were from a culture that couldn't control such an environment without having this option at their disposal.

'It's bigger than I thought,' Feisal exclaimed as he surveyed the town.

'It's going to get a whole lot bigger, I think,' Ologun replied and thought of its possible future. 'I hope my company gets the chance to develop it into a town with real buildings and facilities. Who knows, maybe it'll provide jobs, have its own economy. They did that with Pharant.'

Feisal walked over to the back of his truck, opened the back door, and reached inside. He grabbed a bundle of chopped wood and walked back towards Ologun. 'Yes, I've been there once, and then to Cairo many years ago, when there was money and food and no war.' He gazed into the night, deep in thought at the state of the world as it was today compared to when he was young. *Better days will never be!* 'I think it's time for a nice fire. This place here will be surrounded by thick forests in a few decades, don't you think?' he continued as he crouched to build the fire. He placed a set of bricks in the form of a circle, then began to erect the wood in the shape of a cone.

Ologun laughed at the idea of a town completely enclosed within a forest. 'No, the city would need to be routed south-west from here and towards the lens fields, maybe through the graveyards to the west.'

'City?' Feisal said in jest at Ologun's optimism. 'Larger than Casablanca?'

'Well.' Ologun shrugged.

'What of this graveyard, what is this?' Feisal asked in wonder.

Version

'You see those tall structures over there in the distance?' Ologun pointed to the west and Feisal squinted in that direction. In the last of the evening's fading light, he could just see the silhouettes of many towers. To him they appeared to be a set of evenly spaced trees; sad remnants of a great forest fire which had destroyed and twisted their branches. 'Those are the wind turbines no one could be bothered to tear down. They built thousands of them everywhere, you know.'

'Yes, I remember they weren't as productive.'

'Not as productive as what?' Ologun asked.

'As much as they cost to erect of course.'

'They did well enough before the lenses came,' Ologun argued.

'Have you not finished the fire yet? My mother always say, Haelu, you marry a slow and useless man!'

'Yes, yes, tssk. Give me that,' Feisal complained and took a tray from Haelu. 'Here's your coffee and sweeties.'

Ologun took a metal cup from the tray and relaxed into his chair while Haelu lit the fire just in time to beat the darkness.

'I would have very much liked to see the desert when it had sand,' Feisal said as he sat down.

Ologun turned his head towards the east and, even though he couldn't see anything, the distant rumble of machines could still be heard.

Feisal also turned to listen, then realised what the sound was. 'I think that this flatness is just as enchanting in a way, yet I'm always amazed how men can pillage such a thing so quickly.'

Ologun made a humming noise in agreement and thought the same. In order to create what was referred to as the hard lens, the type mainly used for off-world energy requirements due to their more reliable design, vast amounts of sand had been filtered for quartz and utilised to create the transparent disks to encase billions of antennae which transformed the energy provided by the sun's rays. 'I'm sure a jungle to match that of the Congo would be just as, if not more of, a sight to behold.'

'Yes, that is true,' Feisal said in agreement. 'Yet I think there's a joke in this somewhere, such as where did all the sand go?'

Ologun warmed his hands by the fire, which had now taken hold, and saw that Haelu was again staring at him suspiciously.

'What would a man from the past say to another man from the present?' Feisal said. He stroked his long white beard and his sunken eyes were dark and sparkling from the fire's glow. He lifted a bushy eyebrow and smiled. 'One would say, have you been to the Sahara desert? And the other would say no, but I have been to the Sahara jungle.' He erupted with laughter at his own joke.

Ologun remained straight faced and shook his head. 'That's not anything remotely . . .' then laughed at such a terrible attempt.

Ologun found it odd that, after so many years spent in this place, he hadn't met anyone he considered to be a friend. It wasn't so much that he was alienated or lonely, for really he just preferred his own company. He spent little time with his colleagues out of work hours and found them to be both crude and mundane.

Still, Ologun found that his usual state of existence had changed in the past two days after a solo patrol fifty miles south of the fort and town, which had ended with him being stranded. His vehicle had broken down on the eastern perimeter of a vast lens field, and even though he'd tried to call for assistance, the comms had been powered by the same mechanism that had malfunctioned in the first place. Cursing the technology and the possibly fatal trek back to base, he'd managed to hike a few miles until he'd arrived at the skeletal remains of a wind farm. He'd climbed the stairwell and arrived at its summit to survey his surroundings.

Between the ferocious red glow of the lens fields, and as far as he could see, a wide dirt track headed in geometric fashion straight through the middle and southwards into the distance. The ground quivered with heat and made it so that he thought his mind was playing tricks when he saw the long single file of a caravan trudging towards his direction from the south. After a long and hot hour's wait, the caravan arrived and he'd been aided and rescued by Feisal and his wife. Ologun had seldom met such a chirpy and generous man and, as thanks for such kindness, had brought Feisal food and other provisions that same day. That and the fact Ologun had just started a few days' leave from his duties had ended up as two consecutive dinner invitations.

Ologun felt that Feisal's story was sad but not uncommon. He had worked in Rwanda on one of the algae compounds. That, by all accounts, was a trade which required skill and intelligence. Feisal had been a casualty of progression when his job at a transformer complex which refined and filtered the oil produced by the algae was no longer sustainable. There was just no technology left in the world which required so much oil. What Ologun found difficult to ascertain was what exactly had prompted him to take such a perilous journey all the way to Blessed Earth? When he'd asked Feisal this obvious question, he'd simply stated that it was a secret, which in turn, Ologun had felt, was hint enough for him not to press the man any further.

Ologun felt tired and was preparing to leave when Feisal sprang to his feet. 'More sweeties, coffee?' He dashed into the tent before Ologun could answer. Smoke and the thick smell of burning wood filled the air as he watched a similar scene of camp activity with people huddled around their own fires and various types of stoves across the way. Some were still carrying out various chores while others relaxed and even slept out in the open. In general, they appeared happy and felt safe enough to allow their children to play freely so that even now, they ran amok throughout the camp with a level of energy that only the young possessed.

Ologun wondered at the state of the camp and how none of its residents had even attempted to find homes within the boundaries of the town. So far, they'd remained in a state of readiness that indicated further travel was expected. Many languages and dialects echoed across the site, which Ologun found difficult to understand and he was pleased that so many from all across the continent had pulled together in order to get here; especially aboard such battered and run-down modes of transportation. These people, despite cultural, as well as nationality and ideological, differences were at peace amongst themselves, even those whose countries were still in the states of conflict which had caused them to flee in the first place.

A commotion from somewhere in the camp drew Ologun's attention and, without hesitating, he stood up to make his way towards the noise. He passed the trucks parked to the front of the camp and beyond another row of tents where a crowd of men had gathered. As he approached, Ologun could see that there were two groups and that one of the town's gangs was becoming hostile towards the travellers. *Shit in the fire!* He recognised the men straight away: they all wore jackets of matching camel suede and had draped various styles of black scarf around their necks.

'You're not welcome here! If you stay we'll hurt you!' one of them shouted.

'Kill you!' another one hollered.

Ologun continued towards the men. He noticed they were sizing up their opposition and something would take place at any moment. His main concern was that a number of the gang had brought sticks, stones, chains, metal bars and knives.

He walked amongst them and along the gap the two groups had created, realising that the group of travellers had grown in number. 'We're stopping for a short while, no trouble here.'

As the argument escalated, Ologun identified members of the gang and eventually the leader. 'Yureph, go home and take the rest of them with you,' he ordered.

Yureph looked surprised at seeing Ologun and changed from being outwardly hostile and vocal to sheepish and subdued, and also showed obvious levels of anxiety. Whatever it was he feared, Yureph said a few words to his men and quickly left.

Ologun paid no attention to the mob behind him which stared at him in wonder, perhaps a little too surprised to give thanks, or somewhat disappointed that they hadn't the chance to stand their own ground. Ologun began to make his way home and decided he was in no mood to return to Feisal's camp; he'd make sure he saw them the next evening and apologise for his unannounced departure.

'Ologun,' a woman's voice shouted. He turned to see that Haelu had followed him and groaned with irritation. 'I'm sorry for leaving like that, it's just . . . Please apologise to Feisal for me and thank you for the evening.'

'No need to be this polite,' she said. 'I just wanted to talk to you.'

'Some other time, tomorrow if I'm invited.'

'As suits you best. It is important, so please come.'

Ologun nodded and glanced at the remainder of the crowd who watched his every move, and seemed particularly curious of him. He then made his way toward the town and to the west where the fort was situated.

He woke the next day to sounds resonating from the fort. He'd decided to sleep on a bench situated high above the compound on a lookout tower and within its uppermost sangar that rose two hundred feet above ground level. It was now late morning and relatively hot, yet the fort was still quite busy with many IMC staff going about their business.

Ologun sat up and gazed out from the shadows and across the flats. To the north and less than ten miles away, the forest looked like a distinct barricade that stretched across as far as the eye could see. In front of this, great machines ploughed the golden land, while others planted saplings in uniformed lines in maladroit fashion; gouging with cupped appendages, indelicately plunking the root ball into pockets in the ground and then sifting the excess dirt into place. A workforce of men carried out a task that required more skill as they erected pipes and scaffolding which rose for hundreds of feet above the ground and across the nursery fields. When connected they would spray the land with enriched water from all angles.

To the west, a great expanse containing many fields of various crops sat beneath great rainbows which had been created by massive arcs of water sprayed from rotating pumps. To the south, Ologun could see the wind farm graveyard and, in front of this, the lens fields were illuminated as an angry sea of red.

He then turned his attention to his reality: the IMC camp beneath him. Sitting directly outside the fort's eastern security wall, the shanty town worked its way well beyond and into the horizon.

The fort itself was of a simple design: a basic square with a perimeter wall that was thirty feet in height and made of very tough interlocking metal plates. Ologun observed the guards as they walked across the eastern wall along wire-mesh walkways. Beyond this, the town served as the most chaotic scene of all and one he had never gotten used to. The whole area to the east of the fort was alive with movement and colour. Tents, cabins, caravans and all types of makeshift abodes were strewn out for miles along a very wide lane that was split into sections. There were streets stretched between rows of accommodation and led on to marketplaces, sanitary complexes, and even a section left as open ground so that a sort of grassy parkland had been developed; it was a very busy place in contrast to the lull within the fort.

Many of the town's residents were still queuing along one of the town's most central avenues in order to fill containers with their daily allowance of water. IMC soldiers kept guard over the taps and would lock them away within reinforced sheds when finished. Many were carrying their water home while others carried it to the south of the town and to the allotments where they grew their own food; incredibly there was enough civility here for such a commodity not to be pillaged that often. Ologun could only surmise that enough people here wanted the town to work and that even without IMC intervention, the town's numerous communities punished those who placed this in jeopardy.

Ologun made his way down from the tower and walked out into the blazing sun. He walked past a row of cabins used as offices and then beyond the next few rows of metal freight containers utilized for accommodation.

As an addition to the fort's defensive walls, an extra protective roof had been erected as a port to cover all perimeter buildings. Ologun was one of only several to have had his accommodation set near a wall and under the extra shield. He walked by the mess hall and the gym and entered under the shade of the security port towards his own cubicle.

'Hey, Ghost.' Ologun turned to see that K Green sniper detail were lounging around on the steps leading up to the colonel's office.

'Man, you done three weeks of days and you still have skin like a newborn albino,' one of them shouted.

'Hell, everyone knows he sleeps in a stasis unit, ain't that right, Snowdrop?'

Ologun had already had a few altercations with the man called Mustard. He was built like a block of butter and had strawberry blond hair and a matching handlebar moustache.

'Better than looking like a slapped pig. Shit, Mustard, you look like you've been skinned alive,' Ologun fired back. It was all in good humour, and the group laughed at the jibe.

'Ologun Jowett,' a voice came from above.

Ologun lifted his head to see a man he didn't recognise on the top landing of the stairs. He noticed the man bore the insignia of a colonel. 'Come up here to my office, Sergeant, I need to speak with you.'

Your office? Ologun thought with surprise. He made his way past the sniper team and up the two flights of steps. 'You in for a dickey back ride now, pasty face.'

It was very cool inside the office, almost uncomfortable in comparison to the level of heat outside. 'Please take a seat,' the man offered. 'I'm Colonel Cromak.'

Ologun nodded as he moved towards the main desk situated at the back of the room and sat down opposite Cromak. 'Where's Colonel Ogura?'

'I've been sent to replace Ogura in order to assess each member of staff and oversee the handover.'

'I wasn't aware that another IMC crew were to replace us. Where will we be exchanged to exactly?'

'One thing at a time,' Cromak said. 'The exchange isn't going to be with the IMC. Within the next month GEA will be resuming command of the area and until then we are to work alongside them and bring them up to speed.'

Ologun felt physically sick at this news and sat in silence as he probed the room and clutter. The only light came from a lamp on the desk; its bulb bathed the room a sickly pale green. 'So all this work was for nothing,' he eventually said.

'That is no longer the IMC's concern. Morocco just re-joined the GEA and now own the land as far as the mid-flats, and yes, I know, it's a raw deal considering our investment to get this place up and running properly. The cost to the House of Ecology alone has been significant. I'm sure the GEA has already set out a repayment schedule.' Cromak moved to a cabinet to his left and lifted a file from the drawer.

'That's not what I meant,' Ologun seethed.

'I know,' Cromak quickly intervened. 'Now, I'm not here to discuss politics, so listen up. I've been reviewing everyone's file to see who is fit for purpose because I don't want anyone here who's a liability. Mixing of contractors is a tricky business considering our companies', how shall we say, cultural differences and policy objectives. Now, I know who you are and how much clout you had due to your father. In fact, I've tried to be as objective as possible while reviewing your file, and quite frankly I'm amazed.'

Ologun could see what was coming and held tightly on to what little patience he had left.

'The head peddlers at Control really like to skirt around you, don't they?' Cromak grinned as he sifted through the file. 'Asset control training – failed due to a morality dysfunction. I can tell you what your problem is, son, and it's that you were recruited too late in the day. Christ, you have some real skill at that hunting game don't you? Shame that you had too many ideals roaming in that skull of yours before they programmed you.'

Ologun's heart was beating fast and the coldness of the room failed to stop sweat forming on his brow. He felt that at any moment he'd deck this guy black and blue.

'Thirty eight counts of violent interaction with various sand sniffers,' Cromak continued, shaking his head and chortling away. 'What I don't get is how one man can be such a magnet to so many low-life activities in such a short space of time. I can only assume that you consider yourself some sort of super-regulator the way you've gone about this town.'

'We're meant to provide a safe and controlled environment for the people,' Ologun argued. 'I've done nothing wrong.'

'Subject Twenty Two F,' Cromak said, raising his voice and ignoring Ologun. 'Your statement reads, "I heard a woman scream and a man shouted, 'Hold still, bitch, you love it.' I sought out the source of the noise where a man was clearly attacking a young woman. When I tried to stop this assault, the man attacked me." Obviously the biggest mistake of his life, I mean what in the hell did you do to him? One broken leg, all ribs broken, severe concussion, fractured cheekbone, acute trauma to pelvis, acute trauma to skull, shattered collarbone. Shit, this guy was lucky to have survived.'

'He put up a savage fight,' Ologun quipped in defiance.

'You've managed to notch up the same number of incidences as the entire company combined.' Cromak shrugged and threw the file on to the desk. 'I cannot allow you to stay here during the transfer, you're a spark which would end up losing us the city to a rampaging fire. I'm having you transferred the day after tomorrow, I'm sorry. I've requested that you be sent to Timbuktu for security detail.'

'Timbuktu, that's some kind of joke right?' Ologun said, confused at the order.

'Not at all,' Cromak insisted with all seriousness. 'Continue your leave until tomorrow, and make sure you've packed your kit for when your final shift is completed. You are dismissed, Sergeant Jowett, that will be all.'

Ologun left the office and went straight to his cubicle. His room was fairly neat and tidy, due mainly to the fact that he hardly spent any time there and often slept in other places for three to six hours at a time. He paced the room and thought long and hard about this new turn of events. It was obviously all political nonsense, which he'd never been into, and he found himself at a loss as to his next course of action; if in fact there was to be one at all.

He moved to a small desk to the right of his bed and pulled a comms device from the drawer. He connected a small satellite dish to its box shape, then clicked a digital pad in place on top. 'Put me through to Director Bright,' he said.

The machine's voice responded, 'Time in New York is beyond sociable recommendations, are you positive?'

'Just do it, now,' he ordered the device and paced the room.

A short while later the digipad's screen lit up with the face of a man who had clearly just woken up. 'Who is this? Do you have any idea what—'

'It's me,' Ologun interrupted. He was clearly unsympathetic at having called Bright at such an hour.

'Ologun, God's sakes, bro, you could have waited. Some of us actually sleep, you know.'

'You knew the contract was lost and you didn't tell me,' Ologun fumed.

'Look, bro, it happened two days ago and I've been up to my eyeballs in too many—'

'What the hell's going on?' Ologun demanded to know, uninterested in his excuses. Although Bright was a childhood friend and a valuable contact at Command, he really didn't care to be courteous under the circumstances.

'Look, it's complicated and there's more going on than the Moroccan government's change of heart. Actually that's not the only problem,' Bright said. He rubbed his eyes and lit a cigarette. 'The United States just signed a deal along with Russia for the IMC to build five ships apiece. On top of that they both invested in a significant Martian real-estate deal, and I mean dome, ecology the works.'

Ologun sat on his bed and adjusted the pad to gain a clearer picture of Bright. 'That means absolutely nothing to me.'

'We're not just talking frigate class for Deceiver. Bells and whistles are ablowing for three cruise and two bombardment class. The old superpowers are aching to be back in business.' Bright raised his eyebrows and took a deep drag on his cigarette. 'The GEA is really a public-funded conglomerate implemented by the state of Europe . . .'

'Don't start from the beginning like I'm a child. We went to uni together and did the same courses,' Ologun barked. In reality he knew how it all worked, yet he normally chose to plead ignorance to his level of knowledge.

'Right, right,' Bright said then laughed. 'Japan and China were eager to do the deal, while India and Australia kind of went along with it all. Now the European parliament is playing funny house by cancelling all IMC contracts on any of their assets, they won't even have the IMC provide for their ships, and I mean weapons contracts and all. As far as your lot are concerned, the nearest place the IMC will be allowed in North West Africa is Timbuktu, and only a few ever get to go there.'

'That's where this Cromak is sending me,' Ologun said. 'What's the deal? I had no idea there was a base there.'

'Yeah, there's something going on there all right. Off-world sand-quartz transplants for something, a *lot* of sand, I don't know . . . it's classified.'

'These people in this town are going to die if—'

'Not going to happen, bro,' Bright interrupted. 'One month and the IMC will house them at Section Three, eighty miles south-west of Cairo. Just finalising the transport arrangements now, er well, tomorrow, I mean today.' Bright yawned.

'And if they won't leave?' Ologun asked.

'There's no reason why that would be. The town we made is excellent, large enough for the five million, easy.'

'Five million!' Ologun said, confused at the figure Bright had reeled off.

'That's the figure I have for the town as of March twentieth.'

'No, there's around a hundred thousand . . . if that,' Ologun insisted.

'Well, that's the registered number via the gatehouses. Your men, your tally, bro. Five million are said to be there right now.'

'Whatever, sounds good.' Ologun sighed with some relief. 'Though one month is a long time under the GEA. You remember contemporary tenders?' he continued.

'Yeah, sure, that's always been bullshit speak,' Bright answered and chuckled. He lit another cigarette and swung around in his chair. 'Whatever happened to international community and responsibility, that's what you were gonna ask, right?'

Ologun smirked at Bright's ability to sense he was about to instigate a philosophical conversation. 'Hiding behind the skirt of a business that supposedly floats on the free market under no influence or control,' Ologun reeled off.

'If you don't have the competition or the opposing force, then what's the point? It's all a competition, bro, for better and for worse. Besides, the E in GEA just became Europe instead of Earth as of two days ago. They're going to fold in the next three years, I'm telling you. That leaves just the one,' Bright exclaimed with all certainty.

'GEA are not a company. Our company is not a company. It's Japan and India and . . .'

'Yeah, I know.' Bright mused, cutting Ologun off from a possible rant. 'How come you never came here with me? Hell, bro, you could be a director with your dad's level of clout.' Bright's grin fell away and his face grew pensive. 'You should have taken more time off after the funeral, you know. Shit, bro, you could retire with the wealth he left you. Anyway, I wish you'd give up this crap, you'll get yourself killed or kill someone you shouldn't, being that you're a loon moon and all. Oh, I get the reports of your activities, it's like you're a legend up here, bro. They used to hand around the incident reports like they were comic strips.'

Ologun shook his head and felt more ashamed than anything else. 'Sorry I woke you.'

'No problem. Why don't you take some leave, come see me and the family for a few weeks? H would love to see you. Better still, just retire. Honestly, I miss you, bro.'

'Sure, I'll start with a vacation, see how it goes. Soon.' Ologun smiled.

'Soon,' Bright said.

Ologun leant over and cut the link.

Ologun fell asleep and woke in the early evening feeling groggy. He gathered his things and headed over to the camp in order to advise Feisal to leave; it was apparent that the travellers weren't staying in any case, though he had no idea where they were headed. He sped across the waste ground and arrived to a great commotion where a large crowd had gathered west of the camp. He leapt out of the truck and grabbed the nearest person. 'What happened here?'

Version

The woman said something in a language he didn't understand, yet he could see she was both angry and upset. He pushed through the mob and emerged into a small clearing which revealed his worst fear. Three bodies on the ground were covered in blood-soaked sheets, and a number of men were sitting nearby and being treated for injuries. Ologun approached one of them. 'What happened to you?'

'Those people came back, crept in and did this. My sister's missing.' the man said. 'We're going to town to find her.'

Ologun couldn't grasp how things had got so bad in just one day, and they were getting worse by the minute. 'Don't do that,' he insisted. 'Stay here, I'll go.'

'Who are you?' the man asked.

'I'm the one who's going to make sure you don't get yourself killed.'

'You go by yourself, as one man . . . *you* get killed!'

'Let him go!' a man shouted. Ologun recognised the voice and saw Feisal walking towards him. 'He's Ologun, a genuine friend, and he's a skilled man for these things. That is true, is it not?'

'I think so,' Ologun replied.

'What will you do?' the other man asked, still unsure and anxious about his sister. 'If you go, I will come, along with my brother and cousin.'

'No,' Ologun said forcefully. 'Feisal is right, I know where she might be and I can get in and out without incident.'

'Why has this happened? Where is the law?' the man cried in anger.

By now the mob had turned its attention to the three of them, leaving Ologun feeling exposed and at a loss to answer. 'It's complicated,' he finally stated. The real answer was that budget constraints didn't allow for a full implementation of total law enforcement, so gangs could get away with much, as long as they could avoid upsetting the surrounding community.

A short time later, after Feisal had convinced the travellers not to start something they couldn't win, Ologun travelled back to town. He parked at the fort and set off towards the gang's row of cabins three miles to the east. He walked the streets and through the rows of various huts and trailers. A multitude of thoughts swam through his mind as he took a stealthy approach. His main grief was that the girl was only ten years old and this gang were known for forms of slavery, more specifically the sex trade. He knew his own temperament at the idea of this and hoped to get there soon and before his hand was forced.

He heard voices and hid in an alleyway between five portable cabins, which appeared to be old GEA cabins which had been thrown out of the fort on the IMC's arrival. Several men passed by and all fell silent once again. It was late enough and there were few people about, except that he was in their territory and wasn't sure how they'd react to his being there at this hour.

Ologun had come unarmed. At this moment he didn't trust himself and would rather be caught empty handed than be found brandishing a weapon. More worryingly he felt strange and pent-up to a point he'd never been before. It was anger or something similar, but nowhere near as intense as he'd previously experienced. Right now he had terrible images of things he wanted to do, and which he hoped he'd never be capable of.

It had started with the colonel. He'd had images of trashing the office and killing him in numerous ways, before he'd returned to reality. Then, several times during the remainder of the conversation, he'd thought he would punch him without being able to control his own body. *Maybe I should have reported this!* Time was running out and he cursed that his pattern of thought was so stupid; he could have got a squad out on an official basis and not need worry over this dangerous venture. *It must be the pressure and the news I received today.* Whatever it was had begun to send him into a whole new place which had precluded him from thinking he was still IMC. He felt very much on his own.

Ologun turned a corner and the dusty street looked more like a docking yard with containers piled three to five high in rows. People lived here and had cut through the bottoms and tops of the freight containers so they could live on different levels as if in a house. The metal cuttings had then been used as shutters in front of holes cut for windows, and the excess had been utilized as doors on bolt hinges.

He spotted the gang's row of containers which were interconnected, creating one large building. Running across and exposed in the fullness of moonlight, he made his way to the back of the structure. He stopped to listen and held his nose and mouth from the foul smell of waste dumped at the rear fence. A barking dog, an argument, a baby crying, cats fighting, and then he found it. His heart raced and hoped it wasn't the girl, for way above him and inside the metal container he could hear faint moans and sobbing. The noise was coming from the fifth container; stacked high and around forty feet up. He would have to enter the building and make his way to the top.

He moved to a rear entrance that was a simply cut rectangular hole in the metal. He entered to see a man asleep on a filthy couch at the far end of the room. He was flat on his back snoring, and the noise echoed loudly within the metal enclosure.

Ologun saw a hole in the container's roof leading to the next level and quietly made his way towards a crudely fashioned rope ladder. The place stank and the floor was strewn with mess and rubbish, even dog excrement. He leapt up and grabbed the roof of the container, then peered over on to the next level. Two men at the far end were asleep, sitting against the walls opposite each other, as another slept upright in an old cushioned chair. Opposite his position was another ladder made of wood leading to the third floor.

He did the same again and peeked through the hole. This time there were hatchways on each wall leading off into other containers. Rags had been hung above each of them, obscuring the way except for the light beyond which projected shadows on to the fabric. This cabin was empty apart from a desk where a pile of weapons, such as knives, bats, chains and other barbaric tools, were laid out for quick picking.

The scene on the next floor shocked Ologun as it was used to house the women, who were now asleep on bundles of rags strewn in heaps across the container's floor. This floor, however, was different as the container's far side had been removed and the room appeared to be one long corridor.

Crouching, he made his way to the nearest pile of rags where a woman was asleep on her front and covered by a thin cloth. His eyes adjusted in the darkness as he looked closely at her face and then at her exposed shoulders. Her dark skin made it difficult for him to see her features with much clarity, though he could just make out the bruises and various other wounds that covered her face, neck and arms.

Ologun lifted his focus towards the rest of the cabin and the others who were slightly lit by the moonlight shining through the window ports cut into the container's sides. The sound of voices from above came through the last hatchway above and opposite his position. This time a set of metal steps made of the same material as the containers had been erected, leading up to the light of the next floor.

He crouched for a moment and breathed deeply to calm his nerves. Once again he heard a whimper, followed by the sound of a loud thwack, and then a man's voice. Ologun listened and his mind filled with rage. He took one long, deep breath and made his move.

DESIGNATED ENEMY

He had pretended to be many things in recent days, and it seemed to him that this façade was beneath him, tedious and just rigmarole. Of course it was their doing. 'Keep them alive, keep them occupied any way you can,' they'd insisted, and what for? It was far more efficient to kill the lot of them. Then again he figured that now the threat to the lens had been eradicated, it was all business and no longer practice. That was his main concern and that of the whispers; the crimson and the turn back. Did he misunderstand it? Was he meant to ensure anything? And what of belief without proof?

He continued towards the barricade and across the park then away from the last of the city's buildings. 'I shall negotiate with them,' he'd said to that commander. 'I will make sure we are spared for the moment.' Of course it would never have worked without Ologun's dealings with that sniper. *Use any opportunity as it presents itself.* He had no feelings for what he'd done. The only emotion he felt was that of boredom or irritation; sometimes fun, maybe. *Practice at deception, at gaining control and instilling fear; all can be achieved by misdirection and talking rubbish,* he mused in deep thought. He was glad though. Ologun was coming and the trap was set, but then Ologun seemed to just stop. Well, the killing test had been his brother's idea anyway and Ologun was bound to get the wrong end of the stick. *Yes,* he thought, *Ologun is an animal of sorts and he has a strange set of rules, almost as if he won't kill anyone not worthy, and it was nice to have been worthy for a while.*

It would have been a shame to have blown up that ship, and even worse to have killed the berserker man: he was a great source of entertainment, this Ologun, this entry unit which went on killing sprees.

The turrets on the barricade swivelled to mark him as he approached. Now to him, it was a poor position to be in, to be placed in. He'd had a good run of things by hunting down the first intruders, rendering the ship inoperable and so on and so forth. He'd learned a great deal by breaking the Novex man through physical torture and horrid speak. He'd learned a great deal about things that he'd pretended he wanted to know. The cat and mouse game had been good practice, to learn how to hunt, and had proved difficult with so many on board such a large ship.

He'd had the most fun with the man in the blue wizard's outfit in the docking bays of the ship's lowest deck. He'd been cruel of course. There had been no need to chase the wizard around and spit molecular acid at him. The poor old man had nearly keeled over from exhaustion while scurrying and shouting tongue-tied philosophy regarding his innocence. Still, it had been fascinating to watch his face and skull dissolve when he'd caught him for the last time.

His masterpiece had been the magnetic clasp he'd had those engineers build to capture Ologun. Again he wondered about his interpretation of the man and of those many whispers. Still, that Novex man had had a strange idea regarding a blanket shield and an atomic weapon; too excessive!

In the end he'd tested the slamming bulkheads on the engineers. It was curious how, when faced with certain death from two different threats: himself or the trap, that the human would take the option which allowed them just a few extra moments in the world of the living. Maybe it was a primitive instinct, or was it that they preferred death via an inanimate object?

His face twisted into a smile, which he realised just in time to wipe it away.

'Halt!'

He realised that he'd misjudged his level of trust in his own abilities. He wondered if they'd really believed him; after all, these soldiers would have all known each other or been registered in some way, and so it made sense that they'd wonder who the hell he was and eventually realise him to be an imposter.

On top of the barricade and among the soldiers pointing various weapons at him, he saw the woman. Her face was a picture of malice and fear. He cursed Ologun's timing in that Dark Zone, when he'd interrupted his stealthy operation of disposing of the last spy. *Uh Oh!*

He wasn't sure if he liked or disliked pain, except that every instinct told him to run the other way at seeing every turret point in his direction. He chuckled loudly before being shot to ribbons and thrown thirty feet backwards towards the city.

He lay on the rough sward for some time, bewildered as his body recovered. Tilting his head backwards, his eyes fell on a wide street between the last set of buildings. From his upside down position, he then saw Ologun running down the street towards him. His heart missed a few beats and he couldn't figure out whether he felt fear or excitement. He stood, not knowing what to say or how to say it without having practised the scenario in his head. Ologun came to a halt and crouched at his side, ignoring him, it seemed. 'Well now, I thought you had the intention of wrath, but this is an odd way of proceeding with such an endeavour.'

'Hina,' Ologun whispered. 'Where's your weapon?'

'Is that a personal question?'

'Hina, take this tonfa,' Ologun ordered and handed him the baton.

'This is going to be a long fight if you . . .' Hina then saw that Judith and Ray were crouched behind a few trees in the background and realised something was at hand.

'To your left, seven o'clock, don't draw attention,' Ologun said.

Hina glanced quickly and with as much subtlety as he could. 'It begins,' he said weakly.

Ologun kept glancing, unsure if it could see them.

'It's invisible,' Hina said.

'That's funny because I can see it,' Ologun fired back in annoyance at Hina's sarcasm.

'I mean it would be if you couldn't see it,' Hina whispered.

'What? I swear to God this isn't the time.' Ologun strained, trying to remain quiet.

'The humans can't see it,' Hina added with irritation. 'They assume that we're the same and it's checking us out.'

'Is this what came to Vanguard?'

I don't know, I was blindfolded,' Hina offered. 'This is what the Spectra knows and fears though, I'm sure of it.'

Ologun nodded and turned his attention to the whole area. There were now more of them dropping down on cables of some sort. He'd seen this kind of quick entry before, except that now it was something entirely different and they were coming directly through the star lens, through small apertures they had cut.

Ologun froze as the one ahead of his position strode towards him. Hina was still facing the wrong way and busy monitoring the ones now flanking their position. 'Hina, as soon as I run towards the barricade, you go to your right and for fifty yards.'

Hina nodded. Ologun couldn't quite believe what he was seeing for a number of reasons which had much to do with impossibility, or rather improbability, even after all that had happened over the past few days. He got ready to move as it came closer: the man; the alien. It was bipedal, upright and human in shape; it was puzzling to see something so similar to a man, and yet so big. This was the unnerving part which Ologun had no time to think about. Its armour looked to be white and fleshy, though he could tell it wasn't its real skin. It had legs, feet, knees and hips and everything in order, but no face. As it approached to within ten feet he could see that its mask was a mirror; a substance that reflected his own distorted features right back at him, and he was now becoming more afraid. It lumbered across unhurriedly and towered above him at an estimated and intimidating twelve feet tall. Ologun then thought of something. *What if they're friendly? What if my instincts are just primitive and wrong?*

'They're the designated enemy,' Hina said as though guessing Ologun's thoughts.

It was too much for Ologun to take as it came to within five feet of him. It was clearly going to make contact. He leapt up and darted to his left, sprinting with all his might. The nightmare was enough to make him lose his rhythm as this thing ran parallel to him and matched his pace. The floor thudded as its heavy body bounded along with each step and lunged after him.

Version

The barricade opened fire at Ologun and in turn he panicked, stopping dead in his tracks. A barrage of rounds from the stampede turrets, along with missiles, hit him full on, sending him skidding across the grass. More artillery was fired and some of it hit the creature with little to no effect. It simply stood there, tilting its head, admiring the barricade.

Ologun had had enough. Fear had turned to rage at being sent running away as though he were vulnerable. Maybe it was pride or vanity or competitiveness, but he wouldn't run any more. He stood up and the creature stepped back. It then knelt backwards in some peculiar way – its knees went from being in a forward position to that of the opposite direction; it was truly dual-jointed.

Ologun watched with curiosity for a moment, startled like a deer caught in a spotlight, and did his best to ignore the barricade's defensive fire. The creature looked as though it would pounce at Ologun and he waited, ready to move like a bullfighter.

There was a flash and the creature stood up straight, towering over Ologun who was now completely confused. He could hear the gunfire, the explosions, and could see the creatures using large blades and energy weapons to kill the soldiers. He watched as the tanks fired shells towards the city in blind panic.

Two more of the creatures appeared from above and attacked the vehicles. One grabbed a tank by its treads and flipped it upside down whilst the second pounded at another, destroying its cannons with ease.

Ologun smelled burning flesh and saw smoke rise from beneath his chin. He dropped to his knees and his head automatically flopped forward. It appeared that the creature had fired a weapon at his chest and vaporised everything within his rib cage, which was now just a basket with no organs, no flesh anywhere whatsoever. All he could see was the rising plume and the ashes resting on the redness of his spine.

His body fell backwards on his ankles and he lay there in a daze looking up at the lens. Ologun saw the creature above him looking down; its mask reflecting him in his terrible state. It then stamped down hard, crushing his rib cage flat, before lumbering off southwards towards the city, seemingly satisfied with its apparent kill.

Ologun's eyes moved to his blade, yet he couldn't feel it and waited patiently for his rib cage to inflate and for muscle, along with innards, to grow anew. Heart, lungs, skin, second skin; he jumped up. He took in the sight, which was almost as comical as it was terrifying.

Ray was being thrown and booted around by the creatures in a manner akin to killer whales playing that game with captured seals. Judith fared better and was hacking away at three others until she was blown across the way and through the top branches of a tree. She landed on her head and broke her neck on impact. Hina was by far the best at combat as he elegantly jumped around with martial skill, stabbing the top end of the tonfa into his opponent here and smacking its length across an alien's skull there. He even managed to force a lock on one of the creatures, using the baton as leverage, and snapped one of its collar bones.

Ologun sprinted towards the nearest opponent, the same one which had beaten him a few minutes previously, and ferociously swung the machete. The blade cut upwards and sliced the creature's face in two, breaking both of his own elbows in the process. He ran across to the next one, his arms re-setting as he went.

The creature turned its attention towards him but was too slow to avoid having its leg sliced off at the knee. Ologun rolled over, jumped up, and decapitated it as it hit the floor. The blood was red and Ologun had a fleeting thought that just maybe these things were human; incredibly modified humans. Ologun kept up the pace, dispatched three more and couldn't help but feel overwhelmed as their foothold grew.

There were now sixty of them and more were dropping in and moving to create stronger formations. They surrounded the area and fired blistering bolts of energy which shattered trees and destroyed the buildings.

By now the craft had arrived to join them, and while Hina and Judith had managed to continue the fight, and Ray was still being miserably thrashed all over, the ships showed their true worth. They struggled in their own way as they were so young and these creatures were so very powerful. Creed nipped in and out with diving attacks until it was hit with such force it smashed through the concrete wall of one of the buildings.

The brown one helped Ray finally get to his feet and effectively killed off the group that had oppressed him, while the white one flew at full speed, tearing through one of the enemy's chests and out the other side to gruesome effect, showering the area in red.

The enemy had moved south and on top of the buildings while others moved to the now inactive barricade. They set up what appeared to be their own versions of a turret and fired. One bolt hissed at lightning speed and almost hit Ologun as he flinched for cover. Another hit Ray and obliterated him so that only his head and legs were left. Ologun felt real empathy for him as he hadn't even fought back yet.

More bolts whizzed through and across the open land. One hit a building and sent several of the enemy crashing down as it crumbled. *Idiots*! Ologun realised they had created cross fire, with themselves in the killing ground.

Another bolt hit the white ship aiding Judith. It whirled through the air in a death spin and through the trunk of a mature tree, which exploded into a mass of splinters, before keeling over.

Hina was being aided by a red craft Ologun hadn't seen before. It was truly awesome to watch as it was a trickster which zipped around the back of an enemy to attack, to then hide between buildings, and then ambush the creatures as they manoeuvred around the streets.

Ologun slid across the floor and hacked between one of the creature's legs. He realised that they hadn't uttered a single scream but had remained silent. He'd done this move before and knew it was easier on such great and lumbering beasts. The basin floor was steadily filling with corpses of the enemy, and Ologun realised something had to give. He caught sight of Creed as it crawled across the floor with a broken wing and away from one of the enemy which clobbered at it ferociously with a large blade. He sprinted across, launched himself into the air and landed blade down so that the machete punctured directly through the top of the creature's spine. He grabbed the craft, headed out of the way, and hid it under a bush. *It's wrong to worry,* he thought, as the craft had all the same attributes as himself, yet it just seemed unfair to let it suffer.

Hershal appeared, and behind him the star lens turned dark. Ologun looked up and grew cold at the sight of thousands of craft now swarming across and under the basin's roof. Hershal hadn't been exaggerating about the Spectra creating ships, and en masse. All these infant killing machines were unstoppable. As the hordes of enemy slid down, the craft intercepted. The basin floor was now a pool of rubble and blood, yet the fight continued on.

Ologun looked past the swarm and tried to see the star lens. The thought came to him as an obvious dilemma which caused him to make a dash for the north wall. He negotiated a path, killing several of the enemy as he went, leapt over a burned-out tank and then the barricade wall while decapitating yet another which was firing from a position of cover. He despatched three more creatures, then tripped just as he reached the scaffold. At this, one of the aliens flew over him and lost its balance only to land directly on to the blanket shield. Its body fried on impact and it slumped to the floor a blackened shell.

Ologun rapidly climbed the scaffold to the right side of the blanket shield and towards the star lens. A few of the enemy pursued, yet they were poor climbers and quite slow. He reached a tram which appeared to be heavier and of a far more solid build than any of the others he'd previously seen, and leapt on to its roof.

Seeing the enemy closing in, Ologun sliced one of the joists hanging from the tram's cable and jumped as it swung down lengthways, crushing two of the enemy as they clung to the scaffold.

The fracas below was a flurry of lights and the swarm of craft filled the world with a deafening hum. Even so, Ologun could still hear the sound created by the energy weapons and couldn't quite place it in comparison to anything else he had ever heard: a high-pitched noise which forms in the ear on occasions was the closest he could get. Between the noise of swarm and the enemies' energy weapons, and the sight of red and black everywhere, the fog of war seemed complete. He shimmied across the cable and hacked at the armoured tram's other joist. It fell away, hugging the scaffold and killing yet more of the enemy as they climbed, then a dozen more as it exploded on the basin's floor.

He then made his way across to one of the tram network junction boxes and climbed to stand on top. *This is going to be impossible,* he thought of the massive distance between himself and the star lens. He knew that the chances of jumping the hundred feet to the lens and getting through one of the circular holes the aliens had cut was very slim.

His eyes focused in order to find one of the openings, realising they had somehow managed to enter through the lens without causing decompression; *a link to their ship!* When he found the nearest perforation, Ologun noticed one of the threads used by the creatures for their descent. It was practically invisible, transparent, and appeared organic and gelatinous in substance. He felt this was his chance, for the thread was much closer and would allow him to climb to and through the star lens. He carefully judged its distance and leapt the twenty feet towards the thread.

He was hit by the swarming craft, began to fall, but was then caught and lifted back up and he grabbed hold. Ologun's body filled with pain and his arms ballooned as toxins released by the thread were pumped directly into his hands. He cried out in agony at this new form of attack but managed to hold on amidst the chaos. Once again that mechanism of his creation, his overly acute immune system, went to work and he soon felt relief once more.

He climbed higher until he was within reach of the lens. The heat it produced was blistering at this distance and his body adjusted; he was beginning to feel like a demi-god and couldn't help but think of his body as a separate entity which his mind remotely controlled. This new sensation bordered on ecstasy.

One of the creatures slid down the thread with force, hitting Ologun so that he nearly fell. He hacked at the thing and caused it enough injury that its blood spilt all over him. The skirmish became fraught as the creature stamped down hard on his face and he slipped further down the thread.

Ologun frantically swung the blade and lopped off one of its legs, then an arm; yet, regardless, it was just as determined. Finally it struck Ologun hard enough so that he fell, but not as far as he expected. He lay still for a moment in a state of distraction; he was still only a few yards away from the lens.

His arms explored the strange sensation of pressure that his touch had identified at his sides. Ologun leapt up with surprise and the sight took his breath away. A new layer, created of the plasma in which the Spectra existed, had formed across and directly underneath the star lens. Ologun was now between two massive planes; expanses of which hung parallel to each other. Liquid light beamed from underneath and against the star lens; a level of light that would have instantly blinded any normal person. It was as if he'd reached the corridor to Heaven, which ran its course to infinity.

There was now only silence and light, making it hard to believe that a savage battle was taking place beneath.

'Beautiful, isn't it?'

Ologun turned to see that Hina had joined him. 'I thought I'd seen it all by now,' Ologun said. He felt giddy at the sight and had never felt smaller than this; trapped between two red skies facing each other only twenty feet apart.

'Why did you come up here? Why did you try to reach their ship?' Hina asked.

'I thought they were aboard a scout ship and they shouldn't be allowed to convey this position,' Ologun said. He ran across the field of dense liquid which felt very queer underfoot, as though it would flip or even swallow him at any moment.

'I thought you were done leaping before you looked,' Hina replied.

'You knew these things existed, didn't you? Are they what attacked Vanguard?' Ologun asked, finding the thread and gripping it, ready to complete his task.

'I never saw them, I happened to be blindfolded at the time, remember? They sound the same though.'

'Why is this happening? What happened to provoke all of this?' Ologun enquired, sure there must be some reason behind it all.

'Competition,' Hina said, lifting his hands up as if guessing once again.

'I have to go now,' Ologun argued.

'It's just an idea, burn me at the stake if you will.' Hina chortled. 'You have no idea what's up there or where this ship's going. Even now I can feel it beginning to move, you haven't thought this through. You never think anything through.'

'I was trying for a while, but this is how it is for me. Maybe I'll get it right next time. Make sure that virus Siren created doesn't kill anyone, will you do that?'

'I'll wait until Earth's human population is down to ten billion. How does that sound?'

Ologun had run out of time and hoped he was joking. 'I'll see you later,' he said and began climbing up the thread and towards the lens.

Hordes of the enemy were now dropping down on to the liquid field, burning to death on impact due to the heat created by the two planes.

'We shall see,' Hina said. 'Go. Save humanity from being discovered. Until the turn back.'

Ologun nodded but was none the wiser from the conversation. He climbed upwards, through the lens and out of sight.

SON OF RAGE

The group of men waited for the vehicle to arrive. It sped across the dirt and skidded up next to them in a plume of dust. The man ran to the passenger side and picked the girl up into his arms. He wept with joy and spoke to her in his native tongue, then quickly ushered her away.

Ologun exited the vehicle and moved to its rear. He reached over on to the flatbed and grabbed three sacks of rice along with a large tank of water. 'Take these and head east tonight. Get to Timbuktu, to these co-ordinates,' he added, handing the girl's cousin a digital pad programmed with details for navigation. 'Tell them I sent you.'

The girl's family grabbed the provisions and headed towards their vehicle. 'Thank you,' the cousin said. He held out his hand for Ologun to shake. 'What did you do?'

Ologun shook his hand. 'You really don't want to know. Get going, be gone within the hour and you'll make it.' The man nodded and joined the rest of his family.

Ologun went over to the truck and opened the passenger door to grab a rag from the glove compartment then drenched it with water from a bottle. He scrubbed the seat vigorously to the point where the fabric began to shred. The wind kicked up, blowing dust into his eyes and distracting him. As he rubbed his eyes from the irritation, he lost his temper and kicked the vehicle's passenger door.

'Ologun, are you okay?' a voice asked.

Ologun slammed the door, seeing that once again Haelu had snuck up on him. 'I have to get out of here, I can't stay,' he replied and made his way to the driver's seat.

'Come to ours, Feisal is asleep and we can have that chat,' Haelu offered.

'I can't,' Ologun insisted. The camp was very dark and quiet now with only a few people and a dog visible halfway along the avenue of tents, sitting by an open fire.

'I think you should come. Not all talk is idle and I have things to say,' Haelu insisted.

Ologun finally agreed, set the security lock on the truck and made his way behind Haelu. 'How did you know I was back?' Ologun asked.

'I waited,' Haelu answered.

A fire burned outside the tent when they arrived and Haelu set about making coffee. She didn't ask if he'd like any and simply gave Ologun a metal flask. 'Drink this.'

Ologun accepted and sat on one of the chairs. 'I can't stay long. I have a shift tomorrow, today, I mean,' he said, realising he needed to calm down. It had occurred to him while making his way to Feisal's tent that running away was the worst thing he could do.

Haelu sat her plump frame down into the chair next to him and tied a scarf around her short-cropped hair. 'You're like a lion that roams without a home,' she said.

Ologun rolled his eyes and stood up. 'I really can't stay for this.'

'Please,' Haelu said. 'I understand you find such talk distasteful.'

Ologun sat back down and, out of politeness, waved a hand for her to continue.

'You're also a liar,' she continued.

'Excuse me?' Ologun said in surprise at the remark.

'You're not forty years old,' Haelu smiled, 'thirty or so I think, yet I see much more age in your eyes.'

'Look, Haelu, I'm really tired,' Ologun stated and stood up again.

'Sit down,' Haelu ordered, knowing full well that he at least wanted to stay long enough to rest his mind. 'You're beyond tired, beyond the aid of sleep, and I know this.'

Ologun sat down again, thinking more of the position he was in regarding what he'd just done. He was scared about being a criminal, being found out and hunted down at any time. It was at least a fair distraction to be here and talking instead of pacing his room where he'd be in danger of scheming.

Haelu stoked the fire, threw more wood on the charcoal, then sat back to study Ologun's face. 'I think your second skin has finally worn away and now you are in an impossible place. Such a thing can bring a person closer to what they really are, and I wonder what kind of beast has been hiding in human clothing.' She took a pipe from a pocket in her garment, stuffed it with tobacco, and lit it. She puffed to get it started and added, 'Don't tell my husband.' She winked, smiling wryly at Ologun.

He frowned and smirked after some thought. He still had no idea what she wanted to say.

'My father was a peaceful man. A farmer, a shepherd,' Haelu informed him. 'He took a holiday many years ago when the climate permitted such an indulgence. It was his first, the only time in all his life. On his return journey from Istanbul, he sat in the airport with my mother when terrorists attacked. Hostages were taken and some were executed to show the truth of their threat. Before there was any force used by the authorities, the terrorists killed one hostage every hour.' Haelu puffed on her pipe and blew a large ring of smoke towards the fire. 'When they took my mother, my father rose up in a ferocious rage and killed five of them with his bare hands before they managed to kill him. My mother was two months pregnant with me and so he saved the two of us by providing the authorities with the opportunity to strike.'

Ologun sat wide-eyed at this and Haelu stared deeply into the fire. 'My point is,' she continued. 'I have seen you and you are losing your ability to deceive others and yourself. Some will lose themselves in a crisis, others will save themselves, but you will always charge the chaos when many cannot even think.'

'I get it, really,' Ologun said, thinking she was stating the obvious after what he'd just done in town. 'It doesn't excuse me and you know it.'

'Don't you ever be ashamed,' Haelu insisted. 'You're a good man among many who choose not to control their worst desires.

Version

Sometimes a good man must teach a hard lesson, to provide fairness, especially when so many turn a blind eye.'

'I'll pay the price, nothing's fair,' Ologun said, growing restless and again feeling the fear at the terrible deeds he'd just committed.

'This enterprise with my husband, I fear for him and the others he has convinced. It isn't needed and the risk isn't worth the reward I feel. That is all I will say on the matter.'

'You are right,' Ologun said, knowing now that it was a totally insane idea to raid the food skips and had already pushed it from his mind a few nights earlier. 'Tell Feisal that it's too dangerous and you should leave for wherever it is you were headed as soon as you can. If you need anything, and if I can, I will bring you enough to get you there tomorrow evening. Can you convince him to leave?'

Haelu nodded and smiled in acceptance. 'Good night, Ologun Jowett. Do not mourn those who are destined to cross you, you are not meant to be kind to everyone, for that is unfortunately a fool's game and you do not look like a fool to me. Perhaps in an ideal world you would find happiness and you would be allowed to act as the kind one.' Haelu stood, prompting Ologun to leave without allowing him to question her. She made her way to the tent and turned to Ologun one more time. 'How did you get the girl back?'

'You don't want to know,' Ologun replied. What he really meant was that he didn't want to recall any of it and had blocked it from his mind in some form of denial.

The next day Ologun had some luck for he'd been meant to be on water detail at the far end of town. One of the other sergeants was ill and so he'd taken over his shift and was instead conducting a rapid patrol along the north side of town. He took two soldiers and drove to the north of the fort then took a right at the T-junction.

This was where the twenty-foot security wall made of concrete, which acted as barrier to the forest to the north-west, became a tall wire mesh fence protecting the new plantation which headed east. The truck sped along the dirt track with the fence to the left and the town sat on the right a few miles away in the distance.

Craig Jenkins

The track eventually became a concrete road which gradually inclined so that the vehicle was above ground level. Ologun looked from left to right where the height of the road allowed for a good overview of the town as the truck sped by.

Fifteen miles later and the town had gone from view and the flats of desert land had taken its place. In the far distance he could just make out the enormous vehicles which pillaged the land of sand and loaded dumper trucks to the brim in order for transportation further east. Eventually Ologun pulled up behind a long row of trucks which were accessing one of the few gates in the security fence; they'd brought tonnes of compost and were to offload the contents in large bins located just inside and near a long row of machines parked and ready to be used for plantation work; other trucks brought refined and processed volcanic ash imported directly from Iceland which would enrich the soil further.

Behind this scene of preparation, the mature forest carried on eastward into the distance; in time it would connect to the jungles covering the eastern Sahara and which had been established many years ago. Thousands of birds flocked around the area, in and out of the forest canopy, and were also perched along the industrial machinery. The forest was four hundred miles in depth and the old spray network system must have been in flow as vast clouds of steam rose above the canopy in the tremendous heat, creating a thick mist which drifted softly above the green.

Ologun saw something and strained his eyes towards the second security fence just outside the wall of forest, then studied its front in both directions. He saw it again and recognised it as a tiger. He'd been told that all kinds of animals, which used to reside in other countries and habitats, had been placed there. Orang-utans, gorillas, elephants, various cats and snakes and more; the list was extensive and this place was at least enough to allow them to thrive, regardless of their contrived surroundings. They were secure; well away from any human intervention one way or another.

Some of the sophisticated deterrents against trespassers all across this forest were both lethal and copious; the last surveillance record and body count of trespassers killed in the five-thousand-square-mile stretch of forest was around two thousand: plenty for the wildlife to eat for no one ever went to retrieve them. How these lethal man traps worked and where they were was classified. All anyone knew was that the technology only worked against humans.

Ologun would normally have said something to the soldiers for falling asleep while on patrol. Today he'd allowed them to drop off as soon as they'd left the fort and had no intention of waking them; they appeared hung over and had probably been at the moonshine which was contraband at the fort, as was all alcohol.

It had been three hours since the patrol had begun when Ologun turned the truck around. The second part of the patrol was to head west to the waste bins. He thought of Feisal and their discussions about the place and fought to ignore that other thing on his mind. *They'll think it was a rival gang,* he reasoned and tried to relax. Even if they figured it out, they'd most likely bury it and let him off with a minimum sentence, yet this didn't make him feel any better. Something had happened to him last night which had sent him further than he'd ever gone; too far.

Two hours later the truck reached the T-junction. The town on the left still seemed quiet and there was no indication that anything was wrong; he'd even tried to see if he could spot the gang's set of containers and if anyone was about.

The truck slowed down to allow another patrol vehicle to turn south towards the fort. It stopped and the driver got out; it was Sergeant Andrade.

He ran across the road towards the truck, causing Ologun's heart to beat faster. He had never felt so anxious. 'Ade,' Ologun greeted him as he came to the side of the truck.

'Ologun, Jeffrey, Riddle,' Andrade said, nodding at the others. The soldiers were still snoozing away and jerked awake, thinking they were back at the base. 'Where are we, is this the junction?'

'Ologun,' Andrade said, ignoring the soldiers. 'Some shit happening today for sure.'

Ologun waited then went along with it. 'What's up, Ade?'

'That gang, you know the one who live out by the S1 complex?'

'I know who you mean,' Ologun said. He was shaking and did his best to stay calm and hide his guilt.

'Yeah, well that new guy Cromak is holding everyone as they arrive back at base. He's not even calling anyone in, like he's trying to catch us out or something. Someone said that the entire gang got offed last night. All of 'em been hung like cattle from the roof of their cabins. Some of 'em got really busted up too, and some of the gang's women must have been scared out of their minds 'cause they're saying that some beast came in and attacked, like a creature.'

'What the hell are you talking about, Ade?' Riddle asked.

Ade ignored the man and saw that Ologun was distant in some way. 'Shit, I almost forgot. GEA arrived this morning after shift call. There's something going on at the wastes on the other side of the wall.'

Ologun's heart leapt so hard he felt pins and needles explode in his hands. 'What do you mean?'

'They arrived and closed down the gatehouse just as I was doing my checkpoint. There were about thirty of 'em headed off in there in sharp step, you know?'

Ologun's mind flipped at this. He knew exactly what it was. 'Riddle, Jeffrey, go with Ade back to base. I need to check something out.'

He sat and watched the soldiers leave; they were hardly interested in anything other than themselves and didn't even question Ologun and his business: *maybe they should!* He reached into a compartment next to his seat and lifted the shelf to expose a mini-safe. He typed in the code and reached inside to retrieve his handgun. *Perhaps*, he thought, looking at the weapon, *perhaps I won't be going to Timbuktu.*

Two GEA soldiers were standing outside the gatehouse when he arrived. *At least the gates are open,* he thought. He didn't fancy climbing over the thirty-foot wall, though a few hundred metres further west there were vines which allowed for an easy security breach: the one he had told Feisal about.

He exited the vehicle and walked over to the soldiers.

'What do you want?' one of them asked. The man quickly approached Ologun and he could see that his partner, a female soldier, had released the safety catch to her weapon.

'Just here to complete a checkpoint,' Ologun answered. He surveyed the two of them and could see their level of skill at this encounter. They were making it difficult for him to make any hostile move due to the woman purposefully standing several feet behind as backup.

'Not today,' the man said. He thought about Ologun's presence with suspicion. 'Hold on a minute.' He pressed a finger into the comms device in his ear.

Ologun thought about the situation. So far he was maybe in for losing his career, headed for a gaol term perhaps. This was something else; it was suicide if he made a move at all.

The female soldier must have seen something in Ologun's eyes and immediately lifted her rifle. 'On the ground now.'

Ologun launched himself into the man with enough force to push him backwards towards the woman, creating a domino effect where she tried to find her target but was knocked off balance. Ologun struck the man in the face, then launched at her before she could fire. He knocked her unconscious, then did the same to the other soldier. He ran to the vehicle, grabbed a bundle of detention binds and tied them up. Placing the rest of the binds inside the pocket of his flak jacket, he returned to the truck and retrieved a small case from inside the safe. A number of things raced through his mind as he left the truck and tabbed towards the gatehouse. If he was wrong about what he suspected was going on here, a long prison sentence awaited him. But if he was right, there'd be hell to pay. He'd find out soon enough and was now beyond fear for himself at either outcome.

He approached the gatehouse and slipped by the concrete wall. There was a large warehouse ahead of his position which concerned him, so he hid behind the security cabin. With a quick flick of his head around the corner he spotted a lookout on top of the warehouse roof; the man hadn't spotted him and appeared to be groggy up there in such heat.

Ologun was eighty yards from the building in a position of cover and couldn't risk sprinting across the open ground. He took the case he'd brought, placed it on the ground, opened it and selected a set of subdue class darts. He released the clip from his gun, emptied the round from the chamber, and placed the dart into position in its stead. Taking a deep breath, he launched into a forward roll, came to rest on one knee and fired at the lookout. The man on the roof gripped his neck, slumped down unconscious and was none the wiser to Ologun's presence.

To the left of the warehouse and three hundred yards opposite, different grades of waste vats sat in long rows a hundred feet in length. They were enormous rectangular bins sitting within a compound that carried out five stages of organic waste decomposition. Ologun ran to the first neat row of bins opposite the warehouse. Each bin was twenty feet tall and obscured his vision. He ran to the next row, loaded the magazine to his gun, then ran across a wide lane to the third row. Searching for any hostile forces, he worked his way through each zone where each phase of the cycle was set for creating vast quantities of compost for the plantation. Anything from collected foliage from the forest and farmland, dead wood, and waste food were dumped in these enormous skips then shifted down the line as the matter broke down to become enriched soil. Eventually the skips reached the final zone and the compost was carted off to both the farmlands and nursery fields.

Ologun heard a voice as he approached the last row and hid in order to listen. 'I hereby carry out legal obligations for offences thirty three through forty two, for theft of valuable commodities on behalf of the state of Morocco, which has authorised the use of appropriate sentencing.'

Sentencing! Ologun crept to the edge of the container and peeked round. He couldn't be sure what he felt or thought at the sight. A row of people were kneeling in a long line facing three GEA personnel. He searched their faces, recognising them to be travellers. *Feisal!* Ologun saw him and his anger grew. He couldn't believe that Feisal had done this and cursed himself for ever suggesting such an endeavour.

Version

He left his position of cover and surveyed the area while steadily approaching the soldiers. Many of them were sat in trucks parked behind the prisoners, while others kept guard on foot at either side of the lane. Things were not looking good at all for they were all trapped along the avenue and between the long lines of skips; it was claustrophobic and Ologun knew that if anything went wrong, there would be no escape. There were fifteen prisoners in all who were being shadowed by an equal number of soldiers, one for each of them, and Ologun realised the order of things, picking up pace as he became frantic. 'Wait, wait, I can explain,' he shouted to the soldiers standing before the prisoners.

Ologun recognised that one of them was a commander. The man turned his attention to Ologun in surprise as the other soldiers took position and aim.

'Don't move,' the commander ordered. Three soldiers ran towards Ologun and surrounded him.

'I came to explain the situation, these people are here on my authority,' Ologun said. Sweat had drenched his body and he was even hotter now that he stood in this passage between the rows of vats.

'You have no authority here,' the commander stated coldly. 'Who are you? Check his gear.' He nodded to one of the soldiers, who patted him down then shone a device into his eyes.

'On your knees,' the commander ordered Ologun, who was violently assisted with a rifle butt swung across the back of his legs. He knelt there helplessly as the soldier handed the device to the commander.

'Retinal scan confirms you to be Ologun Jowett. What's an IMC sergeant doing helping such people?' he said, probing the line of prisoners. 'These people are terrorists and thieves. Are you also a terrorist and thief?' he asked rhetorically.

'This is IMC jurisdiction and I will process them, you have no right to be doing this,' Ologun stressed. He searched for Feisal again and saw that his head was held high and his chest was puffed out in defiance. There were men and women of all ages along the row of prisoners; then Ologun spotted a child. 'There is a minor among these people, let them go!' He then thought quickly about what these soldiers were doing. 'What you are doing here is illegal and I shall bear witness.' His voice quivered at his suspicions of what was about to happen.

The commander grinned, raised his hand and dropped it. Ologun's mind reeled and it took what felt like an eternity to re-focus. His ears rang as he stared at the line of people now slumped forward. He couldn't think and watched, totally detached, as the dirt ran red with blood.

Then, just as he heard the sound of a rifle's chamber click behind his head, all his senses fired at once. Ologun tilted his head and reached up and behind for the rifle, pulled it forward and elbowed the soldier in the face. He then leapt to his feet and palmed the next soldier in the nose, smashing the cartilage up into his brain.

Ologun grabbed the nearest gun he saw and aimed it at the commander. He walked forward one step and fired it directly into his face. Things were strange and Ologun's mind had shut down in one way but had amped up in another. He wasn't aware that the soldiers struggled to match his pace and they had trouble finding their mark. To them he was a blur which moved with supernatural ability. They fired in all directions and eventually found themselves to be running low on ammunition. The thought occurred to them a little too late, yet some of the soldiers ran; but there would be no escape.

The sound of clunking was the first thing, a sound at the back of his mind that steadily brought him back from the abyss. His vision grew to encompass his own feet then, in front of them, he saw the sparkling bits of metal, the bullets spattered on the red-stained dirt.

A sensation of motion brought him further back into the clasp of reality and he realised that he'd been banging his head against the side of a skip. He stopped and turned to face the other way. At some point he'd managed to knock the soldiers unconscious. He couldn't remember binding their hands and feet, but they lay trussed up on the ground.

Version

He stepped over the commander's body and saw more slain soldiers; he couldn't remember killing them. He surveyed the long line of prisoners who'd been executed and now lay on their fronts.

The memory of a man came and went when he saw the side of his face as he lay in the dirt. Then something shiny caught his attention. He walked across towards one of the soldiers lying bound and gagged on his back. On the soldier's belt were various tools of barbarism and among the knives and handcuffs he spotted a machete. He unclipped the blade and swung it around, admiring it in the sunlight. He then spotted another item on the belt: a baton, a tonfa, and reached to unhook it. The soldier watched him and made eye contact with him, fully aware of what was about to happen; of what would happen to him.

TIME AND MOTION

He thought back to that day and realised his mind had suppressed the true horror of it. Even in prison and through hours of physical torture and interrogation he'd failed to remember. When on trial, the authorities had hidden the facts of his unspeakable acts by only charging him with twelve counts of murder. This, their greatest lie, had been contrived for a good reason so that he wasn't held accountable for the remaining twenty soldiers and so that his worst crime as butcher wasn't presented to the jury under the clause of diminished responsibility. Now that his mind had finally released its secret and had relented from deceiving him, he was left to face his actions, to face what he truly was.

The smell got to him again. He perceived that he was inside some enormous pit, a stomach, except that it was a ship. Everywhere dripped, and if it didn't drip it pumped, and if it didn't drip or pump it throbbed. The bodies were piled high all around him and he looked above him to the roof of the chamber; the hive. This place was enormous, like being inside the skin of a Zeppelin; yet bigger, much bigger.

He had no idea how long he'd been here, how long it had taken him to kill them all and had no knowledge where in the galaxy he was. He wouldn't know such a thing even if he had a star chart and a marker to point it out.

Through the mucus and the bodies, and along the tubeways of white, which glistened with moisture, he traipsed around aimlessly with his thoughts. These creatures were beautifully evolved and their ship was a great beast which cared for and fed them.

He sat in what he thought was a giant clam, one of the creature's places of rest; for stasis maybe, he wasn't sure. Grabbing his machete, he hacked the head off one of them, peeled off its reflective mask and held its enormous skull on his lap. Two lidless eyes of total blackness, like those of a shark, stared lifelessly back at him. He stroked the pallid skin on the skull one way and then the other; it was smooth when stroked away from the face and strangely coarse with minute spines when brushed forward. It had nostrils and a mouth and two flat bone shields for teeth, yet no ears, not even a pair of holes for anything acoustic.

The loneliness of the place and the silence was now unbearable and he began to feel agoraphobic at the magnitude of the place; this nest of thousands of coves which held cocoons of skin within their solid shells. He threw the skull away and turned his attention to the cocoon he was sitting in.

There were veins or cables of some sort which were attached at the top, and he sent a fine thread of second skin from his sleeve up into it. He focused his mind and attempted to interface with the ship. Nothing. He had killed it and realised that it was the biggest thing he had ever killed; that anyone had ever killed.

'Don't feel ashamed of the things you have done,' someone had once said to him, but he'd forgotten now who'd said it. His mind and soul were torn and he thought himself an animal, a disease only fit for one purpose: to kill. And he thought about the morality of it all.

The Spectra could be accused of leading these beings to within reach of humanity, and yet they had only tried to survive. After all, why should the crocodile be mindful of the bird which cleans its teeth when the hawk circles to attack? As much as he admired these aliens, he was aware of the danger and of their level of sentience. It was only fair to assume that any creature which had imagination would seek to eliminate a plausible threat, to eradicate the competition, and humanity fitted that realm perfectly. In all he could only guess what would happen if these things found Earth or any of her colonies; it was always best to fear the worst and prepare for such an eventuality: the very train of thought which induced paranoia and caused war in the first place.

His second skin transmitted an image from outside the ship. It had hooked into the ship's systems, regardless of it being brain-dead, and he could see a white giant star and then, eventually, an approaching planet.

More systems were accessed and a scan of the planet was conducted. It was a primordial place with many single-cell organisms existing within a toxic atmosphere and underneath yet another ocean; life had not yet made the jump from ocean to land.

Prison! he thought, realising the ship was headed there on some sort of afterlife attempt at vengeance. He was either about to be killed once and for all, or he would survive such an act as an even worse chastisement. He hoped more for one and yet knew the latter to be most likely.

He sat back into the cocoon and relaxed to watch as the ship fired across the stratosphere and descended towards the planet. All the mistakes he'd ever made and every memory was now available so that a few realisations came to him at last. The entity known as Spectra had an idea, would in some afterthought set the five of them up in order to observe. Too much came to light and Ologun felt truly exhausted by it all, yet one thought was held firm; a form of hope. If he ever returned from this, maybe he'd get a few more things right next time.

SPECTRA

Deception can happen by mistake.

When the humans dropped their atomic weapons and brought the entity back from the brink of death, the entity had pretended to need more help. Why? The entity had many objectives; one of which included gathering information. So the habitat the mass of life existed within had one portal left in which to turn and face the star. That was all that was needed in order to feed off solar winds and the rest had simply been a ruse. Trade was a concept quickly learned, even though what had been traded was perhaps unnecessary for either side; yet this was how to build relations, this was how to build trust. And what of the payments made by the entity for energy it did not require?

The first payment was five vessels. These vessels could have been in any organic form and yet they were made to mimic the species which agreed to them.

The second payment was five worlds. These worlds would be off the grid and not on the extensive catalogue of exo-planets created by decades of exploration and research.

The third gift was the death of a planet covered by deep oceans, where those who wanted easy access to precious ores from another universe could siphon off what they needed in order to build an empire. With all these things being offered by an immensely clever entity, what could go wrong?

An ocean of organisms which can pulse in unison to think as one, does not understand culture or ideology. It does not understand greed and selfishness, or altruism and selflessness, or anger, or sadness. It does not comprehend consequence and therefore does not grasp the idea of paranoia or, as some might call it, foresight for insurance and the need to progress in order to survive. Yet it is learning and it has, after many years, just begun to understand.

The faction of humanity it has always dealt with, the only members of humanity it has negotiated with, are prime examples of how difficulties arise and how much mistakes cost. Value is to be interpreted and this entity deals in numbers only.

It doesn't think about the name of the human faction as meaning anything; for this faction, which had five planets marked for territory, ended up with only one. The entity does not factor in the difficulty of travel and the time it takes to traverse the expanse between worlds. It does not ponder how human life is so finite and how so many generations would come and go in order to achieve what it considers a simple set of goals. The failures of this human faction are perplexing and it is even more mystified at the human faction's desire to destroy vast numbers of its own kind.

This entity begins to understand consequence, and is yet unable to use this concept to foresee what the consequences are for what it offered. It couldn't see that giving one faction of humanity the ability to travel vast distances in the shortest possible time would cause such movements; movements towards mass killings and destruction, and movements towards secrets and lies. And for what?

Five planets which can support their own kind in greater numbers, yet they thin out vast numbers of their own kind. There is no sense found among humans and yet these humans are full of so many ideas. Ideas are to be pillaged and plagiarised. Above all, humans are full of concepts and concepts have helped with survival, for humans know how to survive without evolution's aid.

And so the humans are too weak to face those others who are so very much like humanity; and yet the five that were made, one for each world – even though four could not yet be claimed – are not so weak. It is time to retreat and to find distance. It is time to process this new way of existing and hibernate. It is time to leave the humans to their own devices and, with any luck, they would not lose too many of their numbers.

The entity starts to understand that unless the concept of foresight can be mastered, mistakes will be easily made and any initial act could have unexpected outcomes both positive yet against the mean; and oddly, mostly negative.

The entity begins to understand duality as a part of consequence, for these five were designed for something else entirely. The entity begins to understand caution, for caution comes from beginning to understand consequence.

The End

Book 2: Prospect < Earth coming soon

Reviews

If you enjoyed *Version* please consider leaving a rating and review on Amazon – all genuine comments and feedback are welcome.

Reviews and feedback are extremely important to Craig Jenkins, as well as other potential readers, and would be very much appreciated. Thank you.

Craig Jenkins

Read on for an extract of Book 2: Prospect < Earth

VERSION BOOK 2
PROSPECT < EARTH

Prospect<Earth will be available soon.

Craig Jenkins

Version

PROSPECT < EARTH Extract

MONSTER

2424 November 15th
Avatar Operations Control: Algeria.
Avatar Deployment Combat Model: G47.3 12th
Generation Nigeria.
Combat Operation: Rashad.
Parameters of Mission: Eliminate terrorist
threat.
Further Parameters: Classified.

'Okay people, we're approaching Combat Zone Alpha. Suits on and deploy your avatar.'

The hanger bay was one of many housing simulator units used by soldiers to control the combat drones. In other hangers across the field were similar operations using other types of drones. Combat models of aircraft, and dog and ram drones had already been deployed and were headed south with the convoy. There had been a time when less people were needed for the armed forces, as a quantum computer could manage thousands of drones at a time. What had happened in recent times was perhaps more of a choice than a necessity as AI, as limited as it had remained for hundreds of years, had been replaced by the best and most instinctive intelligence of all.

Men and women at the top of their game were now seated in their pods and connected to the various types of drone. They could see, hear and act via the use of the machines, and in this hanger – housing five hundred pods – were the best drones of all: the human drone. Two hangers dedicated to a thousand machines that were designed to manoeuvre as instinctively and fluently as possible for their operators. No one went into combat for real any more; except for those on the African continent who would stand against this flash invasion. They had no such technology, meaning this operation should be swift and encounter no serious opposition.

Colonel Phillips watched as the specialist ensemble of soldiers finished the process of uploading to their machines from within the pod units. He then walked to his own pod, lifted the lid, and sat down within the small chamber. The inside of the metal case was virtually empty apart from a reclining seat with several injection syringes surrounding the headrest. The seat fell back a little and he waited and braced himself for the inevitable first stab of a needle into the top of his neck.

Transfer pads had once been used to interface with the machine. Now, due to some bright spark advising that deep penetration contact with the spinal cord was better, the pads had been replaced with monstrously thick needles. The interface hadn't improved and the only real benefit was that if a person's body flinched or jolted during combat, the pads would no longer fall off or come away from that essential point of contact.

Colonel Phillips felt the back of his neck as a ten-second countdown began. The scars from previous injections were now thick and bulbous, yet the ferocity of the needles would be accurate and puncture the very same locations without any trouble. Phillips inhaled from a small canister to allow a chemical agent to make its way through his body and prevent any bleeding from the injection sites. The first injection was administered: a tiny prick that would numb the rest. A second, third and fourth followed in quick succession.

'Neural synaptic synchronisation complete.'

A fuzzy feeling filled the colonel's head. He opened his eyes, yet they were not his own. He stood up, looked to his left and then his right. A vast proportion of the machines were located on the war path many miles south at the border to Nigeria. His machine, the one he had now become for the operation, stood next to many others on the airfield outside the hanger bay where his actual body was located within the pod. Over a hundred machines began to run at speed towards the jets, and Phillips moved towards his own F250 fighter plane.

'Colonel Phillips, this is Command, patching through Captain Jarvis of Air Drone 2032.'

'Understood,' Phillips said in a hollow, mechanised voice. His machine spoke his thoughts even though the thought projected a response automatically through to the command centre.

'Captain Jarvis. I need a sit rep.'

'Free as a bird and soaring like an eagle, Colonel. Full complement moving on schedule. No sign of hostile forces. One moment – bogey spotted at seven hundred feet, eight klicks south of our location.'

Phillips commanded his machine – seated in the cockpit of the fighter jet – to receive visuals from various drones now surveying the area. Simultaneously he launched the jet vertically up into the air. He set the craft for stratospheric altitude so he could be on site in less than ten minutes. Within seconds the world below became a map and the jet headed south. Phillips watched as the live feed showed him the unknown craft hovering above vast jungle canopy. The view projected into his left eye was quite clear and, on zooming in to gain an even clearer image, Phillips became very concerned.

'Jarvis, what the hell is that? I seem to be having trouble identifying bogey at your location.'

'This is Flag Admiral Dean. Be advised that this is the craft logged from the Earth intrusion on September 18th. Craft is of alien origin, approach with extreme caution.'

'Admiral Dean, this is Colonel Phillips. Why have we not received information on said craft prior to this?'

'All information is classified, you have permission to engage only if fired upon, Colonel. Is that understood?'

'Copy that, Admiral.' Colonel Phillips noted the formation of over eight hundred jets surrounding his own while he thought about this new report of intelligence from Admiral Dean. *Arseholes*! The operation should have been child's play, regardless of the enormous repercussions from other states that had opposed this act of war.

Phillips noted that the Germans had arrived with another squadron of jets equal to his own.

'Colonel Phillips, this is Colonel Weber approaching with Beta Squadron on flank position, please acknowledge.'

'Received and acknowledged. Have you received update on foreign craft?'

'Affirmative. Approaching with caution.'

'Ground Team One, Captain Jones, please give the order to halt all vehicles on encroach path east to west, we have a situation due south of your location,' Phillips said.

'Roger that, Colonel. Bogey has been spotted, convoy will be held until further orders.'

Phillips looked around and saw the mighty force of sixteen hundred jets swarming around him. His jet passed over the mass of vehicles below. Enormous jungle crunchers at the front of the convoy had stopped creating a pass for all combat vehicles, which had also come to a halt. Ahead and hovering above the jungle canopy, thousands of small fighter drones waited. They were small jets which had no human drones on board but combat avatars directly linked to their pilots.

Further ahead of these, motionless and without making any sound, the alien craft hovered and waited. It was jet black with smooth surfaces reflecting the sun as though mirrors. It was strange and yet familiar in a way for it had four wings like a butterfly, except they were sharp and rhomboid in shape and moved at two main points attached to a narrow mid-section. It had a bulbous back end while the top half of what could only be described as its body was narrower with a large sharp harpoon for its head. It could be thought of as a spider with wings and no legs, or another insect perhaps, except this thing was enormous with a wing span of a hundred metres. On the underneath of its body, blue pulsating light emanated through what appeared to be thinner transparent plating that shimmered and rotated. This could be assumed to be its engines or even lungs.

Version

'This is Captain Vale of the gunship *Shadow Light*. Please acknowledge our location at three thousand feet above set jet height of combat zone.'

Three thousand and thirty eight lights winked on the cockpit display of Phillips' jet. Jets and drones alike, all linked to human pilots, confirmed they knew the combat zone parameters beneath the colossal airship that had arrived to offer support.

'Colonel Phillips, this is Captain Jones. Do we have permission to set blanket defence?'

'Position tanks and silos but do not activate unless air support is compromised. I do not want cross-fire zones, no matter how accurate these machines are.'

Phillips sat within his avatar – he had become his machine seated within a jet hovering and waiting as the unusual craft did the very same thing only a few miles away. Thousands of hovering air drones and jets created a deep hum, sounding like a great swarm of bees. On the ground, thousands of combat vehicles, tanks, trucks, dog and ram drones, along with human drones, also waited. Above his position the airship floated as perhaps the most deadly killing machine of all, and further above this there orbited a weapon satellite. A laser cannon held its position as further backup.

There was enough firepower at this location to obliterate a country the size of Nigeria within a few hours and render it a grave of ash. This was not the objective. This operation was meant to be swift and accurate, and cause a minimum of collateral damage. Now Phillips wondered at the thing that had stopped this mighty war machine in its path. The unknown caused fear, and taking a risk might prove lucrative for the timetable of this operation which was slipping away fast. Silence engulfed the world as Colonel Phillips considered that this thing might be destroyed with ease, and it couldn't cover the whole width of the battlefield that stretched across three hundred miles of convoys heading south.

'Captain Jarvis, come in.'

'Received.'

'Order one of your team to send in a drone. Full identification notice protocols need to be followed.'

'Understood.'

An air drone flew ahead over the canopy, its gunmetal jade hull almost disappearing as it shot over the sea of green beneath. Anyone below this machine would also struggle to see it as its hull projected the same colour as the sky through adaptive light emitters. The drone slowed and hovered twenty metres from the alien craft. The alien machine appeared to watch and tilted its attitude towards the human machine.

'This is a message from all allied forces of the United States of America and the United States of Europe. Please identify yourself.'

The alien craft did nothing.

'You are in the direct path . . .'

The alien craft fired a bolt of energy at the drone. It melted and dropped from the sky, hurtling in a molten blob into the forest canopy below.

Phillips gave the order to engage as the craft opened fire on multiple targets as it moved. Faster and faster, more projectiles of energy found targets in all directions. Drones and jets fell from the sky en masse as the hostile craft moved up, down, left and right with impossible and mechanised accuracy as if a dragonfly above a pond.

The swarm of drones and jets fired missiles and fifty calibre rounds from stampede cannons. The airship fired one-tonne bolts that managed to hit the target repeatedly. The alien craft jerked with each impact yet it deflected the rounds and missiles with some sort of shield that could only be seen as fork lightning flashing upside down and away from the alien craft's hull.

The human aircraft continued to fall like molten rain from the sky. Human drone pilots ejected from the jets and parachuted to the ground; there was no sense in wasting the machines by allowing them to crash. Some of the drones were half melted and on fire as they fell to earth, and by now the ground battalions were running around as though an ant's nest had been disturbed.

Tanks, trucks and drones alike were pelted by the debris of their own destroyed air support; the world below was now on fire as the jungle burned. Colonel Phillips took his jet to high altitude and neared the airship for cover. In the medium distance he could see the alien creature hover and fire relentlessly at the allied aircraft. Energy bolt after energy bolt snaked their way with staggering accuracy.

From above, an energy beam shot down and hit the black beast dead on. Its shields shimmered and took the heat blast of over one million degrees. The craft tilted upwards and fired its own narrow blast into the sky. In orbit above the combat zone, the military satellite melted and fell into Earth's atmosphere. It lit up like a flare falling in the night sky.

The craft took more hits from the one-tonne rounds and turned its attention to the airship. As it rose, the Zeppelin-styled military vessel fired a staggering display of missiles and stampede turrets. All found their mark and yet the alien craft appeared completely unscathed.

'We're losing this battle,' Phillips voiced over the comms. 'We need to retreat now.'

The alien craft bombarded the airship from fore to aft down its port flank. The thick metal plating surrounding the ship's inflated innards melted, allowing helium to burst out along the two thousand metres of hull. The ship listed then toppled over. It sank through the air until it eventually hit the ground, crushing hundreds of drone assets. It exploded, releasing a blast that snuffed out the raging inferno taking hold of the jungle in one massive gust.

One of the thousands of bolts the craft fired, headed directly towards Phillips' jet. He manoeuvred but the bolt of light seemed to know where he was headed before he arrived. He hit the ejector seat.

The canopy blew away and he shot out as the jet turned to vapour. Phillips then watched the full horror of the drone massacre from this new and open perspective. He may have been in a drone, had become the very robust drone and was out of danger, yet with such an immersion into technology he felt that he was really there, naked and floating in Hell. As Phillips parachuted to earth, he saw the alien craft move towards him. An eternity crept in as though the world had paused. The craft leapt upon him, was right next to him. It seemed to look at him and tilt itself as though analysing him.

Phillips woke within the metal pod. He was drenched in sweat and his head spun wildly.

Craig Jenkins

He vomited violently and sat for a moment to find his bearings. The pod opened to reveal chaos had erupted at the base. People were running around shouting this and that; Phillips wasn't sure what. He climbed out and grabbed the nearest person he could find.

'What the hell happened?' Phillips screamed.

'World War Four just happened!' the man shouted back.